The Stone Sister is a powerful meditation on family, caregiving, and secrets. Caroline Patterson paints a nuanced portrait of an era, its policies forged with good intentions and devastating consequences. Encompassing many parallels to today, the novel underlines the tragedy of turning away from those who make us uncomfortable.

—Janet Skeslien Charles, *The Paris Library*

Above all, because Caroline Patterson's *The Stone Sister* is a retelling of the author's own painful family history, it represents an extraordinary act of courage. This is a book with a big heart, the characters human, alive and compelling, the heartbreaking subject at its core consequential as blood.

—Kim Zupan,*The Ploughman*

Heart-breaking, riveting, and urgent, *The Stone Sister* explores forces more powerful than love: shame, secrets, expectations. Patterson writes like a dream. Flesh-and-blood characters and stunning prose make her debut an instant classic.

—Diana Spechler, *Skinny: A Novel, Who By Fire*

The Stone Sister is a remarkable story of empathy, sorrow, and tender reflection. It is Caroline Patterson's own story transfigured through fiction into a larger truth. A Downs syndrome baby girl is born to a middle class couple in a small Montana city, hidden away in a mental institution, and deliberately forgotten until her adult sister learns of her existence and begins a painful and meticulous search. Told in the voices of a self-justifying father, a devoted nurse, and a questing sister, the lost child's journey reveals the anguish, fears, and horrors that society inflicts on those who do not fit into its definitions of normal. This is a fable for our time--a story to inform and instruct as traditional ideas of identity and inclusion are being challenged in all corners of our smug old world.

—Annick Smith, *Crossing the Plains with Bruno, Hearth*

THE STONE SISTER

THE STONE SISTER

CAROLINE PATTERSON

BLACK LAWRENCE PRESS

www.blacklawrence.com
Executive Editor: Diane Goettel
Book and Cover Design: Zoe Norvell
Cover Art: "River Road: Milepost 39" by Holly Andres

ISBN: 978-1-62557-146-5

Published 2021 by Black Lawrence Press.

For Jack, Laura, and Caroline Marie Patterson

She was the secret heart that lay under the silences in her family, like the mysterious swath of stone, the batholith, that formed when magma rose to the earth's surface and flowed along a tectonic plate, like milk under a rug, except that it flowed for millions of years, growing harder and thicker until it created a granite slab two miles wide and ten miles deep. Different in texture and appearance than the schists and sandstones around it, the slab went underground and was a vast silent presence beneath the windblown ponderosas and Doug firs. At Homestake Pass, where the soil had worn away, it suddenly appeared: the fields of broken rock exposed and named, appropriately enough, the Dragonback. No one could really explain why, on these cold plains, amid this thin, slanting light, in this place where even the sunshine hurt, the cracked rock appeared like a strange race of people, misshapen and stunted by cold.

CHAPTER ONE

Louise Gustafson liked to think her life began when a screen door banged shut in Blue Earth, Minnesota. Banged shut as she snuck out the back door of the brown Lutheran church blessed by wind and sun and land stretching from horizon to horizon, where her fiancé, the dirt farmer, stood at the altar, stood waiting with his father and his father's father for her to walk up the aisle to join him in growing into the earth, getting smaller and more furrowed each year until they joined the rest of his ancestors buried in dirt, with only their children to cough up their names.

Or that her story began with a slap. Right there in the Plough Bar in the middle of town, when she told her boyfriend she wouldn't marry him even if he held a gun to her head, the bar stool falling back, metal ringing, glasses clinking, Hank Williams on the jukebox, everything growing silent and slow as he stared at her, raised his broad weathered palm, the snap of flesh on flesh, the stain rising on her cheek as the bartender reached across the scarred wooden bar to grab his arm and say, "Not in this place, buddy," and she, Louise Gustafson, picked up her purse and walked out and got into her car and drove west.

But these stories weren't true. She left out of sheer boredom. Blue Earth in summer. Sun drumming the pavement. Her mother sweeping the porch each day with her hymns, certain that Louise wouldn't marry. Louise certain she would be there to ease her mother's dry bones into the earth as old men eyed her with glances that said, *Lift me up in my infirmity.* She had backseat dalliances with the occasional farm boy, but she knew when the time came, their affections would go to the corn silk girls, never a redheaded, sass-talking woman like her who'd gone to nursing school, who'd seen women die, babies born, men cry out in pain.

She left one hot summer day, after her nursing shift at the fan-fluttered wooden box known as the Blue Earth Health Clinic. She left after swabbing down children with chicken pox and tending to an old farmer dying of emphysema and a farmhand with a broken leg. She quit her job and drove home on Highway 90 and thought, *drive. Drive till the money runs out*, and when she said good-bye, her mother said the devil had entered Louise's heart and that she'd pray for her return.

Louise said, *save your breath.*

She drove slowly down the main street of Blue Earth, the broken-down town with a bar and a gas station and the hardware store with the peeling green paint and the redbrick school where hopes were raised and routinely dashed and weeds poked up through the sidewalk and quiet swept the streets. She drove slowly, etching each detail in her mind, then turned onto the highway, adjusted her rearview mirror, and shifted.

The highway was like a river west. She flowed past the flatland, river bottoms, farmland, laid out across the prairie like a black-checked picnic cloth, past small towns like her own, the lives so rooted there, lives of waking up and working and drinking and bedding down again and waking to a certain future. She didn't know what she was driving to, but she didn't care. What she was doing was unforgivable, but she wasn't married, she wasn't pregnant; she was a woman alone and there wasn't a story that fit her out there.

As she drove from Minnesota to South Dakota and from South Dakota to North Dakota, the land rose up around her, rose into small canyons, hills, mountains. As the land rose, so did her spirits.

She overnighted in tourist cabins, where men talked cattle and crop prices with other men, and women cooed to babies, and newlyweds made love cries in the night. She filled her gas tank at stations with the flying tigers where attendants winked at her and asked her where she was headed (*straight to hell*, she wanted to answer, but did only once) or they snapped to attention, scrubbing the windows, and stole looks at her legs.

As she drove, she watched the numbers roll over on her odometer like pages flying from a calendar in a movie, each one measuring how far away she was from her mother's hymns, from the head nurse who watched her with her sour instructions, from the dirt farmer who took her to the Saturday movies and expected to cop a feel in return.

She entered Montana near Glendive, where the oil derricks bobbed up and down like bath toys, and farmers planted spring wheat, tilling up thick rows of dirt behind their tractors, great flocks of birds wheeling around behind them. Occasionally Louise spotted a woman standing in the doorway of a ranch house, her sleeves rolled up her muscled arms, calling a scatter of dogs in the driveway, calling men in to dinner, and Louise wanted to call to her, *hello, good-bye!*

In each town was a life she left behind, ranch wife, librarian, even the whores who disappeared around corners of peeling buildings into alleys where weak lights lit stairways to their rooms. Each tableau a chrysalis she cast off. She wanted to drive west forever. It was a direction she believed in.

The mountains hovered, deep, mysterious, ghost-like. She drove to them, feeling the past strip away from her, the narrow brick school, the nurse's training with its aluminum bedpans and starched white uniforms, the farmers with their pinches and sly remarks, the amputees with their sausage-like limbs and bitter hopes or worse yet, the cheerful ones with their upturned faces and wheelchairs. With every mile, she cast off her own thin dreams of a house and a righteous man and babies and gardens as she drove into this landscape of angles and planes.

Clean, spare lines she could live with.

It was the geometry of starting over.

Helena, Montana, down to her last fifty dollars, she checked into the YWCA, and joined the other stranded women—women without family, women escaping family, women without wits, women whose songs had run out, whose paved roads had suddenly turned to dirt—ruled over by a matron who must have weighed three hundred pounds and had the voice of a sparrow. Here she answered an advertisement in a local newspaper: The Stone Home for Feeble-Minded and Backward Children. Nurses needed, little experience necessary.

When she drove over the hill and down into Stone City, the broad valley reached out to her like a hand. The valley was spotted black and red with cattle, with clumps of pine trees at the foot of the shy, forbidding mountains she later learned were the Elkhorns. A long, silvery river, clotted here and there with moss and cattails, ran parallel to the highway.

Louise drove down the empty main street lined with one-story brick buildings with plate-glass windows—a hardware store, café, and several garages and a market—following signs for the Stone Home. *Why was this called a city?* she wondered. *Why stone?* Her heart thumped. It was cold, high, remote. It was June and snowing. The place enfolded her at once like a lover.

On the outskirts of town, she immediately saw the building, a tall brick Italianate building, so out of character with the one-story Main Street town. It had to be the Stone Home, she thought, wondering at the generosity of a state that provided such a grand place for its feeble-minded children. The building was three stories high with tiled roofs, Italianate cornices, and six-foot plate-glass windows.

It looked like a library. Or a men's club in the middle of London.

Louise was hired for the nursery by the chief of staff, a Dr. Oetzinger, or "Dr. O," as everyone called him. She met him, along with the head nurse and two social workers, around the wide table in the library, sunlight streaming through the long leaded-glass windows to slice the table into triangles of light. On one wall stood a large framed photograph of Sigmund Freud, on another a print of Van Gogh's haystacks.

When she accepted the job, everyone stared across the smooth surface of the table at her, and she tried to read their looks: Astonishment? Sympathy? Amusement?

"Welcome aboard," Dr. O said, after they had hired her to care for eight babies in the nursery. As he said this, his eyes traveled down her body, from her eyes to her lips to her chest, and then discreetly back to his notes. "Louise Gustafson. That sounds like a very sturdy name."

"I'm a very sturdy person, Doctor," she said, and immediately wished she'd kept her mouth shut. It's a place to rest my head for a while, she told herself. Nothing more.

When she stepped back into the hallway, the cacophony of voices shocked her, as patients walked, limped, dawdled in the hallways, the push and thrust of bodies—hands, feet, legs—the body odor and wet diapers, everywhere. There were toddlers, children, young adults, all of them dressed in the same blue serge coveralls and with regulation bowl haircuts. It was as if she had woken up in some kind of Dutch village, except for the nurses in their white uniforms and starched caps and the staff who threaded through the throng in their blue uniforms and another harried-looking doctor in a white coat who rushed upstream against the patients. Two orderlies with broad muscled shoulders and tanned faces supported a man whose face was blank as a pie plate as he flopped one foot in front of the other, like a puppet trying to walk.

Above the chaos was a portrait of a woman in a pale green Victorian dress, Frau Holtzmeier, who gazed down at them through her pince-nez across her forbidding-looking bosom as if they were great curiosities. A bronze plaque beneath the painting stated that she had helped found the school in 1898 for the "care of the unfortunate, because to care for backward children is a mission entrusted to a Christian society by God."

CHAPTER TWO

In January when the town was buried in snow, it was hard to believe Mary's pregnancy began in the season of peonies. A series of storms, three in a row, dumped a record 104 inches, and everything was covered: the cars on the streets were mammoth-like with their humped drifts, the houses like prehistoric animals with glittering teeth at their rooflines, the streets cave-like between the banks of snow that lined the sidewalks. Between storms, there was the weary scrape of people shoveling, the rattle of car chains on the plowed streets.

Bob Carter sat backwards on a spindly chair and watched his wife, Mary, move around the bedroom, looking slightly mammoth-like herself in her white painter's overalls, though he'd never tell her that in a million years, if he knew what was good for him. This was his grandparents' house, built at the crack of a new century after they moved west from Chicago with their sickly baby to start a life out west. He and Mary were repeating the cycle, taking over the house. His father had died a year ago of stomach cancer and, three months later, his mother was institutionalized. Manic-depression, the doctor said. His father's death, people told him in sympathy cards or conversations after church, was a blessing. A blessing for whom? he wondered on his endless drives back and forth from his insurance office to the hospital to the undertaker's to the cemetery, hauling everything from insurance papers to bills, empty vases to the last set of clothes his father had worn. His mother's institutionalization? No one said a word. It was as if she had vanished, though Bob wagered if he stopped anyone in the narthex of the church and asked them where she was, dollar to one, they could tell him. When she was released, they planned for her to come live with them, though the thought filled Bob with dread, his mother with her hand-wringing and endless worry.

But this house, this glorious, four-square, two-story house, was where he and Mary had landed. And now, deep in winter, the grieving and the worry and the funerals were behind them. He and Mary were snowed in. They cleared closets and drawers of his parents' effects so they could move in their belongings: Bob's suits, Mary's dresses, the blanket with the Carter crest Mary's mother wove for them when they got married. Bob's collection of jazz records stood next to the stereo he'd painstakingly set up in the living room, which he'd queued with a record, the Duke of course, on the first night they spent in the house, in September, and as he listened to the speakers crackle to life, he dropped the diamond tip of the needle onto the black vinyl, and his heart flooded at the saxophone's first velvety notes. He scooped Mary up from the prickled horsehair couch and waltzed her across the Oriental carpet.

Moving on with their lives. Every time Mary pulled open a drawer from the oak bookcase that dominated the living room, Bob found more family relics: a great-grandfather's sermons from 1870, his grand-aunt's stereoscopic pictures of catacombs in Rome, and, on the top layer, his grandmother's cookbook for the new Monarch stove with a recipe for, of all things, liver casserole. As he dusted off each item, Mary told him, *toss it Bob. It's filthy.*

Mary was painting an upstairs room, in the southwest corner, for the baby. It was his grandmother's old sewing room, once dominated by a dressmaker's dummy, a cutting table, bolts of cloth and shears, and a large black sewing machine with scrolled writing perched next to the window. He could remember her in here, working, the rat-tat-tatting of the machine as she sewed. *I like to look outside at that lilac bush*, his grandmother said, *to stop and smell it, to rest my eyes, so when I look back down, I can sew my seams straight.*

Mary had him haul the sewing machine and bolts of cloth to the attic, the tables to the garbage. She bought a crib from a used furniture store, cleaned out the closet, scrubbed floors, even sang nursery rhymes. Bob reminded her that the baby wouldn't come out talking. She sang anyway.

Now, a month before her due date, she was painting.

She pointed to the pile of discards.

"This pile needs to go," she said, standing in the middle of the room, paintbrush in one hand, the other on her hip. She had edged the molding in green, but the walls were still a pale blue. The trim she'd planned in white. "And if you get so much as a swipe of dirt on these walls, you're repainting. I just prepped them."

"Yessir," Bob said. He saluted her, and then swatted her rear end with a rolled-up *National Geographic*. "Where do I put this stuff, babe?"

"Away," she said. "In the attic, I guess. Just disappear it."

He grabbed a cardboard box. He folded the front page of the Sunday paper— "U.N. planes pound the Reds 'through daylight and dark' in Korea"—around the stereoscope. There were beer steins he doubted any Methodist in this house had ever used. His father's leather-bound copies of Montana Actuarial Tables from 1929, 1930, and 1931. He wrapped up a china figurine, a shepherdess with lambs curled at her feet, the eyes a pool of blue, his mother's craft project at the hospital. Those bleary eyes bothered him, reminding him of his mother's unfocused stare on her worst days. He filled a box, and at the foot of the stairs to the attic, he pushed the button for the light. He hiked up the steep stairs, his breath frosting the vast, dimly lit, unheated room. It reminded him of the old family meat locker, where his parents had stored the cuts of beef they bought from a ranch down the Bitterroot, its ice-crusted shelves and netted cages of white-wrapped meat. He could just make out the wicker baby carriage, a steamer trunk, an oak writing desk shrouded in dust. The place filled him with a deep tiredness, as if all these family belongings were pulling him toward them, into them, and, much as he appreciated them from a distance, up close these hulking ghosts of past lives and travels made him want to run: he was a man of the present, who believed in moving forward. He set down the cardboard box and clambered down the stairs, snapping off the light on the way out.

"You know what this color is, Bob?" Mary said when he returned. She stood on tiptoe, edging the window in the northeast wall. Outside he could see the brushy outlines of the lilac, its black branches stark shadows against the snow.

"No," Bob said. "What is what?" He was still shaking off the sense that he shouldn't be this way, shouldn't be so silly about a room in what was now his own home.

"Spring green," she said. "I think it is such a hopeful color. Do you like it?" She drew a thin line of green paint along the cornice. "Green, the color of new life."

"It's beautiful," Bob said. "Green like new grass. Green like money."

"Green green the rushes grow," Mary sang, as she dipped the paintbrush in the can and carefully edged the walls, and she continued to hum. "Duh-da, duh, da-duh-duh-duh-duh. I wish I could remember how that all goes. I just remember the end." Green paint oozed down the blue wall until Mary caught it with her brush and spread it across the wall. "One is one and all alone and ever more shall be so."

"You're a merry one," Bob said.

"Ha, ha," Mary said. "Well, I'm nesting. I've read about it you know." She put her brush in the roller pan and turned to face him. "Doctor Spock says all pregnant women experience this incredible activity before birth. It's about lining your nest. Getting your home ready. It's gone on forever—in pregnant humans and animals. It's nature's way."

"Well, God knows, I believe in nature," Bob said. He came up and kissed her.

"If you are going to be dirty, I'm going to make you paint," Mary said.

"Do pregnant fathers experience intense activity too?" Bob said.

She lunged toward him, and he hurried down the stairs before she handed him a paintbrush.

"Ta-duh!" she called him up from his red chair beneath the light in the living room, where he was listening to the evening news. He grumbled. He wanted to hear this editorial about the Fulton Sheen episode earlier in the year when the actor had read Julius Caesar on the air, replacing Soviet officials' names with those of Caesar's minions.

He pushed himself out of the chair, reluctant. He had better not wait. Not now. Not when all was going so smoothly. That Mary was flushed and happy was good enough for him—her face pinked throughout the day as he checked in on her, edging the trim, rollering the walls, until the light flushed the western sky, then dimmed the room, and she had to turn on the bare light to finish.

He took the stairs, two at a time, and stood at the door. Mary was just stepping on the lid of the paint can to close it. The walls were light green with white trim. She had pushed the white crib decorated with baby chicks and ducklings and rabbits against one wall and had already hung the stiff white curtains at the window.

She came to stand next to him in the doorway.

"Do you like it?" she said.

"It is magnificent," Bob said. Bob looked over at the crib and tried to imagine the small humped form, the chest moving up and down with breath, under the woven blanket in blue or pink. His child. Mary's child. Their child.

Nothing there. He shook his head. He might as well imagine what it was like landing on the moon. Say something, he told himself. Mary caught him in these pauses, springing on him as if they were proof of his disloyalty. She needed so much reassurance these days. No, you don't look big as a barn. Yes, you are beautiful. No, I don't think that you will forget our child in the bathtub. "You'll be a damn good mom," he said quickly.

This time, she didn't notice any pause. "I'm taking a bath," she said. "My back hurts. My feet hurt. My arms hurt. I think even my toenails hurt."

Bob wandered back down to his book and his radio, where the Jack Benny show was just finishing up and the twang of the Singing Pioneers was just starting. His heart sank. He always found them cloying with their gosh-darns and howdy-dos. God knows, he had enough of cowboys around here. He snapped off the dial and watched the yellow glow of the tubes fade as the singers were pledging their love to the ground. As soon as they could afford it, he wanted a television, but Mary forbade it. Arnie Brechbill says you can buy it on time, he told her. Television! she said. Do you think we can afford a console at several hundred dollars? That's practically the cost of my delivery, for God's sake.

He wandered back upstairs and opened the bathroom to a cloud of steam. "Mary? Are you in here?"

Mary lay up to her neck in the hot water, her sinewy body blurred in the steam.

"Bob, you know perfectly well you can see me." She balled up the washcloth and threw it at him.

He picked it up and set it in the hamper. "You've marked me, woman."

"You deserve it," she said and slid into the water.

From his perch on the toilet, he studied her. Her hair swirled the water, black seaweed against the white porcelain. Mary, his Mary, with her slash of cheekbones, brown eyes, the thin mobile mouth, quick to laugh, quick to anger. He thought of the two of them, traveling down the coast to San Francisco after all the funerals, the song in his head, "Pennsylvania Station 'Bout a Quarter to Eight," as she threw up by the side of the road. The trip was like a rite of passage for him, he had said good-bye to his father and mother, and now he was on an interstate, the yellow lines ticking away like musical notes on a grand score, his beautiful wife, his Buick, a child on the way, the war over and won, and in his head, in time to the rubber tires slicking the pavement, he could hear the orchestra run the scale from F to C, then pause as the men's chorus shouted out: "Pennsylvania 6-500!"

How did he do it, Glenn, how did he find those sounds?

He'd first seen her in the University of Montana choir, singing, transfigured with joy, and everything bad in his life was erased by her face: the fear as he stood on the deck of that Merchant Marine ship, gliding into the Okinawa Harbor the day after Armistice, the Japanese artillery trained on them, each dark barrel a question of life or death, the water parting at the thick iron hull of the Liberty ship and rippling out to shore as they stood, hearts thumping loud as gunshot. His father telling him the money he sent home during the war was gone, he used it to pay the mortgage because he'd had no income for the past four years, no one was buying insurance during a war, he was so sorry, and his tears—the shame of them—and the afternoons of his mother in her armchair, motionless except for her wringing hands as she cried, *Bobby boy, you are too young for the world.* Bob saying, *Stop, Mother. I'm a man now.*

All that disappeared when Bob saw Mary's face as she sang Verdi's *Requiem*, her red lips, her slender body shaped by these notes, towering notes of music built like a cathedral, and Bob knew she had to be his.

His parents didn't see this immediately. He was their prize, the bright boy with his slicked-back hair and good grades. They were polite to Mary, but he knew they didn't quite approve. He was their Bobby boy, the one who drove his mother nearly mad when he was in the war. It wasn't until Mary lived with them when her school funding ran out, helping his mother cook dinner each night, assuring her that Bob was home safe, fetching his mother novels and prescriptions, fetching his mother home when, in a mania, she'd decided to go buy herself a new wardrobe for fall at the Mercantile, saving his father from the shame that had been his since Bob had been away at the war. Each night, when Bob came home from work, Mary would be setting the table, his dad reading and his mother working away at a needlepoint of black flowers on a dark blue background, or was it blue flowers on a black background? It was as if Mary restored them to better versions of themselves.

Now she was his. Mary, with her round, white belly, pregnant with his child. A dash of green paint on her forearm. There was a burst of water as she rose up from the tub, streaming, to face him. She put her hand on his. "The water is delicious. My back is killing me."

"You don't need to do all this work," Bob said. "The baby doesn't give a damn about clean curtains or even a painted room."

She smiled up at him, absently, and then she sat back down again, the water sloshing back and forth as she settled in. She looked at her stomach, rising out of the bathwater like a rounded flesh island. She studied her nipples that, early on, had changed from pink to brown. "Bob?"

"Hmm?"

"Are you excited?"

Bob looked at her face, pink from steam, the lashes black. "I guess I'm a little scared."

"Scared?" She slid back down into the water until it framed her face, a perfect oval. "Of a little baby? You? You've sailed Liberty ships around the world and fought the Japanese—and now you're scared of a little baby?"

"Well, yes." He turned away from her and looked out at the moon just glazing the window. "Is that so bad?" He wondered, fleetingly, if anything scared Mary, remembering their honeymoon, when they were camping under the ponderosa trees next to Coeur d'Alene Lake when a car full of drunk high schools kids pulled into the campsite next to them and started carrying on, breaking beer bottles, whooping and shouting. They huddled in their bags until Mary finally said, "Bob, this is my honeymoon, and I've had it." "Mary," Bob said. "Just let 'em alone. They're kids. They'll leave in a bit." "No," she said. "I'm done here." She stood up, pulled a shirt over her pajamas, unzipped the tent, and, with her feet in Bob's hiking boots, marched over to the kids gathered around a campfire. Bob limped along the gravel road in his bare feet and came up on her just as she was telling the kids that her husband had a pistol and if they didn't pack up and get out of here, he'd damn well use it. One of the kids, an older boy, surveyed Mary from head to toe, and gave her a sly grin. He threw his beer bottle into the woods. In the glare of the headlights, Bob followed its glittering arc into the trees. "Okay, little Momma," the kid shrugged and turned to the others. "Don't sweat your pretty little head." He slid into the driver's seat and slammed the door, and the others followed suit. The car peeled out, washing the campsite in the glow of red taillights. Bob had never felt so useless in his life.

"How could you be scared of a little baby?" she said. "Silly, silly Bob."

"I'm afraid of babies. I'm afraid I'll hurt it," Bob jiggled the toilet handle, looking around the old bathroom with its oak wainscoting and high ceiling. "What if I drop it?"

"You won't drop it, dummy." She smiled at him and cocked her head, as she floated, staring up at the ceiling. "It's *your* baby. You'll diaper it and feed it and rock it. It'll be perfectly natural."

"Maybe for you," Bob said. He couldn't explain the dread he felt, how he worried that he would hold it too tight and crush it or forget to feed it or worse—just walk off. "I'm not good with little things. These hands—" He held out his hands to her as if they could make his point. His hands were thick-fingered and broad-palmed; to his mind, his hands could carry a briefcase or sign a contract or do figures, but his hands were not delicate enough for a baby. "They're just so clumsy—"

Mary sat up and laughed, the water slopping from one side of the tub to the other. "Stop. You're the father. You'll be fine." Bob felt a hitch of irritation. Why did she think everything would be fine?

Why was she always so supremely calm just as they were on the brink of this new life? They'd just been reborn as adults in this lovely old home, a child on the way, and this would be his family, the one he had seen dimly in the back of his mind all those nights he was on watch, as the moon pearled the ocean, as he watched the skies for dark shapes, or the water for mysterious bulges, wondering if this calm were it or the moment just before the ship upended in a blaze of fire.

He wanted to touch the taut flesh of her stomach, the turned-out belly button, the nipples that had recently turned a deep brown. He touched her left breast. The nipple stiffened and he felt himself stiffen in response.

"You goat," Mary laughed. "Come 'ere."

He knelt by the side of the tub and she took both of his hands in hers.

"This is our baby," Mary said. "We'll do this together."

She took his hands and placed them on her stomach.

The flesh was pink, firm, taut. A brown line ran from her navel to the scrabble of pubic hair.

"Well?" she said.

"Well what?" Bob said.

"Wait a minute." She studied his face.

He waited, looking out the window at the snow falling, at the moon that was three-quarters full, a gibbous moon that shone through the bare branches of the scarlet oak tree—the scarlet oak his great-grandfather had grafted onto a maple so that it would survive. It was an ugly moon, he thought. A sloppy, misshapen crescent.

"Keep your hands there," Mary said.

"What?" Bob wanted to pull his hands away. The room was too hot, too close—the whole thing some kind of test he was failing. The pipes squeaked. The house ticked.

He could hear Mary breathing.

Then he felt it. A kick. It was light, sure, like a knock against a curtain. Then another kick.

"My God," he whispered.

"Isn't it thrilling?" she whispered.

"Amazing," he said, but the word that came to him was *engulfed*.

That night, as Mary rested in front of a tepee-shaped stack of logs burning brightly in the fireplace, Bob took down his grandmother's cast-iron skillet. He peeled off six strips of bacon and set them cooking, watching the sides curl as they popped and hissed in the skillet. At the wide porcelain sink, where he remembered his grandmother up to her elbows in soapy dishwater or her arms coated in flour as she kneaded bread dough in a stoneware bowl, he grated potatoes into cold water. He chopped onions, tears swelling at his eyes, and sniffed.

"What's wrong?" Mary called.

"I'm weeping."

"What?"

"Onions."

The crackle of onions in lard, the potatoes, his spatula turning and turning, as the heat from the stove glazed his face. He glanced out the kitchen window. The snow was coming faster now and he was supposed to be up in Seeley on Monday, God knows what the roads would be like, but never mind, Monday was miles away. He wouldn't think about that now, only about this meal—the bacon nearly ready, the potatoes crisping nicely, and in a minute, he would crack the eggs and cook them in that bacon grease, two for Mary, three for him, and serve it all, bright against the red Fiesta ware plates.

The kettle screeched as Mary set the long oak table in the dining room. Bob could hear her moving about, humming as silverware thunked on the table, spoon, fork, knife, the whisper of napkins. How many nights on that ship—sailing into Manila Bay, bringing in munitions, hoping they wouldn't be shelled, or sailing out of Australia hoping they wouldn't be seen by a Japanese spitfire—had he hoped for this? Three eggs, a pile of crisp browns, flanked by bacon. Two black cups of coffee.

And a home, where his beautiful wife was singing.

The following Monday morning, Mary boiled beef bones for soup. Bob drove to Seeley Lake to visit Pete Donetello's logging company, to write him a liability policy, hoping like hell he didn't get killed on the way, the logging trucks bearing down, chains rattling, passing him in a whoosh of blinding snow, bearing loads of Douglas fir and ponderosa pine on their way to the tepee burners in Bridger and Spurlock that would keep firing through winter, spring, summer, and fall, keeping loggers and skidders in the woods, the millworkers on the lines carving the massive trees into lumber. He tried to make out the side of the road, the dark shapes emerging from the grey clouds, lights wavering, and then passing him, as snow blanketed the windshield, faster than the wipers could sweep the glass clean. Now and then, Bob glanced sideways at the road to keep from being hypnotized by the oncoming snow.

Pete had a small mill in Seeley, a six-man operation, but he needed insurance so Bob had agreed to come up and write it for him. Pete had never finished grade school, but he was one of the shrewdest businessmen Bob knew. He earned enough to support himself and his family, winning bids on timber sales because he kept his ear to the ground and listened to men talk in bars, sipping on one beer all night, as the loggers around him spilled their secrets in a river of whisky, underbidding logging outfits twice his size almost every time at the bank. He bought land on either side of him, logged it carefully, and used the money to buy more, yet he and his wife Cora and their son Donny continued to live in a log cabin he'd built when he moved to the area right after the war.

When Bob asked Pete why he didn't buy a new place, he looked at him blankly.

"Shit, Bob, if I did that, I couldn't piss off the porch," Pete said.

As Bob drove, he wondered what his mother was doing at this minute, if it was snowing like this in Warm Springs, and at the thought of her, felt the familiar sadness and strangulation. *If only.* A grandchild on the way, her son established in business, and still the dark clouds, he thought. He stared ahead, making certain he stayed inside the tracks of the car ahead of him, the forests a dark blur on either side. He remembered the day he'd come home from grade school, his mother, Beatrice, meeting him at the door and telling him she had a surprise. *What?* he'd asked. *No questions*, she'd responded, as she slipped a cookie in his hand. They walked several blocks from their house to the railroad station. He looked up at her, so tall, her dark hair swept up in a twist, her eyes burning, a smile lighting her face. "What?" he'd asked her. "What?"

"Promise me first you will not tell your father," she said.

With a tweak in his stomach, he promised.

She took him to the depot and there they met someone, an old high school boyfriend, who was an engineer. "I'm Erwin," the man said and extended his hand. Bob solemnly shook it. The man was right out of a storybook, with his grease-stained railroad cap, his thick bristly cheeks. "Your mother says you're something of an engineer." He remembered looking from Erwin to his mother, thinking the arrangement was somewhat strange. They smiled back at him. No man had ever spoken to him like this.

"He doesn't know what to make of this," his mother said. She was laughing differently, her voice light and carefree in a way that made him want to snare it and bring it back to the lower sound of the mother he knew.

"It's okay, Robert," The man said. "I know your father. I've known your mother since I was a boy your age. She just wants you to have a little fun. Are we okay here?"

Bob nodded.

"A serious fella," the man said to his mother.

"He watches out for me," his mother said. "He's a good boy, that Bobby."

Erwin, his mother, and Bob walked along the embankment, the sounds of the crunching gravel filling the silence between them. Bob looked out to the river, where a long line of freight trains—S&O Freights, Great Northern, the Milwaukee—brown and rust-colored, seemed to stretch along the curves of the river for miles. When they reached the black locomotive, panting along the tracks, Erwin stood to one side as his mother climbed up the iron steps, followed by Bob. Erwin followed them into the cab and turned a wheel to lock the door behind them. The reek of diesel and oil filled the cab. Bob studied the array of gauges before him, measuring things like fuel, speed, and oil pressure.

"Ready?" Erwin said, and when Bob nodded, he took his hand and switched a few levers, and slowly they began to move down the track.

His mother smiled down at him.

The creaking engine, the slow curve of the tracks slid inside him, and as they picked up steam, headed east for the Hellgate Canyon. Bob couldn't stop grinning

"You like this?" his mother said. "Are you having fun? I wanted to do something really special for you and I came up with this."

He shook his head, afraid to take his eyes from the tracks.

"I think your kid has a knack for this," Erwin said.

Beatrice tipped her head back, laughing. "Figures I'd have an engineer as a son," she said. "You always told me I lived too much in my head."

He remembered the excitement of shifting the levers forward, the way his mother and Erwin leaned forward as well, toward the windshield, leaning with him, as they moved down the track, and the vague feeling in his stomach that this much fun came with some kind of price.

"Ah, Beatrice." Erwin smiled and slid his eyes over to her. "Do not fear the mechanical world."

Something was going on over his head and he didn't like it. "I want to reverse," Bob said, and the engineer moved his hand to brake. "We can do that, my friend. Pull this up."

Bob pulled on the brake.

The lever would not budge.

"Pull harder," Erwin said. "You have to pull that thing till you think your eyes will pop out of your head."

Bob grabbed the rusted brake in both hands and pulled back on it, this time with his ninety-eight pounds, and slowly, the lever ground back, and there was a shriek and a jerk as the wheels ground to a stop.

The cab filled with a sudden, alarming silence.

"Don't know your own strength, do ya, boy?" Erwin laughed his hearty, booming laugh. "This is a specimen of a boy you have here, Beatrice. You better keep a close eye on him."

Beatrice laughed.

The man placed Bob's hand on another switch and pressed it forward, and slowly they moved back to the railroad station in reverse. "The boy's going to be the strongman at the Western Montana Fair impressing his girlfriends."

"My boy will be known for his brains," Beatrice said primly. "Not his brawn."

"Oh Bea," Erwin said. "You always were such an egghead."

His mother, of all things, stuck her tongue out.

Where was that Beatrice? he thought, the one that made up these adventures, then went through with them—his father laughing at the table that night as Beatrice told him about the engineer and Bob driving the train. He didn't seem to mind, so much, the old boyfriend, although, Bob noticed, his voice had a hitch in it when he asked how Erwin was, and his mother's voice grew cagey and she waved her hand as if Erwin were a fly she was swatting away.

That's what he wanted for this child, he thought, as the wipers swished a fan-shaped clearing in the windshield. Moments like that. A mother who would lean down and whisper, *You can go to the moon, if you want to.*

Bob arrived in Seeley Lake, two hours later than he'd expected, and slowly eased the car down the snowy dirt road to Pete's cabin, hoping like hell he'd be able to get back out. He hiked through the snow to the front porch and knocked, snow capping the shoulders of his Harris Tweed. There were garbled voices inside, and he hoped he hadn't arrived during some kind of family trouble.

Pete opened the door. Notes from a soprano spilled out from the warm cabin, the voice high and round and clear. "*Chi il bel sogno, di Doretta*?" rang into the snow-muffled forest and a meadow where a lone horse was hunkered down in a small shed, its head bent, its mane white.

Bob stood, stunned. He might have expected "Your Cheatin' Heart." Or "Jumbalaya." Not opera.

Pete laughed.

"Damn, Pete," Bob said. "Puccini?"

"Maria Callas," Pete said. "I wisht I coulda taken a picture of your face. But for Christ's sake, come in or you'll freeze your ass off.

Bob stamped his feet, brushed off his coat, and stepped around the large dog lying in the middle of the hooked rug as Maria Callas hit a high C and held it. Bob remembered Pete was originally from Italy, though he had been in the states since he was a child and only the faintest trace of an accent.

Pete walked over to the turntable and lifted the needle off the 78. The room was shocked quiet. Bob began hearing other sounds, the hissing coffeepot, the crackling woodstove, the clatter of the record as Pete plucked it off the turntable and slid it back in its cover.

Pete poured him a cup of coffee and set it on the table, not asking.

Bob sat down. He loved Pete's directness, his gruff voice and the way his gnarled hands gripped his coffee cup, sure, steady, straight up—without the tentativeness that permeated everything in his own family.

Cora came in the back door, dressed in men's boots and a coat, her black curls sticking out of a stocking cap. "Bob!" she cried and hugged him, then immediately went to fetch plates, forks, and—she announced—raisin sour cream pie. "Where's your manners, Pete? You didn't offer the man pie?" She sat him down at the table and set out the sugar bowl and cream pitcher. "You and that damn opera." She turned to Bob. "Good lord, we barely heard you knocking—and me, starved for company!"

"Danny, come have pie with Mr. Carter," Cora called to a room in the back where Bob could hear some muffled music.

Danny emerged from his room, a gangly kid with a cowlick and a hawkish nose.

"Damn kid," Pete said. "Always listening to some fool guitar player."

"It's not some fool guitar player, Dad." Danny said. "It's Elvis."

"Hey Danny," Bob said, shaking Danny's outstretched hand. "So you like Elvis Presley?"

"I'm a fool for him, Mr. Carter," Danny said. Bob laughed as Cora and Pete rolled their eyes. Danny bowed his head, giving Robert a view of the pale scalp beneath his crew cut. "I know the words to everything he wrote."

He stood in front of Bob, hands dangling at his sides like long extension cords, while his father looked up at him like he was some kind of strange animal. Cora tugged his flannel shirt and handed him a fork and a plate of pie. "You're excused."

"Nice to see you, Mr. Carter," Danny said, and they heard the door close softly behind him, then the scratch of the needle on the record as the music swelled again.

"Danny plays basketball." Cora thrust a picture of the five-member Seeley Lake basketball team in Bob's hand. He could see Danny in front, his legs like tamarack poles sticking out of his black trunks.

Bob felt the day closing in. He had to get home by seven. He had volunteered to work as a timer at the Kiwanis basketball games held in underprivileged schools, the boys with their thin, malnourished faces and their gritty drives down the echoey grade school gyms. He had to get back on the road before dark. He got out his briefcase and laid out the insurance papers on the blue-flowered oilcloth, next to his empty pie plate. He explained to Pete how he had two sets of insurance papers, one to insure the stud mill, the other for the tepee burner, at a reasonable replacement value for both of $300,000. "I'd add $100,000 bringing your replacement value for both to $400,000 and insure it for that amount," Bob said. "$100,000 more will cost you just $150 more a month. And you'll be glad if something happens. Mills, you know, are very flammable."

As he talked Bob fiddled with the salt and pepper shakers at the table—a tiny rooster and chicken. He saw Pete studying his hands. They were freckled, sprinkled with brown hairs, square at the fingertips, nails clipped, unscarred, and soft. They were not a workingman's hands. This was Montana, where a man's hands were supposed to be calloused, toughened by work and weather. He was not that kind of man, a man that other men looked to, admired, took stock of. He never had been. He was quiet, retiring. His weapon was his brains.

Pete waved at the papers—his fingers tracing the blocks of words. He studied Bob's face. "What is all this crap—" he said.

"Pete—" Cora said, her voice low.

"In plain English?" Bob asked.

"Well, probably not Italian," Pete grinned. "Comprende?"

"Basically, this crap says that if a fire destroys the mill and if it hasn't been set by you, you're covered up to 80 percent of damages."

"Is that as good as I can expect for what they gouge me each month?"

"It's about as good as you'll do."

"You sure as hell wouldn't lie to me, would you, friend?" Pete leaned so close to Bob that he could see the hair follicles on Pete's nose. His eyes were blue and sharp as glass. I would hate, Bob thought, to be on the wrong side of this man.

"I'd be afraid to," Bob said.

Pete laughed. "I believe ya."

Bob pushed the papers toward him. "Read these. This is for the mill; this says that you are insured if the mill burns down." He pointed to the signature line and drew a large X. He uncapped his pen. "Name and date."

Pete Donatello. His signature seemed so unlike him, Bob thought, the letters large and awkward, tilted slightly backwards. He paused, ink puddling on the white paper, then added the date: "January 5, 1953."

Bob moved another contract toward him. "This says you are insured if one of your workers sues you." Again, he drew a large X at the signature line.

Pete pointed a weathered finger at Bob. "I'd kick their asses if they did."

"This," Bob said, "protects your home if your business gets sued." He looked at the documents as he imagined Pete saw them—Pete who spent his life in the woods or on the green chain picking out imperfect boards or in the tepee burner, stripping the thick knobby bark off Douglas fir, these trees where bears scratched for cambium and squirrels chattered down generations of families, stripping them bare and slick and giving them dimensions—4 x 6, 8 x 10—so they easily stacked and could be shipped around the world on trucks and railway cars to build houses, all this contained in these documents grey with words, with the clauses and indemnities, with whereases, wherefores, and whereofs.

"Jesus," Pete said, taking his eyes from Bob's hands to his face. "There are too many fucking lawyers in this world."

Bob tipped back his head and laughed. "You damn right about that. That's why you have to protect yourself."

"If I played it safe," Pete said, "I wouldn't have anything." He flipped one page, then another. "I don't know anything about this—" He flipped another page. "Or this." He flipped another page. "Or this."

He looked Bob in the eye. "So you're telling me it ain't just me and my chainsaw anymore?"

"It's a different world out there, Pete."

"Helluva thing," Pete grumbled and scrawled his name on the signature line as the stove popped and Cora, over the clatter at the sink, reminded him not to swear.

At the door, Bob rested his fingers on the wooden handle. He turned back to the room he loved so well, wondering if, in another lifetime, he could live like this: the log cabin, the oilcloth table, the pie, Cora; why did it seem so much simpler? Pete handed him his hat, and then Bob did just what he told himself he wouldn't do—he blurted, "Mary's expecting." Cora clasped her hands and hugged him with surprising fierceness. Pete pumped his arm up and down, then told him to wait as he went to the back room to get something. He disappeared into Danny's room and returned with something he pressed into Bob's palm.

It was a gold St. Christopher medal.

"You know this guy is usually the patron saint of travelers," Pete said. "But it started when he found a lost child and carried it across a river."

Bob clasped his hands around the smooth, round pendant. He left the two of them framed in the doorway, trudging back to his car through snow-laden tamaracks, trying to retrace his steps to keep the snow from going over the top of his rubber galoshes.

It didn't occur to him until he was miles down the highway, following cars south on the plowed roads along the snowbanks, past the tiny town of Seeley Lake, a resort town with its one café, three bars, and a tackle shop, dark in winter and surly in summer when droves of summer folk arrived with their fancy cars and lake cabins and money the locals unhappily depended on, and three deer paused, then leapt across the highway in front of him, the movements liquid, effortless, as they disappeared ghost-like into the black lodgepole, and he geared down and the car began to slide, his heart bunching in fear, and he turned into it and the car righted itself and he avoided going into the ditch. Of course, he thought, as he corrected the skid, how could he be so dumb. It was plain as the nose on his face. Pete asked him all those questions—what does this say, what does this mean—because he couldn't read. The only letters he knew were those in his name: Pete Donatello.

CHAPTER THREE

The Prairie-style house Elizabeth inherited from her parents was filled from basement to attic with four generations' worth of Carter furniture, mail, knickknacks, letters, magazines, trunks, dolls, lead soldiers, cookbooks, baby buggies, and sermons. When she and Tom first moved in, she was comforted by the clutter. It was a way of summoning her parents. Her father had died three years ago of heart failure, sitting at the breakfast table on the morning of his June birthday, the next minute slumped over his eggs. Her mother followed a year later; complications stemming from a broken hip. Elizabeth had been comforted by the sight of her mother's army of vitamin bottles, her father's collection of World War II miniature tanks, all facing west, as if he were preparing to do battle with an army of mice.

Now, she hated all of it. The stuff was paralyzing, as if it buried her along with her parents, like those Egyptian kings who took their servants, horses, and armies along with them when they died.

Garbage bags were her salvation. Throwing things out was her war against death. It was a way of rescuing one more molecule of air in the house, a way of claiming it as her own.

She shook a sack open and began to toss.

As each clean surface emerged, Elizabeth felt cut to some essential shape.

Who needs history? she thought. What is the past but some old story that wraps itself around you until you can no longer see, seaweed that pulls you underwater, robbing you of breath? Her past, her newspaper job at the *Chicago Tribune*, which she'd abandoned to come home to take care of her parents, was the most recent history she'd like to run from. Here she was, right back in the arms of her more distant past. Ugh.

She buried her grief in housework, as had generations of women before her. She stared at the stacks of magazines in the upstairs hallway—*Fortune*, *Time*, *National Geographic*, *Good Housekeeping* dating back ten years. She tossed. First, *Time*. Enron's collapse, *thunk*. Saddam Hussein's capture, *bang*. She trashed whole years. 1988, 1987, history. She threw away a blue ceramic Dutch boy and girl with ghastly grey faces and listened to them break in two, satisfied. Each item she threw away energized her, and as she cleared one surface, she looked to the next: a cluttered tabletop, an overstuffed cupboard. All just waiting for her.

She was vacuuming out the hallway, sucking out decades-old mouse poop, when the vacuum suddenly quit.

She whirled around.

Tom stood behind her, the vacuum cord dangling from his hand.

The room grew quiet, dust floating down around them.

"Elizabeth, it's one-thirty in the morning."

"I can't sleep," she said. "And they say when you can't sleep, you should get up and make yourself useful. So I decided to clean—I mean look at all these magazines, these bags of stuff I'm getting rid of—"

"Elizabeth, you are vacuuming." Tom had a look on his face that Elizabeth read as a kind of bemused wonder. "Don't you need to work in the morning?"

"I'll be fine," she said. "I'll drink coffee. I'm so excited about what I'm getting done."

"Well," he said calmly. "I would be too, if it were two in the afternoon. But vacuuming at one-thirty in the morning is not useful. In fact, it is the opposite of useful." He pointed to her with the vacuum plug. "What is useful at one-thirty in the morning is sleep. I have to teach in the morning, in case you've forgotten."

"Look at these shelves!" Elizabeth whirled around and showed him the bare boards, the clean floor of the closet she had cleaned. "Remember that junk in here? We can store things now! And look—there are even shelves here we didn't know about."

He looked at her hands, grey with dirt. "Elizabeth—"

She had a dropping feeling in her stomach, as if she had come down in elevation too quickly. "What?"

"This is out of control," he said softly. He dropped the plug and slowly wound the cord around the vacuum handle.

"I know. I can't explain it."

"It's got to stop." Tom said.

Elizabeth's face grew hot.

Tom came over and took her hand off the vacuum. He grabbed her around the waist, plunked her down into an overstuffed chair, and pulled her onto his lap. Elizabeth put her head on his shoulder.

All I do is clean, Elizabeth emailed Karen, January 2, 1996. *It's the only thing that makes me feel good. God, there's a lot of stuff here.*

Clean away, Karen replied, *it's about as healthy an obsession as you can get. And you've got a great place to exercise it—is there a closet there that isn't filled? A drawer that isn't stuffed? Maybe you are just exorcising your grief. It must be harder for you, surrounded by all of Mom and Dad's stuff every day.*

She woke, consumed by panic. She climbed out of bed and crept downstairs to the kitchen, put the teakettle on, waited for the water to boil. She looked at the freckled Formica, the stove with two working burners that was the height of fashion in the 1950s. Suddenly she was shot with the loss of her parents—she missed seeing them around this table, her father with his nubby cardigan and thick glasses, her mother in her red sweater and strands of white hairs, looking up, smiling as she moved her walker across the kitchen. The house still had their sweet, slightly acrid smell of fried meat, floor wax, and furniture polish.

What was that song she used to sing? "Love Wanders on Every Road"?

She drank her mug of tea in the stillness of the kitchen. A dog barked down the street. The neighbor's bathroom light clicked on and, minutes later, clicked off. Weariness stole over her, then was quickly replaced by a kind of internal humming, like an engine starting up again, and she pushed herself out of the chair and walked upstairs.

She climbed up the stairs to the attic, past a pair of wooden crutches and hideous portraits by a relative who was more successful in the meat packing business. The smell of dust and moldering clothes was sharp, thick, inviting, a smell as old as imagination itself. This was the place she and Karen had played as children, dressing up in beaded gowns and leather gloves, looking at daguerreotypes of family, faces resolute as they stared up from brocade-covered albums, the aunts like black crows, the ancient-looking children, the boys in short pants, the girls in ringlets, the stern fathers with monocles and broad unsmiling faces. This was the place the two of them came that day in May, when her mother dressed them for the Penney's photographer, Elizabeth in her pale green top and skirt with rickrack trim, Karen in a plaid sundress. They'd found the Christmas toys their mother had bought on sale and stored away for the next Christmas: a dollhouse with real furniture for Karen, a sad-eyed doll with long blonde hair that came with her own sleeping bag for Elizabeth.

While the two of them were covered in dust and that particular timelessness associated with guilty pleasure, their mother was riding Elizabeth's Schwinn around the neighborhood, frantically calling them. Then she remembered the attic. There they were: faces smudged, dresses filthy, Karen decorating the living room of the dollhouse, and Elizabeth putting the blue riding coat on the Samantha doll and tucking her into her sleeping bag. Their parents had taken them into their bedroom and spanked them as they faced one another. At first, it seemed very funny to Elizabeth, until it made her mother spank her harder.

She gingerly touched a white-faced china boy doll with magenta lips that looked like something out of a nightmare.

Nearby was a rack of cheap, matching cardboard boxes that Elizabeth recognized as one of her mother's attempts to get organized. She unloaded the boxes from the racks and opened them, tossing the threadbare girdles, underwear with stretched-out elastic, torn T-shirts into her sack. Check carbons, bound together by a silver clip.

As she was about to toss them in the sack, her father's handwriting stopped her. It was pinched, squarish, small, the awkward scrawl of a left-hander forced to write with the opposite hand.

Each one written to the State of Montana for amounts ranging from $40 to $60.

Oh God, Elizabeth thought. She remembered her father's voice, soft, his head sideways on the white pillow, the heart monitor beeping.

"I wasn't always good to your sister." he said. "Daddy, Karen loves you," she said. "No," he shook his head, his voice urgent. "Listen to me. There is another Elizabeth. Another sister. I always thought it was better not to tell you. Now I'm telling you." "Why keep her a secret?" she asked him. Her father looked at her, his eyes distant. "That's what we did in those days. To protect you."

Oh my God, her sister Karen wrote back. *We have a sister?*

And then the news was lost in the chaos of grieving, settling the estate, and then her mother passed and the cycle began again. She'd told Ruth when they were out for a drink one night. When Ruth started to pepper her with questions: Is she still living? What's her name? Don't you want to find her? Elizabeth knew it was a mistake. I don't know. I don't know, she kept saying, wishing that Ruth would stop asking her questions, wishing that she had never brought it up.

She put the checks back in the box and shut the lid.

She climbed downstairs, washed her face and hands, and got into bed beside Tom, curling into his reassuring, furnace-like warmth, her head on his back. She dreamt she was being chased by an invisible dreaded pursuer, disguising herself to throw the pursuer off track, but every time this invisible being sniffed her out and was once again chasing her.

CHAPTER FOUR

"Did you come on a train, Miss Gustafson?" Willy said to Louise as she steered her Rambler past the white cottages bordering the dirt road. A man with a florid complexion and round face, Willard, the staff told her, was only mildly retarded and allowed to move with some freedom around the campus, doing odd jobs, helping with new staff members. He was telling her about a train ride he'd taken to Billings, Montana, where the conductor had taken him up front to ride in the engine.

"No, Willard," she told him. "I drove."

"Do you know trains are my favorite thing?" Willard said. He leaned closer to look at her. His large, wet lips made her nervous.

"I do," Louise said as she steered around a rock.

"Why didn't you take a train, Miss Gustafson?"

"I needed my car here, Willard," she said. It was strange, she thought, driving in the car with a man her age and speaking to him like a child. She glanced at his hands as he rubbed them together, hoping he wouldn't touch her. Part of her thought, okay Louise, this is the real deal here. And another part of her thought, he could just reach over and strangle me. Right now. Just like that.

They had passed the cottages where, Willard told her, he and the patients stayed and were headed farther out toward some log cabins, farther along the dirt road, near the base of the mountains.

"There it is!" Willard shouted, pointing out the window. "See the one with the porch, Miss Gustafson? It's the one with the porch."

She steered her car in that direction, following ruts in the grass. Stopping in front of the cabin, Louise cut the engine and pulled up the brake, dust floating around them like smoke. In minutes, she thought, I will be behind that door. Alone.

"You know, Miss Gustafson?" Willard said turning to her in the sudden quiet. "I would have taken the train here if I was you. I like trains."

Louise looked back at him. "You are a determined conversationalist, Willard. I like that about you."

Willard stared at her. "Nobody said that about me before, Miss Gustafson."

"Is that right, Willard?"

"Should I say thank you?" he asked.

"I'm not sure," she said and smiled.

"I'm glad you smiled," he said. "It's the first time. You look nicer now."

When they stepped out of the car she could see another set of two-story cabins across the river.

"Are those part of the hospital?" she asked.

"Yes, Miss Gustafson, they are." Willard's voice grew quiet. "Them's Ward Two."

"What's Ward Two?"

"Them's the ones sit naked on the floor, Miss Gustafson. The ones that throw furniture."

"Oh?"

"The ones they tie up at night," Willard said. "You don't want to know about them."

"I see," Louise said and pulled her sweater tight around her. She looked from the cabins across the river to the one in front of her. Her cabin. Built of rough-sawn lumber, it had two windows in front that shone blankly in the late day sun. The porch was piled with at least a cord of split wood. She unlatched the door and pushed it open. It was cool inside, with a narrow frame bed, army surplus no doubt, a rickety dresser, horse-collar mirror, rocking chair, and bookcase. There was a propane cookstove, a sink stained with rust, a wood box. Rough, but it was hers and hers alone.

Willard brought in her suitcases, groaning as he lifted them out of the trunk of the Rambler, his face redder with each trip to the car. When he had hauled the three suitcases and the hatbox of pictures inside, he stood next to the door, his hands dangling at his sides. "Well, home sweet home, Miss Gustafson."

Louise wondered if he expected her to ask him in, but she'd had enough. "Thank you, Willard. We'll visit another time."

"Ok-kay." Willard looked at his shoes, which were, Louise was surprised to see, brand new Romeos, an odd choice for ranch country.

"Your help was invaluable."

"It's good-bye now, Miss Gustafson." He lifted his head, his face brightening. "But you know what you need here, Miss Gustafson?"

"What's that, Willard?"

"A phonograph."

"Is that so?"

"Play some music. Some waltzes. Blue Danube. Turkey in the Straw."

"I'll take that into consideration."

"And you know what else?

"You got me on my toes, Willard."

"You need a garden."

"A fine idea, Willard." *Go now, Willard,* she thought.

"Carrots and lettuce, radishes... I grow beets real good, Miss Gustafson."

"Beets would be lovely," she said, with what she hoped sounded like finality.

It worked. He turned to go, and she watched his broad back as he walked across the field, hitching up the straps on his overalls. She could hear him talking as he walked along the side of the hayfield, "Carrots. Beets. Some nice broccoli and cauly-flowers."

She shut the door and sat on the rocking chair, padded with a print of cowboys on horses, and tried to ignore the sodden dust balls in the corners of the room. As she sat, she felt the road running through her, the tires on the pavement, the plains, the wheat fields, the slow-eyed cattle, the faces of the children that streamed past her in the hallways, wide eyes spaced too far apart—something about them reminded her of the prairie—and their hands touching her, pawing her, wanting something from her.

She closed her eyes on the steady, faraway gurgle of the river, and distant thud of Willard's footsteps as he crossed the field to his cottage.

The quiet was a song in her head. Water, bird cries, heartbeats, breath.

Finally, Louise pushed herself out of the chair and went to make a fire in the woodstove, crumpling an old *Stone City Register* with headlines about a train derailment that happened near a bridge in

Basin, the conductor and two brakemen killed. Foul play suspected. She stacked kindling and watched it burn, the crackling warmth rising into the room as she unpacked, putting the picture of her mother on the dresser, then turning it around. She did not want her mother—even in a photograph—to see her room here. She did not want to see her mother in her room here. That—the hymns, the gruel of her girlhood, that was behind her. She set her clothes in the drawers, her fan quilt on the bed, her Aunt Viveca's treasured silver mirror and brushes on the dresser, and the Marie Antoinette china doll on the washstand. The last thing she did was thumbtack her favorite picture over her bed: a tiny print of Renoir's woman ironing, the blue shadows, the strong, sweaty forearms as the woman pushed the warm iron across the cloth.

When she finished unpacking, she stood at the window looking out over the fields, graying in the dusk, the pools of light gathering at the red brick building and the one-story cottages where the patients would be bedding down by now. In a day, she would be in those rooms, soothing crying children, getting them to eat, pulling up blankets, holding bottles, singing lullabies. But not now.

She pressed her nose to the cool glass. She came to this place from Blue Earth, Minnesota. Cold enough in winter to get frostbitten in five minutes. Hot enough in summer to imagine hell. She got out early and left. This was her story now, and she grabbed hold of it, in her cabin along the Stone River.

A dog barked. Stopped. Barked again. The mountains hunkered down in the distance. Louise Gustafson in Montana. Thirty years old. Too old to be married. Too young to be an old maid. Not innocent. Not guilty. Her breasts touched the cool pane of glass. Stars pricked the black sky.

CHAPTER FIVE

The idea for the snowshoeing trip came up when he was timing at the Kiwanis basketball game between the Lowell Loggers and the Roosevelt Redskins. Held in the brightly polished Roosevelt gym, it was the third game of the six-game elementary school tourney between fifth-grade teams. Lowell was surging ahead at halftime, 45 to 36, the tough Northside boys, Arnie Brechbill told Bob, who was keeping score on his right. Arnie should know, having grown up there before starting as a teller at the bank, before moving up the ranks. The boys were huddled with their teacher-coaches, pulling at their heavy cotton shorts and pennies over their T-shirts as they nodded and the coaches talked. Dick Anderson, who was recording the score on Bob's other side, tried to slip him a flask, but Bob would have none of it, though he smiled to let Dick know he didn't mind. "Hey," Dick said, "Arnie and I and a couple of guys—we're snowshoeing in to Cecil's cabin for the weekend and we want you to come."

The referee sounded the whistle and the game resumed, and

this time the Roosevelt Redskins put a little more effort into it, their center scoring a basket as their coach leapt from the bleachers to congratulate him.

Dick nudged him.

"Think about it," Dick said as Bob pressed down the button on the stopwatch.

"Mary's due soon," Bob said. "I don't know."

"Hey man," Dick said. "The noose is tightening, this might be your last gasp, if you know what I mean. First it's love, then it's marriage..."

Bob smiled and clicked the stopwatch again.

The referee blew the whistle and the boys lined up at the baskets. The Lowell Loggers had the shot. Bob watched as a scrawny kid, with cut-off athletic socks as wristbands, stood at the center and looked up at the net as if it were the moon. Poor kid, Bob thought. He'll be lucky to get the damn thing halfway to the basket.

The kid lobbed the ball and it thudded, cruelly, at half court. The other boys yelled encouragement, throwing their arms in the air as they cheered, then hunching down again, all concentration.

On the second shot, the kid looked up. He crouched. He held the ball and looked up again, mumbling. He's praying, Bob realized. He watched the boy bend his knees and then jump, stretching out as far as he could and heaving the ball in the air, and this time the ball hit the rim of the basket and wobbled, teetered this way and that, before it dropped smoothly into the net.

The boy leapt into the air, his hand in a fist, shrieking. His teammates surrounded him, jumping, patting him on the back, voices cracking, until the whistle sent them back into formation.

Bob, Dick Anderson, and Arnie Brechbill piled into Cecil's Jeep. The trunk was heaped with army surplus backpacks, food, snowshoes, thermoses, whisky, matches, and fudge that Dick's wife had made, chocolate chip cookies from Mary. Cecil's wife was mad about the whole venture because Cecil didn't ask her about the trip, just made an announcement, so she took off for a shopping trip to Spokane, charging everything to Cecil. Arnie's wife—well, Arnie told them it was a surprise. They were so bundled up in scarves, hats, coats, long underwear, and boots that by the time they got to Bridger's city limits, they were all sweating and shouting at Cecil to roll down the windows.

"Jesus, Cecil," Arnie said, wiping his brow. "Turn down the heater."

"Now boys," Bob said. "If you're going to fight…"

Dick, who was in back next to Bob, leaned forward with his flask. "Medicine, boys. It'll make you behave."

They all took a swig, Bob too this time, glad Mary wasn't here to see this. As the car moved down the highway and wound up through the canyons along the frozen Blackfoot River, he was happy to be here with his friends on this sparkling January morning. The green and grey shales of the river canyon shone against the white snow, offset by red willows and Doug firs. The Jeep hummed along, past the Miller homestead with its log cabin and barn still in the family, past the Herefords bunched against the cold in Potomac, splotches of brown and white against the vast snow-covered pastures, past the old Abbott homestead, long abandoned, but the house, shed, barn, and cold storage so well built they would not fall down.

They stopped for coffee at Clearwater, a gas station and tiny café, where a few ranchers were gathered at the lunch counter.

"Howdy boys," said one fellow, who looked up from his coffee cup. "How're the roads?" The man looked at them in their sporting wear, hats, and coats and his eyes said *city folk*, and they looked back at him in his cowboy hat, Wranglers, leather gloves, and canvas coat and their eyes said *ranchers*.

"Slicker 'n deer guts on a doorknob," Bob said.

The old man laughed and looked up at him. "Not bad."

Dick held out his flask and offered the old man a drink.

"Don't mind if I do," the old guy said. "It'll warm me up faster 'n this coffee, that's for sure. What are you fellas doing out here anyway?"

"Snowshoeing," Arnie said. "Cecil's got a cabin at Lindburgh Lake, and we're snowshoeing in.

"You're crazy," the man said. "Why would you choose to go out in this?"

"It's fun?" Arnie said. He elbowed Cecil. "At least that's what Cecil tells us."

The man turned fully around and stared at Arnie. "Fun? For fun?"

"Because we want to get away from our wives?" Cecil said.

"Okay," the man said. "Now that's a reason I can live with."

The men filled their thermoses, ate some apple pie that had been sitting just a bit too long Bob thought, the crust powdery and stale, before they loaded up the car again and headed toward Seeley.

Bob asked them to stop at the mill, insisting that they meet Pete. "You'll love him!" he said. "He's a wonderful man."

As soon as they piled out of the car, where the tepee burner sent a full plume of smoke in the air, he knew it was a mistake. It wasn't that they weren't polite. Arnie, Cecil, and Dick shook Pete's hands. Pete took them on a quick tour of the mill and showed them the tepee burner and told them his story about coming from Italy to New York, then across the United States on a train before he landed in Helena, where he told them about sawyering in the woods west. They nodded, asked a few questions, but in their restlessness Bob could sense their lack of interest. How could he tell them about the surprise of the opera, Pete's log house, and Cora, wonderful Cora. Dick offered him a swig, but Pete abstained.

"Pete loves opera," Bob said.

"Man," Arnie said. He made a face. "That stuff hurts my ears."

Bob clapped his hands. "I guess we'd better go." He knew this was a bad idea. "We'd best be getting into that cabin before it gets dark. We sure as hell don't want to get lost."

Everyone, Pete included, looked relieved.

All was chaos as they unloaded the car, shouldered their packs, tied the cooler on the sled, strapped on the snowshoes, and grabbed ski poles, and then, with a final *thunk* as Cecil slammed the lid of the trunk, they set off. At early afternoon, the light was still good, but thinning, slanting now through the Doug firs and thin tamaracks as they set out along the unplowed road. Cecil said it was approximately a mile and a half to the cabin. He led the way, his red cap and wool jacket bright in the graying light. Arnie followed, whistling, and Dick was behind him, his collar up, stopping every once in a while to take a swig from his flask. "Are we there yet?" Dick called out. The men laughed. Bob was at the rear, pulling the sled that carried their food.

He settled into an easy rhythm, listening to the whoosh of the snowshoes, the men's breathing, the trees whispering as they swayed in the wind. The air was so pure, the quiet so profound. Maybe this was the reason he was here: to experience quiet. Mary hadn't been too happy about it. Growing up as she had in a world of women, she didn't trust him with men, didn't trust their drinking and loud voices. It's my time, she said. What if I go into labor and you aren't here? How will I get word to you? It's just overnight, he said. I'll be back the next night, safe and sound. These are church men, Kiwanis buddies. I'm trying to get out before the baby comes so I can be with you, Mary, he'd said. She frowned, but he knew all was well when she touched the tip of his nose and said, "Oh, just go."

They followed the cabin road, past a tangle of deadfalls, past a small, iced-over creek. As they neared a meadow, Cecil stopped and turned around and pointed. At the meadow's edge, a moose stood, head down, grazing. Arnie adjusted his backpack, the canvas scratching, and the moose's head shot up. The antlers were enormous, cupped and fringed and wide as platters, Bob thought, as he watched the moose turn its head to the right and the left, listening.

The men stood still on the road above, watching. The moose bent its head down again and began to graze on the willows. It pawed the ground, then grazed some more.

After a minute, Dick said in a stage whisper. "Cecil, I have to pee."

"Good God, Dick."

"Cecil," Dick said again. "Can I pee now? Have we watched the moose long enough?"

"Oh for God's sake, Dick," Cecil said. "If you didn't drink so much, you wouldn't have to pee so much."

The silence in the forest seemed to angle in toward them, until Dick said, "Cecil, you're hurting my feelings, not to mention my bladder."

The men laughed. The moose lifted its head and loped on its long knobby legs across the meadow. Dick unzipped his fly and peed with abandon, the urine yellow and arcing, before it tunneled into the snow.

It was Dick's idea to snowshoe along the lake. "Cecil, it would be so much faster," he said, pointing to the frozen water. "I mean, look, we are on the road above, circling it, but the lake is smaller in circumference. It will save us so much time."

"Dick, I don't know if it's safe." Cecil said, continuing on the road. "I mean I know it's frozen and all, but there's always cracks."

"Look at it, guys!" Dick said, throwing out his arm. "It's solid. And in half the time it will take us trudging on this road, we could be in that cabin before a roaring fire."

Bob had to admit that sounded good. They'd been going for an hour and a half with no cabin in sight, and he was tired and sweaty and his feet were numb.

"What do you think, Bob?"

"If we stayed on the edges, it seems like it would be okay," Bob said. "The ice is thicker there."

Arnie agreed. One by one, they turned off the road, stepping over snow-covered deadfalls and old stumps as they moved through the forest, branches snapping, to the lake's edge, Bob sidestepping with the sled to keep it from sliding down the hill and dumping all of their food.

The stillness of the lake was so profound it seemed to run through each of them like a kind of holiness as they gazed out on the wide expanse of ice, the narrow snow-covered docks jutting from shore, the timber-covered mountains in the distance that sloped right down to the water. The four of them stood still, looking out at the wind-whipped ice.

"God, this is beautiful," Cecil said. "Sometimes, Dick, you have a thought in your head."

The rest of them laughed.

Dick jigged his feet up and down in his snowshoes. Then he shed his pack and took off down the slope, crashing along the shore and out onto the lake.

"Dick, you're crazy," Bob yelled. The others laughed, Arnie elbowed Cecil, and Cecil nodded his head. "Okay, I take that back about you and your thoughts."

As Dick kept going, past the shoreline, past the dock where someone had left an inner tube that was transformed into a perfect snow-covered doughnut, their laughter thinned.

There was a crack, like a rifle shot. Suddenly Dick was uneven, one leg immersed in the lake, the other straddling the ice.

"Oh Jesus Christ," Cecil said.

"We should get a branch," Bob said. "The ice'll break if we go out."

Bob unstrapped his snowshoes and stomped into the woods, digging into the deadfall for a branch. All the while, Dick was sitting on the ice, trying to pull his leg out of the hole.

"Hold still," Cecil said. "If you keep moving, you'll break the ice more, you idiot."

Arnie was standing by. "What can I do? Should I go back and get someone?"

"No," Cecil said. "Stay here. That's a good way to get yourself killed."

Bob dragged the branch down to the water, stomping through thigh-deep snow till he reached the lake. He gingerly stepped out on the frozen surface, beaten by the wind into a whorled, bumpy surface. He knew at some point he should lie down and extend the branch to Dick—spread his body weight across the ice—but he inched forward, past the dock, toward Dick who was sitting, saying, "Guys. I'm feeling really bad. Guys."

"Shut up, Dick," Cecil shouted. "We don't want to hear it."

There were calculations here. The distance from where he would be, prone on the ice with his branch, and where Dick was, splayed, one foot in the icy water. He was probably twelve feet away. Did Bob have the strength to pull him out? Would the ice crack as he pulled?

Should he even be doing this, Mary home alone, a child on the way, his mother by herself trying to survive the clouds of Lithium? And what about his own life?

He inched forward.

"Lie down as much as you can, Dick," Bob said. "It distributes your weight."

Dick carefully lay down on his side. He had managed to slip his right leg and snowshoe out of the hole in the ice and pull them alongside his left leg. He looked at Bob. His face was slack with fear.

"I'm just going to drag you." Bob said. He realized that someone really should have tied a rope about his waist, in case he went down, but it was too late.

He thrust the branch to Dick. Dick grabbed it. Bob began to pull.

"Damn you're a heavy bastard," Bob said. It was difficult to get traction, pulling from this angle, and at first, Bob couldn't move him. He tried scooting down the ice and jerking the branch. Dick moved just a little. He scooted again and jerked the stick. Dick moved again, his pants sliding on the ice, and Bob used the moment of the slide to pull him again.

Arnie and Cecil cheered from the shore.

When Bob reached the dock, he was able to stand on it, turn around, and pull the branch from behind, and, at last, Dick was back on shore. He was shivering. His right leg and boot were soaked. But he was all right. He stood up, brushed himself off, and faced them all.

"Well, I do feel a bit foolish," he said. "My apologies to you all."

"You *are* a damn fool," Cecil said. "But we've got to get you warm. We're close now, so you'd better snowshoe like a son-of-a-bitch if you don't want to freeze to death."

By the evening, as they gathered in front of the large stone fireplace where Cecil had coaxed the logs into a roaring fire, drinking cups of coffee laced with Dick's whisky, all was forgiven. The rest of the cabin was shadowy—the two bedrooms with army cots and army-issue wool blankets where they would sleep, the rough-planked walls hung with fishing poles, nets, and oars, and the windows where thick muslin curtains were drawn. At a large Monarch propane stove that Cecil lit with matches, he uncovered and heated up Arnie's wife's surprise: beef bourguignon, complete with pearl onions, carrots, and baby potatoes. Bob thought he might weep, the stew was so thick and delicious, sopping up the gravy with white bread.

"Your wife is a great cook, Arnie," Bob said.

"That she is," Arnie said. "I'm very blessed. She likes to cook, sew, and other things as well."

"It's the other things," Cecil mused, "that endear us so..."

"Though she won't let me get the new Buick Skylark," Arnie said.

"At least you have a television," Bob said. "Mary forbids it. Radio, she says, is all we need. All the Shakespeare productions they're doing now—right from New York City. And this new *Victory at Sea* production. She's worried about the money."

"It's what they always say," Dick said, having come out of his pout. "Until they're buying dresses."

"Or shoes," Bob said. "Then all bets are off."

"Sure enough," Cecil said. "It's the cost of hamburger, heating oil, the mortgage."

"Not to mention diapers," Dick, who was the father of two, said. "Holy shit, I mean, how can such a tiny human excrete so much. Cecil? You're the doctor."

"It is a medical mystery," Cecil said. "The tinier the human, more excrement produced."

"Not exactly what we fought for, eh boys?" said Dick. He offered them a sip from his flask.

"Or exactly what we fought for," Bob said. He accepted the flask from Dick and felt the pleasant burn of whisky spin through him. "Those nights on that ship, keeping watch, hoping like hell there wasn't a submarine as we sailed from Sidney to Okinawa, damn, all I hoped for was this."

Arnie, who was fighter pilot in the Battle of Normandy, said, "Those French women were pretty friendly, as I recall."

"So were the Australians," Bob said. "I nearly married one, till we sailed out."

"Some of us were almost married too," Dick cried, laughing. "I was almost married in Italy. In Anzio. Nettuno. And oh my God, the wine."

Arnie started telling them about his ranch house, the master bedroom with a bathroom, two bedrooms, an eat-in kitchen, and a two-car garage, for which he had only one car. That Skylark, he said, would just slip in the other side so beautifully.

Cecil chimed in to complain that his wife told him he couldn't get a new car because of the mortgage on their new house, a brick two-story house up in the hills, with wall-to-wall carpet, new furnace, and a romper room in the basement.

"Hell," Dick said. "We won the war. You should have a new car."

"If only it were that simple," Cecil laughed and poked the fire, then added another log, blowing on it just a bit so that the flames rose higher.

"At least, my friends, we have our lives—whether we have the cars, televisions, or houses we want," Arnie said. "So many guys didn't make it."

"Amen to that, buddy," Dick said. "God bless 'em."

They held up their coffee mugs and toasted one another, all of them looking into the fire, as a log shifted and sparked and ricocheted among the ashes.

Bob looked around at his friends: their faces ruddy with cold and whisky, their wool shirts rolled up to expose their muscled forearms, their wool-stockinged feet stretched toward the fire. Cecil the doctor, Bob the insurance man, Dick the lawyer, and Arnie the banker. Just like the children's nursery rhyme. He sat back and warmed his hand around his coffee mug. He felt as if they were all now on the deck of a ship, this one a dark, sleek modern ship, venturing into new waters together, fathers, husbands, friends, peering ahead to the moon-laced waters together, and he took another sip of the bitter coffee and felt his heart expand at Dick's deep laugh, Arnie's humming, and Cecil's measured voice saying, "I'm turning in, boys."

Bob was the breakfast cook: making cowboy coffee, and using an eggshell to settle the coffee grounds, serving up the others while he fried the bacon and stirred the pancake batter. Cecil had risen with him. Dick, who'd been snoring like a freight train in the bunk above, stopping every time Bob gave him a kick, snorting and turning over before he'd start up again, was still in bed. Arnie had read old issues of *Field and Stream* all night on the couch, his feet tucked in a blanket. Bob tested the griddle, flecking some water across it to see if it was ready, and when it skittered, watching the batter bubble up as he dished it onto the skillet.

He served up a stack of buttermilk pancakes, a nest of bacon, and coffee to the men around the fireplace. They were talking about childbirth.

"Cover your ears, Bob," Dick said. "This isn't anything you want to hear, since you're in for it soon enough, brother."

"What are you talking about?" Cecil said. "It's not like you were anywhere nearby, Mr. What-do-you-have-to-complain-about?"

"Too many secretions. Not enough sex," Dick said. "If you must know."

Cecil rolled his eyes. "Don't listen to him, Bob. His wife has had two beautiful babies, just a bit of ether, no forceps, easy deliveries, and all this guy did was go visit the nearest tavern until I called him and he could come and pass out cigars in the waiting room."

"I hated it," Arnie said. "The waiting. I hated being in that waiting room. Knowing she had to do all that."

"What are you, a weirdo?" Dick said. "You think you could help?"

"Well, I'd like to be with her, is that a crime?"

"Stick to printing money, Arnie," Dick said. "You're getting strange on us."

By the time Bob was home, curled in bed next to Mary, the snowshoes put away, the thermos rinsed and drained in the rack, his smoke-infused clothes in the basement next to the washer, all thoughts of babies and houses and mortgages slipped into the soft, warm sensation of Mary's skin, her breasts, the tautness of her belly. "I really missed you," he whispered, but she was far away in sleep and didn't hear him, only covered her head with the sheet and burrowed down next to him.

CHAPTER SIX

Elizabeth's body was one world. Breathless, thrumming blood, an ocean of nausea that rose from her toes and prickled the backs of her legs and engulfed her morning, noon, night. Her breasts seemed to belong to her ten-year-old self—swollen and sore to the touch, the nipples turning from pink to brown. Her stomach seemed enormous to her when she turned sideways, the way it swelled out of her hips, though no one so far had seemed to notice that she didn't tuck in her shirt anymore and favored loose dresses. And the nausea, the constant rising and falling, overshadowing, mind-clouding nausea, like a background noise that some days she could live with and on others, couldn't. It seemed that if she turned toward it or if there was a certain smell—say the acrid, oily steam of hot dogs cooking—she would succumb to it immediately, barely making it to a bathroom safely before she retched until her throat burned. Other days, she could move through it and around in it, the strange push of blood through her, like a river swollen with snowmelt.

In the newsroom of the *Bridger Chronicle*, she was immersed in a familiar world: the sharp smell of newsprint, the police scanner chattering, computer keys clacking, phones ringing and voices murmuring as reporters laughed among themselves or into receivers cradled into their necks as they typed, the *phhhiipp* of the pneumatic tube carrying stories to typesetting, and the presses in the basement that hummed and sang as they ran the ads first, then classifieds, and finally at night the dailies, the bitter smell of burnt coffee, shoes tapping back and forth across the linoleum floors and the front doors wheezing open and shut, open and shut, and that sensation of weariness that settled over her as she opened the gate that led into the newsroom, hung up her coat, put her purse in the bottom drawer of her desk, and turned on her desktop, saying hello to Clayton on her right, Miriam on her left, as her computer blinked to life.

Clayton, of course, was working on the assignment she wanted, the one about the colony of rhesus monkeys housed at a research lab at Fort Bridger. He'd told her how the professor had shown him how the monkeys were held in rows of wire cages, none of them allowed to see humans—he had to wear a mask to go see the monkeys in their cages. They were fed, Clayton told her, on "Purina Monkey Chow." As he spoke, Clayton stepped over to her desk, and stood over her. "Monkeys, you know, are very hierarchical," he said, looking down at her breasts. "When the male dies, the colony is in complete disarray."

"Clayton, I know you want me to read into that," she said. "But I really have a lot of work to do now. And you have your monkeys, dear."

Clayton touched the bridge of his glasses to push them back on his nose. "But if a dominant male attacks a baby, the females attack him."

"Well, then," she said. "You're learning a lot, aren't you?"

"Just sayin.'" Clayton thankfully was moving to his desk. "I'm telling you, testosterone is really something to watch out for."

"I'll keep that in mind," Elizabeth said and rolled her eyes at Miriam, the eternally cheerful woman next to her, who was assigned to the zoning commission, where there was always a fight about something—this time the definition of a family, telling her the last zoning commission meeting was so contentious, the commissioners had called in the police. "I mean all of these people are standing up in the meeting, all upset because these four bald white guys think 'three or more unrelated people sharing a dwelling' is violating some family rule and they should be fined or sent to jail." She opened her desk drawer, threw her purse inside, and slammed it. "Lord, we might as well just start packing our jails with all the slumlords in this town."

"I'll volunteer mine," Clayton said, as he dialed the phone.

Ruth, the city editor, came out of her office and asked Elizabeth to come into the narrow glass cubicle Ruth called her "clean, well-lighted place." She settled herself behind the desk, shoving her glasses up on her head. "I know you were mad about that monkey story," she said. "But I have something I think you'll like."

"Hey, I'm all ears." Elizabeth looked through the window at Clayton who, although he was on the phone, was looking at her, smiling, as if the two of them were having a moment. God, what an annoying man, she thought. She'd love to make him eat shit.

"It's about a Down syndrome girl," Ruth said, running a hand through her short black hair. "Isn't that the right term now?"

Elizabeth nodded, her heart sinking. "It's Down syndrome, not retarded. God, the psychological association used to use the categories imbecile, moron, idiot."

Ruth folded her hands together and stared at Elizabeth. "I know you are thinking I want you to write a feel-good piece. But this piece is about this test case in California. She's thirty-five, Down syndrome. She's an activist—she even attended Bush's signing of the Americans with Disabilities Act. She graduated from high school. She needed a new heart and lung. And guess what? She got rejected."

Elizabeth stared at her. "Why?"

"The surgeons at Stanford and UC–San Diego denied her a transplant because they didn't think she's smart enough—until they were embarrassed into it when the news broke nationally." Ruth wiggled her pencil between her fingers. "Bastards. Her parents were supposed to institutionalize her here. They moved to California instead after they heard some bad reports about the Stone Home. You okay with this?" She handed Elizabeth the wire copy.

Elizabeth pushed herself out of the chair.

"I mean," Ruth paused. "Didn't you tell me you had a sister who'd been institutionalized?"

The sounds from the newsroom roared in Elizabeth's ears, and Ruth seemed to grow far away from her.

"Yeah," Elizabeth. "I do. That's about all I know." She edged toward the door, hoping Ruth would stop talking and she could settle back in her desk, cocooned by tea and routine: making calls to sources and asking questions, typing answers and fitting together words like puzzle pieces to make a story.

She waited at the kettle for that whoosh of noise as the water heated to boiling. This was the beginning of the hunt: her pensive cup of tea. She called directory assistance for a Jensen in Sacramento, then checked with the California state library for the name and number of a California disabled rights group and the hospitals that had rejected her for the transplants: Stanford and the University of California at San Diego. She had an afternoon of work in front of her. Between calls, she drew the thin red string from a package of saltines and bit into a cracker. She had never appreciated saltines till now: their existential flat, salty, crispy blandness.

"Whatcha doin'?" Clayton watched her chew. "Do I need to know about it?"

"Probably not," Elizabeth said as she dunked the tea bag in the hot water. "Story about a Down syndrome girl."

"Hmmph," Clayton said, pleased, heading out, and Elizabeth watched his back recede out the door. Through the front window, she saw him jaywalk across the street and head straight for the local dive, the Hamburger Ace. The thought of the hamburger, overcooked so it was slightly crunchy with its slop of ketchup, chopped onions, mayonnaise, and melted Velveeta on a bun made her stomach rise, and she quickly took another sip of tea to settle things.

The director of the California Center for Disabled Rights told her what an abomination he thought it was that the doctors refused to operate on this woman because they deemed her "not smart." What about their civil rights? Wasn't this the 1990s, not the 1890s? What did this say about how we treat Down syndrome patients? "People think just because we've stopped calling patients with Down syndrome retarded that somehow we're done with them."

Then he told her to call Nancy Jensen herself, telling her that she spoke slowly, but very clearly.

She first called the surgeon at Stanford Medical Center who rejected Nancy Jensen's application. Out of town, a receptionist told her, a lie of course, and Elizabeth called his office number to see if she could schedule an emergency appointment, and his assistant said, you bet. At least, she thought, the doctor at UC–San Diego had the balls to answer her calls.

"Look, I know you smell a story here," he said when he came on the line. "But the woman at age thirty-five was near the end of her life for a Down syndrome person. We made that call and, okay, we were pressured to change. But I stand by that call. Do you have any idea how complicated this is, post-surgery? Any idea?"

"Why don't you tell me?" Elizabeth said.

He sighed. "Medication morning, noon, and night. It's hard for a regular person to keep it straight. Watching the patient's diet. Their exercise."

Elizabeth smiled into the phone and kept her voice light. "I thought Medicaid hired a caseworker to help her with this?"

"You open this door," the surgeon said, "and you'll be sorry. God, we can hardly keep up with the healthy ones! We have to make judgment calls every day—and it may look easy to you, but we have to take a lot of things into consideration. Is our society going to pay to fix every broken person that walks in the door of the hospital? Really?"

She thanked him for talking to her and signed off, the phone hot on her ear. She pushed herself back from the desk. "Cauliflower ear," she said to Miriam, as she massaged the sore lobe. "I'll be back in a minute."

She zipped herself into her parka, donned her ski hat and gloves, and walked out the front door, the sudden quiet clapping her ears. She walked along a brick street that dipped down to the river, past a mural of a wagon wheel flanked by wheat painted on the side of a building, past a ramshackle house with a cock-eyed television antenna on the roof, and another row of old brick railroad workers' houses fronted by a frosty yard decorated by a lone snowman with a cap from the local football team.

She had ten minutes to walk, to think how she'd call the national disabled-rights magazine, *Mainstream,* which broke the story, then the press agent for the California Medicaid system. She had a few more hours to finish the story, due at four.

She stepped carefully along the icy path. Blocks of ice moved slowly in the river. The water was pewter-colored, slow as an afterthought. *This is your river, baby,* she thought, as she held her stomach. She talked to her baby here. *This is a part of you. This is where your grandfather came and tossed pebbles and wrote letters home and said, this is the place we come to cut out all worrying. I can't wait to meet you.*

In the pictures her father had showed her, her great-grandfather looked so resolute, as if he knew the size and shape of his world, with his thick white hair and bald pate and dark round glasses as he stared straight into the camera. His son and grandson were taller and softer: the dark-haired, dimpled, blue-eyed Dandy, her grandfather, and then her father, the chubbier, round-faced man who was called Bobby-Boy by his great-aunts until he came home sobered by World War II. And this other sister. Was she out there, like this Nancy, walking a dog, rallying for her rights?

She walked past a man jogging, his black-and-white border collie smiling at his side.

She started back up the hill, planting each foot on the snow so she wouldn't slip, heading back to the newsroom to finish her story.

Nancy Jensen spelled her name out for Elizabeth. She told her that with her new heart, she could now walk her dog and do water aerobics. "My dog is a brown lab. His name is Snickers," she said.

"Can you tell me about the transplant?" Elizabeth said.

Nancy told her how the nurses helped her go to sleep so it wouldn't hurt when the doctors cut her, and when she woke up she felt sore. "I had on the biggest bandage ever," she said. "It made me cry." She went on to tell Elizabeth how she had to take many pills and sleep long days in the hospital. The nurses were so nice, especially

Daisy, and brought her dinner and 7-Up. And she had balloons.

Elizabeth asked her where this happened. Nancy carefully told her it was Stanford Hospital. "The buildings were white. Tall," Nancy said. "There was a big dish like a giant Frisbee on the hill." About San Diego, where she saw white sailboats, she said, "The doctor said I couldn't get a heart because I wasn't smart." She giggled. "I saw a giraffe there."

"They say you are breaking barriers," Elizabeth said. "Breaking barriers for the disabled with this transplant."

Nancy was quiet. "I didn't break anything."

"What I mean is that you are standing up for what is right," Elizabeth said. Amazing, she thought, how filled with euphemisms English is. Standing up. Breaking barriers. How could she simply say she admired her? "You are a hero," Elizabeth said.

"Like Superman?" Nancy giggled again.

"Like Superman," Elizabeth said.

Elizabeth wrapped up the story by three-thirty, running it by Ruth for a quick check, then by the copy desk who corrected a few dangling participles, and she was able to send it in the tube to typesetting by four, before she felt swept over by an exhaustion that often visited her this time of day, so she snuck into the break room, wrapped herself in her coat, and lay on the couch. She was drifting off, despite the sounds of the refrigerator opening and closing and Clayton telling Miriam how he thought the rhesus piece guaranteed him newspaper's association prize this year, when Nancy's even voice came back to her.

"Can I ask you something?" Nancy said. "'Kay?"

"Okay," Elizabeth said.

"Are you scared of me?"

"I don't think so," Elizabeth said. "Why do you ask that?"

"Because you talk really loud. Like you are afraid."

CHAPTER SEVEN

When she was introduced as the new nurse in the nursery at the Monday morning meeting, Louise saw the look that scattered through staff members. She knew immediately the nursery was the test job: Survive it, you stayed. Don't survive it, you're down the road. As the others discussed budgets and medications, Dr. Oetzinger eyed her afresh—her face, her neck, her breasts—as if he were sizing her up all over again.

While Charlene, the head nurse, talked, the staff held coffee cups and doodled on steno pads as the sun shone on the old fireplace at the end of the room. Louise looked around the room as her new colleagues went on to discuss individual cases—the fifty-year-old man caught masturbating in the dining room and whether or not the seizure that Sandra Wittpenn had last Sunday was real or was she faking it to get out of sowing the winter wheat in the school's fields.

Above the table hung another portrait of Frau Holtzmeier, the school's benefactor, the wife of a wealthy cattle baron from eastern

Montana. She looked a bit like a Hereford herself, Louise thought, her large head and wrinkled neck rising up out of a large bosom clad in brown velvet. Her eyes were clear, green, and penetrating, her shock of white hair swept up in a bun. *To all my little lambs, one and all,* the plaque read, *may thy comforts of the Lord shine upon ye and release thee from darkness. Frau Holtzmeier.*

Louise snapped back to attention.

Charlene, whose hair looked like a roll of barbed wire, read a list of surgeries: how a certain Kyle Daniels had the "procedure"—a lobotomy, Charlene explained in a nod to her—because he had been "increasingly violent." She read on: there were several "tube ties" on severely retarded female patients, and a few others who had been moved from one cottage to another because of behavioral issues. "We had to isolate Isabella Klack again," she said to the Indian woman with the long braid who sat next to Louise and had not said a word the entire meeting.

"Why?" said the director, Mr. Roberts, a large officious man in a white coat with a large brown and meticulously waved mustache.

"Inappropriate use of feces."

"What'd she do?"

"She drew on the walls with her B.M.," Charlene said.

Several staff members groaned. "Jesus," someone muttered. "I thought we got her to stop that."

"Kind of like a Poop-casso," the director said and looked over his glasses at the room.

A titter.

"You bet, Larry," Charlene looked at him, her voice was flat. "A regular Rembrandt."

A large man at the end of the table said to Louise. "You'll have to excuse us, Miss Gustafson. Some of us around here think our little jokes keep us sane."

Louise smiled, but said nothing.

"The question is," Charlene continued. "Do we isolate her again or give her more Luminal?"

Dr. O looked at the nurse, then down at the file. "How much is she on now?"

"In the 300s—," Charlene said. "And remember, she doesn't do well in isolation. Last time she pulled her eyebrows out."

"Try 350," Dr. O said.

One of the nurses announced the arrival of the state inspection board that next Tuesday, and how all buildings, cottages, and group meeting rooms needed to be cleaned, and the residents bathed and dressed.

There was a pause and Dr. O cleared his throat. "And now—" said Doctor O, who had landed here from the University of Michigan, because, Charlene had told her, he liked rocks. Rocks? Louise said. Rocks, the nurse said. He's a paleo-whatchamacallit. "Good news, everyone. Next week, for the first time in this joint, we get an EEG."

Everyone looked at him.

"Ah yes, the blank stare," he said. "Such a familiar and comforting sight." A shock of black hair fell into his eyes. He shook it aside and looked down the row of nurses. "This will help us diagnose those with epilepsy, you see. Spikes and slow waves, the classic brain wave of the epileptic. We can sort out the cases, and figure how better to treat them." He looked around the room. "Thought you might be interested. Though, of course, the bright light in your eyes tells me I might be mistaken."

Charlene nodded.

"What is an EEG?" Louise asked. Immediately she knew, from the looks cast her way, that the question was a mistake. Brown-noser, obstructionist, the stares said. The meeting was nearly over, the other looks said.

"Do I—" Dr. O looked over at Louise, "detect that rare and wonderful thing, curiosity?"

Oh God, Louise thought. I've done it this time.

"An EEG is an electroencephalogram. It measures brain waves. It is used to diagnose epilepsy. Right, Charlene?"

"Right, Dr. O," she said.

"Such eager faces. Sigh..." he said to the rest of the staff with a smile. "Meeting dismissed. And don't worry—your doughnuts are out there, waiting for you."

Louise walked out of the meeting room with Anna Windy Boy, her steps nearly soundless in her leather moccasins. Her black hair hung down her back in a long shining braid, her eyes dark.

The hallway was long and echoey with eighteen-foot-ceilings and faded brocade wallpaper, a red that had faded to pink. Louise put her square-palmed, blunt-fingered hand on the wall: she had worker's hands. She thought of the thousands of hands along these walls. Closest to the ground would be the soft, pudgy children's hands with their thin pink fingernails and pale half-moons, fat dirty hands with torn cuticles and ragged nails. Above those, the secretaries and nurses' hands, some clean-scrubbed, others with scarlet nails. Above them, the large calloused hands of the men who worked on the farm, nails bitten to the quick, and the scrubbed hands and neatly clipped nails of the doctors. She imagined all the years of hands down this hallway, touching the curlicues, the dots on the wallpaper, as the fingers swept or scraped along, where a Victorian print hung, the same one that hung in her bedroom as a child: the black-and-white image of a girl praying at an open window as fat, translucent cupids spilled down from heaven to greet her. Why were the Victorians so preoccupied with children and death? Louise wondered. Why would anyone in their right mind hang a picture like that here? What are they trying to tell these children, anyway?

As she and Anna walked by the picture, Anna was so quiet Louise felt she could hear her own heartbeat.

Louise wanted to reach over and rip the ridiculous picture from the wall. She looked away. Gather yourself, she thought. This is how you get yourself in trouble. She turned to Anna and said, "So you've worked here a long time?"

"Five years," Anna said.

"Where is everyone? It is so quiet."

"Training," Anna said. Her voice was soft and precise. "They have morning training in manners, basic math, and reading—as much as some of them are able."

They walked, not talking, for a few more steps, the sounds of their footsteps between them.

"Who made your moccasins?" Louise said. "They're beautiful."

"I did," she said.

"You made them?" Louise knelt down to touch the intricate pink and green beads and porcupine quills that made up the pink roses, the petals stitched in four shades of green. "You stitched all that?"

She shrugged. "It's what I do."

"How long did it take you?" Louise said.

"A winter," Anna said. "Not much else to do up on the Rocky Boy."

Louise laughed. "In Blue Earth, you play cribbage, sew, pray, or drink."

Anna smiled a quiet, slow-spreading smile. "In Box Elder, you can do all that in one night."

The cries reached them first, the sharp mewling of the newborns, the more substantial cries of the three-month-olds, pure outrage from the six-month-olds, and the sturdy howl of one- and two-year-olds. As they walked in, the room was alive with the delicate, unearthly energy of babies: their crying, gurgling, screaming. The pungent brew of talcum powder, diaper rash ointment that smelled like fish oil, shit, urine, and sour milk gagged her. Eight cribs lined the walls, and in most of them a baby stood at the rails and cried, the mouths a succession of black Os.

A baby in a red fuzzy sleeper reached through a crib's white slats. Near her, a boy in a blue striped onesie stared blankly at them, weeping, then plunked down on his large padded bottom, his hair sticking out from his head in wet tufts. Another gripped the rails of the crib and rocked back and forth as she cried. In five cheap bassinets made of plastic etched to look like wicker—donated by some Ladies' Aid Society—babies too young to lift their heads sobbed. Saddest of all was the one bassinet where a baby in a sleeper decorated with printed trucks lay staring.

The boy in the red sleeper had the protruding forehead of an encephalitic. The other kid, Louise observed, who was sitting down, was clearly mongoloid, with his tilted eyes and flat face. In the bassinets, some of the babies had missing limbs, protruding foreheads, or mangled lips and flat faces. The child on its back simply shook.

Lord, Louise said, though she wasn't the praying type.

An infant stared up at her from a bassinet.

"You the new one?" the nurse said. She stood, straight as a birch limb, her thick blonde hair plaited in two straight braids. She picked up the red-sleepered child, sniffed his bottom, and began to pat him. "I'm Margaret."

Anna introduced Louise, touched her arm, and disappeared down the hall.

"Thank God you're here." Margaret plunked the child in Louise's arms and turned to fetch another. "I'm about to lose my mind."

As the morning wore on, Margaret and Louise worked the room as fast as they could, moving from baby to baby, diapering, feeding, rocking. Louise held the convulsive baby, feeling the strength of his tiny arms and legs as they twitched and jerked, and she had the strongest urge to still them and wondered what in his body commanded him to make these movements, to flinch and jerk this way. She picked him up and took him to the rocking chair, where she started to sing, "Rock-A-Bye, Baby."

"Don't," Margaret snapped. "We don't got time. You start that and pretty soon they'll all be wantin' it and we'll be sunk."

"He's convulsing," Louise said, stung.

"He always convulsing," she said. "We got three babies to change and three more to feed."

Louise blinked her eyes clear. She put the baby back in his bassinet and picked up another child, this one a girl with twisted limbs, pulling off her urine-soaked diaper. The child flailed as she howled, and Louise wiped her bottom and dusted it with powder and wrapped her up again, setting her in her crib with a bottle propped in her mouth. Thankfully, the child sucked the milk, contented.

The sudden absence of noise was such a tonic Louise thought she'd weep.

Then she cleaned the bed of the one-year-old boy who had thrown up all over himself and his bed. Louise moved him to an empty bassinet, and as she put him down, his dark eyes studied her face and Louise called him by his name, Timothy. "Hi, Timothy," she said. He couldn't talk back—his vocal cords had not developed correctly Margaret told her—but his arm twitched. Paraplegic. It was like that all morning: babies, diapers, urine, feces, vomit, each task so immediate, each solution so temporary.

At noon, a scrawny young nurse in training came to relieve Margaret and Louise so they could go to lunch. Louise followed Margaret to the mess hall. There, they stood in line holding out their trays for baloney sandwiches and tomato soup and cookies. They carried their trays to long wooden tables surrounded by the other nurses who were also dressed in white uniforms decorated with stains that varied by the age of their patients: spit up and excrement for the baby nurses, food stains for those who worked with the younger kids and adults.

They joined a table with several other nurses and when they sat, Margaret said, "You made it through your first morning. And you stayed. Now all you have to do is get twice as fast and three times as tough." She looked to the nurse next to her. "Right, ladies?"

One of the nurses looked up, studied Louise's face, said, "That's about it," and smiled, turning her attention back to her soup.

Tomato soup. Creamy, rich, comforting, Louise thought, as Margaret began to talk. "This is the lay of the land here, kid. That there—" she pointed with her soup spoon to the head table where Dr. O sat with the hospital director and Charlene. "That's the head table. You may talk to them on rounds, but you never ever talk to them in here. Dr. O, he don't care. The hospital director, Roberts, he's an ass. But Charlene—sittin' at the head table is her be-all and end-all and do not for-get it."

Louise bit into the grilled cheese sandwich, feeling the rich gooey cheese melting between the soft homemade bread.

"That table. What shall we tell her about them?" Margaret pointed her spoon to a table where three rough-looking men sat smoking.

Two were large, heavily bearded men, and one was a scrawny bow-legged cowboy.

"Watch out?" offered one nurse.

"Turn the other way?" said another nurse.

Margaret laughed. "Those guys who look like ranch hands?" she said, as she set down her spoon and lowered her voice. "Them's Ward Two guys. Don't mess with them. They deal with the guys who have the brains of animals, who throw furniture, even eat furniture, and have to be tied in their beds. They're strong as bulls and mean as snakes and you don't want to mess with 'em."

"Got it." Louise tore off another bite of the sandwich, hoping beyond hope she could finish.

Margaret slurped some soup, small red wings forming at the edge of her lips. "Those ladies—ranch wives." Margaret pointed her spoon to a group of middle-aged women who were eating out of black lunchboxes. "They're part saint. They deal with the non-ambulatory patients in the basement here, changing diapers, cleaning up shit, bathing and feeding them. Those women are tougher 'n nails, don't mess with them neither. And that motley crew next to them—" Margaret pointed to a group of teenaged girls and boys sitting with some beat-up-looking older men. "They're staff who get hired for loose ends. You ask me—they're either too young and dumb or old and beat-up to do much of anything else. But then—" Margaret laughed, a loud braying laugh, "nobody did ever ask me."

After lunch everyone got out crossword puzzles, knitting, unfinished letters home, and novels, to fill out the hour before they had to go back.

Louise hadn't thought to bring anything, so she looked over Margaret's shoulder and helped with her puzzle, filling in "orts," for "leftovers" and "Mitchell" for the author of *Gone with the Wind.*

When the bell rang to signal the end of lunch hour, the staff rose from the tables with a weary scrape of chairs, lunch trays banging as, one by one, they slid them through a small window into the kitchen.

Louise was headed out of the room to the stairs when Dr. O caught her arm.

"How was the first day?" he said.

"Satisfactory," Louise said. "As first days go."

He laughed. His dark blue eyes bore into hers. "You look like you are paying attention. I like that," he said and turned to hurry away, his footsteps tapping on the linoleum floor.

CHAPTER EIGHT

A tap on the arm. February 4, 1953.

From the jumble of sheets and blankets, Mary's hair fell around her face as she bent toward him, buried as he was in a cave of wool blankets and dreams. Her face—her lovely face—a moon above the bed.

"My water broke," she whispered to him.

He stared at her a moment, then over at the clock. 5:15 A.M. "It's early."

"I know, silly," Mary said. "Babies don't come on schedule."

"But it *is* early," he said. He threw off the covers and leapt out of bed. "I thought the baby was due next month. What? What do I do?"

"It's fine." She laughed and held her hand out. "Stop. Relax. It's okay. Let's have coffee and some breakfast. The baby's not coming this second. Let's enjoy this—" She smiled again and flopped back on the pillows. "Let's enjoy this moment. The two of us, alone for the last time."

Bob sat on the edge of the bed. He turned to her, her hair spread against the pillow framing her lovely face, and as he watched, she grimaced and her back arched.

He stood up. "What! What is it?"

She arched her back, clenching her teeth, pursing her lips together to blow out a long stream of air. Then she collapsed back onto the pillow again. "It's okay. It's a contraction. I've been having them for a while."

"I don't know, Mary. I don't think this is a good idea. You always think you know the best thing, but you don't always."

"Ahh," Mary waved her hand at him, her face opening up again as the contraction passed. She threw back the covers, swung her feet over the bed, and walked to sit on the overstuffed chair by the bedroom window. She parted the curtains to look out on the silent street, the cars heaped under their blankets of snow, the sidewalks untrodden, snow shovels leaning on front porches, waiting. She pulled her hair to one side and rocked forward to tuck her legs under her. "This is so beautiful, Bob. It's like the whole world is waiting."

"Well, I'm waiting too," Bob said. "Waiting for you to go to the hospital."

She looked back at him. "The contractions are still pretty mild."

Bob studied her as he dressed. Her face was calm, regal even, her eyes dark and distant as if she were already a country apart from him. "Shouldn't we be going to the hospital? Now?"

"Sit down." Mary's eyes were black, fierce. "We have time. They're still a long way apart, Bob. They'll just send me home."

"You're so damn stubborn, Mary," Bob dressed, zipping his pants with a loud, decisive-sounding *zzzzzt.* "We have to go. You need doctors, nurses, a hospital—not me." He buttoned his shirt, his fingers thick.

Mary turned from the window to face him with that pale, calm, inscrutable face. "Bob."

"What?"

"I'm not ready for this. I can't do it." She stared up at him. There was a look in her eyes he'd never seen before.

"What is it?" he said. "You're scaring me to death."

"I'm not ready for this, Bob. I know I act all confident and all, I'm not. Ready, that is. At all."

"Well, it doesn't matter if you're ready," Bob laughed. "That baby's on its way."

Mary's eyes glistened. "I don't want to do this," she gulped. "What do I know about babies? What do I know about being a mother? Goddamn it, Bob, I don't even like children."

She wept, gulping draughts of air.

"Mary." Bob came over and sat on the arm of the chair and began rubbing her back. "Of course you are scared. You've never done this. But women before you have done this and women after you will do this—women a whole lot dumber than you and women a whole lot weaker than you—and I bet most of them felt like you do."

She stared at him, squeezing his arm as another contraction passed through her. "And? Your point?"

"You've got me."

She looked over at him. "And?"

"Well, doesn't that make you feel better?" He reached out to her and wiped the tears that trailed down her face. "Nothing great happens without fear."

"When it's your turn to do this," she said, "you can give me advice."

"Look, I'm trying here," Bob said and laughed, and then stopped. He'd never seen her so panicked. He knelt beside her chair and followed her eyes out the window. "Look, it's snowing again, Mary-bear.

It's snowing. I'd better go start the car and get it all warmed up for you. Can you believe it? Today we are parents? Look, I've never done this before and I'm as scared as you are but we have each other and we will do this, we will, I know we will." An ordinary winter, he thought, with the snow piling outside their window, the sound of the plow scraping the streets and the slow jingle of snow chains now and then, the whiteness and cold, their lives revolving and churning forward. He took her hand in his. "You'll be fine, Mar-bear. Fine. You'll be a hell of a mother. I promise you. We have this great house and we're going to have this beautiful baby and we have each other."

"I'll probably forget to feed it," she said. "Or I'll forget it in a car, like that woman we read about in the paper." She sniffed. "Remember that?"

"That's silly," Bob said and rose to his feet. "Look. Come in the living room. I'll make a fire and make you coffee, and then we'll go to the hospital, agreed?" He held out his hand and thought: This was his lovely Mary, his travel companion, his wife who had vomited as they traveled down the California coast and threatened hoodlums in the campground with his nonexistent pistol and now she wouldn't go to the hospital because, in the last moment she, his calm ship, his safe harbor, his moon across the dark water, was suddenly terrified of a tiny baby.

He seated Mary in the rocker, opposite the fireplace. She pulled a blanket up over her lap. Bob balled up the newspaper—the headlines touting Eisenhower's election address—made a tepee of kindling and held a match to it. As the match flamed the paper, then the kindling, and lit the larch, the two of them sat in the dark living room. After a few minutes, he excused himself and went to the kitchen to spoon coffee into the percolator and stood, transfixed by the small explosions of water in the glass knob at the top of the pot that seemed to say, this is the day, this is the day. When it stopped perking, he brought her a cup.

Mary rocked back and forth. Every so often she delicately set down her cup, stretched her legs and groaned, gripping her stomach, and cried, a long, keening, wild sound that made the hairs on the back of his neck stand straight up and sent his heart on a run.

"Now?" he asked. "Shall we go now?"

Pennsylvania Station 'bout a quarter to eight! He remembered the swing trio the two of them saw in San Francisco, the thrill of the smoky bar, how the men played back and forth, the bassist played to the drums, the drums to the saxophone player who tipped his head back and grinned, and plunged down a stairwell of sound that wrung Bob's heart out. As he looked at Mary that night, he felt so filled with the openness of the road, and as he studied her from her black hair and white slender neck and full breasts down to her slim ankles and feet, his body filled with the heat and fullness of her, and then the drummer took over and it was all about the rhythm of the waves on the shore, his hips against hers, and how when he heard that wild arpeggio he just wanted to get up and drive, the music hopping up in his blood. An odd thing, he thought, to come back to him, this day in February, when his child was on its way.

The spasm passed and she was Mary again, rocking. She lifted her coffee cup to her lips. The neighbor's dog barked. The newspaper thumped against the door, and milk bottles rattled as the milkman set them on the porch, two worlds colliding, the outside world awakening to a day of winter in February in Bridger and their private world on the brink of an earthquake.

Bob knew he couldn't budge her until she was ready. At last, she lifted her eyes to his and said, "Okay, Bob. It's time."

"Train's a-rolling." Bob said as he ran to the kitchen to find his keys. He felt as if a large motor were starting up inside himself, clanking to life, all metal rods and gear trains and pistons creaking and groaning as it picked up speed. He thought of all those nights on the bridge, standing watch over hundreds of sleeping men and munitions as they moved south through the dark chop of ocean where a yellow moon lit an uneven pathway. *Pennsylvania 6-500!* and all that it represented—that's why he was there, on that dark bridge, defending the subways and the bright crowds and women with lipstick and his mother who scowled when he put on that glossy black record with those bleating saxophones and those thundering, thundering drums.

The two of them drove to the hospital through the hushed subzero winter morning, bound together by the warm car, heater running, wipers swishing to and fro, tires whooshing the packed snow, bound together by the knowledge that their lives were about to change forever. Bob wished the drive were longer, except that, next to him, Mary's groans split the quiet, and he squeezed her hand as he drove, one hand on the wheel, from Edith Street to Higgins where the plow had already cleared a track, and across the bridge over the ice-clotted river. He parked at the hospital door, walked inside to tell the nuns Mary was in labor.

A large nun with a deeply lined, freckled face came outside with him. "Calm down, Papa, baby's not going to be born on the sidewalk," she said as she patted his arm. She pushed the wheelchair through snow to the edge of the passenger side of the car. As she and Bob helped Mary into the wheelchair, Bob noticed her hands were broad and thick-fingered. "Hello, Mama," she spoke to Mary in a voice Bob thought must be wearied from helping so many others in pain. "Let's get you more comfortable, Mama, this baby is coming our way." Bob saw the look of relief on Mary's face at her calm and he stepped aside as the nun pushed her through the snow-covered sidewalk into the hospital. As they entered the foyer, other nuns in grey habits flocked around and whisked the wheelchair off behind two metal doors that whooshed shut behind them.

"She'll be fine," the nun with the freckled face came back out to tell him. "The doctors will give her ether for the pain. She'll drift off a bit, and soon you'll be a papa. You're in good hands. I've done this many times. I'll take you to the waiting room."

She walked him down the long cold hallway, where nuns moved in and out of examining rooms, their heavy cotton habits swishing.

The waiting room was a meager affair: a few turquoise leather chairs, a table scattered with newspapers.

"Here you go, Papa." The nun showed him to a chair. "Make yourself comfortable. Get coffee. Sandwiches. You'll be here awhile. I'll bring you news as I have it." She patted his arm. "I say this to all the papas. But be calm. God has a grand design."

Bob sat in the turquoise leather chair until she had moved down the hall and out of sight. She was annoying with her pats and her papas and her grand designs. As soon as her grey habit disappeared around a corner, he popped up, walking in the other direction to the cafeteria, where another set of nuns tended giant urns of coffee. He chose a white cup and saucer. A young nun with hollowed eyes poured him a cup and he sat at a long table drinking it, listening to the chink of the cup in the saucer, feeling the thin coffee warm him. *Papa.* He wouldn't be a papa. He was a *dad.*

Outside, dark, snow-bellied clouds humped over the mountains, the snowflakes pelting down and piling up in drifts outside the front doors, until the cold sucked him inside out, his hands, feet, nostrils, eyeballs, and he headed back to the waiting room.

He thought of his father growing cold in the ground and wished he were here with him, waiting, his father who always calmed things, kept excitement from building just in case it tripped into something else, one of his mother's manias, for example. He thought of his mother, Beatrice, God bless her, tucked in her strange room in the mental hospital, in her sea of Lithium, her eyes as vague as the china dolls she painted in crafts class, and was relieved and guilty to be away from her.

Returning to the waiting room, he sat on the turquoise seat across from another man and opened a paper. He read a piece about a North Sea flood that killed three hundred people in Britain, three thousand in the Netherlands, not to mention those lost when the *Princess Victoria* ferry went down in the Irish Sea. When Bob stood up to pace, the other man in the waiting room glanced at him.

"First child?" he asked Bob.

When Bob nodded, he waved at him, suddenly expansive. "Sit down, relax. Pick up another section. You're gonna be here a while, pal, so you might as well take a load off. I been through this three times."

Bob sat across from him and the man handed him more newspaper. This time, he read about Senator Finn McCarthy's participation in the Mothers March Against Polio. The Little Liz cartoon that said, "Most women fall into one of three classes—the beautiful, the intelligent and the majority." The curious new item: Pink Elephant Invades Jail, a one-column item about a pink elephant from the Hunt Brothers Circus, bound for Chicago, that showed up in a jail in Fort Wayne, Indiana, "because it was the only place trainer Roy Bush could find to bed it down."

A nurse popped out into the waiting room to tell him that Mary's contractions were coming closer and closer and that it would be anytime now.

As the hospital settled from the squeak of early morning to the late afternoon hum, Bob consumed five cups of acidic coffee, two egg salad sandwiches, and one piece of sour cherry pie. As he moved through this vast expanse of time—it seemed to him that he lived for several days during these hours—it was strange to him that just on the other side of this hospital door, Mary was undergoing this intense physical transformation, contractions, birth. A child was coming out of her, for God's sake, how did a female body do that anyway, moving that head through the narrow tunnel, the blood, the fluids. And for him this white expanse of nothingness, of twitchy, leg-giggling, head-scratching, pacing worry: How was she? How was the baby? Would she survive? Was it a boy? Girl? When he pictured himself as a father, saw himself sitting up on a Flexible Flyer, laughing, with a child between his legs, as they sped down a snowy hill past his old school, shrieking.

He was drifting off for the third time that day, his legs crossed, his head tilted backwards, when the doctor came in. It was Cecil, ruddier-looking than usual in his blue scrubs. "Hey old man," Cecil patted him on the back. "How are you weathering all this? It's not your turn yet."

Bob gave him a wan smile. "Right now, I wish I were back at your cabin."

"Soon enough, old boy." Cecil said. "Soon enough."

Cecil fetched the other man in the waiting room, and the man saluted Bob on his way out of the room. "Here's to number four," the man said. "Good luck, pal."

When Cecil finally returned, Bob knew from his pallor that something was wrong. His breezy, joking manner was gone, his face was taut. "Just follow me, Bob," he said.

"Cecil, say something." Bob touched the sleeve of his scrubs.

"Mary's fine." Cecil turned to him. "Mary's just fine."

Now, Bob thought, he could breathe. The two of them were silent, as they pushed through the silver doors separating the waiting room from the operating theater and continued down the hospital corridor, their feet scuffing the green linoleum, nuns scurrying past them, avoiding their eyes, ominous as owls in their grey habits, and thoughts streamed through Bob—*the baby has died, oh my God*—until his legs went wooden and the hallway blurred into streaks of white and green.

He walked into Room 122 and saw Mary, alive, her hair wet and black against the white bed. He went limp with relief. She was strung with IVs, her face pale, black circles like commas under her eyes, but she was alive. Bob bent over and kissed her.

"Thank God," he whispered. "You've done it, babe."

Her slim fingers circled his wrist. She closed her eyes and fell asleep.

His eyes met Cecil's. "She had a difficult delivery," Cecil said. "Some of the anesthesia's still wearing off. It'll take her awhile to wake up."

"But she's okay?"

"She'll be sore from the delivery—she had an episiotomy—but there are complications," Cecil said. "Complications that we'll be dealing with in the next few days. But all in all, your wife is healthy and fine."

"Okay?" Bob said. "And—"

"Come with me." Cecil took him by the elbow and Bob followed the green flap of Cecil's coat, past stretchers of new patients, casts in traction, hung with IVs, and families holding vases of flowers, past halls, candy-stripers whisking in and out of rooms holding charts, the whirr and buzz of machinery and coughing patients and brightly lit nurse's stations with their message boards and ringing phones.

Bob followed Cecil's narrow, green-jacketed back, wondering how he could have trusted him, and, at this moment hating him for his God-like sureness, his command in this world, of his wife, of his child, when Bob's world was tilting and spinning. Bob kept walking, past rooms where he noticed, in a blur, the name of his first-grade teacher, an old high school friend, a nightmare walk past the sick and dying.

Cecil stopped and waited for Bob at the doorway of a glass-fronted nursery. "This is where I'm taking you." He stood to one side and let Bob pass into the room ahead of him. In this room where the sweetness of baby powder vied with the sour smell of ointment, bassinets of tiny newborns were lined up against the windows. Each was tagged with a last name—Brown, McKay, O'Reskovitch. A rosy-cheeked nurse—Bob remembered, years later, her nametag said Iris—moved slowly over each one, adjusting sheets, checking diapers, pulling small knitted caps of blue or pink down over the babies' heads.

She looked up as they entered the nursery. "This is Mr. Carter," the doctor said.

"My prayers are with you, Mr. Carter," she said, and bowed her head and moved out of the room. "Please let me know if you want or need anything."

Bob followed the doctor to the bassinet marked "Baby Girl Carter." His heart slammed against his ribs. He stopped. The baby lay on her back under the pink blanket. She was wide-eyed. Flat-faced.

"This is your child," the doctor said.

"Hi baby." Bob stared at her. The child stared back.

"Something's wrong," Bob looked back at Cecil. "What is it? What aren't you telling me?" The mewling cries of the babies grew louder and seemed to circle his head like blackbirds. The room seemed to shrink from him. "Hi baby," he said to this creature below him. The child was so far, far away from him, this blur of pink.

"She's mongoloid," Cecil said. "I'm so, so sorry Bob. I couldn't have predicted it. I know it's a shock." He went on talking, his mouth opening and shutting, opening and shutting, Bob focusing on a piece of spittle that stretched from Cecil's upper lip to the lower.

Finally he stopped and stood beside Bob, silent. He patted his back. He, too, slipped out of the room, leaving Bob with five babies and the tiny malformed child that was his.

"Baby girl Carter," Bob said.

He stared down at her. He studied her fingers, the translucent fingernails.

"Baby," Bob said. "Girl."

The baby turned her head toward the sound of his voice, the mouth puckering.

"Hey, baby girl," Bob said.

The bluish fingers curled in a fist. Her head was black, downy. She had his round nose, and a round, dished-in face. Her almond-shaped eyes, so much like Mary's, were slightly too far apart.

Bile rose up in the back of his throat.

The baby opened her mouth to cry.

The tiny pink mouth opened into an O. A void.

This was his child.

His face went numb. He couldn't feel his feet or hands.

He looked out the window of the nursery, and the nurse, Iris, was there.

She hurried in. "Do you want to hold her?" she said. "Can I help you?"

He stared at her.

"Mr. Carter? Are you all right? Do you want me to get someone?"

He shook his head. He turned on his heel. He walked down the line of infants, O'Reskovitch, McKay, Brown, then burst out of the nursery and blazed down the hall, walking faster and faster, breaking into a run, the linoleum tiles blurring, face burning, some rough-faced man saying, "Watch it mister," when Bob bumped him. He was searching for a bathroom, shame prickling the back of his neck and weakening his knees and he knew he was not going to make it, not going to find a bathroom, not going to hide his sickness, and he grabbed the wide-draped grey sleeve of a nun's habit and said to the blue eyes framed in grey curls, "Save me," and she grabbed him before he vomited, and then there was nothing. He fainted dead away, all 225 pounds of him, dead weight against this sixty-two-year-old nurse who, she said later, thought it was a good thing she was used to wrestling her father—a railroad man—or "I'd a buckled." In the room where he was taken to recover, Mary was wheeled in to visit him that night, and the two of them held hands in silence as the day fell and the nurses walked, carrying trays of dinner, water pitchers and medications, the rubber soles of their shoes squeaking.

CHAPTER NINE

Of course, she hadn't planned the pregnancy. She and Tom had been married six months. She'd been on the pill. Then came the sinus infection and antibiotics. The face aches waned, and the nausea began. She noticed it first walking to work when she happened to look over the fence into a yard where there was a dead cedar waxwing, its white and grey feathers, its tufted head and yellow-tipped tail feathers tucked underneath a mountain ash tree, a red berry still pinned in its red beak. She might have known what happened: flocks of cedar waxwings descended in February every year, got drunk on wizened berries, swooping in grey rushes from yard to yard around the city, every so often flying into a window.

She couldn't take her eyes off it, its neck turned at a wrong angle, face down there in pink snow.

Her face flushed, her stomach rushed up through her throat, and she began to retch, right there on the sidewalk. She tried to get over a nearby alley, to hide herself, just as a kid on a dirt bike zoomed past her. "Gross, lady," he yelled.

Ruth, the city editor, took one look at her when she walked to her desk and told her to go home. "I can cover you, no sweat," she said. "You look like you've seen a ghost."

"Well, thanks," Elizabeth said. "I love compliments."

"You're pale as skim milk, kid. It's dead here anyway," Ruth said. "Mr. Big Shot is at a Sunshine Rotary meeting and several of the reporters are on assignment, so scoot before someone thinks of some way to object." Mr. Big Shot was Ruth's name for their boss, who'd been head accountant at the Helena paper before he was promoted to publisher in Bridger.

Elizabeth smiled, too weak to protest.

She'd been hired as a general assignment reporter two years ago, covering city council meetings, then the budget wrangling at the university and the usual scandals with the football team who couldn't seem to keep their dicks in their pants, but she was hankering for bigger stories. She told Ruth about the investigative pieces she'd helped with at the *Chicago Tribune* and Ruth was sympathetic but practical. "We don't have the staff for those big investigative pieces, hon. But I love your feisty spirit."

Every time Ruth said that, Elizabeth felt she died a little death.

She walked the four blocks to what was now her home, her stomach still churning, her vision hazy, avoiding the yard where the cedar waxwing still lay. She passed the large white Victorian house with a makeshift fence—remembering the old man and the woman with round glasses and a bun who lived there, the woman always out sweeping the porch. The place was rumored to belong to a group of people who had once been part of a commune at Rainbow Creek in the sixties. Supposedly, they'd had several children together. She rarely saw anyone come in or out of the house, she just noticed that their refurbished school bus gravitated from the front to the side street every now and then.

As a child, she and Karen had wound trails through this neighborhood playing, with strict instructions to stay away from the ditch with its tangle of bushes and sleeping hoboes, to stay away from the railroad below with the trains heading west and east with their cargoes of lumber. The alley and the yards, however, were theirs and they knew every path and back way through them, through overgrown lilacs bordering the edge of the ditch (the forest they called it) and the alleyway past Mr. Babin, with his mean eyes and blue coveralls as they played pirates and frontier children, picking acorns and chestnuts and storing them in jars she found in the basement, acorns that later grew grey with mold. The thought of mold sent up a shiver. She bent over and wretched again.

By the time she made it to the house, she had vomited five times. "I have the flu," she told Tom, when she phoned him from bed.

Until it happened the next day. And the next.

"Darling," Tom said to her after five days. "I don't think this is the flu. I think you might be preggers."

How she hated that word. Preggers. It sounded like some kind of instant food.

After the doctor's appointment, she met him at the Derby, a dark local bar with a moose with the requisite hat, a carved oak bar, booths with leather banquettes and red guttering candles.

After Tom ordered a beer at the bar, he slid into the booth next to her. She cupped her hands around the candle, feeling the indentations of the warm glass, as she stared at the flame flickering inside. She looked up to study her dark-haired, broad-shouldered husband.

"Well?" Tom said. He crossed his arms and smiled his beautiful smile.

"I'm pregnant," she said. Her heart skipped.

Tom leaned to her. "Really?"

"Really."

"Elizabeth. That's amazing." He stared at her. "Oh my God. I'm just a little freaked out."

He held up his glass to toast her bottle of root beer.

"Oh my God," Elizabeth said. "If you think you are freaked out, try being me, asshole. Freaked out. Big time."

This was not the plan. The plan was that they'd establish themselves: Tom at his new teaching job, Elizabeth at the paper, get the house mucked out, take some river trips, travel overseas—France, then Germany. "I'm not ready for this, Tom. I don't think we should go ahead with this."

"No, don't say that." Tom took her hands in his. "Hey, it'll be all right. I'm just a little freaked out. I want you to do what feels right, but we can still have our plan. We'll just do it with a baby. Babies are little. We can travel with a baby."

"Tom." Elizabeth felt her stomach rising. She slid out of the booth and down the aisle, swerving around the waiter with a large tray full of drinks, and made it to the bathroom just in time.

When she returned, Tom had ordered her a 7-Up. A beautiful, clear, sparkling glass, with ice. The sweet, cold soda slid down her throat and coated her stomach.

"I'm trying not to feel incredibly trapped here," she said.

"It's only a trap if you let it be," he said.

"Drink your beer," she said. "When did you get to be so wise?" How could she explain to him what it was like being back in her hometown? How she hated it so much sometimes, like the town had sent her away, to the city, to a great job, only to reel her back in, *ha ha ha*. How the familiar bumpy sidewalks and streetlights and misspelled street names in cement were on some days a comfort and on others, excruciating. "The thing is, Tom, I just don't know who I am right now. Two years ago, I was a journalist in Chicago, living in a high-rise. Now my parents have died. I live in my childhood home. I'm married. I'm pregnant."

Tom stroked her hand. "At least you aren't barefoot, dear."

Elizabeth burst into tears. "You drive me crazy."

"You said that when we first met, you know."

Elizabeth laughed. She remembered that party, a cookout at a campsite, the Blackfoot River. By that point she'd been living at home for a year, camped out at her parents' house, trying to reassemble her life, when her friend Molly called her and told her it was summer, it was time for her to get her butt in gear, she needed to have some fun. She told Molly she was too depressed for fun. Molly told her she didn't care, she was going to make her come out anyway, then picked her up in her red Toyota truck. They started with Budweisers at the Derby, where a garage band was playing while a few dogs wandered in and out. Then Molly said it was time to leave. She rolled down the pickup's windows and, with a six pack of beer at their feet, the two of them drove through the hot evening down the windy road along the Blackfoot River. Green water snaked through the canyon, tamaracks marching up the rocky slopes, and by the time they arrived at Johnsrud Park for the cookout, she knew Molly was right. She had been by herself too long. There was a large bonfire at a campsite and people drinking beer and roasting hot dogs, throwing Frisbees and swimming in the green rocky water, small groups of people disappearing into the cab of a Dodge pickup to smoke joints. Tom was the fire tender, a large man with a brown beard. They shared a beer. He asked her if she wanted to go for a swim, and she waded into the water with him and when she started to slip on a rock, he held out his hand to steady her. *What am I doing?* she kept saying to herself. *Why am I doing this?* When she pulled her hand out of his to dive in the water, stroking over to the other side, Tom was next to her, his arms plowing through the water in a butterfly stroke. "Hey, you know how to swim," he said, when they reached the opposite shore and sat, side by side, watching the party. She smiled. "So do you." "It's funny watching a party from this shore," Tom said. "People look so silly, don't they, kind of like ducks." She threw her head back and laughed. She realized she hadn't laughed in a very long time. "I always thought that about my parents' bridge parties—the way the sound started, swelled, and died down—sounded just like ducks." She smiled at him. "You know, this is not the plan: I didn't think I would ever be back here, back in Montana. I wanted to live in Chicago, I wanted to leave this place forever." "I left the east to come here," Tom said. "For exactly this: the rivers, the trees, for women who like to swim in rivers." Tom touched her arm. "Your arms are stippled." "Nice word," she said. "Oh I haven't even begun," Tom said, "with the big words." "You could drive me crazy, you know," she said. Of course, she did sleep with him, but not for several weeks, after they'd hiked up to the giant L on the side of the mountain named for a circus elephant and looked down over the long Bridger Valley that ran south with the railroad, wound with rivers and maple-lined streets and wide empty hillsides that rose up around them like friends. He took her to his favorite gyro place. The two of them packed a canoe and traveled down the Flathead River, where in a tent, facing a white cliff where swallows wove in and out of mud nests, beneath a gibbous moon, they made love for the first time.

That all seemed so long ago. She reached beyond the candle to take Tom's hands in hers. Broad and brown and strong. "You seem so sure."

"We'll do this babe." He looked at her and shook his head. "Still. Oh my God. I can't believe it. I really can't believe it."

"We can't tell anyone, Tom," Elizabeth. "It's too soon. Promise me. I'm still not sure I'm even okay with this."

"I won't tell a soul. But Elizabeth. Really. This is great news. We'll be parents."

"We're barely married, Tom. Barely. Don't you worry about that? I feel like we don't know each other well enough yet."

"Elizabeth," Tom said. "What I love about you is how much you think about things. But honestly, do you think anyone is ever ready for a child? Really?"

Elizabeth stared at the candle flame, then at the bar mirror where she could see Tom's back and her own narrow face. "Well, I guess we do have nine months, don't we?" she said. She knit her fingers into his and squeezed his hand.

"Well there you go," Tom said and walked over to the bar where she could hear him tell the bartender. "Hit me again," he knocked smartly on the wooden bar. "I'm going to be a dad."

That night, at home, Elizabeth thought, well, hell, if he's telling the bartender, I'm at least going to tell my sister. She went into her room, shut the door, and turned on her computer. While she waited for her email to load, she looked at her desk: the stones she had gathered from Lake Superior, smooth and round and flat, the picture of herself at Saugatuck, sunglasses on her forehead, tanned, taken just after her first month at the *Tribune*. She fingered the graduation tassels from Northwestern hanging from the architect's lamp over the desk. Talismans, they were. Talismans from a life she had left behind. A sorrow pierced her at the life she wouldn't have now: that reporter with the curly hair, those Danish modern sofas, the high-rise, that cool sophistication, free from the bindweed of history and inheritance.

When the email envelope showed up, she punched the New button and began to type.

> *February 18, 1996*
>
> *Dear Karen, You won't believe this. I thought perhaps I had the flu. Well, you guessed it already I bet. I'm pregnant. No, it wasn't planned...the doctor says that sometimes antibiotics can weaken the effects of the pill in some women, and guess who is that woman? Yours truly. Yes I am freaked out. No this wasn't the plan. Tom is great. Yours in nausea and soda crackers,*
>
> *Elizabeth*

Elizabeth wandered downstairs to fold a basket of laundry, brought it back upstairs and crammed the sheet sets in the already overstuffed linen closet. She stopped by the bathroom to throw up. By the time she'd returned to her desk, Karen's response was in the inbox.

> *Oh, Elizabeth, I'm so so so happy for you! What spectacular news. I'm praying for you tonight, and I will every night, that things will go well. Mom and Dad would have been so happy and I know they are up in heaven, just smiling down at you. Don't worry about not feeling ready: nobody feels ready and that is why God designed us to have nine months to think about it. Good plan, huh? I'm here for you day and night and ask me anything and I'll help you. About the morning sickness, it is a drag, but like you said, soda crackers help a lot and ginger ale (ginger is supposed to be good for nausea) and I haven't told anyone not Bill or the girls, I promise, and won't till you tell me but I'm just bursting, I'm so happy. I have so many things of the girls'*

to pass on, so please don't buy anything till you talk to me. Love and so so so many kisses,

Karen

CHAPTER TEN

That night, as Louise neared her cabin, she could see the shape of a man, moving about the snow in some strange version of duck-duck-goose. Her heart clanged as she drew closer until she realized it was Willard stamping through the snow at the side of her cabin. His feet were wet from tramping down the snow in the shape of a square. At his feet were a scattering of seed packets.

"What are you doing, Willard?" she said. "I would guess a garden, but it's January."

"I'm planning you a garden, Miss Gustafson," Willard said. He stood straight, wiped his sweaty brow with his hand.

"But Willard, aren't you cold? Lord, honey, it's nearly zero. And you didn't ask me if I wanted a garden."

His face fell. "But remember, we said beets? Squash?"

"That's right." A long weariness flowed through Louise. "That seems like years ago."

"Miss Gustafson," he said. His voice was patient. "I know it is snow time now. But in spring, I will plant a garden for you. With lettuce, cauly-flower. Carrots."

She went in the cabin, exhausted. She could see her breath. She poked at the coals in the stove, opened the wood heater and tossed in a log. She pressed her face against the glass and looked out at Willard, who was eyeing the square garden, his foot on the shovel, his face red, and she could see how his face had fallen and he was beginning to cry. Oh my God, she thought. Not now. She wanted to crawl into bed and sleep and sleep and sleep while the wind hushed the ponderosas outside.

She drew a breath and watched it fog the glass.

Then she pulled open the door.

"Did you get seeds for carrots?" she said. "Spinach?"

His smile was jack-o'lanterned by missing teeth. He held out the seed packets to her, a peace offering, the small rectangles with their pictured promises of radishes, corns, beans.

Willard showed her the square he had outlined in the snow using the edges of his shovel. He planted the shovel, jumped on it, and it bounced off the frozen earth with a clanking sound.

Louise kneeled nearby and tried to pull out a long-frozen cord of binder weed, but her hands froze.

"I think it's quittin' time, Willard," she said. "We'll have to dig the rest in spring. Ground's too frozen." She looked at his face, round and red and streaked with sweat. "Do you want a cup of tea?"

"Yes, Miss Gustafson," he said and followed her into the cabin.

Once inside, she regretted asking him. He looked large and uncomfortable inside the small room as he picked up the black-and-white photograph of her mother, her hair marcelled in stiff waves, her lips curved into a smile. He looked from the photograph to Louise and back again. "Your mama looks mean. And weak."

"Weak?" Louise said. She looked at the photograph again. Willard was right. There was something weak in the way her mother's chin slid into her neck, the way her burning eyes tried to make up for that weak spirit, something that had taken her, Louise, years to learn.

"You are very perceptive, Willard," she said. She thought of her mother's latest letters, her mother imploring her to come back, her mother asking her what kind of a daughter just picked up and left her mother to fend for herself, alone, in the cold, only the meanest neighbors to look out for her?

She dunked the tea ball in the cup and the water darkened into a deep green. "How did you see that, Willard?"

"'Cause she ain't looking at the camera, she's lookin' away."

"What does that tell you?"

"She don't like the light, Miss Gustafson. Animals don't like the light are generally mean ones."

When Louise handed him his tea, he gulped it down so fast she was worried he'd be burned. "Don't drink so fast," she said. "You'll burn yourself."

"No fear, Miss Gustafson," he said. He gulped his tea again. "I'm really 'preciating this, the tea and your pictures."

"You'll have to come again, Willard."

He set his cup gently on a stack of books. "Have you read these? This one?" He held up a thick volume, *Anna Karenina.*

"I have. It is a wonderful book."

He bowed his head as he backed out the door, rubbing his hands together, and stepped outside, where he immediately looked more comfortable. He stood quietly for a minute, surveying his snow-etched plot under the star-strewn sky.

Louise stepped out with him, shut the door, and stood by Willard's side. The sight of the snow garden, tromped into six rows, each one with a seed packet lying nearby—it filled her with a deep pleasure.

"It's beautiful," Louise said. "No one has ever made me a snow garden before."

Above, dark snow-bellied clouds were washing into the valley. Goosebumps prickled her spine. She could hear someone calling in the distance.

"This row, Miss Gustafson—" He stood over the garden with its snowy rows and seed packets, and pointed to the first row. "This is for carrots and beets." He pointed to the next. "This, for lettuce. Tomatoes."

"We got our whole spring ahead of us, Willard. But they're calling you. You'd better go."

He bowed his head. "Yes, Miss Gustafson." Then he scampered across the field as fast as a two-hundred-and-fifty-pound man could, his feet crunching through the snow. "Good night," he called, without turning around, the moonlight shining off the back pockets of his overalls.

"We did good, didn't we, Miss Gustafson?" he called. "Didn't we do good?"

CHAPTER ELEVEN

It was a time Bob remembered in black and white. Newspapers and televisions were black and white. Politics, black and white with the occasional red. It was the time of loyalty tests, red-baiting. Even the more moderate Eisenhower was trying to keep peace between the Republicans on a witch hunt for communists and Democrats who were still mourning Adlai Stevenson's lost bid for the presidency. Even the world outside the living room window was a study in contrasts in mid-February 1953, with its black-striped branches and skies with low-hanging, snow-bellied clouds. And during this time, he and his wife got into their four-door Buick sedan and crossed into a world of alcohol and antiseptic, a world of sorrow staged in white. Mary dressed in one of her beautiful suits, green merino wool, nipped in at the waist, her hair the color of ravens, her slash of red lipstick, and Bob in his stiff Harris tweed still smelling of mothballs from the hall closet, a suit that his father bought him on a rare family trip to Vancouver, Canada, a suit that marked his rite of passage into the world of men.

Sorrow, he thought, drained color from everything.

Bob and Mary were in Cecil's office, sitting on two black leather chairs, facing the examining table. The room was white. To his right, on a set of metal chests, sat tongue depressors in a glass jar, next to it cotton balls. He put his hand on Mary's hand. Her fingers so slender. So cold. Mary, who was not talking, not weeping, just sitting, her face rigid, pale, her tears sealed up inside her as she slowly turned to stone.

In other times, he and Cecil would be easy with one another, making small talk about the next Kiwanis meeting or joking about their trip to the cabin, but all that casual talk was gone. Dr. Babcock, as Cecil was to them here, was warm but professional.

"As I told Bob at the hospital, Mary, there is a lot to discuss about your baby," Cecil said. "Your child has mongoloidism and will need to be institutionalized."

"It's a requirement?" Mary said.

"Absolutely," Cecil said. "I know this is hard, and some mothers do not comply, but it is best for you and best for the child to be in a place where she is with doctors and nurses who are equipped to help her. To be with other patients who are like her so she will feel as if she belongs. It is the best thing you can do as a mother."

Dr. Babcock's ruddy face was clean-shaven, his eyes a surprise of icy blue. He wore a string tie of black braided leather. Bob studied Cecil's string tie. It was fastened with an eagle clasp that was cut from a silver dollar.

"I'm so sorry," Cecil said. "This is not the news I wanted to bring you. But I feel it is best to face it squarely and consider our options."

How did Cecil, Bob wondered, cut out the eagle from the silver dollar? What tool did he use so that each detail was so precise—the feathered wings, the beak, the pointed talons? What were the odds, he thought, that his hand would slip? Bob shook himself. Did he come home each night, eat supper, then go down to his basement to work on it, the precision of cutting out each talon and wing wiping away days like this when he had to tell patients that they had cancer? Or that their child was defective. This was a side of Cecil—big, calm, steady Cecil—that he had not known before.

Mary was silent.

"This is the best thing," the doctor said. "We'll keep her here at the hospital until there is a spot for her. Then you can drive her there. She'll be taken care of. And the two of you can move on with your lives. You can put this behind you."

Bob could see a lazy drift of snow through the outside window. He turned to Mary. She was watching it as well.

"I know this sounds cold, but this is what we do in these cases." Cecil hugged their file to his chest. "There are more of these than you know. Other parents, patients of mine, people that you know, who have done this, and now they have full, happy lives. They've gone on. They've gone ahead and had more children. Normal children."

In the silence, Bob could hear shoes tapping by in the hallway, the squeak and whir of wheels on a gurney, the whisper of gowns, habits, feet, ghosts, voices telling him *This is your child Bob, this child.*

He stared at Cecil's string tie again to anchor himself. Had he ever cut a talon off as he carved out his silver dollars? Severed the bulb-like head? The wetter Bob's cheeks were, the stonier Mary grew. It was like some kind of riddle.

"Drive her there?" Mary said finally. "How would we drive her there?"

"You'll have to drive the baby to the state hospital." Cecil said. "We have no other way of getting her there. By law, that is what you have to do unless you make the decision to keep her home."

Bob reached to take Mary's hand in his, looking down at her

slender, tapered fingers. He traced the thin vein that flowed between her knuckles to her ring finger where her engagement ring, the diamond given to him by his grandmother, slipped to the side.

"We'll keep her here until they have a spot for her," the doctor said. His voice was slow, patient, as if he were speaking to a child. "I know this is a shock. I know this is not what a new parent wants to hear. But we'll get through this."

She peered sideways at Cecil through the curtain of her hair.

Cecil touched her forearm. "There will be other children."

The doctor leaned forward, his elbows propped on his knees, his fingers knit together as if he were a supplicant. "This is best," he said softly. He looked first to Mary, then Bob. "For you. And you. You're not alone, you know."

Mary let the word hang there in the air between them, and Bob finally turned his entire body in the chair to stare at her. What he saw thrilled and frightened him: the old Mary, her eyes boring into the doctor's as if they were two warriors facing one another. "You're telling me to bring my two-day-old daughter to a bunch of strangers in an institution to bring her up because it would be good for her?"

"Your daughter is not a normal child. She is a mongoloid. She is severely retarded." Cecil said. "These are not normal circumstances."

Mary sank back. Her eyes seemed to dim.

Cecil looked away from her glance. "That's my recommendation. That's the state's recommendation."

The room grew quiet.

"I think—" Bob said. "What Dr. Babcock is telling us, Mary, is that this is better for everyone."

The sentence floated down into the room. So much delicacy. The smell of alcohol. Combs in their solution. Fluorescent lights bleaching the room of color. The thrumming.

"You will have more family," Cecil said. "You'll have healthy children that can feed themselves, clothe themselves, grow up to be adults. Not children that will be children forever. By Montana law, these kids belong in the state hospital. It's your choice, of course, but most parents opt to commit them to the state hospital, where they can get the best care."

My husband has a pistol and he'll shoot, Bob remembered Mary saying that night in the campground as the teenagers partied in the campsite next to them—and one of the rowdies took a look at her, turned back to his buddies, and they packed up and left. But this was different. She was pale, her skin burnished, her beauty intensified by grief. Something was hardening in her. Something he couldn't identify.

"They have special programs," Bob said. "Nurses. Special teachers, where they can be among children just like themselves."

"You're telling me this is best," Mary said. "Can you guarantee that, you two? Can you look me in the eye and tell me that's best?"

"I'm telling you, that it's best. For you. For her." Cecil looked her straight in the eyes.

Mary pinched her lips shut and sat in the chair, her hands in her lap.

Cecil stood up, his bolo tie swinging from side to side.

Mary looked from Bob to Cecil and back to Bob. He could see she was deciding something, and for the rest of his life he would wonder what it was but he would always be afraid to know. She smoothed her dress and said, "Okay then."

They named her Elizabeth Finch Carter, after Bob's grandmother. As they waited for news from the institution, they went back to lives disfigured by the absence of the child they had just made room for—Mary sleeping long days, Bob lost in work, trying to sell business insurance to guarantee farmers and business owners against all odds: windstorms, earthquakes, hail, ice, and injured workers. His business was the business of calculating worth against accident, the business of sizing up buildings made of wood and brick against the forces of wind, rain, snow, in an eternal contest to see what indeed would win. That was his work: insuring his clients against the odds that a tree would fall on their home, or that a worker's hand would be cut off on the green line in the mill, betting life against death, health against illness.

The baby stayed in the hospital nursery with the nuns for fourteen days as they waited for an opening at the Stone Home, previously known as the School for Backward Children, the institution nearly a century old. When Bob thought of that name, he pictured a caveman drawing of giant stick children, walking backward in a line. He asked himself, *This is where you want your daughter to live?* He replaced that with the thought of clean, ironed sheets. Nurses with starched hats. Trays of healthy, nutritious foods neatly divided meals into squares of proteins, carbohydrates, starches, and sugars.

Mary went to the hospital to nurse the baby several times a day at first, but the nuns quickly bottle-trained the child, so her visits tapered off. Each visit dragged her so far underwater it took hours to reach her afterward, until finally, she found it easier not to go. Each time she drove back and forth, she thought the world looked like the inside of an iron lung: breathing its breaths of exhaust from cars and humans alike, encased in grey cement and clouds.

Bob couldn't bring himself to go back. It wasn't for lack of trying: He'd go to the hospital, walk to the nursery, walk to the door, even spy the bassinet, marked Baby Girl Carter, and then he couldn't go farther, his heart pounding so hard in his chest he couldn't breathe and he had to sit in the hall and gather himself, while the black-winged nurses fluttered past, some occasionally stopping by to see if he needed help.

At the Methodist Church, the first Sunday after the birth, he decided to attend alone. When Arnie and his wife asked him about Mary, he demurred, then noticed Arnie's wife elbowing Arnie in the side. "Oh, right," Arnie said. "I'm sorry." There had been no birth announcement, delicately left out of the papers by the nuns. Dick Anderson came up and patted him on the back. The Tuesday Kiwanis meeting was a tonic, and Bob lost himself in its structure, the Pledge of Allegiance, the group prayer, the group singing "God Bless America," the comforting gravy-laden food and the political science professor's program on "Communism Here and Abroad." Mary shut the door to the baby's room. She started attending choir practice on Wednesday nights, where she was seated in the soprano section next to Gladys McBride, who took a motherly interest in her, and she started up with her women's club activities, serving as secretary, always, with her superior shorthand skills.

People were kind and favored them with silence.

CHAPTER TWELVE

She moved the roller through the paint, pushing it back and forth through the pan until the white fur cylinder was coated yellow. Yellow, the color of butter. She kept rolling, watching creamy paint ooze back into the pan, dripping like thick tears. She looked at the wall. She'd already painted it once—a base white, the coating the paint store recommended for covering up that Delft blue—oh so, so blue—her mother had painted when Elizabeth was a teenager, inspired by the trip to Europe the family had taken in 1970, sighing, *Isn't that just the color of happiness?* Elizabeth and Karen looked at one another and rolled their eyes. She had also painted that oak bedroom set white with gold trim. She hung a print of Renoir's *The Seine* on her wall, hoping, Elizabeth suspected, that the image of the two young women sitting in the red boat rowing, backs straight, might inspire Elizabeth to have better posture. Her mother had also acquired a Louis XV–style chaise lounge, painted in blue and black with clusters of flowers at each corner. Upholstered in tattered silk, and purchased from the estate of a long-departed lumber baron, Elizabeth wondered what had possessed her mother to buy the half-chair, half-couch that dominated the room. Clearly she yearned for some kind of leisure that her life was missing, with her endless sweeping, folding, vacuuming, and cooking—or was her mother bringing some elegance into their lives? Either way, she and Tom were hauling it off to an antiques store somewhere.

Elizabeth stood, ready to paint the walls. She had taped the baseboards and molding. Those, she'd finish later in a soft cream. She'd covered the chaise with a drop cloth and moved it to the center of the room. She would replace the brocade curtains her mother had had a dressmaker sew with something simpler: cream-colored linen, perhaps.

Elizabeth began to roll, watching the yellow light the wall. This room had been her great-grandmother's sewing room, then her room, and now, in eight months, it would be her child's room.

She had worked hard to find this yellow: Yellows were either too acidic and harsh or too orangey, and the one she wanted was pale. She bought seven samples, trying them one after another until Tom told her she could have painted the entire room for the same cost, and that maybe she could settle on one soon. Perhaps? She found the color in, of all things, a package of ancient Jordan almonds tucked in her father's rolltop desk. Among the pastel blues and greens was the perfect light pale yellow—and she brought it into the paint store and the salesman matched the color, and she began rolling that day.

Of course, she never imagined she'd be back in this room, back in this house, back in Bridger, Montana. She remembered that morning, moving quickly down the sidewalk to the white Gothic *Tribune* tower that overshadowed the streets, past the brass cornerstone and swinging doors into the wide echoey lobby with its exhibit of rocks—everything from a stone from Jesus's grotto to a moon rock—and into the sudden hush of the elevator. It was packed. There was a sportswriter picking something out of his teeth, two disc jockeys from WGN, executives in their double-breasted wool suits, and secretaries in silk blouses and high, belted pants, all of them watching the buttons light their way up the floors, doors dinging as people entered or exited. On the thirty-fifth floor, Elizabeth pushed past everyone to get off, moving to the newsroom past pictures of reporters who'd won Illinois Association of Journalism Awards, Tribune Journalism Awards, and Pulitzers, reporting on the rioting at the Democratic Convention. Every time she passed them, she thought, *Maybe someday I'll be on that wall.* She opened the door to the newsroom, moving past the rows of reporters, telephones ringing, men talking, teletype chattering, making her way to her desk against the very back of the room, when Dave, the managing editor, tapped her on her shoulder.

"I need to talk with you," he said.

She followed him into his office, a glassed-in cubicle with a desk and two chairs.

"Sit," he said. He shook the knot on his tie to loosen it. "I need to tell you something. Something has happened at home."

"Home?" She looked at the picture of the blonde woman, his wife, with her perfectly coiffed head, flanked by a boy and girl standing sentry over his left shoulder, on the bookcase behind his desk. His eyes followed her glance.

"Not my home. Your home."

Her heart froze. "*My* home?"

It was her father. He'd had a heart attack. She flew home in time to see him in the hospital, to bring him ice chips and cups of broth, taking turns with her mother and Karen to sit with him, read him the daily newspaper, until the night he was feeling so good he insisted they all go home and get some sleep—especially you Mary, he said, pointing at his wife. And then, when they were all home sleeping, he died. She'd stayed to help her mother with the care of his body, the interment, the funeral, where an inordinate number of people from Bridger showed up, their doctor Cecil Babcock and her father's client Pete Donatello and hundreds of others who told her how he had helped them through church or work or just as neighbors—as Mrs. Larsen, the neighbor from the alley, telling her that, long after her husband had died, *Your father helped me with a little something every Christmas. You probably don't know that, dear.*

After a month of writing thank yous, settling her mother in, asking her if she was all right alone, Elizabeth returned to Chicago. "I'm back," she announced to her editor, who assigned her to work with an investigative journalist who was doing a series on the meat-packing industry, specifically Vann Meats, one of the largest meat production companies in the Midwest. She'd never forget their first meeting in the elegant board room of the Tribune Building, when the company janitors wheeled in boxes and boxes of Vann Meats production records.

"We're cutting our teeth on this story," the reporter said, looking into her eyes. His were very blue. She suspected he knew that. "No one can help me like you can."

She had the sense that probably many people could help him, but he was so powerful, with his reportage on disease in Africa and the crisis in public education in inner-city Chicago.

That's when he showed her the boxes. "You're my runner," he said, and he carefully explained to her, as he bored his blue eyes into hers, that it was her job to track the meat: from the pig to the ham to whatever happened to the rest of it.

"What do I do?" she said.

"Just look at the records," he said. "See if there's a pattern. We think they are putting meat by-products—tails, entrails, hooves—in the spreads and spam, but we have to prove it. That's where you come in. You get to look at every single one of these reports." He patted the pile of boxes on the table. "Have at it, kid." He flashed his smile at her, and then he shut the door behind him.

She picked up one box from the stack and set it onto the large mahogany conference table. She sat with her box, staring back at the chairs. "Wish me luck everyone," she to the twelve red leather chairs around the table. "I'll answer questions when I'm dead."

After a month, however, she had found a pattern. She made a chart labeled with hog numbers and tracked them through the assembly line: slaughtering, butchering, rendering, processing. It was clear where each hog went—things got fuzzier in the records as the carcass moved on down the line. About that time, the reporter showed up in the board room, flashing his smile, asking her for any leads. She told him to start interviewing employees who worked in processing and rendering. "Nice work," he said, looking at her with interest. "We should get a beer sometime."

She looked up from the pile of files on the desk. "Sure," she said. "Anytime."

The paint went on so smoothly; the wall was the color of very pale jonquils. Always buy good paint, her father had said. It pays for itself. She rolled a second line down from the molding, listening to the paint squelch as it coated the wall, a comforting sound, trying to resist the urge to roll up and down, up and down. Keep the paint moving in the same direction, he told her. You get better coverage that way.

The story was really breaking—a disgruntled line worker who had been denied a promotion was telling Barry how hooves, bones, ears, and pig tails were thrown in a Vat #30. "We all know what Vat #30 is at Vann's. Once you work there, you never eat that shit again. Rumor is they throw union workers in there." He laughed so hard he couldn't stop coughing. She and the reporter were back in the conference room, playing the interview over again to see if they could pick up anything else he had said, when the city editor caught up with her.

This time, it was her mother, he said when they were back in the office, with the beneficent blonde family ever smiling over his shoulder. Her mother had fallen and the doctors were worried. Elizabeth needed to get home at once.

She died, Elizabeth figured, at the moment when Elizabeth's flight was rising over O'Hare, above the shining lake, the towers, the traffic, the endless shuttling back and forth of the L, the city disappearing into a flashing of lights and reflections before they disappeared into the clouds.

"Maybe it is better this way," Karen said as she greeted her at the airport, the two of them weeping. "I don't know how else to process it."

After the funeral, and the casseroles, and the endless visits from women from her mother's symphony and women's groups, arriving in pairs and sitting with them on the porch or around the tea table, Elizabeth and Karen gathered at the lawyer's office. Her parents had left her the home. They had left Karen rental properties that would provide her with income for her growing family.

She sat with her sister in the park outside the sleek brick and glass lawyer's office. "I don't want it," she said. "I don't want it. I feel like it is suffocating me."

"Elizabeth." Karen put her arm around her. "Think about it. It is a beautiful house. It was mom and dad's, but you can make it yours."

"But what about you?" Elizabeth said.

"I don't live here," Karen said. "My husband has a job in Choteau. We're raising kids where he has work. You're flexible. You can relocate. Or sell that dang place. I don't care. It's yours to decide, kid. It's your inheritance."

Your inheritance, Elizabeth thought, as she set the roller in the pan and reached for the paintbrush. She needed to trim out the window. As she brushed, she could see deer moving across the yard: a doe and two fawns that gamboled after her until the doe turned back and stared and the fawns stilled. At the sidewalk, a young man on a bicycle wearing a green backpack stopped and stared. The doe stared back at him. Slowly he put his foot on a pedal and cycled off. The doe sauntered back to her fawns, and Elizabeth watched as the doe tucked them into a leaf pile in the yard. The doe wandered off down the alley, past the dented garbage cans.

The afternoon light slanted through the west window as she started on the third wall. She remembered falling in love with a cheap white bedroom set at a nearby furniture store and begging her parents to buy it. Elizabeth imagined herself on that gold-trimmed bed, reading, drinking a Coca-Cola, rolling her hair up, somehow becoming a real teenager, like one she had seen in *Life* magazine once.

No, her mother said again. You have a perfectly good bed. We can't afford a new bed for you.

That Christmas, among the presents under the tree, Elizabeth's mother gave her a sack containing a can of white paint, with a smaller can of gold enamel for the dresser knobs.

Thank you, Elizabeth held the sack and tried not to cry. *It's just what I wanted.*

Her mother worked tirelessly—painting the furniture, upholstering the chaise lounge, having matching curtains made, writing her sister in Casper, Wyoming, that she was undergoing "a home remodeling project in Elizabeth's room! Out with the child's, in with the princess room!" Elizabeth tolerated it all, but the thought of her mother's work made her tear up now. She knew when she was at school, her mother often napped on her bed, enjoying her handiwork.

There were moments she sorrowed over the gulf that had always existed between her and her mother. But there were moments when that gap seemed to close up, when her mother told her things about how her own mother didn't tell her about sex, not a thing, or how her mother had sewn her wedding dress when she was thousands of miles away simply from her measurements—a pure satin wedding dress at that—and how when they were married the photographer took picture after picture at the wedding but all they were left with was a snap some family member had taken because he put film upside down in the camera. Then, when Elizabeth would come to her for something: advice about a boyfriend or teacher, her usual mother would be back, cold, remote, and snapping back at her: "Oh, for goodness sakes, Elizabeth. You'll figure it out."

By the time she finished rolling the third wall, she heard Tom coming in the back door. "Up here," she shouted.

He came up the stairs, two stairs at a time.

"Wow," he said. His large frame filled out the doorway. He had on a red Henley shirt, and she could see a few chest hairs peeking through. He ran a hand through his brown hair. "This color is beautiful. Vast improvement over Delft blue, don't you think?"

She set the roller in the pan and walked over to kiss him. "You're not just saying that because I had to try out seven pints of paint to get it right?"

Tom smiled. “Not even.” He grabbed her around the waist. “Hey kid,” he pulled her closer to him where she could smell his smell—soap and sweat and something piney—and he kissed her. “You need to open a window. Fumes, right?”

CHAPTER THIRTEEN

In many ways, Louise thought her story started again on February 15, 1953: the day the new baby arrived. It was mid-winter. Below zero. Snow barreling down from the Arctic to blast the windows. She picked up the infant from the elaborate bassinet, this time an expensive one with ribbons and real wicker and the softest, finest cotton, with the tag, "Carter infant, six weeks." She was tiny, just a newborn. She lifted the child out of the bassinet, supporting her downy head. The child was so small, she could hold her along her forearm, with her scrawny legs and thin neck and bright eyes—eyes that bored right into her. Elizabeth Carter.

How could a tiny child bear a name that long? Lizzie, she thought. I'll call her Lizzie. Later on, she would know her mistake, would know it would have been better to call her the Carter infant. To honor that long, multi-syllable name that seemed so ill-fitting. To rename her, she would learn, was to crack open stone.

She held her in the crook of her arm and tried to feed her a bottle, but the flat-faced child kept turning away.

"Doc says she probably won't make it," Margaret said.

"Why?"

"Failure to thrive," she said. "Happens with mongoloids."

"Nonsense." Louise dipped her finger in the bottle and put it in the infant's mouth. She felt the infant suck at her finger, but Margaret was right. Her sucking was weak. "What's wrong with her?"

"Happens sometimes when babies go from breast to bottle."

"Did the mother breast-feed her?"

"Records said she didn't. But you never really know," Margaret said, as she slung a one-year-old easily on her shoulder and started to dance from foot to foot, patting his back. "You have to burp them, by the way, after a bottle. You got the diapering down cold—but this is important or we'll have a whole nursery of bawling babies."

Louise dipped her finger in the milk again. "C'mon, Lizzie," she said, looking down at the bright-eyes baby, its tiny face, the otherworldly stare, the suck like a faint kiss.

She had to move on, so she laid her back in the bassinet and the child stared up at her, the clear blue eyes staring out of her flat face, before they fluttered shut.

At noon, she and Margaret joined the others in the cafeteria where a woman in a window handed them trays of sandwiches made with beef raised on the ranch and bread baked by the patients, thick white fresh bread, and chocolate chip cookies, which they carried to long, wooden tables.

At the end of the day, when Louise stepped outside to walk back to her cabin, she couldn't believe the world was still there: that there was snow, birds wheeling in the bright cold sky, the crackle of ice on the ground, and quiet, oh God love her, quiet. She walked home through soft snow, stumbling occasionally on the frozen furrows of the fields that had been plowed for spring planting. She could see her cabin in the distance, but she felt as if she were swimming in a sea of snow and ice and dirt, and that she would never reach that log haven, safe from the sounds of crying.

Failure to thrive.

What the hell was that anyway?

Leave her alone, Margaret had told her several times. Don't get attached. Doctor says she ain't gonna make it anyway.

Those eyes looking up at her, penetrating, ancient, like the gazes of children who peered out of old photographs, children in mining camps, in front of homesteader shacks, in grim western towns perched at the brink of poverty. There were the eyes of children who knew and accepted their fate.

She walked faster.

She could feel that whisper of a suck at her finger.

Let her go, the other nurses warned. *We know. We all have them. The ones at our heartstrings. But you have to let them go. You have a job to do.*

She could feel the noise of the children in the hallways surround her, the children in their blue uniforms and bowl cuts moving about, some talking, some groaning, some crying, some laughing, as they went to classes on basket making or hygiene or exercise. All that noise. That want. That need.

She kept on walking. When she looked back, she could see footprints in the snow. Some were intact, a perfect outline of her foot, even the tread of the shoe intact. Others were collapsed, filled with dirt and rocks.

Slowly she was getting closer to the cabin.

The child is weak, she thought. *She's not getting enough food.*

The eyes again. Round. Wide-spaced as the plains. Blank. Maybe it is better if she goes, she thought. Save her from this institution.

From knowing her family abandoned her. She thought of her in the bassinet with the stitching, Lizzie, and her mother breast-feeding her once, hiding it from the father.

What the hell, she thought. Just dip my finger in milk, then cereal, and let her suck it. It can't hurt anything.

The next day, after she'd fed, cleaned, and changed the babies in the nursery and the noise had subsided and Margaret went out for a cigarette, she cut the top of a nipple and mixed some cereal with milk, picked up Lizzie, took her to the rocking chair, and told her, "Let's try this, kid." Her voice was quieter than a whisper. "Drink now, baby girl."

At first, the baby turned away.

Louise opened the bottle to the side, dipped her finger into the milk-cereal, and put it in the child's mouth, feeling the faint suck.

Her large, veined, freckled finger. The small rosebud mouth.

The child closed her mouth around her finger again.

After she fed Lizzie with her finger several times, Louise screwed the nipple on the bottle again and tried to feed it to the baby. She turned her head away. Louise shook a drop on her finger and inserted it in Lizzie's mouth, then quickly slid the bottle in right after it before the baby had time to turn away. She was fitful, staring up at Louise with those tilted blue eyes. But she drank.

Louise leaned back in the chair and rocked, holding the bottle upright as Lizzie drank, her cheeks moving in and out, fanning Louise's heart.

Several months later, in the middle of a routine April morning, Louise and Margaret stood over the bassinet of the palsied baby, helpless. Margaret sponged his forehead, while Louise tried to hold down his limbs, grey as clouds, as he seized again and again. At last, he turned his head to the side, spittle flecking his lips, and died.

She released his arms and stood up, looking down at him, hands dangling at her sides. She felt Margaret straighten up next to her.

After a moment, Margaret leaned down and drew his eyelids down over his eyes.

The encephalitic baby cried. A one-year-old stood and rocked the sides of his crib. Then all eight babies began to wail. The room stank of urine.

They stood there.

"My God," Louise said.

Margaret lifted her eyes from the child, now stiffening, to Louise's face. Her eyes, cold stones. She said, "You don't still believe that shit, do you?"

CHAPTER FOURTEEN

Mary and Bob were in sudden, close proximity after weeks of moving from hospital to home and back again. Through the roar of the Buick's heater, Bob heard Mary's breathing, could see her fingers moving as she tucked the blanket around the baby, adjusted her scarf, pulled down the rearview mirror to check her lipstick. The infant murmured, shifting in her bundle of blankets. They had picked her up in the nursery and moved on to Cecil's office, signing papers for her release, papers that recognized them as parents, and papers that recognized the child as a ward of the Stone Home for the Mentally Retarded, even negotiated the awkward moment when some fool woman stopped them—mistakenly identifying them as a happy young couple heading home from the hospital with their newborn and began to gush, "Let me see the little darling," and Mary looked at her sharply and Bob said, "We're in a hurry, ma'am," and they rushed past the hurt on her face and out the door to the shock of the below-zero, snowbound world and into the upholstered intimacy of the car.

The child's face screwed up and she was about to cry when she was startled quiet by the grinding sound of the car starting. Bob shifted into first, pulled away from the curb, but as he headed toward the highway that would take them up over Beavertail Pass to the place that would house this child for the rest of her life, he felt suddenly panicked, as if he'd left something behind. He patted his pants for his wallet. His keys were in the ignition. Mary was beside him. He glanced over at the child's dish-shaped face, the slanted eyes. This was it. He had to be ready now.

Mary stared straight ahead, her profile etched against the frost-crusted side window, inscrutable.

Bob launched the car onto the highway behind a logging truck, loaded with Douglas fir, correcting for the skid. They headed east into the ice-bound, unblinking morning.

The road was rutted, glittering here and there with black ice. As they drove, they passed cars scattered this way and that in the ditches. An ambulance tore past them at Bonner, heading for the hospital they'd just abandoned. They slowed when they came to the wreck—a head-on between a Chevrolet van and a Ford truck, its load of hay now spilling across the embankment. With a shudder, Bob saw the driver's side smashed flat.

At Beavertail Hill, a whiteout. Bob inched the car forward. The snow blew directly into the windshield, each flake large and hypnotizing, flying into them as if from some deep, bottomless well. Bob kept moving his eyes from the rearview mirror to the road to the side mirror to keep from feeling dizzy, to keep from feeling he would fall into a dream and off the side of the road, a dream where the sun was shining and the road was clear and his wife was beside him, glowing, with a baby with rounded checks.

When the snow cleared a moment, Bob saw, in a nearby meadow, trees that had lived a lifetime in wind, bent and gnarled.

"This is a terrible storm," Mary said. It was the first thing she had said since Bridger. "You can barely see the road. Should we turn back?"

"No," Bob said. "Let's just keep moving."

As if she could sense their nervousness, the baby whimpered. Her eyes opened. Her face flushed red, and then her cry blossomed into the furious, bleating, skin-crawling sound of a newborn.

The windshield fogged.

Bob tried to drive as he polished the glass with his leather glove, leaning close to the windshield to try to make out the shadows ahead of him. Were they cars? Trucks? Were the three of them going to be crushed, another road fatality, like so many in storms like this, family of three killed on ice-bound road in head-on?

Ah-ahhh. Ah-ahhh. The baby kept crying, her face changing from red to light violet.

Mary took over clearing the windshield. The baby grew quiet and Mary looked down at her, just as the child screwed up her face and wailed until her fists shook. *Ah-ahh. Ah-ahhh.*

"Can't you do something, Mary?" He patted the bundle in Mary's arms. "Shh, baby. Shhh."

The child cried harder.

It was as if their entire world had shrunk down to this sound: *ah-ahh, ah-ahh.*

A logging truck passed them, in a *whoosh* immersing them in a cloud of blinding snow. The child began to scream.

"Oh my God," Mary said. "I can't take it."

The baby's cries now were desperate, two-punch, her tiny face moist with tears.

"Bob. I'm going to lose my mind," Mary said, her voice quiet with panic. "We have to stop this crying."

Heart pounding, Bob turned on the blinkers and eased the car over to the side of the road, praying that someone didn't come barreling up behind them to send them into the ditch. He looked at the rearview mirror glanced back at the road shrouded in clouds behind them.

"Can you be fast?" He looked at Mary.

Mary cradled the child in her arms, swinging her from side to side like a rocking cradle. "Tsk, tsk," she said. "There, there." The baby stopped and sniffed. Then Mary held up the child to her nose and sniffed.

"Oh for heaven's sake, she's dirty. Turn the heat up, I've got to change her," she said. "I can't believe I'm so dumb." Mary hauled out the diapers and the dry towels. She laid the baby out on her coat on the seat beside her. Her hands moved quickly to unsnap the safety pins and the wet diaper. Suddenly, the naked child was on the leather seat between them, startling with her slender blue-veined body, her pink vagina, her fists curled, her blue-veined legs pulled tightly to her stomach. She cried her wet, braying cry, and Mary was talking to her, saying, *now-now, it's all right, it's going to be all right* as she folded the soft clean diaper across her belly, where the black stump still adorned the child's belly button, pinning up one side, then the other. She guided her arms and legs back into the fuzzy yellow sleeper, snapped it up, wrapped her tightly in the blanket decorated with red and blue and green elephants, embroidered by a neighbor, and set her pink cap on her head. As the smell of urine filled their car, another car appeared out of the clouds on the highway moving toward them. It edged slowly past, then became a dark shape, disappearing into the flurry of snow, honking as if to ask, *why would anyone in their right mind stop here?*

Mary pulled a bottle from a diaper bag, a shower gift sent over from Warm Springs by Bob's mother, crooked her arm, settled the baby, and fed her a bottle. Suddenly, mercifully, the car was filled with the rhythmic kiss of the baby's sucking, her eyes flickering.

They drove on, inching their way over the Garnet Mountains and across the wide plains at Drummond where Bob had to steer against the wind. He saw the grey shapes of cows, barns, and houses in the sheeting snow and wondered if this is how the child would remember them—dark shapes looming over her like those cars passing them on the highway.

"Worst I've ever driven in," Mary said finally. "At least the baby's asleep."

"Thank God for small miracles." Elizabeth Finch Carter, Bob thought as he looked at the child, asleep in Mary's arms, her fingers relaxed, her lips fluttering, and he felt a hand close around his heart.

At the sign for the Stone Home, just after Butte, he felt weak with relief.

"I feel like I've aged ten years," Bob said. "That was a hellish drive."

"Let's just get through this," Mary said. Her mouth was set. The child was sleeping in her arms. She sat, erect, in the seat next to him, but she might as well have been miles away. "I never thought I would be doing this," she said. "Never."

"You know what Cecil said," Bob replied.

"Yes, I know what Cecil said," she snapped. "But I'm not Cecil. Cecil didn't just give birth and have to give up a baby now, did he?"

Bob skidded to a stop at the stop sign.

"We don't have to do this," he said. "Are you changing your mind?"

"No." Mary tipped her chin up. She looked down at the baby. She lifted her up and smelled the top of her head. Then she looked back out the window. "Let's go, Bob."

They passed slowly through Stone City, past a small café, where a young girl with long braids stood in the window looking out at the snow, licking a large ice cream cone. Why wasn't she in school? Bob wondered. Why didn't she have a sweater on? The thought of eating something cold in this weather made him shiver, even inside his thick wool coat. They drove slowly, looking for a sign that would direct them to the Stone Home. The baby woke and began to fuss. At last, as they passed the low brick buildings of the downtown and headed out of town, they saw the entrance gate for the Stone Home.

Mary stayed in the car, engine running, with the child. Bob walked into the building, past a receptionist with large dark circles under her eyes who turned away from him as he entered, cradling the phone under her chin, her voice lowering suddenly. The room was warm, a fire crackling in the fireplace, some potted ferns, and a few landscape reproductions on the walls, the air greyed. Was he imagining that? Was it the lack of fluorescent lighting, which they were putting in all the buildings now in downtown Bridger? Bob was aware of the sounds of people from other floors, murmurs, and he was relieved when a nurse dressed in a white starched uniform with a white nurses' cap perched on her head came briskly down the hallway and asked him if he needed assistance.

When Bob explained who he was and that he was looking for Doctor Oetzinger, she knew immediately what it was about. Her tone softened and she asked him to wait. She asked if he was alone—or did he want to bring his family inside?

"I have to get my wife and the child," he said, and hurried outside.

Inside the cocoon of the fogged-up Buick, Mary held the bottle upright, as the heater hummed and the baby nestled in her arms. Bob opened the door and slid in next to them.

"They're ready for us," Bob said.

Mary looked at him. "Okay."

She held Elizabeth to her, pulling the swaddling blanket close around the child's face, and bent down and kissed the top of her head.

Mary pulled on her hat. She draped her coat over her shoulders and buttoned it up around the baby, the arms hanging limply at her sides. She slid across the seat, opened the door, and got out. As she stood, her black hair snaked out into the wind, and she bent down and hurried toward the door.

In the sudden warmth of the lobby, Bob lifted the coat from her shoulders before he took off his own, hanging them on wooden hangers before he and Mary settled in large leather chairs to wait for the doctor. There was a large carved oak fireplace, with an oil portrait of a certain Frau Holtzmeier, a benefactor of the Stone Home, dressed in green silk with a broad, imposing chest. Bob held his hands out to the fire as it popped and crackled, his fingers tingling. The child started to cry. Mary bounced it, holding it close, as she walked over to the fire and stood there, swaying.

"She's cold," she said to Bob. Her face was drawn. He knew that Mary was telling him something. What was it? That none of this was her idea? That they had time now to change their minds—to turn around, take the baby and run?

He wanted to remind her about what the doctor said. He wanted to remind her about the law. He wanted to remind her about how they really didn't have much choice. In fact, when he thought about it, choice was their enemy here. Black and white. Right and wrong. It was a simple decision. It was the law.

Mary patted the baby on her shoulder as she moved about, her galoshes squeaking. The baby's cries echoed off the high walls.

The beginning of a headache drummed against Bob's temples.

The receptionist was talking on the phone, her lips curving, red, as she laughed at something, her hand over her mouth, eyes cast politely away from them.

Mary walked over and stared Bob in the face, and he could see her red lipstick and black hair and dark eyes, how lovely, how startlingly beautiful she was as she offered him the child, saying simply. "I have to use the ladies' room."

"Okay," Bob said and stood there.

"That means, Bob," she said, using both hands to offer him the child, "that you need to hold the baby."

He reached out and took the child into the crook of his arm, and listened to the dimming click of Mary's heels.

"*Sh-sh*," he said to the screwed-up face, the purple vein pulsing in the forehead. "Don't cry." Bob smelled the child, the dewy, slightly decayed smell like overripe fruit. He saw the black hair feathering her head, the tiny purple-tinged fingers gathered in a fist, the narrow eyes, tilted. The child turned her eyes toward his voice.

"Oh God," Bob said. He walked, around and around, jiggling her, feeling the bulk of her six pounds, two ounces wriggling, the weight of a large file: Northwestern Insurance/Donatello Logging.

"Please don't cry," Bob said, his heart pounding as he walked and jiggled and wondered where Mary was and what was taking her so long and whether she was applying her lipstick, perhaps she was enjoying sounds of the baby's cries ratcheting up higher and higher, cries that were building like psi in his brain and his skull and his spine.

He glanced again at the receptionist, who was also clearly ignoring him. "Of course you feel that way," she cooed softly into the phone. "She was *so* wrong to do that."

Well, Bob thought. I'm not going to give her the pleasure of watching me suffer. He looked for someplace quiet, someplace he could get away, when he spotted a phone booth and headed over to it. He sat inside, folded the doors shut, the baby in his lap. "Okay, kid," Bob said, looking at the child in his arms. "We're in this together and we've got to make the best of it." He put the child to his shoulder and patted its bottom. The child kept crying. "'Ain't she sweet. She's a walkin' down the street.'" His mind went blank: he couldn't remember the words.

The baby arched its back and shrieked.

His mind turned red. Where was Mary? He looked out into the room. It was empty.

"Okay, princess. So how about, 'Cigarette holder, which wags me.'"

More crying, but a curious change in tone.

"Over my shoulder..." He turned sideways as he patted her back, taking in the blue eyes, the flat face as he hummed a tune, jostling her to get her to stop crying. "C'mon little one, you gotta love the Duke."

"Huh-ha-huh-ha-huh...out steppin," The fists gripped, the body clenched as he patted the baby's flannelled back."

Suddenly, miraculously, Elizabeth Finch Carter hiccupped. Bob turned her over to face her—holding her along his forearm—as her eyelids fluttered, and as quickly as she was consumed with fury, she was consumed by sleep.

"Good girl." He placed her back on his shoulder. "Good taste."

When he emerged from the phone booth, the receptionist arched her eyebrows at him. "The doctor will see you now. Your wife is already in there."

"Duke Ellington," he said to her.

Another office, another doctor, this one surrounded by built-in shelves of medical books with titles like *Afflictions of the Mind*, the *Psychology of Dementia*, and *Mongoloidism Explained*. On top of the bookcase was a pair of scales, used in early-day Montana to measure gold dust. The physician's name was Doctor Oetzinger, but he told Bob and Mary that most folks just called him "Dr. O."

As Bob held the baby, heavy with sleep, and Mary sat next to him, her back not touching the chair, rigid as a tamarack, Dr. O told them what would be done for the child, and how she would have a nurse who would tend her in the nursery, and when she was older and able she would learn the basics of toileting and dressing herself, the most that could be hoped for.

Mary's face was drawn, only a muscle in her cheek twitching. She unbuckled the jacket of her suit. She'd worn a red sweater over her skirt as her stomach was not quite back to its usual flatness. Her sweater had some decorative pom-poms on the collar, and, through her rubber galoshes, Bob could see the faint outline of her black high heels.

As the doctor talked about exercise rooms and training programs, Bob focused on a sign above the doctor's desk: Plan ahead, the letters squeezed together, the "d" dropped down on the line below. It was supposed to be funny, but it infuriated Bob.

The doctor took a yellow pad from his desk drawer and dated it: 2/15/53. He began asking questions: family names, births, deaths, strokes, heart attacks, the crazy ones, the tragic ones, the ones who just kept carrying on, holding up the branches for the rest of the motley crew. The family tree, Bob's mother's nervous breakdown, Mary's sister's suicide, the squares for the men, the circles for women, writing out, Bob could see, a family tree that looked, if you asked him, like a hangman's chart or a stick Christmas tree, hung with deaths and births and sorrows, lit with the occasional joys of babies that lived, babies that were healthy and normal.

Mary's voice grew thick as she described her miscarriages one and two. "Tell her about the sickness, Mary," Bob said. "She was pregnant, we were on a trip, and she was so sick."

"I couldn't keep food down," Mary said quietly. "We were traveling and every time I ate, I threw up."

"Acute morning sickness." The doctor shook his head. "That happens."

Bob leaned forward. "Wouldn't that be the cause of this, doctor? The child not getting nourishment? Wouldn't that affect the child this way? Is that what caused this mongoloidism, doctor?"

"Not necessarily, Mr. Carter," Dr. O said, looking from Bob to Mary. "Mental retardation and mongoloidism are complicated. We don't know enough about them right now—there's a lot of new research out there and we're trying to figure out if it is genetic or caused by something in the environment. We think it might be an extra chromosome, but we're not sure. It's a very interesting field." Bob saw him write: "Get chromosomes on pt on arrival."

Then the doctor got up and asked to examine the child.

Bob laid her on the examining table and watched as a nurse came in the room and carefully undid everything Mary had done just an hour before—the blanket, sleeper, the diaper—until the child was squirming on the starched white cloth, wriggling and crying.

Dr. O talked to her, as his fingers poked and probed her, *You're mad, you're mad as a wet hen, aren't you babe*, he said, his deep voice soft as he examined her mouth, her ears, her throat, and felt her glands, and used his rubber mallet to scrape along the soles of her feet, which barely twitched.

"This is very hard," he said, as he worked. "She has the rounded eyes and the flattened face of a mongoloid—John Langdon Down in 1866 discovered the syndrome in Surrey, England, and some think it should be called after him. But my guess, by her responses, is that the child is also very retarded."

"How can you tell?" Mary said sharply.

"See those reflexes." He tapped the knee, which barely jerked. He scraped the bottom of the child's foot again. "Very little response.

We don't like to see that in babies. Of course, it is hard to say at such a young age, but I see a lot of retarded newborns, Mrs. Carter."

"Also," he said. "Watch this." He waved his hand in front of the child's eyes.

"See how slow she is to blink?" he said. "Not a good sign. And this loose skin—he pinched skin along the child's belly. We associate this lack of tone with mongoloidism as well, folks."

Dr. O put the diaper, then the sleeper printed with bunnies back on the child, his hands working slowly and deliberately around the pins and zippers. He handed the child to Mary. He put a hand on Mary's back and patted her. "She would be a lot of work for you, Mary. A perpetual child. Here, at least, we know how to take care of retarded kids. We can train them, school them—we have classes on etiquette, reading and writing, even basic tasks, some of our folks can go on to work on the farm or in restaurants—and you can go on, have more children, get on with your life. We're doing research here," he said, "so perhaps one day we'll know even more about how to help these children."

"They deserve our compassion," Bob said.

Dr. O and Mary looked over at him. "I'll be in touch, Bob," Dr. O told them. "I want to give you some time." He left the room, the door clicking softly behind him.

"It's best," Bob said, "if we make this short."

"Of course," Mary said. She held the child, patted it, kissed her head, took a long look at her face, the blue eyes staring back. "Lizzie Finch Carter," she said. She handed the child to Bob. "Bye, Lizzie," he said, then he opened the door to let the nurse know they were ready.

Bob offered the child to the nurse.

The nurse's three-cornered hat skewed sideways as she settled the child on her shoulder. She looked at both of them, but said nothing.

Mary turned her face from Bob, her hands shaking as she gathered up her purse. Bob touched the flannel-clad back of the child and nodded to the nurse and whispered, "Thank you." She opened the door and left, silent on her white rubber soles.

On the drive home, they didn't speak. Mary's face was in profile against the white-frosted car window, her straight nose tipped red, her lips thin, her face drawn, her hair spilling across the wide black hood of her coat. Bob said, "It's the best thing, Mary. I know it's hard." He glanced out at the cattle along the road, the relieved look of them as they grazed along trails of hay scattered in the snow, the sun glinting off the white-covered hills in the distance. She slowly unwrapped the scarf from her neck, then wound it around herself again, this time tighter.

"I think it's best. I really do," Bob said. He looked in the rearview mirror at the truck barreling down on them and started the wipers to prepare for the blast of snow that would blind them when the truck passed.

Mary continued looking out the window.

Bob looked over her shoulder to see what she was watching: the rancher framed in the doorway of his red barn, the road sign to a town called Opportunity—the sweet, doomed sound of it, some pioneer lured west by the promise of a free homestead of 160 acres—the sight of a horse shaking its mane in the wind, then picking its way across a snow-covered pasture.

As the car fell into the skid, Bob could see the pasture on one side, the sheared-off rock on the other. Steer into the skid, he told himself. Never brake. He was trying to steer into the skid, but the car kept fishtailing toward the rock wall. *Fishtailing*, he thought. What a strange and wonderful word, and he pictured a speckled green cutthroat, dead, frozen into a curve, just as the car started to right itself.

He pumped the brake. The engine choked to a stop. The car bisected the yellow line. The road, mercifully, was empty.

"Jesus," Bob said. "Are you all right, Mary?"

Mary held her hands to her mouth, her face wet, her eyes on the road, and nodded her head, up and down. She looked at him, her brown eyes bright and hard.

"We're gonna make it, Mary. Remember that."

Mary let out a strangled sob. "Bob, goddamn it, we're in the middle of the road."

Bob pumped the gas, turned the key again, and the engine caught. Mary let out a breath, as he shifted into first gear and turned the steering wheel so the car was headed in the right direction, moving slowly to avoid another skid, feeling Mary's eyes on the road, on him, on the steering wheel.

They rode the rest of the way in silence, stopping once for coffee in Deer Lodge. It was the longest drive of Bob's life: He felt as if he would remember every snow-covered willow, cottonwood, barn, plow, combine, and hollow-eyed cow along that snowpacked two-lane highway for the rest of his life.

CHAPTER FIFTEEN

A quarter-sized stain against the crotch of her underwear. Bright red. Fierce. The color of something dying. Elizabeth stared at the blood as she sat on the toilet in the ladies room of the *Bridger Chronicle.* She had been sitting there long enough to hear Miriam come in, talking about the snow-snarled traffic on Reserve and how the shithead of a managing editor was making everyone file their stories early, voices floating in and out between toilets flushing and faucets turning on and off and the whoosh of the door swinging open and shut.

After a long while, she heard the door open again. Ruth called her name.

Elizabeth paused.

"Call my husband," Elizabeth said. She could not get up, could not leave this stall. Bad news was on its way, but she wasn't going to move, for fear it would pounce.

"What's going on?" Ruth said. Her voice was quiet. "Tell me."

"I can't, I'm sorry," Elizabeth said. She stared at the green metal door. If I tell you this, she thought, it is really happening.

"It's okay," Ruth said. "I'll call Tom. I'm sorry, Elizabeth. I don't know what's going on, but it must be awful."

Elizabeth heard a drop of water plink from a faucet onto the ceramic bowl of the sink. Drip for drip, water for blood. She sat, her head between her hands, her elbows resting on her legs, willing herself numb. After a long while, she heard her husband, Tom, the deep tones of his voice in concert with Ruth's, so smooth and capable and in control that Elizabeth knew Ruth was scared shitless. "Thanks, thanks for everything," he said to Ruth, his voice muffled, then loud as he neared her stall. "I'll take care of her now."

Elizabeth started to shake.

The tap of his footsteps on the black-and-white tiles.

"Elizabeth?" His voiced echoed.

The sound punctured her heart.

"We need to get you to the doctor, hon."

Elizabeth did not answer him. She stared at her feet, feeling the cold drip of blood between her legs, clouding the water rose, pink, fuchsia, maroon.

"Elizabeth."

His voice, insistent, soft.

She did not answer.

He rattled the door. "Elizabeth. C'mon. Let me help you."

His face appeared under the door.

Elizabeth looked at him, the mouth where the eyes should be, the eyes where the mouth should be.

"C'mon," he said. "Open up."

Feb. 20, 1996. I lost the baby, she e-mailed her sister Karen, who lived in Choteau with her two children and husband, each green word so upright and blinking on the black computer screen in front of her. "*Oh Lizzie,*" Karen wrote back. "*I am so so sorry. I wish I could be there to hug you. I'm crying while I write this, because I can't imagine anything more painful. I know how much you wanted this child. The kids send their love. I'll pray for you. I know it doesn't seem like it now, but God probably had a reason for all of this. We don't always understand his greater plan. I love you. Hang in there.*"

If only, Elizabeth thought, she'd just say, *I'm sorry. That sucks.* What kind of a God would make a plan like this anyway? Piper—that's what she had planned to name the child if it was a girl—was now a knot-sized piece of flesh she had to flush down the toilet. What kind of a plan was that?

She took a two-week leave and spent the time watching the sun creep across the white ceiling, the snow melt from the mountain ash trees, the clusters of robins and cedar waxwings fighting over the fermented red berries and occasionally thumping the window in a drunken frenzy. She watched Hitchcock films and read thick novels about English families come to rack and ruin because of unfortunate marriages. Tom went back and forth to his job as a schoolteacher at Hastings, a private elementary school in Bridger, hailed as progressive, alternative, or hippie, depending on who was talking. She lay on the floor of the room that she had painted yellow—the baby's room—and stared at the ceiling. She held a photograph of her parents—her father in his dark wool business suit, her mother in a plaid blazer, the studio lights bleaching their skin color to a whitish green.

At least, she thought, they didn't have to bear my disappointment.

At least, she thought, I didn't have to bear their disappointment.

The one thing she did each day was drag herself out of bed to slap something in the crockpot so Tom had a meal at day's end, though it was food she would have complained about at any other time—sloppy Joes, stringy beef stew made with cream of mushroom soup, chicken stew made with canned cream of celery—but Tom bless his heart didn't complain, and as they stared at each other from opposite ends of the long oak table, he smiled at her, lifted his glass in a toast, and dug in.

The days of going to the gym, visiting friends, sitting on the thick leather sofa in their living room and drinking red wine seemed to belong in another century. What about investigating a story? Riding the El to the Art Institute? Gone. Elizabeth tried to remember what she used to laugh about. Her publisher's tanning bed tans? At least he cared about something. The neighbor who mowed his lawn twice a week in precise rectangles? At least he had a routine. The woman in advertising who changed her hair with each new boyfriend—pageboy, flip, shag—to mark the transition from bartender to college professor, poet to real estate salesman? At least she had style.

This family thing isn't what I'm good at, she wrote Karen. *I never should have come home. This isn't working for me. This house. This job at the paper. None of it.*

When she told Tom how she felt, he brought home St. John's Wort, an herb said to be good for depression. He purchased a new color TV, complete with a remote. After several days he came to her, on the sofa, took the channel changer, snapped off the television, and said, "C'mon, Elizabeth, I want to show you something."

He took her by the hand and led her out to the front flower beds, pushed aside the dead leaves until the naked points of daffodils and fragile green-white crocuses emerged. "Your flowers are coming up."

She looked down at the white, transparent heads of the crocuses, thinking how pale and eerie they were.

How closely, she thought, the unborn resemble the dead.

"I'm sorry," Elizabeth smiled weakly. "All I want to do is snap their little heads off."

"Jesus." He went inside, slamming the door behind him.

It was time, she knew, to go back to work.

CHAPTER SIXTEEN

Louise dedicated herself to Lizzie, to feeding her, day after day—waiting till Margaret walked out for her cigarette break to feed her a second bottle of cereal. Her cheeks grew fat, her face plump and round. At six months, she started lifting her head. At one year, she started pulling herself up, standing at her crib. Lizzie slowly began to experiment with crawling. Her shiny brown hair was straight and framed her round face. While other children tolerated Louise's touch, her diapering and feeding and occasional attempts at play, when Louise reached for Lizzie, her eyes shone and she held out her arms and smiled her broad smile punctuated by one tooth, then two.

"Don't get too close, it will only cause trouble," Margaret cautioned Louise as they sat in the cafeteria with their cups of weak coffee, sun flooding through the basement windows. They were gathered for a short coffee break with the other nurses from the children's and teenagers' cottages and the aides from the blind and non-ambulatory cottages. Someone had brought in a transistor and propped it on the counter, and they could hear the faint sounds of "Ain't Nothing But a Hound Dog." Across the table, a nurse was painting another woman's nails red.

Of course, they both knew that this warning was a joke. All staff fraternized with the patients. Everyone knew which staff was connected to which patients, and the administration turned a blind eye to the whole thing—they had to in an institution with nearly eight hundred patients and just enough staff to treat half that many. Willy and Lizzie belonged to Louise. Margaret had a brood: three little girls with palsy whom she called Flopsy, Mopsy, and Cottontail and several boys with missing limbs she called her Howdy-Doody Boys. Her jokes were savage, Louise noted, but so was her love for these children, and Margaret almost strangled an attendant who put one of her boys in the bathtub and went off to have a cigarette, getting back just in time to keep the kid from drowning. Anna watched over an eleven-year-old Assiniboine girl, Mary Kicking Horse, whose father gave her up when her mother was killed in a car accident, and a Salish girl named Belle Star who had mongoloidism, a sprite of a child, whose long black braids hung like bell pulls from her impish face, as ethereal as Lizzie was round and sturdy.

They called them the hidden children. They included the child of a prominent judge and his wife; a paraplegic ten-year-old born to a prominent Montana State University history professor and his wife who wasn't expected to live out the year; a severely retarded boy born to the U.S. congressman who originally hailed from Butte; even a pair of severely retarded twins born to some "muckety-muck," as Charlene described him, of the Great Northern Railway. Like old manor houses where servants were named for their masters, the children were sometimes known by their parents' occupations: "the judge's child" or "the railroad twins." Louise and the other nurses read about the parents' goings-on in the newspapers, while she and her friends wiped the drool from their children's chins, cleaned up their shit, and put them to bed each night. They had charts where they recorded the parents' gifts when they arrived: the giant Easter baskets bought by guilt, the castoffs from the "normal" children, or the beautifully stitched dresses, the toys from expensive department stores—the Paris Gibson in Great Falls, the Bridger Mercantile—the Hudson Bay blankets and expensive cotton sheets that sometimes didn't make it to the patients. The nurses wrote letters about the size, weight, and condition of these children as well as their recent accomplishments—sitting up, toileting, using table manners, tracing the occasional shape of a pumpkin—letters that were read with varying degrees of interest at carved mahogany dining tables or on the oilcloth-covered tables in farmhouse kitchens or in lavish private offices, before they were locked in desk drawers, underwear drawers, filing cabinets.

Castoffs. That's what these children were to them. Practice for more perfect models.

Look at the mimeographed newsletters the place sent out, Louise thought. From the outside the Stone Home might appear like some kind of private school with its Thanksgiving tracing of pilgrims and pumpkins. The cottages, where patients were grouped by age, had sweet little names like Robin and Wren and Bluebird, and on top of life training, the staff taught the patients songs and stories, and the newsletters announced things like "Halloween found our boys very enthusiastic about the parties at the schools" and "a very happy birthday party was given by the Recreation Department" and in "primary trainable" they had been doing a unit on "how the farmer raises livestock and supplies us with basic food and how the ranch garden produces things like carrots and beets and potatoes."

But there was no news—no seasonal cutouts—for the basements

where the non-ambs were stuck, where the air reeked of piss and shit and the staff had to clothespin their noses to work, where the doctor yelled on his weekly ward visits, "Jesus Christ, open the fucking windows, the smell is ungodly!" his cursing shocking the nurses as he examined his patients and took tests for his genetic studies. And Cottage Number Two. No bird name there, Louise noted. That's where they stuck the male nurses, stove-up vets, or ex-ranch hands, because that's where the patients, all men, all two- and three-hundred pounds, had to be strapped in bed or they ate their own shit. Billy Meakins was famous for eating his shoes—laces, leather, and all—one pair a year that arrived each Christmas, and his father a successful doctor in Billings and all.

Sometimes Louise resented the children. They all did. Sometimes the children seemed like a giant pulsing, howling mass of endless needs and wants and all she could do was walk the path home and hope that, the next day, she would walk back. So many of them, the nurses said, so few of us.

Cynicism, after all, was their backbone.

Lizzie, with her round blue eyes and soft brown hair and chubby arms, dimpled at the elbows. As Louise held her, that day, Lizzie reached up and touched her cheek.

Don't get attached. On the way back to the nursery, she cared what Margaret said. Then she got back to the nursery and all hell had broken loose. Babies were standing, lying, crawling around their cribs, and all were crying, the sound like a buzz saw along her spine as Louise sprang into action, stripping the infants' wet sleepers and diapers and drying and powdering them and re-diapering them as fast as she could and giving the ones that could feed themselves bottles.

When that was done, she started feeding the infants, rocking one after the other in the chair, until she got to Elizabeth.

She had to feed the others—the kid with the Thalidomide arm, the quadriplegic, the encephalitic baby. She had to weigh the six-month-olds.

But Lizzie was crying. And she didn't care, suddenly, about the others. Babies were always crying, always wet, always hungry, and she was always overwhelmed. So why not make one child, hers, happy. It was the least she could do, her payback for long hours, crappy money, sore feet.

When she finished her bottle, Louise put her back in her crib. Lizzie's face crumpled and she began to cry.

"Hush now," she said.

The sound of the crying seemed to crawl up her neck, flush her cheeks.

Louise made the mistake of looking in the crib at Lizzie. The baby held out her arms and cried harder.

"Sh-sh," Louise said. "Sh-sh, Lizzie, go to sleep." She stroked her downy head—was there anything softer than baby hair?—glad as hell that Margaret wasn't here to witness this, as it was completely against regulations.

Lizzie's eyes drooped.

Shhh, she said. She slowly withdrew her hand. Tiptoed away.

A loud screech rose from the crib. When Louise peered over the railing, Lizzie's round face was red with fury.

"*Sh-sh,*" she said, helpless, as she weighed a six-month-old. Ten pounds, six ounces. Or was it six pounds, ten ounces. She couldn't remember. The crying drilled out her brain. She bundled up the baby in a cotton flannel blanket and stuck a pacifier in his mouth, his eyes widening.

"Lizzie," Louise peered into the crib. Her voice was stern. She imagined her face, a big red cloud of flesh with a black spot opening and closing. "Stop crying, you're fine, go to sleep."

Lizzie continued crying, the raw sound triggering misery in crib after crib that just minutes before had quieted into a dull hiccuppy peace.

"Peace!" Louise shouted. "Shut your goddamn traps."

She was sweating, her hands shaking.

Lizzie stared back at her, her mouth a perfect O.

A pure still moment.

And then that nerve-shattering sound again.

What could Louise do? She picked Lizzie up and carried her as she finished her other chores, diapering and feeding the others as best she could, one-handed, hoping beyond hope she could quiet the room before Margaret came back to scold her, to see her face, tear-streaked and red, to tell her about the dangers of becoming too attached and how that could compromise her nursing abilities. She held Lizzie until she fell asleep, held her until her own back and shoulders were fiery with pain—and at last, she set her in her crib and she did not awaken.

That day, she knew, was the beginning of her downfall. The beginning of Louise and Lizzie. Lizzie and Louise.

CHAPTER SEVENTEEN

Mary was next to him in their new Studebaker, the first car they owned that was less than ten years old. They traveled down Highway 200 from Bridger to Seeley Lake during a late February thaw. Pete had called and asked him to come up and take a look at the new tepee burner. He'd just had it constructed, with the help of a local contractor and a loan from the bank, and he wanted Bob to see it. Pete was starting a small mill, telling Bob he was getting too old to down trees. "Widowmakers," Pete told him, the name loggers used for dangerous trees, "don't get their names from nowhere and I don't aim to be another statistic." When Bob mentioned the idea to Mary over breakfast, she brightened. It was an excuse to get out of town, to get away from the grief that dogged their days and nights. "Of course," she tipping her coffee cup from side to side, watching the dark liquid slosh up the white side of the cup and back the other before looking back at Bob. "Of course I'll go see his tepee burner. Who doesn't love Pete? And God knows, I could use a change of scene."

Of course, Bob had mentioned to Pete everything that had

happened to the child. He didn't want slipups. This was a voyage of discovery. He was trying to find his wife.

Beside him, Mary was quiet. The two of them had survived dismantling the nursery. Bob took down the crib, storing the mattress and frame in the attic, another trip to the frozen zone of family detritus. Mary went back to work part-time at the dress store downtown, coming home the first week with most of her paycheck on her back—a beautifully tailored grey wool dress and slacks she had slimmed down enough to wear again—but Bob enjoyed all of it: she was stunning with her black hair spun back on her head, the grey wool with the narrow darts setting off her slim hips. "You are exquisite," he said, and she just looked at him, even in bed when he put his arm around her slender waist and pulled her toward him. She patted him on the head. "Good-night Robert," she said, before turning away. "Good night. I love you. Don't fret."

Don't fret?

Bob's mother was still in the state hospital, where he drove every other week to take her out for lunch at the Goosetown Café in nearby Anaconda, with its wall-sized photograph of the Pintler Mountains and an ancient-looking waitress who addressed them "Can I help youse guys?" and they ordered the gravy-covered pasties. After a shock treatment and Lithium, the doctors insisted his mother was doing fine and might be able to be moved to a nursing home soon. They were watching her closely.

"Shall we lunch in Potomac?" Bob glanced at Mary as they headed down the highway, which hugged the grey-green Blackfoot River. She fiddled with a button on her coat. "That little spot on the Blackfoot with the great burgers?"

"Doesn't matter," Mary said with her careful smile. "Whatever."

"You don't sound enthusiastic," Bob said.

"I'm not as hungry as you are." She shrugged and looked out at the river as the road wound along it, the water bright and glittering where it flowed next to the iced-over sections, the banks of striated red rock along the road cuts layered with sediment.

The Blackfoot Tavern was small. A large man dressed in a white greasy apron greeted them when they walked in, but after they ordered, he didn't say another word, the room filled with the sizzling of burgers and the distant cries of a baby in the glassed-in front room behind the grill that overlooked the river. The smell of frying meat was soothing, but the quiet was unnerving, so they ate quickly and left enough money to cover the bill on the table, the man looking up from his newspaper and nodding when they walked out.

As they wound into the hills past the experimental forest at Lubrecht (What is an experimental forest anyway, Bob wondered. A forest that was trying to be a forest?), past pastures of Herefords and Black Angus, he and Mary talked about the Christmas parties they'd attended, who was building a new house or moving out to the more fashionable subdivisions in the hills, who'd had new jobs, promotions, who was moving out of town, who was dating whom among their single friends. The conversation was easy, Bob thought, like the good old days, roving from topic to topic, little of this, little of that, on this sunny winter day, good friends and a good meal on the road up ahead of them. The one topic they avoided was that of children. Who was pregnant. Who just had children. Did they want children? Did they dream of her? Of that child? Babies. Offspring.

Off-limits.

At the Seeley turnoff, Bob slowed down, set the turn signal, and patted Mary's hand. "You watch, Mary." He studied her face before he turned onto the highway that would take them north to the lake country. "This is going to be our year. I just feel it. How do you feel?"

"Dandy." She offered him a weak smile.

She was in that place again where he couldn't reach her. It was as if she were on an island, and he could see her from a boat, but a large lake of choppy ice-blue water lay between them.

"Talk to me," Bob said. "Don't you think we're coming through this?"

"Maybe," she looked at him. "I've got my job, Bob. I've got symphony association, and the women's auxiliary, and I'm busy. I'm doing what I can." She lifted her chin and set her lips in a straight line.

She looked out the window at the wide pastures, where a few desultory cows were standing, watching them pass. "I'm just glad for a drive. Isn't it lovely we have sun for a change?"

He forced himself not to say more, not to push her, much as he wanted to ask what she was thinking, did she love him still, did she think about the baby? Why didn't she let him in? Let him comfort her, talk to her? Why this remoteness, when he was there for her? "We'll be there soon," he said. "I'm really looking forward to seeing these two. Wait till you taste Cora's pie."

Mary smiled as if that was the sorriest excuse for conversation she'd ever heard. "I've been hearing about this pie," she patted his arm.

Mary, are you in there? he wanted to ask her, the easy, funny Mary, not this sealed-in, pursed-lip person in the car next to him.

They drove on as the road dipped down to Salmon Lake, spreading out before them, a white plane of ice. Here and there were circles of men sitting on lawn chairs, bundled up and drinking from thermos cups, and fishing from holes augered in the ice, surrounded by green ice chests.

"Remember that time I took you fishing on the Blackfoot?" Bob said. "With Cecil and Arnie?"

Mary smiled. "Do I ever."

"We had to teach you how to bait the hook with worms, and while Cecil and Arnie were doing their fly-fishing thing, you caught the biggest brookie anyone had ever pulled out of Scotty Brown Bridge and we cooked it and ate it right there by the river?"

"That was the last time I fished," Mary said. "You never took me again."

Bob laughed. "Well, it's hard to top that."

Of course, what neither of them said but they both understood was that, right afterward, Mary was pregnant. That understanding turned around in the air between them as the car bore through the thick Douglas fir forests that lined the road, slowing as they reached the town of Seeley, with its gas station, grocery store, tackle shop, and Deeno's Bar, frequented by lake people in the summer and locals in the winter.

Bob turned down Boy Scout Road in Seeley, and there was the tepee burner, the steel sides and wire mesh top smoke-stained but still shiny in places, the conveyer belt running out of a small door in the cone three-quarters of the way up. The tepee burner was surrounded by log decks on one side and stacks of newly drying boards on the other.

When Bob pulled up, Pete walked out of the mill and over to their car. "Welcome!" he said, holding out his arms. "Welcome to the money pit." He smiled and motioned for Mary to unroll the passenger-side window, and Bob watched in fascination as she complied.

"Mary!" Pete's voice boomed through the car as he peered through the passenger window. "Bob, you hound dog, you brought the most beautiful woman in Montana! You really class up this joint. *Bella donna*," he said, leaning over to buss her on the cheek. He drew back. "Do you know what that means?"

"No?"

"Beautiful woman," he kissed his hands. "But I better stop before this guy punches me."

Bob laughed when Mary turned bright red.

"But guess what I can tell you about my mill?"

"What?" she said. Her eyes widened.

"You'll be bored stiff!"

"Ha, ha," a smile flashed across Mary's face as warm and welcome as winter sun, and Bob jumped out at that moment to walk around the car and shake Pete's hand. "Let's see this thing, Mr. Donatello."

Pete guided them to a parking place, and when the two of them stepped out of the car to join him, Pete held his arms out to indicate the sawmill, the conveyer belt that carried the sawdust to the tepee burner, and the office built on the far side of the sawmill with the hand-painted "Office" sign, the muddy yard with its web of tire tracks, the logging deck where piles of shaggy Douglas firs lay waiting to be fed into the mill. "Ain't America great?" Pete said.

Bob patted him on the back. "Congratulations, Pete. This was a lot of hard work." His heart swelled as he looked around, knowing he had some small part in helping Pete create his business, Pete with his knotted hands, his saw, the long days at the scarred kitchen table where the two of them worked on the business insurance and bank loans. "You did it. You made this."

Pete held his arms around Bob and Mary. "This is us," he whispered. "You helped me make this happen, Robert, so this belongs to you too."

As they entered the entrance to the mill, the shriek of the saws was overwhelming. *Cover your ears,* Pete said, pointing to the ear plugs in at least a few men's ears. The shrill ring of metal against wood ran through him, and Bob could tell by Mary's pinched face that it was painful for her too. How could these men endure it, day after day? Bob was aware the three of them were an odd trio—Pete in suspenders and stagged-off jeans, Mary in her black wool coat and leather gloves, and Bob in his Harris tweed. As they walked through the mill on the dirt floor, men in their striped logging shirts and stagged-off black logger's jeans glanced up at them and their looks said, *city folks*. The tang of sawdust rose, pungent and sweet, as men, intent and relaxed at once, watched as boards came down the line on a conveyor belt from the deafening saw, and every once in a while one of the men plucked a misshapen board off the line and tossed it into a pile. In the sawmill section of the mill, giant saws split and quartered the Douglas fir trees, transforming them from round logs into square lumber, from trees to boards—8 by 6s, 8 by 10s, and 8 by 12s—the saws screaming and shrieking as if this were a task almost too much for them, raining sawdust that the men below swept into piles that were conveyed to the tepee burner. Bob took them next to the tepee burner to glimpse the pale, pungent piles of sawdust that glowed red hot and smoky. The smell of dust and pine resin was so overwhelmingly sharp and sweet and sour it turned Bob's stomach.

"What's your output?" Bob shouted when they were outside again.

"5,000 board feet in an eight-hour day," Pete yelled. "That is if there aren't any men sick. Or power outages. Or breakdowns. And that—my friend—are some big ifs."

"So this is what a $50,000 loan will get ya," Bob yelled.

"That and about five men and a dozen headaches," Pete yelled back.

"What kind of saw?" Bob said, pointing at the circular saw with its hooked, silver teeth.

"We're a circular sawmill," Pete said. "I'd love to go gang-circular, but I can't afford it, Bob. One day, maybe, but I'd have to retrofit the whole damn thing. It's that sash-gang saw that's the ticket on this

Doug fir, slices it up like a knife through butter."

"Doesn't exactly *sound* like a knife through butter," Bob said.

In the back of the mill, men stacked the clean boards on the back of a semi, the naked pine gleaming in the morning sun.

"These are the 8 by 10s, off to market," Pete said, his hands stroking a board, pale yellow and pungent. "$2 a board. And 1954 is lookin' to be a swell year, Bob."

"It's amazing," Mary said dreamily. "Watching them go in the front, these huge ancient logs, covered with bark, homes to birds and chipmunks and squirrels and out they come, like this, ready to be homes." She reached out and touched the lumber where it lay on top of the truck. "Shiny, long, and squared up on the sides."

Pete looked at her, quiet for a minute, and then he laughed up at the man who was stacking the logs on the truck. "Hey, Harley! This missus here thinks your boards are pretty as a baby!"

The man called Harley looked down at Mary and grinned. "Thanks, Missus." He crossed his heart with his hand and bowed, keeping an eye on the line, and said, "That means a lot, coming from a pretty lady like you."

"Nonsense." She batted at the air and laughed, but Bob noticed that she flushed pink.

In the office, a trailer lined with cheap wooden paneling, an oil burner stove glowed orange in the corner. Above a dented metal desk hung a Stihl saw calendar featuring a busty ski maiden in a ski coat and furred hood and bikini bottoms holding a giant chainsaw. A large woman with a helmet of blonde-grey hair sat at a large black typewriter, her dress draped over the sides of her chair like a tent. The tapping of the keys paused as they walked in the door.

"Pearl?" Pete said. "Do we have coffee?"

"Honey, we always have coffee. Pete lives on coffee."

"Don't bother for my sake," Mary said. "I'm fine."

"I can always use coffee." Bob said.

"The question is," Pearl continued, "cups. Clean cups, that is." She heaved herself out of the chair, picked up a couple of translucent peach-colored cups that looked as if they hadn't been washed for several weeks. "God, these look like they've been buried in mud."

"I mean, where else could a dago who can't read go to start his own mill, can you tell me that? Sure as hell not in Italy, if you excuse me," Pete nodded to Mary. "I mean, did you see that tepee burner out there? It's still shiny! And that beautiful saw?" He kissed his finger. "*Bellissimo! Or Bellisima,* I should say."

This was the first time Bob had heard Pete admit he couldn't read.

Pearl returned carrying three cups of coffee. "Pete," she said as she handed Mary, then Bob, then Pete a cup. "If you're giving them your America is Great speech, you're boring these nice people. Cream, anyone?"

"Shall I put on our office music, Pearl?" Pete winked at Bob and Mary, after they told Pearl they didn't take anything in their coffee.

"Oh, my lord, no!" Pearl said. "That shrieking opera! You put that on and I'm walkin', Pete Donatello."

Pete grinned at them and disappeared in the back. They heard the squeak of a record player coming to life and the scratch of a needle on a record, then the opening bars of "*Aida*."

"Peeeet!" Pearl bellowed. "I'm getting my coat on!"

There was a scratch as the needle came off the record. Pete reappeared, laughing.

"He does this," she said to them, shaking her head, though Bob could see she clearly loved this game. "You'd think the man had a business to run." She walked to her typewriter and sat down. She stuck an invoice in the typewriter roller and rolled it up, squaring her shoulders as she pressed in the knobs so she could type *Donatello Logging* on the address section.

"Now, Pete, get out of here." She turned to him, her hands poised over the keys. "Some of us are working. See what I have to put up with, folks?" She smiled at Bob, then Mary, before she began punching the keys, her voice in tandem with the staccato tapping. "Lovely to meet you."

Pete piled in the car with them, Mary insisting that he sit up front. As they drove the mile up the road, Pete peppered Bob with questions about the car, what kind of horsepower the engine had, what kind of mileage it got. In the backseat, Mary focused on the contrast of Pete's rough red hands to the smooth tan leather of the dashboard.

Pete's cabin was perched on a dirt road without a name. There were no names on these roads, Pete had pointed out to Bob, because there were no strangers in this sparsely settled country. Bob knew Pete's road was the one past the failed motel that looked over the meadow, past the sign featuring the ten commandments, past the boarded-up six-sided log restaurant, the first left past the house and barn surrounded by a convertible with a smashed-in roof and a Ford half-ton on blocks.

As they drove, Pete described how he built his cabin, when he first arrived after the war, with his bare hands and all the whisky he could provide a few sawyers he befriended in Deeno's, the local bar, the gang of them felling logs, skinning them, and notching each so they fit together, then polishing the insides (*Cora wouldn't live with me if I didn't*) and cutting the diamond windows on either side of the front doors (*they were the biggest diamonds I could afford*) and a large picture window that overlooked the meadow to the west. When Danny came along, he added an extra bedroom with lighter, newer Douglas fir planks.

He grew quiet when they pulled up the long driveway, snow packed down, fishtailing just a bit at the curve, and came to a stop under a large blue spruce. "Let's get you inside," he said. He held the door open for Mary, studying her face. "How are we, Missus?" Pete seemed awkward. Bob wondered if his jocular self had suddenly drained away because, away from the noise of the men and the mill, he was overcome by the knowledge of what had just happened to her.

"I'm just fine, Pete," Mary said, her voice clipped. She refused his extended hand, as she slid out of the backseat and stood up.

Pete's hand dropped to his side.

In the awkward silence, Bob said, "Well, gang, are we ready to go in?"

Pete studied Mary's face. He looked over at Bob as if he were seeking some kind of clue.

"Yes." She lifted her head.

He touched her sleeve as they walked the slushy path to the door, giving her a sidelong look, but she kept her head focused on her boots, on following Pete, and as they walked, the shushing of their feet in the snow seemed so loud to him, almost a rebuke. *Why can't everything just be nice?* he wanted to plead.

When they arrived at the cabin door, Pete turned and smiled at them. "This is the old homestead," he said. "The old humble, is that what they say?"

Mary smiled.

"Look, I made you smile again," Pete said.

And this time, thankfully, Bob thought, she kept smiling.

He spun around and lifted the cast-iron latch on the door, and there was his wife, Cora, wiping her hands on her apron. She took Mary by the hands. "Mary," she said and looked her fully in the face. "You are every bit as lovely as Pete has told me you were. Now you two—" she pulled Bob by the sleeve of his coat. "You both get in out of that cold weather and make yourselves at home. I know Pete's been putting you to sleep about board feet and headsaws."

"Sash-gang saw, mio bambino," Pete said as he wandered off and disappeared behind a door. They heard a whine of phonograph tubes heating up, then the scratch of a needle on a record, and the opening lines of Catalani's "Ebben! Ne andrò lontana," sung in translation, *"Well then! I'll take off far way, like the echo of a pious bell."*

Mary's eyes shone dangerously, but Cora sprang into action. "Sit down," Cora said to Mary, taking her coat. "You need pie and coffee."

"Oh no," Mary said to her. "We couldn't. Or at least I couldn't. We just had a burger."

"Nonsense. Everyone needs pie. The world needs pie."

"Listen," Bob looked at her. "Mary, it is useless to protest. One is powerless under the spell of Cora."

"In that case," Mary said, "I surrender." Cora took Mary by the hand and led her to the table that Bob knew so well, the oilcloth that had been scrubbed for so many years he could barely see the print below, the window frames with brightly colored flower boxes worn to an almost abstract pattern of blues, red, greens, and yellows.

Cora handed her the pie and Mary accepted the plate and fork.

He took his apple pie from Cora. In between the fluted, sugar-sparkled crust, the filling was thick with apple freckled with nutmeg and cinnamon, and he sat next to Mary forking the heavenly concoction into his mouth.

"This is divine, Cora," Mary said. "I wish I had the knack for pie. Cookies, yes. Not pie. I don't have the patience. I roll out dough and it sticks to the roller. The fillings end up pasty and bad. I can't do crusts. I just can't do it."

"Nonsense," Cora said. "The key is bear fat. Bear fat makes

wonderful crusts. And refrigerating them before you roll them out."

"Bear fat?" Mary said, startled.

"Best lard in the world," Cora said. "Makes the lightest crusts."

"Yeah, Bob," Pete said. "Wait till I take you bear hunting, old man."

"I don't know, Pete," Bob said. "Mary may have to stick with cookies." He smiled.

A few minutes later, Pete took him into the back room of knotty pine and showed him to a worn chair decorated with hunting dogs. The room was simple: a cedar dresser topped with a simple round mirror, a closet with a hand-sewn curtain on a rod. A ceramic figurine of a milkmaid surrounded by sheep and a framed picture of Danny standing ready to throw a basket stood on the dresser.

"Where's Danny tonight?" Bob asked.

"Out with his buddies." Pete said. His face darkened. "Probably drinkin' beer, drivin' too fast. I worry about that kid, Bob. You raise 'em thinking you're doing everything right—and they're good kids, and the next thing you know they're drinking and wild and makin' trouble and you tell 'em one thing and they hit this age—teenagers—and all they do is the opposite. He's going into the army, though, soon as he's done with school."

Out the window, tamaracks swayed in the wind, making it seem, for a moment, like the room itself was moving in the deep, snowy night.

"I'm sure he's a good kid," Bob said. "I don't know teenagers, but you two are good people."

"I don't know, Bob. I'm about done with him. He sasses me somethin' terrible. His mother defends him, but right now I think he's a little punk." Pete shook his head. He closed the door and sat down on the bed across from Bob, put his hands on either side of him. "But that's not what I wanted to talk with you about," he said. "I gotta a problem. I ain't even told Cora."

"Money?"

"Not directly."

Then he told Bob about his bids on lumber sales at the First Northwest Bank. Every time he bid on a sale, one of his competitors came in just $500 under his bid.

"It's happened three times," Pete said. "I bid $4,000 on the Tin Cup Creek sale. And Darby Creek Lumber comes in at $3,500. I hire another saw and raise my price to $4,500, and bid on Monture Creek. Shit—outbid by Darby Creek by $500. So I take a higher loan, raise my price again, and bid on Owl Creek sale. Beauty of a sale, flat land, big Doug firs, easy to get in and out, and I bid $5,500, barely making a dime, and guess what?" Pete glared at him.

"Darby Creek wins out again." Bob said.

"$5,000." Pete rolled up his sleeves. "I got to win a bid, Bob. I got four men at that mill depending on me. Not to mention their families."

"It's always Darby Creek?" Bob said.

"Always," he said.

"Where'd you get the loan for the bid?" Bob studied Pete's hawk-like face as he talked, his dark, fierce eyebrows, his hands thick and scarred from years of working in the woods, and felt a rush of warmth for him. He would do anything for Pete. Bob knew the score, the bank men in their fancy suits and their well-fed bellies, their shiny shoes, martini lunches, and steak-fed advisory boards, knowing that what they saw when they looked at Pete, with his stagged-off logger pants, his weather-beaten face, asking for a loan for a logging sale to beat Darby Lumber—*this hick from Seeley Lake who will never figure out what's what.* Bob knew these men. He lunched with them at Kiwanis. He heard them talk at the symphony. He listened to their pompous jokes.

"First Northwest Bank," he said. Then he looked at Bob. His lip curved up in a smile. "You got something, dontcha? I knew it, Bob. You're smart like a fox."

"I have an idea," Bob said, and told him how they would go out of town, to Hamilton, to get the loan to put up the bid.

"Damn!" Pete knocked his fist into his palm. "And when they open the bid, surprise, Darby Creek Mill!"

They walked into the front room, laughing, and Cora and Mary looked up from their cards, Mary placing a peg in the cribbage board. A fire crackled and popped as a log shifted in the fireplace.

"What are you two scheming about?" Cora laughed.

"Screwing Darby Lumber," Pete said.

"I knew you were up to no good," Cora said. "Mary here has been telling me the gossip about Bridger high society—the ladies who buy dresses, wear them once, then return them, and the new hemlines that are four inches above the knees—" She and Mary laughed, and Bob envied and was relieved by their easy camaraderie.

"I'm afraid," Cora said and laughed, "I don't have much good gossip to trade. The biggest news here was that when they did the school play, 'The Christmas Gift,' they were lighting a candle on stage and lit the music teacher's wig on fire and a volunteer firefighter in the audience had to douse her with a pitcher of water. But the play went on!"

Mary laughed and rose from the table and moved to the fire, holding her hands out to the flames. "This feels so good, doesn't it, Bob? We should light up our fireplace more often."

"We should probably hit the road," Bob said, watching the firelight gild her face and hands. "It starts icing up."

Mary started to move toward her coat, when Cora stood up. "Oh no," she said simply. "It's Saturday night. The roads are bad. I'm making you stay."

Mary lifted her eyebrows and looked at Bob.

Bob laughed and said to Cora, "On what grounds are you making us stay?"

"On the grounds that I already made dinner and that it's a long drive and once it snows, we're here. We get three-foot drifts and can't get out and Pete and I see a lot of each other—so we need you. You are our Saturday night entertainment. So—" Cora clapped her hands and started to set the table. "It's settled."

"Look," Pete said. "I'm putting on some more music. Mushy stuff."

"What now?"

"'Song to the Moon,'" he said. "Dvorak." Bob hear the *tchh* of the needle on the record and then the lush soprano of Dolores Wilson singing, *Oh moon, high in the deep sky, your light sees faraway places.*

"You're being too nice," Mary said.

"I'm being practical," Cora said, getting up from the table and opening the oven door to peer in. "I've made a stew and—" she held up a towel over a pan of white circles of dough, "I have biscuits rising and more pie. Please stay the night. It's pure idiocy to drive these roads at night. If the drunks don't getcha, the deer will. Look—" she walked to a knotty pine doorway and held it open. It was their son, Danny's, room, with his basketball trophies. "I made up the bed—Danny's staying overnight with friends."

Where is my lover? the voice rang from the dark, whirring record player in the shadowy cabin as Bob listened to the words. *Tell him, silvery moon that my arms shall hold him, that between sleeping and waking...*

Mary looked at Bob. He sensed a loosening in her, a desire to nestle in the warmth of these two wonderful people in this cabin with the venison stew and homemade biscuits and pie, and later on, he would mark this day as a new beginning of their life together.

"Shall I set the table?" Bob said.

Oh, silver moon, do not fade!

Bob helped Pete put in a bid for $7,500 on a sale up Froze Out Creek, $7,000 from First Northwest Bank, and another $1,000 from Bitterroot Bank of Montana. When the bids were opened at the Forest Service, Darby Lumber had come in at $6,999. Pete won the bid, and when he was down in Bridger, they celebrated with a drink at the Florence Hotel Bar, before Pete headed back north.

Pete stood at the polished oak bar, surveying the dimmed gas lights, black leather banquettes curved around round wooden tables with guttering red candles where a few bankers in their pinstriped suits were huddled in conversation, and a man with a woman in a bright blue silk dress sipped drinks underneath frosted windows where street scenes were transformed into wet blurs of yellows, greens, greys, and blacks.

"You sure I belong here?" Pete said.

"We'll tell 'em you're in oil," Bob laughed.

Bob asked the bartender for a beer for himself and a shot of Johnny Walker Red for Pete, and carried them to a table when they were poured.

Pete still looked nervous, but he sat down opposite Bob. He put his weathered face in his hands and then looked up at Bob. "You figured it from the start, Bob," Pete said. "Goddamn it. Someone on their board was tippin' them off."

Bob sipped his beer and felt the comforting slide of liquid from his throat to his belly.

"Damn, Bob, you're a good man, to help a dumb logger like me." He reached out his hand, the shirt uncovering just a bit of his scarred forearm.

Bob shook his hand. "You're dumb as a fox, Mr. Donatello," Bob said. "Your praise means everything to me."

"To Donatello Logging," Pete said. "To outbidding those other sons-of-bitches!"

They toasted glasses.

"And Mary, Bob?" Pete's voice was soft as he rocked his shot glass side to side. "How is she?"

"Oh, Pete," Bob stared into his beer glass. "She doesn't lose a step: she's back at the dress shop, she's working the symphony, she's—"

"She's hurting," Pete said. "Losing a baby, it's hard on a woman. Some advice?" Someone shouted from the back, oddly enough one of the bankers, and Pete sat quietly until the bar quieted down again. "Just let 'er ride it out," he said. "Don't pressure her. Beautiful woman like her, you don't want to back her into a corner."

CHAPTER EIGHTEEN

Elizabeth avoided the looks of sympathy that, in an office that cashed in on death, disfigurement, and injury on a daily basis, were fleeting anyway. She carried a coffee cup to her desk. She could drink coffee now; at least there was that consolation. There was a flower waiting. From Ruth, of course. *For new beginnings,* the card said, in her loopy cursive: *Love, Ruth.*

She warmed her hands around her coffee cup, comforted by its rich, bitter smell and the chaos of the ringing phones, clacking computer keys, slamming file drawers, and the constant ebb and flow of conversation. Clayton, thank God, was out on assignment. In front of her was a stack of newspapers. On each paper, Ruth had circled stories on her beat to help her get caught up, circled leads off the wire and some local interest stories—a man injured in a karate class claiming workman's comp (smiley-face on that one), a first-grader with leukemia who made a video for his family to watch after his death. At the bottom of the pile was yesterday's paper. On the front page, above the fold, was the top half of Rosie Valera. Elizabeth unfolded the paper and there was the rest of her, head to toe, from her platinum blonde hair, and the red-sequined dress tight across her well-advertised bosom all the way down to her strappy silver sandals. Over her head was the 20-point headline: "Starlet Dead from Pill Overdose."

Clipped to the page was a memo: "Mandatory Editorial Meeting, today, 2 P.M.," with the words "everyone must attend" in bold caps.

Elizabeth walked to Ruth's office and held up the story. "What?"

"Welcome back," Ruth grinned. She pointed to her watch and nodded toward the bathroom. "Meet me there in five minutes?"

Elizabeth got there before Ruth. It was the first time she'd been in the bathroom since she'd lost the child, and she could feel herself begin to tear up. *Shake it off. If you start, you'll be doing this all day.*

Thankfully, Ruth swept in, looking under the stalls. She told her that the publisher, Lyle Short, unbeknownst to all, had the hots for Rosie Valera, a slutty starlet with a big derriere and 42 DD chest, so when the news came over the wire about her suicide, he declared the story front-page news. He and Ruth had an epic fight about the story's placement, right down to the copy deadline. Finally, Ruth said, she threw up her hands and said, "Fine. Print it. But don't come whining to me later." She instructed layout to print the starlet's picture above the fold at twice the normal size and to give the story top billing.

Letters to the editor had been pouring in: Didn't the newspaper print news anymore? Was this the *Bridger Chronicle*'s idea of a top story? What kind of message was this to send to today's youth?

"Of course, I'll probably be fired," Ruth said. She looked down at her shoes—scuffed navy blue Hush Puppies. She looked up and grinned. "But honestly, it was so worth it."

Elizabeth walked back to her desk, nearly losing it when she passed the tanned publisher with his slicked-back hair headed her way, pulling at his suit jacket so it didn't bunch. She dialed the local dry cleaner to track a story on the dumping of cleaning fluids into the water system. She asked the owner questions. Did he know the city/county health department had found dry-cleaning chemicals in the water table underneath his establishment? Did he know these fluids were toxic to native trout? the man's voice clenched. That report must be wrong, he said. She felt the old gears of her life clicking into place, gaining traction and she thought, *I can do this. I can get through this day.*

It was only on the drive back home in the quiet of the car on the rain-washed streets that a hollowness opened up inside her again like a night-blooming flower.

Tom wasn't home yet. She wandered into the living room and switched on the television—more news about mad cow disease. She quickly switched it back off. Elizabeth climbed the stairs to look again at the yellow room. It still smelled of new paint, still had the freshness of a buttercup. Bad idea. She pulled the door closed. She could call Molly and meet her for a drink, but she didn't want to talk. She could call Ruth to talk, but she really wanted a drink. She walked downstairs, threw on her coat and went to walk on the path by the river, hoping the cool air, the sight of the snowline creeping down the mountains, would clear her head.

Elizabeth headed east on the path that wound along the old railroad bed, her feet crunching the gravel, watching the river, high on its banks, the water carrying logs and branches as it powered west, muddy and green and swirling. Absence is presence—who said that? Did that even make sense? But as she walked in the late evening, the mist rising off the banks, she could feel them around her in the haze gathering in the sweet-smelling cottonwoods and willow bushes. Her mother, her father. Her sister. She missed the weight in her belly, of knowing that the child would anchor her here. They were the past; her child would have been the future.

Back home, she made herself tea and hiked up to the attic. She located the check carbons again and brought them down to the kitchen, so she could sit near the heater. She snapped on a lamp. As she studied the carbons, the evening skies grew dark around her and the hum of traffic grew louder on the street.

The Stone Home for the Mentally Retarded.

She flipped through the stacks of carbons beginning in the year 1954 and ending in 1974. They were written to the Stone Home for the Mentally Retarded, later the Stone Home for Developmentally Disabled.

In the memo line was her name: Elizabeth Carter. She found notes on several, written in her father's pinched hand. *The dresses that you requested will be arriving soon. Did you get the Easter basket? Letter to follow.*

She got up to get honey for her tea, plucking the plastic bear from its sticky corner in the cupboard and staring at the thick gold stream as it oozed from the spout into her cup. She stirred it into her tea.

Elizabeth Carter. The name had to be a mistake.

She went back to the kitchen table and picked up the check carbons again. There it was in the memo line of the large square business checks her father insisted on using: Elizabeth Carter, written in her father's odd handwriting: half-printing, half-cursive. What must he have felt as he wrote these checks every month, every year, every decade?

She had the sense of things flying apart and coming together at once, a dawning like a slow paralysis. Elizabeth Carter. Her sister, who had her same name. She was born in Bridger, Montana, in 1953. She grew up at the Stone Home in Stone City. And in between these facts hung a life.

She held the dusty check carbons, numb, picturing the time when she was five and she told her friend Sally that she had an older sister. Sally said it was a lie—like the one Sally had told about a king living in her basement. In 1961, she figured, this Elizabeth was eight years old. In 1968, when man first landed on the moon, Elizabeth remembered watching the television footage with her parents and her sister in a hotel room in New York City. Where was this other Elizabeth? In 1970, she graduated from eighth grade. In 1974, high school. In 1978, her parents flew to Maine to watch her graduate from Colby College.

A jumble of images ran through her mind as she sat there: her second-grade teacher crying when Kennedy was shot, the nubby texture of a hotel bedspread in New York, the scratchy white lace dress she wore for eighth-grade graduation, the strangeness of seeing her parents, looking small and vulnerable among the well-heeled Easterners at Colby. All of it moving forward like a puppet play while in the background a whole different show was being played out, this show about another girl named Elizabeth Carter who was three years older in the Stone Home for the Mentally Retarded, a story contained in the border of these check carbons from the Western Montana Bank of Bridger.

Or saying good-night to her father, who, night after night, would be working at his rolltop desk in his study, a desk he was thrilled to find at an auction, and as he looked down at Elizabeth from his large, fabric-covered check register, his face was lined and his hair tousled as he said, his voice weary, "Good night pumpkin. Don't let the bedbugs bite."

"Pumpkin," she'd say. "I'm not a pumpkin."

"Oh yes you are," he'd say and reach over and tug her braid. She kissed him good-night, and as she turned to go to bed, he swatted her on her red-flannel bottom.

Who was that father?

She was flipping through the check carbons when she heard the hum of Tom's Subaru in the driveway and the squeaking of the garage door as it slowly lifted on its tracks. She began to shake. Was it cold? Shock? Somehow, she felt she'd had some sense about this sister all along. Her existence seemed to explain certain inexplicable moments in her past: the disappearance of her mother and father on some weekend trips. The time she was pretending, at five, that she had an older sister and no one knows about her and her mother overheard and turned to her, startled, and said, "Stop! Stop that game at once." Or, years later, when she saw her name on a list of unclaimed items published by the State of Montana in the local newspaper and called the published number, the receptionist at the Department of Health and Human Services said her name was right, but the social security number didn't match. Perhaps it was that extra beat of breath when her grandmother told her how special she was, how very special she was to her mother and father.

Tom sighed as he came in the back door and flung his backpack on the dryer. "Why's it so dark in here? Hey, what's for dinner?"

Elizabeth rose and turned on the overhead lights in the kitchen. "Holy shit, Tom. You won't believe this."

"What?" He appeared in the doorway of the kitchen, his cheeks ruddy as he unwound the scarf from his neck.

She walked over and pulled him by the sleeve of his coat to the table. "Look at this."

He leafed through the copies, uncomprehending. "I know you told me about a sister that you thought was out there—Stone Home, I see." He grew quiet as he sat down to study each carbon more carefully. His head jerked back in surprise. "Oh jeez, Elizabeth. Holy shit."

"Right?" Her heart flooded. "I mean, Tom, this is huge. I have a sister who was put in at birth—hell, raised her whole life in an institution, for God's sake. And my father never told anyone. That in and of itself is strange. But then they go on and have another child, me, and give her the same fucking name? That's bizarre."

"It's very weird."

"I mean it's strange enough to know I even have another sister, one I didn't know about. And now, she has my name?"

She rose to go to the counter to start dinner, and Tom got up and stopped her. He wrapped his arms around her. She was held still for a moment, enveloped in his arms, in his familiar scent of soap and clean air, but she pushed herself away.

She *had* an older sister—that in itself was stupendous. A sister, a doppleganger, a complete stranger—and the two of them were bound by that twisting double-helix of DNA.

Aren't secrets in a family like a spider's web—light, invisible sticky lines that bind people together forever?

It was as if, at that moment, a sinkhole opened up beneath her feet and threatened to engulf her, her life. "Right, Tom?"

"It's bizarre. I don't know what to tell you. Families are strange." He kissed her head and set his scarf on the counter.

It felt to Elizabeth as if everything that had gone before was a rickety construction sitting on top of this knowledge. Her life—her career, her marriage, her attempts at a family, her childhood as one of two daughters born to successful businessman Bob Carter and his wife, Mary, active in numerous causes—was built on top of this other Elizabeth Carter who lived miles down the road in a place called the Stone Home.

CHAPTER NINETEEN

Let's get out of this loony bin, Margaret told Louise, so the three of them—Anna, Margaret, and Louise—donned their rayon print dresses and piled in Louise's Rambler to drive to the May Day dance at the Helena Fairgrounds.

It was a warm night. As Louise drove out the gates of the Stone Home, the window down, Anna, who was in front with Louise, turned to pass a bottle of beer back to Margaret as the hot wind blew up their dresses and raked their hair.

"Good-night you," Margaret called, looking back at the cottages and waving, laughing. "Pee away!"

"Good-night, my sweets," Anna cried and blew them a kiss.

They drove down the road, past dark brooding barns and cows that looked dully up at them. Late day sun lay gold and heavy on the fields where older boys and men were checking to see if the hard winter wheat was ready for harvest, their humped backs backlit by the sun as they moved up and down the rows, circled by a black shepherd and red border collie. As Louise eased the Rambler onto Highway 91, which wound along the Stone River, the women could see the distant porch of Cottage Two, where staff members sat smoking, and Anna and Margaret stuck their arms out the window and waved at them too.

The highway was surrounded by steep forested hillsides of Douglas fir and tamarack. The alpine fir were dark and mysterious, studded by tractor-sized boulders known as a "erratics." Where the country widened out, they passed a log cabin, a stout ranch house surrounded by a jackleg fence, and an old homesteader's shack, outhouse, and barn, sliding log by log back into the earth.

Anna sat next to Louise, wearing a red rayon dress. Her hair was plaited, of course, and curved around her neck to hang down her chest, nearly touching her belt.

"Nice dress," Louise said.

"Well, you look a lot like a girl, yourself, kid," Anna said. Her smile broke across her face like a sun. "You clean up nicely."

"You gonna dance?" Louise said, smiling at her before looking back to the road.

"Go on," Anna said. "I probably won't go."

"What do you mean—not go?" Louise asked, and then realized she knew the answer and she shouldn't have asked Anna to spell it out. Dances were for white girls.

"You in your nice dress," Anna said. "You gonna find yourself a cowboy?"

Louise smoothed the skirt of her one nice dress—daisy-flowered and fitted with giant square buttons up the bias, which she had bought for a date with a man in Blue Earth. She'd spent money on this dress, ordering it from a catalog, sending it back to get the right size, her mother shaking her head, saying *You could have sewn yourself a perfectly fine dress for half that money, Louise Gustafson, if not for that pride in you.* "Probably not, Anna. Boys don't ask me to dance. I remind them of their mothers."

"Go on!" Anna pretended to punch her in the arm. "You'll have 'em eatin' out of the palm of your hand."

"You watch. They'll look at me. Whistle, maybe. Kiss me. But they won't ask me to dance."

"Kiss you?" Margaret leaned over from the backseat. "What's this about kissing you? Has Dr. O tried to kiss you?"

"No," Louise said. "Is there something I need to know?"

"Don't worry, he hasn't tried that yet on me," Margaret says. "He won't. But I hear he's a heck of a kisser." There was a bright fatalism in her voice Louise recognized from Blue Earth. There was something so cheerful and doomed about country girls—they expected nothing to turn out: girls got pregnant before they got married, bad guys always won, and the good things that happened were only a trick, an omen that more bad luck was on its way. "Me—" Margaret added. "I'm gonna find me a ranch boy that's a hell of a kisser."

"You, Margaret, are a wild woman," Louise shouted and pressed down the accelerator until they were going ninety and Anna yipped as the hot wind and the sound of the slicking pavement ran through the car, young women on a sultry night in Montana, heading to a dance, their veins thrilling to the love of pure motion.

At the Helena Fairgrounds, Louise parked the Rambler and pulled up the brake. One by one, Margaret, Louise, and Anna pushed open the heavy car doors and stepped carefully into the newly mowed pasture, taking care not to let the bristly shorn grass run their nylons, checking one another for smeared lipstick and drooping slips.

As they sauntered toward the sounds of music from the

fairground pavilion, a Thunderbird pulled up next to them and several men in bomber jackets piled out, looking slantwise at them, cooing; the tallest one, with black, slicked-back hair, nodding curtly, "Evenin' ladies," he said. He hung back to watch them walk ahead of him, their dresses swaying.

They paid twenty-five cents to a woman at the ticket counter, who hesitated only when it came to Anna.

"No Indians," she said.

The two of them crowded around Anna. Margaret was looking eagerly past her into the dance. "I knew this would happen. C'mon, I don't want to mess up your big night," Anna said. "You guys go. I'll meet you back here."

"No," Louise said. She glared back at the woman. "She's my sister visiting from out of town. Italian." The woman grudgingly took the quarter and handed her a ticket.

The band was the Rockets, a foursome with suit jackets, black glasses, bob cuts, and guitars, drums, and a vocalist who kept up a refrain, "C'mon baby, Vulcan-ize me!" On the sawdust floors of the pavilion, young women in shirtwaist dresses or wide skirts did the twist with young cowboys or soldiers back from Korea.

At first, Louise, Anna, and Margaret danced among themselves, doing the Boogie Woogie Blues, the Shake Rattle and Roll. Then a ruddy-faced cowboy who came up to Margaret's shoulder asked her to dance and the two of them whirled away, doing an awkward two-step to Ray Charles's "Mess Around." Anna danced with an Air Force lieutenant, natty in his blue uniform, the two of them making an odd couple, Anna just up to his chin with her long braid swinging like a rope every time the serviceman spun her around. Louise danced with a man who she thought looked vaguely like a weasel. He was surprisingly strong as he pulled her to him, and she watched his narrow leather shoes as the two of them whirled around the room.

When the band took a break—the singer shouting into the mic, "Stay tuned for more Vulcan-i-zation Nation!" before they stepped off the stage—the group went out back by Prickly Pear Creek and sat under the chokecherry bushes. The men drank Jim Beam straight from the bottle; Margaret, Louise, and Anna were drinking paper cups of beer. They were reclining in a row along the grass, staring up at the North Star, the faint Big Dipper just appearing over the mountains.

"Where you girls from?" Margaret's cowboy friend asked.

"Stone Home," Margaret said.

"With them retards?" he said.

"That's right," she said. "We herd 'em. Feed 'em. Round 'em up and put 'em to bed at night." She sat up and looked at him. "Probably like you do with them Herefords."

They all laughed and settled back again to lie in the grass and watch the moon slide up and over the tip of the Sleeping Giant, a local mountain shaped like a man lying on his back that, with his hooked nose and pot belly and barrel chest, looked as if he were as drunk as they were.

"What d'ya think he'd say to us if he could come down here right now?" Louise finally said.

The cowboy dipped his hat and said, "He'd come down and say, 'you little shits.'"

They all laughed so hard that Margaret began rolling down the hill.

Later in the evening, Louise was in a rodeo chute with the man with the slicked-back hair, and he was pressing her against a post and kissing her—really kissing her—running his hand along her spine, the hair on the back of her neck prickling, and she was kissing him back, her body blending into his. How long had it been? Sweat, skin, heat, pulse, and she looked up and right in her face was Margaret's. *Margaret?* Louise straightened up. "Margaret, what are you doing here?" just as the man moved away, disappearing into the crowd, Margaret bending into her and saying, "Louise! I've been looking everywhere for you!"

Louise bent back into the moment, aware that the lights were coming on, the band was putting away the instruments, and, in the distance, car engines were revving. As Louise straightened her dress and ran a hand through her hair, Margaret leaned over the whitewashed chute again. "I can't find Anna."

She and Margaret scoured the sheep shed and the cow barn and called her, but Anna was nowhere to be found. They got in the Rambler and followed the line of cars driving out from the fairgrounds and slowly drove the ash-lined streets of Helena, from the mansions on the west side, to the downtown where the lights were still on because it was Saturday night, to the east side where the homes were smaller, stopping when they thought they saw a figure Anna's size. It was just a kid, walking home. They were driving to the police station, when Louise had an idea.

"Suppose that air force cadet carried her off?" Margaret said.

"The airport," Louise said. "It's a hunch. Let's go there."

"Airport," Margaret said. "That's crazy."

"It's the quiet ones that always surprise you," Louise said.

They drove to the small wooden building that constituted the airport with its runway punctuated every so often by weeds. They walked from the car into the hangar, and spotted a 1954 de Havilland DHC-3.

Louise knocked on the door to the cockpit and it swung open. Seated inside were Anna and the pilot, the latter looking a bit sheepish. Anna, however, smiled broadly. "He's a pilot," she said to Louise and Margaret, as if that explained everything.

"Jesus Anna," Louise said. "You scared the wits out of us! We thought something happened to you."

She and the pilot looked at each other and smiled. There was a pause. "It did," she said. "This is Larry. He told me he would teach me to fly."

Later, when the three of them were back in the Rambler and they were driving back to the Stone Home, drinking whisky that Margaret pinched from the cowboy, Anna told them, out of nowhere, "Of course, I had to let him feel me up."

"You had to what?" Louise said.

"Let him feel me up."

"Anna! Jesus."

Margaret leaned forward from the back and looked at Anna, who was sitting calmly in the front seat, her hands folded. *How could you do that*? Margaret's face said, though to her credit she kept her mouth shut.

"It's all about going fast enough to get enough air under the wing to give you lift," Anna said. "It's so simple, really."

"Well, you got flying lessons," Margaret said, taking a gulp from the whisky bottle and wincing. "We got smeared lipstick."

"I liked him," Anna said. "Even though he's air force and South Dakota. And white."

"You can pay for lessons," Louise said.

"I'm gonna get my license," Anna said. "And fly me right out of that hell hole, you two watch."

At the mention of the Stone Home, the car went quiet.

"Ugh," Margaret said. "Did you have to mention that?"

In twelve hours they would be back on shift. They could feel the weight of the next few precious hours suspended between them in the dark car—how they would take baths, wash and iron clothes, take a nap or read a novel until Sunday night came with its attendant sadness and the weekend closed down and they surrendered themselves to Monday, when the work week began again.

"Where's the whisky?" Louise said. "I have to wash my mouth out."

As she drove toward the Elkhorn Mountains, they drank in earnest, passing the bottle back and forth, their faces shining in the glow of the dashboard. The more they drank, the more they confessed about their sexual adventures: a kiss here, stroke there, a touch to the mons Venus, the mention of which vibrated the air with desire.

They passed the whisky bottle back and forth, the fire burning their throats and loosening their tongues; the night seemed a great wheel of hope and youth and love, moving through them like a river, slow and liquid and hilarious, so that when Louise turned off the road to the driveway that led to the Stone Home and the car began to bounce and turn, instead of shrieking as the car began to roll, Louise, Margaret, and Anna began laughing. Then the laughter stopped as the motion became unfamiliar, unrecognizable, Louise's head flopping forward, then backward as she gripped the steering wheel, Margaret coming straight across the backseat to the front, Anna flung beneath the seat, a whirl of purses thunking, arms and legs churning, the car body scraping against rocks, moving slower and slower as the dice on the rearview mirror were flung back and forth, back and forth, Margaret yelling, "Jesus! Oh Jesus! Oh Jesus!"

The car bumped. There was a loud crunching sound. The engine quit. Then it was silent. Beyond them, a twittering.

Louise felt a goose egg growing on her scalp where she'd bumped her head on the steering wheel.

"Anna?" she said. She felt in the dark next to her for Anna's arm.

“I’m here. I’m fine,” Anna threaded her fingers in Louise’s. She was still on the floor.

“Margaret?” Louise said.

“I’m so goddamn alive.” Margaret said. She was draped over the seat, her head in the front, her legs in the back. “What the hell, Louise Gustafson, were you thinking?”

“We’re in a haystack,” Louise said slowly. She studied the cross-hatching of hay that filled the windshield in front of her.

Margaret started to laugh. She pushed herself off the front seat with her hands and landed with a plop on the backseat. “Like little boy fucking blue.”

Louise turned the key in the ignition. The engine turned over. She backed up the car over the rocky field. She drove over the field to a low point in the embankment, and headed back up to the road.

“I’m getting out of this car,” Margaret said. “I am not driving with you.”

“You go, I go,” Anna said.

“Two against one,” Margaret said.

As the Rambler’s tires spit gravel behind them, Margaret and Anna walked in the glow of the headlights on the silvery road to the Stone Home, trying to ignore the dark weight of the buildings ahead of them, a few lights blinking on then off from the dormitory windows. Louise watched them in front of her, the silhouette of Anna’s slighter form next to Margaret’s tall, angular body, the two of them facing forward, walking. *My friends*, she thought, and wanted to come to a grand conclusion about love and near-death experiences, but she was too drunk. *My friends*, she whispered, and the words seemed enough.

She awoke to a knock. For a moment, she lay still, thinking she was dreaming and if she lay still, didn't move a single finger, the dream would disappear. The knock came again.

"Who is it?"

"Dr. O."

"Dr. O?"

"Can you open the door?"

She wrapped the quilt around her and stepped to the door, and there he was, waiting on the step, the moonlight glinting off his glasses. "Can I talk to you?"

"I was sleeping."

"I could come back," he said, looking at her, her quilt, the doorstep, the handle.

Years later, Louise would come to know this look, the coyness of it, how he meant to imply she had a choice, but she really didn't, he was the one choreographing things here in the moonlight. He was always the one choreographing things.

"You're tired," he said softly. "I'll come back."

"I'll make tea," she said, sighing.

"Just a cup," he said delicately and parked himself in a chair in front of the fireplace.

CHAPTER TWENTY

The world was slush, punctuated by the slump of snow sliding down from the roof and the sudden uptick in the obituaries and every day another neighbor planning to move on from Bridger, to bigger cities, better jobs, more interesting friends—plans that would dissipate with the arrival of good weather, barbeques, and trips to the lake—they were merely the plans that sustained them during the slop and grey of March.

When Bob arrived home for lunch, Mary was at the kitchen table, weeping. Still in her flannel pajamas, where, it seemed, she had been since the morning mail, her hair still x'd in pin curls, the shine of night cream on her face, her nose tipped red. She was pregnant again, one month in, battling waves of nausea that overtook her in the mornings, despite tea, ginger ale, and soda crackers.

"What?" Bob said, dropping his hat and briefcase in the hallway as soon as he saw her. He hurried to the kitchen. "What is it? What happened?"

Mary's glance wandered from his face to his shoes as if she could not figure out how he got there, much less fully dressed, then she looked back to the kitchen table where sugar spilled across the piles of mail, the flyers from the outdoor store advertising winter parkas and twill surcoats for $10 and sleds for $1.50.

She picked up an envelope and held it out to him. As she did, the sleeve of her red flannel pajamas fell back from her long white arm, her hand raised as if in supplication. Except that Mary was never a supplicant and as she turned her face to him, he could see it was hardening again, from the almond-shaped eyes to the carved cheekbones, the mouth growing small and pinched as she said, "Here. Read this."

"What is it?" Bob said, his breath catching when he saw the return address: Stone Home. He reached out for the letter and she pulled it away from him. "Bad news? What is it Mary? The doctor said she was in the best of hands."

"You bet," Mary pulled the letter to her heart. With her other hand, she traced a circle in the spilled sugar on the table. The drip of the snowmelt sounded between them. "Dr. Babcock said, 'She is in the best of hands.' Dr. O said, 'She is in the best of hands.' But whose hands, Bob? Certainly not mine."

She looked at him.

He looked back at her.

"Whose good hands are these, Bob, can you tell me that?"

"Mary," Bob held out his hand. "Give me that letter."

The carbon was dated, March 10, 1954, from a nurse named Louise Gustafson.

"Patient 1147. Elizabeth Carter. B.D. 2/4/53," the carbon read. *Spruce Cottage. Louise Gustafson, RN. Elizabeth is a very cute little Mongoloid girl. She is a quiet sleeper and has learned to feed herself. Very trainable. Recognizes verbal commands and loves to be sung to. Should send to speech therapy as she has very charming way of letting you know what she wants. Recognizes verbal praise and commands. Has had two grand mal seizures. We are giving her Haldol for her seizures. She also seems to have a sensitivity to milk as a bottle of milk seems to make her throw up. We have switched her formula and she is doing much better…*

"See, Mary. This is good," Bob said. "She is doing well. Sleeping well. She likes to be sung to. She's had some seizures, but they've given her medication—"

"Keep reading," Mary said.

"What is it?"

"Your mother."

"My mother what?"

"Keep reading."

He sat down across the table from Mary and continued to read the letter. …*We have had a request from the Elk Meadows Asylum (which is located approximately an hour north of here in Warm Springs) from a Mrs. Beatrice Carter, who wishes to see Elizabeth. Claims to be a grandmother. We cannot grant this request without your permission. So, with this update on your daughter, we are sending you this permission form. It is up to you. Also, please send more clothing as Elizabeth is growing quickly and running out of sleepers. I'd advise purchasing 18 and 24 month sizes so she can grow into them. Can you please answer quickly as we are having to cut the feet out of her current sleepers?*

He set the letter on the lazy Susan and the two of them watched it spin around the table.

"What do you want to do?" Bob said. He erased from his mind the image of the child wearing a sleeper with the feet cut out.

"I don't know," Mary stared across the table at him and patted her belly. "I am consumed with nausea. No thought. I have no thoughts."

"I feel as if I could take a long sleep right now," Bob said. "Like my body was made of lead." It was true, somehow the letter seemed to just drain him, in spite of his lectures to Mary about how, a year after the traumatic birth of the child, all this was past them and they were reinventing their lives, starting over, and they had this new child to think about, plan for.

"Do you want mother to see her? It might be good for her."

"For whom?" Mary lifted her head and looked sharply at him. "For your mother? Or the child? For me?"

"Mary," he reached across the table to take her hand, feeling the delicacy of her finger bones. "We have to move on here. Remember what the doctor said? He said to go on. Start over. Have another child. We are having another child—and this child deserves all of us. All of us, Mary. This has happened to others: the Simpsons, the Coxes—and look at their families now. You'd never know."

"I know," Mary said. "The doctor said to move on, forget about her. Shake it off like a bad dream. I'm trying, Robert."

"Mary—"

"Move on with that?" she said, and looked at him, her gaze scalding. "This annoying mourning?"

"We are not giving up our lives to this," Bob said, looking out at the mountain ash berries, bright red against the grey March sky. He could hear the water dripping from the eaves, the dim click of the furnace going on, a deep buzzing in his head as the room grew distant and an enormous weariness washed over him. He thought if he had to, he would describe it as a tiredness of the ages, his weariness of this same room, this argument, his voice.

When he did speak, he seemed to hear himself from a thousand miles away, Mary's face trained on him, her eyes pained and desperate and cold all at once, as Bob spoke of the happy things that awaited them, the spring coming, the trip to Lolo Hot Springs with friends, and this summer, Seattle. He kept talking, saying whatever came into his head, and the words seemed to stretch out, each word heavier and heavier, until the weight of the cheer he was trying to provide was simply too much for him.

"Stop!" Mary put her hands over her ears. She ran her hands through her hair, brushed the sugar off the table, and stood up. She folded the letter and put it back in the envelope and handed it to Bob. "Let your mother see her. It will give her a goddamn project. I have to go to work now. I only have a month before I'm really showing."

She turned away from Bob. She opened her robe, wrapped it around herself again, and retied it. From that angle, he studied Mary's silhouette, her arched nose, her strong chin, chiseled against the brown cabinets, and he thought at another time, in another century, she would have been a beautiful warrior princess. But in the 1950s, there wasn't much call for warrior princesses. He was an insurance broker; she was a dress saleswoman. And his mother was at him again, always messing things up just when some equilibrium had been established.

"I'll answer this Louise Gustafson," Bob said to Mary, but what he really wanted to say was that he wanted this child to go away, he didn't want to know how much she weighed or when she had her last seizure or how she was learning to tie her shoes or to sing a lullaby or whatever, he just wanted to be happy again. Didn't he deserve it? Didn't he work hard and try to be a good husband and help his wife recover from this? Wasn't that enough?

"Fine," Mary said, her voice trailing behind her as she walked up the stairs.

Never, ever again, he wrote Louise Gustafson, underlining the last ever, *write me at home. Please direct all future correspondence to my office: 460 Edith Street, Bridger, Montana. I feel very strongly about this.*

My wife finds this correspondence very upsetting. Secondly, you have my permission to allow my mother to visit the child. Sincerely, Robert Carter

P.S. I will have my secretary order some sleepers from Sears and have them sent forthwith.

That night, he dreamt he was in a room where the water was leaking. *The water is leaking*, he was saying to someone, but no one else seemed to notice. He grew increasingly panicked as water began overflowing the sink, the tub, then dripping down a ceiling. *It's leaking!* he woke up shouting, his heart pounding in his chest.

A few days later, just as things had righted themselves, Mary was back at work, telling him over meatloaf and potatoes at dinner about putting tulip print dresses in the shop window, boys lined up outside laughing and pointing at the bare-breasted mannequins, before she shooed them away. As he ate, Bob let the sounds of her talk wash over him. He was clearing the table, carrying the dishes out to the sink to wash them and set them in the drain to dry, when he saw his mother's letter propped up on the counter. His heart sank. Oh God. His mother.

He grabbed the letter, and told Mary he had to look up something in his office, taking the stairs two at a time.

In his office, he left the door open a crack so Mary wouldn't be suspicious. She had a habit—he wondered if she was aware of it—of knocking on his door every time he shut it completely. What did she think he was doing? Looking at *Playboys*? Masturbating? Good Lord. He flushed, knowing that he had to do that in the dark of the car or his office, after the secretaries had left and he locked the door, and thought about women with sulky eyes fingering themselves through flimsy lingerie.

He sat down and stared at the return address on the familiar light blue envelope. Mrs. Robert Carter, 460 Edith, Bridger, Montana. The sight of his father's name gave him a pang. He missed his father, with his round glasses, his easy way of asking Bob his opinion about things: Eisenhower, the Korean War, the new subdivisions going up in the canyons around town, his sly stories about Mrs. O'Leary, who was in her cups when he tried to give her a Christmas ham and she was too embarrassed to answer the door and she shouted to him, "I'm not home." He missed the comfort of knowing his father was there, that he had help with his mother, and the support of the man who raised him, who knew him as a boy.

The address blurred for a moment, then came back into focus. He slit open the letter. He unfolded it and looked at her handwriting, spider-like, blotches of ink here and there, and no salutation, just Bob, as if they'd just seen one another just days ago.

The usual patter about the hospital, the bland meals, how the Lithium dried out her mouth and made her so thirsty. She asked when he was coming to visit and how she looked forward to it, and described her neighbor whom she visited regularly, and the chemical compound of Lithium—did he remember she had been summa cum laude in chemistry in college?—and how she appreciated the gifts of *Time* and *Life* and the books, *The Caine Mutiny,* which she felt wasn't her cup of tea, and *My Cousin Rachel,* which she loved and could he send her more Daphne du Maurier? *Your daughter*, she wrote at the bottom, *is lovely. Sweet and pink-faced. I can't always get a ride there, but when I do, I have to say it gives me such joy just to hold her, Robert. I know you don't approve. I know you want this all to go away. But you have to understand what it is like for me. I'm lonely here. I miss my family. She is my family. She needs me. Sometimes I can soothe her when the other nurses can't. I sing her that old lullaby that you used to love, "All the Pretty Little Horses."*

Bob put his head in his hands, his heart slamming his chest. Even in her reduced state, she had the power to infuriate him. Thank God Mary hadn't read this. Just when he thought he had everything settled, his mother had to go gum up the works. Why would she do this? He had written her that the child was a ward of the state, and that was that. They had to move on with their lives.

Yes, he knew he should visit his mother more. He wasn't doing what he should. But he had to make a living, bring in the cash to support this whole enterprise. And just as he was feeling on top of things, getting the house settled, getting Mary feeling better, getting his father's estate settled, his mother kept opening this door, the door to this child that he kept trying to close. Did she know how the knowledge of her squeezed his heart? Did she have any concept of how he was scrambling?

He stood up and looked out the window at the backyard, at the winter-stripped apple tree, at the tangle of bushes around the ditches, and the Milwaukee Railroad below, where, in several hours, they would be hitching and unhitching the freight cars. Beyond that was the Clark Fork River. Bob folded his arms and leaned on the windowsill. He had half a mind to get in a canoe and dip his paddle in the river and go with that current, down to where it joined the Bitterroot and on out to the mouth of the Columbia where it dumped into the sea. Maybe the old explorers had it right, heading out into unknown territory, freeing themselves of the web of family and obligation and debt and just striking out into the unknown, damn the odds.

He came back to his desk and looked again at the letter. He wrote his mother and told her he loved her. He told her he was glad she was well. He told her, *I have to be strict here, Mother, you must limit these visits. We are trying to put this behind us.*

He put the letter in an envelope and rummaged through his desk for a stamp. He then paid the monthly bill for her care at the Elk River Mental Hospital as well as the bill for the Stone Home for the Mentally Retarded. He'd drop them in the mailbox at the corner so they wouldn't attract the postman's attention.

Downstairs, Mary was just settling in on the couch with a needlepoint. She'd taken up the dreadful art, that of his mother and her mother before her, her needle and black thread punching through the tan netting, her wrist flicking as she pulled the thread through. "See what I'm making?" She held up a picture of pale pansies on a black background.

Hideous, Bob thought, but he nodded and said, "That's really something, the pink and violet pansies."

"Liar," Mary said.

Bob opened the doors to the television. He'd found it at the Mercantile, marked down forty percent in the after-Christmas sale, good walnut cabinet, Magnavox. The deliveryman even set the thing up.

"What were you doing up there?" she said, taking another stitch.

"Just bills," he said. He focused on the set, watching the static roll down the screen as it turned a kind of mossy green, then a picture began to tilt into view.

"What did your mother have to say?"

"The usual," he said. "Craft class. Medications. Her friend from across the hall."

A package of Lucky Strikes came into view on the screen, then a man in a suit talking gravely about the health benefits of the cigarette before there was another long screen shot of the cigarette itself. Then after the intro, Jack Benny appeared, walking across a stage, his hands in his suit jacket.

"Ahh," Bob said, hoping Mary was done asking questions and that he'd done a good enough job hiding the letter away. "It's Jack Benny."

Sunday in the narthex after church, the minister asked after his mother and there was a pause that, Bob felt, seemed to contain another question and his stomach began to twist until the minister asked if Bob would take a look at fire and liability policies for the church. When they finally escaped and were having grilled cheese sandwiches and soup in the dining room, Bob told Mary he thought they needed to have a party.

"It's the ides of March, Mary," Bob said. "We've got to do something to cheer ourselves up, to give ourselves something else to think of besides the next snowfall, or shoveling, or the latest raid in Korea."

"A party?" Mary looked at him. He could hear the dread dropping down through her voice. She was not a fan of entertaining; she had told him she couldn't think of things to converse about, she couldn't cook, and no one liked her dessert. "Like a dinner party?"

"We owe people—the Andersons have had us. Arnie and his wife, too. We really need to repay them."

She scowled. "I know. I'm so bad."

"Look," he put his hand on hers. "We'll have a hobo party. We did it at the Methodist church when I was a kid. I'll make stew. You make a salad and dessert. It's easy and really fun."

Which was how Bob found himself answering the door wearing a holey undershirt and a pair of green canvas pants, sizes too big, held up by rope. Mary was next to him, her front teeth blacked out, dressed in a ragged blue polka-dotted dress, a tattered broom at her side. Cecil wore patched jeans and a shirt with straw sticking out, shoes that flapped at the front, and a large red nose. Cecil's wife drew black half-circles under her eyes and wore a red nose and red-striped pajama pants and a corncob pipe in her mouth. Arnie wore striped overalls and carried a hobo stick. Arnie's wife had on a torn flannel shirt over a stained skirt, with flannel underwear instead of nylons. Dick Anderson came in a tattered raincoat and a fedora with a flower in it, crashed in the front door with a ceramic jug of moonshine, marked in chalk with XX's, passing it around to the men as the wives looked on. "Let me just say," Bob said to them, as he let them in the door, one by one. "You all look like hell. Dick, that jug takes the cake. Lord, Cecil, where'd you get those shoes? Now, let's go eat. I'll play you a little jazz."

They sat around the table, where Mary, who had gotten into the spirit, placed nametags scrawled in charcoal and a flickering lantern in the center of the butcher paper that lined the table. The table was set with tin plates and cups and old dented camping silverware Bob had found in the basement.

Bob handed out bottles of Great Falls Select for the men before he seated himself at the head of the table. Mary circled the table, pouring iced tea into tin cups for the women. Bob looked at the table full of his family and friends. Their faces were shining, happy—here they were, he thought, the big war behind them, everyone moving forward in their work, their lives, with families and houses, cars and televisions, all of them back here, alive, laughing, the scrapes of forks ringing on the tin.

"You know, on the railroad tracks along the river, the real hoboes used to put their mark so that the others knew to come to the back door for food," Bob passed the bowl of stew to Cecil on his left, the garlic bread to Arnie's wife on his right.

"Well, I ain't sharin' mine," Dick said, and cupped his hands around his bowl.

"Me neither," said his wife—and pointed her fork at Dick. "So stay away from mine, if you know what is good for you, mister."

"You know," Arnie said. "There's a big difference in the camps between hoboes and tramps. Hoboes worked—just took long vacations. Tramps never worked."

"So which category are you in, Arnie?" Bob said.

"I'm looking for that long vacation. Sun. Surf. Women." Arnie said. "California. Hawaii."

Arnie's wife looked at him from across the table. "Not so fast, buddy. You've got a wife and a mortgage to pay."

"Aw, Mom," Arnie said. Arnie and his wife were from the Midwest and they called each other "Mom" and "Dad." "Always punching holes in my dreams."

Everyone laughed. Bob grabbed the serving bowl to fill it with stew again in the kitchen, when there was a knock at the door.

"You expecting someone?" Bob looked up at Mary at the opposite end of the table.

"Not a soul," she said.

"A hobo, perhaps?" Cecil said, and the others laughed.

"Feel like a little freight-hopping, Arnie?" Dick said. "It might be that vacation you were looking for."

"Dick, I don't think you'd be able to get yourself down to the tracks," his wife quipped. "Much less up onto the car."

As the others laughed, Bob set the bowl on the table and excused himself.

It was Duane Larsen, his neighbor, dressed in his dark blue coveralls. He lived with his wife in a small preformed cement-block house on the corner and worked as a mechanic at the Chevron station down the street. Bob invited him in. "Prepare yourself, Duane, we're having a hobo party."

Duane looked shocked as he surveyed the crowd at the table in their patched jackets with their blacked-out teeth and corncob pipes.

"This is a what?" he asked.

"A hobo party," Cecil's wife called out. "We dress like bums."

"Why would you do that?" Duane said, looking around at the flushed faces around the table filled with bowls of bread and thick, glistening stew. Bob watched him cast his eyes around the room, at the red and blue scrolled wallpaper, the plate railings, the cast-iron stove, the television set off in the living room.

"We're just having a bit of harmless fun, Mr. Larsen," Bob said.

"Beats me." He shook his head. "But someone's blocked my car in."

CHAPTER TWENTY-ONE

After work, she slowly sauntered home, drinking in the spring sun on her face, enjoying the chartreuse line of maples along the streets, the lilacs sending up their light sweet scent, the few gardens of crocuses and tulips coming on strong, wishing that she had gotten her shit together to plant tulip and daffodil bulbs last fall, but hey. She'd been in the midst of a crisis. She swung in the back door, heading for the kitchen and a beer on the porch, when Tom shouted from inside the house.

"Elizabeth," Tom said. "Did you forget about the potluck?"

"Shit." Elizabeth realized with a shock that she had completely forgotten about the May Day potluck at Tom's school. She joined Tom in the bathroom, passed a washcloth over her face, and on the way out the door, grabbed a bowl. At the Stop 'N Shop, she bought deli potato salad and dumped it into the bowl for her potluck contribution, and they drove to the school, now a good forty-five minutes late.

Fortunately, she knew, as Tom parallel parked between a Subaru with a "Keep Whirled Peas" bumper sticker and a Volkswagen van with a kayak on top, everything at this school ran late.

Faculty, staff, and parents, who looked as if they were gathered for a peasant harvest festival with their Guatemalan shirts and Tibetan vests and long skirts—although Elizabeth suspected half of these people had trust funds somewhere on the East Coast—were lined up at long oak tables laden with heavy wooden bowls of couscous salad, pesto pasta, tomatoes and feta cheese and leafy greens, and, at the end, a lone bucket of fried chicken—the food she was really lusting for—brought by some hapless parent who wouldn't last a year here.

They sat at long tables decorated with children's handprints, artworks adorned with poems titled "I feel free when… " and "Justice is within me when…"

Amber, the school administrator, stood at the head of the table and hushed the room. "We are ushering in the season of light," she said. "So I'd like a moment of peace to welcome the mother of all life: the sun." The adults held still, but the peace was a restless one, as the children squawked and squirmed.

She looked out to the crowd. "Brightness is here within us, my friends. And soon we will be surrounded by it!" She tossed back her mop of grey hair. "Now, as my mother said, eat!"

Voices rose, as did the din of silverware clattering against the tin plates that they would later wash in shifts.

Elizabeth and Tom sat across from Nonny, the slender, dark-eyed English teacher at this school. In the privacy of Tom and Elizabeth's living room, the three of them had spent hours telling stories about this place, its preciousness, the parent meetings about whether it was right for the boys to play with swords and the significance of a child-sized ironing board in the play area and what that said about women and subjugation when, in the end, they tossed it out because it was pink and molded plastic. In spite of their complaints, Tom and Nonny loved the school: its liberal idealism and academic freedom, the clapboard house, the small brook running through the playground shaded by cottonwood trees. Sometimes, Elizabeth suspected, they loved it because it represented the childhood they wanted and never had.

"Happy spring, guys," Nonny lifted her wine glass to Elizabeth's. "To Bacchus, Eros, and whatever god rules good gardens." Her hair was blonde and grey, her skin weathered, and her glance piercing and kind.

They toasted, their cheap glasses thunking amid the murmur of conversation around them. Kids shrieked on the swing set as they sailed back and forth, chains squeaking. Several boys kicked a soccer ball in the long grass near the front gate. In the rare warmth of spring, parents lingered at the long tables. Several mothers were nursing, a few were laughing, heads tilted back, taking long slow sips of sparkling cider. A toddler held the finger of his father as the two of them slowly circled the playground. Amber went from parent to parent, talking about this child or that.

Elizabeth asked about Nonny's girlfriend, Lucinda.

Nonny looked uncomfortable. "She's busy tonight."

Tom looked at Nonny and cocked his head. "Nonny—are you telling the truth?"

"No," Nonny's face cleared. "She's home studying ways to get back at me for wrecking her car."

"Pour her more wine." Elizabeth topped off her glass and Nonny's. "We want details." Nonny's mishaps with her car were legendary. Her car, an embattled blue Subaru Legacy, had certainly earned its name. She'd run into a mailbox, she'd torn the taillights out by hooking her mother's bumper, and—though it was not her fault—she had been hit by a runaway cart outside the grocery store.

Tom shook his head. "What'd you do—?"

"Okay, asshole." She looked at Tom, then Elizabeth. "It was like this. I was driving on Pattee Drive and it started raining, raining hard, and then the wipers were hung up on something. I parked at the edge of the road and got out to clear them, when the car started rolling forward. I chased it, but the car picked up speed and I couldn't catch it, and it plowed into another car."

Tom put his hand on her arm. "Oh, Nonny."

"There's more," she said grimly. "Then the car rolled down the hill and into someone's garage."

Tom whistled. "Jesus. Didn't you put the parking brake on?"

She looked at him as if to say, *What do you think, asshole?*

"Tom." A girl of twelve appeared by Tom's side and studied Elizabeth with frank curiosity. Tom introduced her to Elizabeth as one of his best students.

The young girl's face was slender and she had a waist-length gold braid. Her eyes were deep-set, blue, and there was something mesmerizing about the way she fixed her gaze on Elizabeth that was both fierce and shy at once, like a wild animal's.

"Kiera is my best student," Tom said. "She's in seventh grade and she wrote the most dynamite paper on pioneer women in Montana that I've read from a student. Though we do not make value judgments, do we Kiera?"

She basked in that for a moment, and then wandered over to a group of girls. She climbed up the stone wall that bordered the schoolyard and began to walk, her arms out, one foot in front of the other, clearly conscious that she was being watched as she moved toward the group of gnarled apple trees at the fence's corner. Her balance was sure, her step light. She was walking, Elizabeth thought, as if to show the world how young she was, moving down that rock wall in perfect balance, her braid swaying back and forth as she moved.

When her friends called up to her, she paused, looked at them, poised, mid-step, then she lifted her head, laughed, and moved on.

Elizabeth felt a hole opening up inside her.

As she watched the girl in the deepening twilight, Elizabeth thought, *I used to be like her, so confident, doing arias, singing lieder, stepping lightly on and off the stage. Where is that girl?* She wished that growing up was as easy as the straight line of that rock wall, connecting that girl she had been—singing on the stage with her father in the audience—to the woman she was now, sitting at a table, disappointed, drinking wine.

Elizabeth watched as the young girl reached the grey branches that covered the far end of the wall. She put one foot on a branch, testing her weight on it, then changed her mind and withdrew it. She turned around, stood on the wall as if she were contemplating walking back, then jumped lightly to the ground and was swallowed up by a group of girls.

And then, because it was a lovely evening in May, the beginning of the lingering season in this town, not a time for bitter words and self-recrimination, she murmured, "Ah youth," and set down her wine with a sigh that was supposed to sound exaggerated and self-mocking and instead came out broken-sounding.

Tom looked at her sharply for a moment.

She picked up her fork and split a potato in two and brought it to her mouth.

Back at the house, she'd just had time to quickly apply a few strokes of fresh makeup in the bathroom mirror before she and Tom rushed to the potluck. Tom, standing in his bold Guatemalan shirt, had leaned against the doorjamb, eyes fixed on her.

"What's up?" Elizabeth had said.

"I like to watch you."

She'd turned away from the mirror and pointed her eyeliner at him. "You just think if you say things like that you are going to get laid."

"A man can try," he'd said and shrugged.

She had laughed, a bottomless, heady feeling, then turned back to the mirror and carefully drew a black line on the lid of the other eye.

"You never told me about Kiera," Elizabeth said on the car ride home that night, as they wound through the streets in the dusk.

"I guess I didn't," Tom said, his eyes on the street as he turned from Third Street onto Mount Avenue, heading back to the university neighborhood.

Elizabeth studied him, his steady profile, the way he so solidly occupied space. His self-possession was something that had always moved her about him.

"It's obvious she means something to you," Elizabeth said.

"Of course she means something to me, Lisbeth," he said and paused. "She's my student."

Tom called Elizabeth "Lisbeth" when he was trying to make a point, and Elizabeth knew that the point now was this was none of her business. But it *was* her business, goddamn it. She was his wife and whatever happened to him was her business, boundaries and all that bullshit be damned. So she persisted. "It just seems odd, that's all," she said, keeping her voice even-sounding.

"Well, nothing's going on, if that's what you mean," Tom said, looking over at Elizabeth as he shifted into third gear as they headed down Mount. "Good God, Elizabeth, she's twelve. Do you think I'm weird enough to go after a twelve-year-old?"

"No."

"Well, why are you doing this?"

"I don't know."

"C'mon, Elizabeth. She's like a daughter to me."

Like the daughter you can't give me, Elizabeth heard. *Like the daughter I can't have.* The windshield blurred.

"What?" Tom looked over. "Oh, don't cry. Please don't cry."

"It just seems odd that you didn't say something before."

Tom stopped the car at the light and shifted down. "We've had a lot going on."

They sat in silence as the light turned from red to green. Elizabeth watched Tom shift into first, then second, his hands on the gear shift, strong, muscular, capable.

They drove through the university neighborhood, under the canopy of maple trees that were planted at the instigation of her great-grandfather, trying to make the streets of this dry western town look more like the orderly, tree-lined boulevards of Chicago's prosperous neighborhoods.

As they drove home, they passed the century-old Hammond Park where ghosts of picnics, baseball games, and swim-suited toddlers seemed to swarm the wet grass, and where the band shell cupped the darkness like a hand and light pooled under the streetlights. Tom pulled over the car and pulled up the brake.

"What is it, Elizabeth?" he said. "Something's wrong."

She looked out at the night-darkened street, the houses with lamplight burning in bedroom windows, downstairs panes washed in the blue glow of television.

"What's up with you?" Tom crossed his arms. "C'mon babe."

Love stabbed her fiercely at that moment.

Elizabeth didn't want to cry. She looked into Tom's face, the brown hair that waved over his forward and the green eyes and the prickly chin, remembering the photo he had showed her once of himself on the farm at twelve feeding a bottle to a lamb, his back straight, his look of steadfastness, even then. He hated the photo for the religious fervor it ignited in his mother. She loved it for the way it shadowed the man he had become: steady, back-straight, and tender.

"Talk to me." He lifted a hair away from Elizabeth's face and peered at her. His voice was soft. "You need to tell me what's going on."

"I don't know." Elizabeth's voice wavered. "I honestly fucking don't know, Tom. I think I'm losing it. I mean I look out there and you are just moving on, living your life, but I don't know. I don't seem able to—engage."

"Tell me about it."

"I can't."

"Try," he said. He watched a red Volkswagen van pull out of the driveway across from them.

"I don't want to try again," Elizabeth blurted. "I don't want to have sex. I know you do, I know you want a child, and I want a child, but I can't bear another disappointment. Right now, all I want to do is find my sister."

"So go to Choteau," Tom said. "Go see Karen. Nobody's pressuring you, Elizabeth. C'mon. We don't have to try again right now. Nobody's telling you that. Slow down. We'll get through this."

"Not that sister. The other one." Elizabeth ran her finger over the reptilian plastic of the dashboard.

He looked sharply at her.

The pause between them lengthened, the wind shushing the trees, a dog barking somewhere.

"Holy shit." He shook his head. "It's so weird, isn't it? Suddenly a sister just arrives in your life." He stared out the windshield.

"I don't even know if she's alive," Elizabeth said.

"Oh my God, Elizabeth. I know you just found this out, but in the day to day, I keep forgetting it. No wonder you've been strange lately."

"I've been strange lately?"

"Kind of. It's understandable. You've had a lot going on."

"I didn't think I'd been that strange."

Tom laughed and slipped his hand in hers. She studied his face in the darkness, the grey hair at his temples and his broad shoulders, and something loosened in her chest and her words tumbled forward, fast and easy. Several kids floated across the grass of the park, laughing, moving back and forth, drinking something out of a bottle tucked in a sack.

"I have to find her," Elizabeth said.

"So find her," Tom said.

She looked at him. "I will."

Outside, the teenagers were on the swings, the chains of the metal grating against the metal bars of the swing set, creaking forward and backward as the kids pumped their legs, going higher and higher, shouting, and the slow squeak of metal on metal seemed to be the sound of her heart opening, shutting, opening, shutting.

CHAPTER TWENTY-TWO

At the beginning, Louise and Dr. O exchanged long looks at staff meetings or had lingering conversations about the thalidomide baby or the child missing half her brain, or the phenylketonuria babies—with severe brain damage—from the mining country in Butte, the two of them trailing their fingers over the patient files, adjusting paper clips and clamps, folding over the edges of forms and files as they talked. At the lunch line in the cafeteria, as they waited for white plates of meatloaf with gravy or ruby red Jell-O, he touched her at the waist, the touch burning through her until the next glance, the next weighted word.

Ridiculous, Louise would tell herself as she walked across the shorn fields each night, the prick of the stubble across her bare feet some kind of penance, as she looked over to the wheat fields where the older boys in their blue serge uniforms and bowl cuts were harvesting wheat that would be threshed and milled into flour and baked into bread for the patients.

Damn idiot, she whispered, watching other patients bend forward, rope the hay bales and lift them onto the wooden bed of a truck, the sound of their groans echoing across the field. There was a soothing choreography to their work, the way the men raked the hay into long rows and the baler swept the hay from the ground and cut and compressed it, leaving behind neat rectangles. Another team followed with a flatbed pickup, heaving hay bales up and over the sides, the sun glancing off the cab, all of it captured by the light slanting down through this valley.

Watching them, she hated herself for the way she spent staff meetings noticing the hairs on Dr. O's tanned fingers or the sturdy masculinity of his black glasses when he slipped them out of his white jacket and onto his face to read charts.

For Christ's sake, you have responsibilities, she told herself under her breath, several days later, when he rolled up his sleeves to brown muscled forearms and her stomach grew weak.

She resisted him until the day in the nursery—she was there to check on Lizzie with the five-year-olds—when Lizzie seized and Louise was trying to care for her while a three-year-old boy was strapped to the changing table.

A gurgling sound rose from Lizzie's throat. A girl began to cry, and then another. Lizzie began to grow stiff.

Louise lifted Lizzie up and laid her on a blanket on the floor. She covered her with another blanket and sat, cross-legged, putting Lizzie's head in her lap. She called the other twelve children to her, and told them it was time for a story.

"She sounds like a toilet flushing, Miss Gustafson," one child whined. "Make it stop!"

"Once upon a time," Louise yelled. "C'mon. I'm telling a story."

The children looked at her, quiet, sullen, as they circled around her. "Once upon a time there was a woodcutter who had two children, whom he loved very much, but when his wife died he remarried an evil woman and he had to send his children out to the woods for food."

The children whimpered, still scared, but they gathered around her. Two girls lay down and began to suck their thumbs.

"They secretly dropped stones along the path on their way into the woods, so, when the moon came out, the two children followed the stones home."

Lizzie went limp. The stench of her urine rose to Louise's nostrils and kept her focused. The kid on the changing table thrashed his legs. Poor kid, Lizzie remembered thinking, his bottom must be so cold, but she didn't dare get up and get him yet.

"And when they got home, their father was so glad to see them and their evil stepmother was gone."

Two boys wrestled quietly, punching each other, but listening.

"And the children all got candy," she said.

"Candy!" Mary said and jumped up, her braids flapping.

"Candy!" the boys cried.

She heard someone clear his throat. When Louise looked back at the doorway, Dr. O was standing there. He was silhouetted in the light from the hallway, his glasses glinting.

"You were remarkable," Dr. O said to her as he tended to Lizzie, putting antiseptic on her cuts and giving her a shot of phenobarbital to make sure she would sleep and suggesting that she wear a helmet to protect her head. Louise diapered up the boy on the table and lifted him to his wheelchair. "You really were, you know," Dr. O said. "Handling all those kids by yourself. Calming them, telling that story. You have a gift, you know, Louise." He touched the inside of her wrist. "Truly."

She thanked him.

Candy, the children sighed.

"Who does she see?" Dr. O said.

"Doctor Spitz, from Helena. He comes down."

"Oh, God. He's doesn't know shit. What's he got her on?"

"Luminal. What does that do?"

"It dopes them down—but sometimes way too much. Sometimes they docs use it as patient control, more than seizure control. And sometimes there aren't a lot of other options, either, in their defense," Dr. O said, taking Lizzie's face in his hands and turning it from one side to the other, opening her eyes to check her pupils, tapping her knees with his reflex hammer. Lizzie was so exhausted, Louise noticed, she didn't wake up. "Let me give you a tip. When they don't know what to do here—and I'm as guilty as the rest—they just sedate 'em. She needs Dilantin. Let me take care of her. I'll make it my personal mission."

Later she would hate herself for the way her body leaned into his.

For falling for his bait, that yes, she should move with Lizzie, taking over the five-year-olds, moving out of the baby room, leaving the infants to Margaret and a new assistant, so she could help with the older children, with whom she had a God-given talent. She would hate herself for allowing him to see the soft white underbelly of her heart.

He took her hiking to Ringing Rocks, a spot just up Pipestone Pass. She stopped, pressed her back against a quartz monzonite boulder—Roger would tell her later it was a rock special to this area, the magma shoved upward by volcanic eruptions seventy million years ago—and as she started to drink her canteen, he took it from her, screwed on the top, threw it aside where it skittered as it landed, and pressed himself into her, his mouth firm and hot, his hands moving quickly up her shirt.

"Surprise," he said.

"Surprise," she said.

He stood up, pulled out a chocolate bar and broke it into exact squares of chocolate.

"You're a very precise man, Roger," Louise said.

"I'm always—" he said, "—always measuring things."

He slid a square of chocolate into her mouth and kissed her, the rich round sweetness mingling with the kiss and the liquid call of a nearby robin.

They made love standing up, their shorts ringing their ankles, Roger pinning her against the rough rock, the sun warming her, coaxing the sweetness out of the ponderosas, the dry smell of dirt rising as he cried out, pressing himself against her, and Louise felt the past drop away.

When they were finished, they put themselves back together. Roger took her hand and led her to the top of the pass, a place he knew about, one of the world's geological wonders called Ringing Rocks, where they took hammers to the rocks, ringing out tunes on that ancient batholith. They played the Alphabet Song. They played "Row, Row, Row Your Boat."

Roger chanted a tune he'd made up. "From the cracks comes the mines. From the mines comes the lead. From the lead comes sick babies, and those, my dear Louise, are what you and I deal with each day."

She tapped *ba-da-bum, ba-da-bum.*

He rang, *Ba-bum. Ba-bum.*

Their hammers echoed across the eerie granitic landscape, where she was, of course, falling in love.

The cabin, he said, was a precaution. A place he knew about, tucked in the hills just beyond her own cabin, away from prying eyes, a place they could arrive separately and leave separately. The first Saturday, after she'd finished dusting and sweeping her own place, doing a quick wash of her uniforms and underwear and pinning them out on the clothesline, she set out from her own cabin to the woods behind it, following a skinny game trail tramped down in sagebrush and needle grass. She walked straight back as Roger had told her to do, looking behind her to see if anyone was watching. She turned back once and stopped where she could see the Stone Home campus spread before her, the staff cabins below her, the fields of wheat where the patients and staff continued to stack bales, farther out the white cottages nestled in their web of dirt roads. Beyond that, to the west, she could see the dim grey building of Diamond Bar Ranch, a hot springs resort for movie stars and wealthy out-of-towners, where, in the old days, it was rumored men lost entire ranches in days-long poker games and women prostitutes lived on the third floor, descending only in the evening after dinner and drinks. One lady of the evening, it was rumored, was killed by her lover and came back as a ghost to haunt the place.

She hiked up higher and, just as she was about to give up, the cabin came into view. It was a tiny homesteader's shack he'd found near what must have been an old silver claim, the door to the mine boarded shut and spray-painted Keep Out.

She opened the wooden door to the small square room, complete with a woodstove and a kitchen hutch, a window, a rickety metal-frame bed, a washstand. A mouse skittered across the floor. She threw her backpack at it, and it peeped and dove through a hole in the wall.

Where was Roger?

She sat at the edge of the bed, the springs squeaking.

This was a mistake. She should go back. Just leave before he got here, before he stepped in the door. She got up. She picked up her backpack from the floor, and was turning around to open the door when it opened instead.

Roger, of course, out of breath.

"I got held up," he said. "One of the non-ambs had an emergency and I had to check in. But I'm here now."

He walked to kiss her, easing the straps of her backpack off her back.

"I don't know," she said, "if this is such a good idea."

But he was already kissing her lips, her face, her neck. "It's *such* a good idea," he said, nudging her toward the bed. "Such a very, very good idea," he said through the tangle of clothes and limbs and kisses.

Afterward, they sat at the rickety table, across from one another, as the sun burned across the Elkhorns and the fire settled to coals. Louise was shuffling through a deck of cards they'd found in the hutch, Roger waiting for her to deal.

"Hearts? Concentration?" Louise said. "What shall we play?"

"Five-card stud," Roger said. He adjusted the glasses on his nose and rested his elbows on the table.

"What do we bet with?" Louise said.

"Our clothes?" Roger grinned.

"No way," Louise said. She set down the cards to pull a blanket around her. "Too cold."

He looked around the cabin. "Dust motes? Splinters?" He walked to the hutch and pulled open a drawer. "I got it! Silverware. Spoons for nickels. Forks for dimes. Knives for quarters. What do you say?"

She anted up a spoon and dealt out five cards to each of them. She didn't have much—just a pair of twos—but when Roger asked to draw three more cards, she increased the bet from one spoon to a fork. When he got his new cards, he met her bet and increased it by another spoon.

"What do you have, Roger?" she said. She studied his eyes above the fan of cards he held before his face.

"It's a secret," he said. His eyes glittered. "You know I love my secrets."

"You're bluffing me, Roger." She grinned. "You're trying to get me to fold."

"Well," he stared at her over the cards. "Are you? Are you going to fold?"

"Not on your life." She raised the bet another spoon.

He laughed. "I should have known." He thunked his spoon down on the pile of silverware in the middle of the table. "I don't think you give up on anything."

"Is that a compliment?"

"I guess it is."

"You guess?"

"Yes. It is. You are fierce, Louise Gustafson," he said, and he leaned across the table to kiss her.

And, even though she won the hand, her pair of twos beating out his queen, as she raked in her winnings, seven spoons and two forks, and Roger took the cards to deal out the next hand, and they continued to play, laughing as the piles of silverware grew on her side of the table, until dark when the two of them left, Louise first, then Roger, using flashlights to follow the deer path down the mountain and back to their separate homes—her cabin, his residence in the doctor's quarters across the road from the hospital—that word *secrets* sent a chilling breeze through her.

CHAPTER TWENTY-THREE

When Bob arrived at the Elk Park Mental Hospital to pick up his mother for the Easter weekend, she was dressed and ready for him. She perched on the edge of her bed, dressed in a flowered chintz dress, her hair done, wearing a pink cloche hat, with matching scarf and gloves. She was very still as he walked in, and he could see how beautiful she was, her hair swept up underneath her hat, her dark eyes composed for a change instead of swimmy as they got when her mania set in. She started to rise as he came across the tile floor toward her, and he motioned to her to sit back down.

"Robert," she said. "Bobby Boy."

His heart sank. Why did his mother insist on calling him that?

"You look lovely, Mother," he said. "How are you?"

"Oh," she said. "What can I say? That the shock treatment was a walk in the park?"

He smiled and sat on the chair next to the bed. They stayed on neutral topics for a few minutes: the warming of the weather, the new calves Bob saw along the road along with a few foals, and the news of the Queen's upcoming coronation in June. "She will be anointed with holy oil and wear a robe of ermine," his mother said. "It's almost like a fairy tale, if you believe in such things." She put her hand on her heart and sighed. Then she straightened up and looked him dead in the eye. "I rocked her and sang to her, Robert."

"Mother." Anger flushed through him. "I'm glad for you. But we're trying to put that behind us."

"She's your flesh and blood, Bob."

"It's my decision, and you need to respect it." Bob stood up and walked to the door, clenching and unclenching his hands. "Are you ready to go, Mother? Do you have your bag packed? We need to get on the road and get going. We can talk in the car."

"Robert." Beatrice sat up straighter. "She's just a toddler. She sang, 'Twinkle, Twinkle,' but she can't remember all the words, so she just sings twinkle for all the words. It's so cute. She has your coloring—freckles, brown hair. Mary's eyes."

"Mother, focus," Bob said. He took a deep breath and exhaled slowly. His face was hot, tight, his throat constricted. "You are on one of your highs, I can tell. Listen to me. We need to get on the road before the early afternoon because Mary is expecting us for dinner." He walked over and picked up her black leather suitcase from a closet and set it on the bed while she continued to talk. He wanted to get out of the place, the sounds of the patients, the bursts of crazy laughter, the smell of floor wax and antiseptic and urine, and the sharp tang of hot water heat that boiled inside his head and squeezed his stomach, as his mother nattered on about the child's singing and how she hugged her, and when she left she called her the "soft lady." "Bring the soft lady back," his mother said, repeating the child's words until he thought he would scream. A headache knotted the back of his skull and bloomed across his temples.

"Ready?" he said, his voice sharp.

His mother looked at him, wounded.

"Your pajamas?" Bob said.

Beatrice's eyes teared. "My what?"

"Pajamas," he said. He moved over to sit beside her on the bed. "C'mon Mother, focus."

"Behind the door." Her voice wobbled. She turned her head from him. "Look, I'm trying to help."

"I'm sorry," he said. "Sorry, sorry sorry. I didn't mean to interrupt."

"I'm an old woman," she said. "Foundations, top drawer to the left of the closet."

"Did you do anything else with her?" Bob asked, cornered.

"No."

"Why don't you tell me now? C'mon Mother."

Beatrice pursed her lips.

Before he had arrived at his mother's room, he stopped by the doctor's for a quick update, the doctor telling him he thought his mother was responding well to the Lithium, improving after the last shock treatment. *I know,* he said, *you don't sanction them, but the visits to the child help her.* She was regularly participating in crafts class, reading books and memorizing the first line of the periodic table that she used to know in its entirety, moving on to the second. She was working on the other forty-nine, telling him the other day that she had always been partial to the alkali metals.

As Bob and Beatrice walked down the hallway, decorated with pictures of chicks hatching out of eggs and Easter bunnies springing out of brightly colored baskets, they passed rooms where patients stared dully out the windows, or were talking to no one in particular. "Happy Easter,

Mrs. Carter," a dark-haired nurse at the station said as they walked by.

"Happy Easter to you, Lorraine." Bob's mother nodded her head grandly as they walked past, and he noticed how stately she looked at that moment with her white wool coat and her jet earrings, her nylons wheezing against one another as she moved back into the world, and how the other patients watched her with a mixture of longing and dread.

It was a beautiful drive back to Bridger, the sun warming the pastures that were greening on the edges, the mother cows circling their spindly calves, the snow still capping the tops of the Tobacco Root, Pintler, and Sapphire mountains as they headed west, the tires slicking the highway, the world sounding wet and ripe and breathing after the great stillness of winter.

"They say she likes music, Robert," Beatrice said.

"Hmm," Bob adjusted the rearview mirror.

"And I could tell when I sang to her that she liked it. I told her who I was and she called me the soft lady."

"You told me that, Mother." Bob concentrated on the highway. He was going to just stay calm, plow through this, a Liberty ship, steady in dark water.

"And Mary? How is Mary feeling about this?"

"Mary is sad, Mother." Bob turned on the radio to see if there was any chance they could catch an errant radio station, but no luck. Static, as he spun the tuning dial from one end to the other. "Can we talk about something else?"

Beatrice touched his arm. "Robert?"

"Yes," he said, the tone in his mother's voice soft, old, familiar, a knife gutting him.

"Don't you think about her?"

"No," Bob said. "Not really." It was a lie, but not a lie. He didn't think about her. He was intent on putting this child behind him, on thinking about the new life growing in Mary's belly. "The doctor said to move on," he said. "So Mary and I are trying to put all that behind us and start over. I don't think thoughts about her." That was the truth, he thought. Instead, she was like a cloud at times, enveloping him.

"Oh." Beatrice cleared her throat and looked out the window.

She was blessedly quiet, Bob thought, just the growl of the motor filling the space between them.

"It's nice to be with you, Bobby." She sighed. "It's so nice to be out of that hospital."

"They're taking care of you, Mother." He patted her hand.

"I know," she said. "But sometimes I just want to see the sky. Do you miss Dad?" she asked, staring ahead.

"Every day."

"Me too."

In that silence, Bob felt his father's presence between them, calm in his charcoal tweed coat, his steady gaze, his touch connecting the two of them as they rolled down this grey ribbon of highway.

He pulled over in Drummond for lunch at the Wagon Wheel Café. The place was packed with ranchers, their cowboy hats hung by the door, the windows sweating with heat, the room alive with the smell of sizzling grease and easy conversation. As they waited for hot roast beef sandwiches—the best kind, Bob thought, salivating, with thick hunks of beef and white spongy bread smothered in rich brown gravy—a young girl who appeared to be around five wandered in and came up to Beatrice.

"Ma'am?" she said.

"What is it dear?" Beatrice gazed down her white wool jacket at her.

Bob felt a dropping sensation in his gut.

"Can you see something?"

Beatrice looked at the girl. "What would you like me to see?"

"Come see—" the girl said. Her face was round and freckled and two brown braids hung on either side like rope cords.

Beatrice looked at him and cocked her head. "She's so sweet, Bob."

Couldn't he just once sit and enjoy his goddamn sandwich?

He helped his mother up from the oilcloth table and they followed the girl outside, where a cool wind was blowing, and around the back of the restaurant, past a rusted combine and a tire-less pickup truck set up on blocks. The girl skipped over to a wire cage up on two cement blocks and stopped.

"My rabbit," she said. She opened the cage and pulled out a large black rabbit, which pedaled the air with its feet, claws out. "Want to pet it?"

"Look dear," Beatrice looked at Bob. "She has a rabbit."

"Very nice," Bob said, looking longingly back at the restaurant, where it was warm and, by now, most likely, his sandwich was waiting. "What's its name?"

"Nibs," the girl said and smiled. "Like the licorice. Get it? Want to hold it?"

"That's fine," Bob said. "I'd better get back. Our food is coming. Don't want that gravy to get cold."

The girl looked at him again. "Please mister?"

"Oh honey, I think it's time for my lunch."

"Robert." Beatrice looked at him, her voice fierce in a way he had not heard it for years. "Hold the damn rabbit."

Bob held the rabbit stiffly, stroking its soft fur. The rabbit's long ears lay against its back in fear, its eyes darting. He could feel its claws digging into his arms through his suit jacket. When he felt he had petted the rabbit a sufficient amount of time, he handed it back to the girl and said, "I think we'd better be getting back."

“Thanks mister,” the girl said as she carefully put it back in the cage and fastened the latch.

The three of them started back to the café, the gravel scattering under their feet, the noon sun warming Robert’s head, the little girl skipping out in front of them, her arms swinging from side to side for momentum. Beatrice looked at him as she picked her way over the uneven ground in her pumps. “I may be old and crazy,” she said, her earrings glittering in the late-day sun. “But honestly, Robert, sometimes you’re just pathetic.”

CHAPTER TWENTY-FOUR

When Elizabeth Carter opened the copper doors of the Bridger County Courthouse, she was greeted by the smell of floor wax and dust. She took the marble stairs, two at a time, her steps slicing the silence, looking at the murals lining the courthouse dome—Edgar Paxson's paintings of Meriwether Lewis and William Clark shaking hands with the Salish Indians. *Walk away,* she wanted to shout to the Salish, who reached out their arms in welcome. *Those white men are the harbingers of doom.* Paxson had paid her great-aunt for his daughter's piano lessons with a painting. *Indian, Crow-type,* it said on the back, scrawled in pencil. Her great-aunt, she thought, had certainly gotten the better end of that deal.

When she reached the Clerk and Recorder's office, she stopped to catch her breath, her heart hammering her chest. She opened the oak door. Over the marble counter was the picture of her great-grandfather, District Judge Robert Carter, his round-rimmed spectacles, his thick white hair parted exactly in the middle. He was the enterprising one who had set out from Chicago to this mountain town, so his five-year-old son, who was in failing health, could heal.

"My name is Elizabeth Carter," she said to the clerk who asked for identification. "I'm looking for a birth certificate of an Elizabeth Carter."

"Your birth certificate?" the clerk said. Her hair was curled back from her face like rolls of sausages. Her eyelids were powdered with shadow, the color of the ocean in furniture store paintings.

"It's not mine," Elizabeth said. "It's my sister's."

"Your sister has the same name?" the clerk looked at her for the first time.

Elizabeth shrugged. "Weird, huh?"

She waited for ten minutes, until the clerk reemerged with a paper in her hand and set it on the counter. Elizabeth paid $3.25 for the Certificate of Live Birth from the State of Montana. She sat down on a bench, under her great-grandfather's picture, and as the sounds of clicking keyboards and ringing phones and slamming file drawers faded into a distance, she read the blurry birth certificate, stamped "Informational Copy Only."

Under name, it read: Elizabeth Finch Carter. The child's middle name—Finch—was her mother's maiden name, she realized with a shock. Under facility name, it said: St. Dominick's Hospital, Bridger, Montana. Date of Birth: February 4, 1953.

Elizabeth took out a scrap of paper and did the math: 1988 minus 1953. If she was still alive, she was thirty-five years old. Certifier's name, Cecil Babcock, M.D. The same doctor who, three years later, delivered her.

Father's name: Robert James Carter. Mother's: Mary Hope Carter.

Mother, 26 years of age, father, 28. No other children.

Length of pregnancy: 33 weeks. Weight: 6 pounds 2 ounces.

Length: 15 inches.

Notes: Mongoloidism.

On line 25d of the certificate under the heading, Future Home of the Child, there was the blurred typewritten word: *Withdrawn*.

She walked home in a daze, across the bridge spanning the river where green cottonwoods overshadowed water roiling with snowmelt, passing college students bicycling slowly home from classes, trying to avoid patches of ice. She walked past the red brick high school where the students hung in the alleys smoking cigarettes and playing hacky sack, past the bakery where the yeasty smell of the afternoon loaves perfumed the air, and the grade school playground surrounded by mothers in Subarus, waiting for the children to spill through the doors.

Home, at last, she walked up the driveway, past dog shit moldering in the yard—she'd have to talk with her neighbors about picking up their Labrador's poop—and into the kitchen, where she tossed her coat onto a chair. She sorted through the mail on the dining room table—a running shoe sale at the outdoor store, a pamphlet from the local gym, and a few restaurant fliers promoting St. Patrick's Day.

She had to tell her sister.

She climbed upstairs to her study and turned on her computer. The neighbor children across the street were playing—a blonde boy and his slender younger sister. The girl was shimmying up the light pole while her brother circled her on his bicycle, shouting.

Without typing a word, Elizabeth turned her computer off and searched for the phone. It was where it always was, in Tom's study on a pile of student papers.

"I found her," Elizabeth said, sitting on Tom's chair and staring out at the telephone wires drooping over the backyard.

"Found who? Hi, Elizabeth."

"Our sister."

"You *found* her?"

"Karen, she has my name." Elizabeth stared at the rug between her feet.

Okay, honey, she could hear Karen saying to one of her daughters. *You go ahead and color that while I talk with Aunt Elizabeth for a minute? Goldfish? Of course.* There was the sound of a drawer opening and something being poured—"Sorry about this," Karen said. "I'm trying to buy myself some time here."

"No hurry," Elizabeth said. "Give them kisses."

"Aunt Elizabeth sends kisses." Elizabeth could hear Karen talking to the girls. "Okay, now," Karen spoke directly to her. "Shoot. I may not have much time."

Elizabeth told her the date of their sister's birth, how she weighed six pounds and two ounces, she wasn't full term, and then—she was *withdrawn.* "I mean I told you what Dad said, that we had this sister. But not only did we have a sister, she was alive the whole time we were growing up, Karen. She was alive. She had my name. Jesus." She felt badly about saying Jesus—she knew Karen was religious and didn't like to hear her Lord's name in vain, but it seemed to pop out of Elizabeth's mouth, unbidden, when she talked with her sister.

"Why didn't they tell us?" Karen said. "Why do you think they covered it up?"

"Exactly!" Elizabeth said. "It just pisses me off. Why leave us to figure this out after they were gone? Why just cut her out like that?"

Karen was silent. "I mean, it reorders everything. You are a second child, not a first. I'm a third child, not a second."

"Well, I'm going to find her," Elizabeth said.

Karen paused. "Wait. Wait and see how you feel, Elizabeth.

Maybe there is something we just don't know yet. Maybe they had their reasons." Just then Jessie grabbed the phone and said, "Hello 'Lisbeth. I'm eating crackers. And my mom is going to put me in my underpants."

Elizabeth laughed. "Well Jessie. You are a mighty grown woman."

"Daddy says I'm big as a bear cub. Mom says I have to say bye-bye. Bye-bye."

"I gotta go," Karen said when she took back the phone. "Jessie has to go to Kindermusik and Bill will be home soon and I need to get a start on supper. I want to think about this more. Can I call you back?"

Elizabeth said of course and pressed the off button on the phone.

It rang in her hand just as she was setting it down.

"You know," Karen's voice was tentative. "Just a quick thought and then I gotta go. Maybe you shouldn't pursue this, Elizabeth. I mean, you've just gone through a shock yourself. You're not on an even keel yet. Maybe you should just let it go."

"I know what you mean," Elizabeth said. "But Karen, she was our sister. She had my name. And you know me. Once I get a bone in my teeth, I can't let up."

"This is different," Karen said. "You don't know what's at the end of this. They may have had their reasons and maybe we just need to respect that and not ask questions. Maybe we are not supposed to ask why."

"I'm a journalist, Karen," she murmured. "I ask why for a living."

Karen's voice dimmed as she moved away from the phone. "Jessie—time out in the chair, I'm counting. Oh my stars, she's drawing on the wall... I just get on the phone and all hell breaks loose." Her voice was back, strong and clear. "Maybe they weren't ready. This was just what people did then. Maybe Dad thought that, if they had other children, this was the way he could give them a better life, just to put this behind him. I mean, they would have had to do so much for her—it's not like now with all the programs and government help. Cold, I know, but a hard choice. Elizabeth, they made their peace with it, maybe we should too. They were wonderful parents to us, and we need to respect that it was a different time then. That's what people did. Maybe we need to leave the past in the past."

"That's the oldest argument in the book," Elizabeth said. "I respect your opinion, but I'm not going to abide by it."

"I hope you know what you're doing," Karen said, her voice sharp. "I gotta go."

Elizabeth stared at the dark computer screen in front of her. Maybe Karen was right. Elizabeth was always the child who went too far, who asked too much, who couldn't leave things undone. Karen's words rang in her ears. *Maybe we need to leave the past in the past.* Jesus. Isn't that what she'd spent her whole professional life working against? Weren't these secrets at the bottom of each painful family dinner, the long pauses, the thickness in the air comprised of all the things that couldn't be said—her grandmother's mental illness, her mother's deep coldness, and now this, a missing sister—and the fact that it wasn't polite to talk about anything that meant anything, until conversations wheeled dully around weather and school and schedules like the hands on a clock. Her father grew angrier as she grew older, raging at the television as the world seemed to spin out of control with news of student strikes, civil rights, and anti-war protest marches, each act of civil disobedience registering as some kind of personal affront.

CHAPTER TWENTY-FIVE

Several months into the affair, they rode horses to Potosi Hot Springs. Potosi, which he told Louise meant snake in Spanish. Later, she learned, it was a Quechuan word for "great thunderous noise."

The horses were fast, a bay and a chestnut, pounding up the road, stirring dust up around their hooves as they galloped past Pony, an old silver mining town in the Tobacco Root Mountains with Victorian homes that sported peeling paint and carved gables and wide porches and long elegant windows looking out on dirt streets. They rode farther into the mountains, winding around the narrow road lined with ponderosa pines. As she rode behind Roger, she watched him, sitting up straight in the saddle, reins in his hand, his black cowboy boots firm in the stirrups.

Roger tied his horse to a tree, then went to Louise, took her reins and led her horse to another and tied it up. He helped her down and over to the pool, and kissed her. Then, carefully hanging each item of clothing on a low-hanging branch of a ponderosa, he unzipped her jeans and took off her shirt, bra, and underwear. Her skin prickled with cold, her nipples hard as stone, her belly flat as prairie. The horses dipped their heads and grazed, nickering, as she undressed him: the flannel shirt, jeans, the clean undershirt smelling of soap and sweat.

"Hey—" he said as she took off his glasses and carefully hung them on a branch. "I'm blind without those, you know."

"Well, I've got you where I want you then," she said. "Naked and vulnerable."

He laughed and looked down to at the water.

The two of them slipped into the hot pool next to the creek and sat down. The water came up to Louise's chin. She rested her head on the bank. The bottom was slightly offputting, mucky and soft, but the warm water melted away the stiffness in her muscles. After Roger got in, Louise climbed into his arms, tangling her legs in his like green-white roots, their faces cold as they kissed, and then he pressed her against the back of the pool and she could feel the dirt and rocks and roots against her back.

Afterwards, they sat on the bank, naked, their feet dangling in the warm water.

After a while Louise began to tell him about Lizzie, how she had taught her the alphabet and how to say "Please" and "Thank you" and how to pick up after herself. "She calls me Lolo."

"You know Louise—" His voice grew quiet.

Her skin prickled.

"What?"

"Nothing." He shook himself. "Must have gotten a chill." He slipped back into the water.

"What is it, Roger?" She looked down at him where he rested in the shallow pool. His eyes were distant. He was distracted, his mind no longer here with her, that was clear. "What is it?"

"Nothing."

"You know something you don't want to tell me." She splashed water on his face and watched him duck it. "What is it?"

He stood up, grabbed his glasses from the branch, and put them on. He sat back down on the edge of the pool, put his feet back in the warm water, swishing them for a minute, staring at them. Then he looked sharply at her. "We can't keep these kids anymore," he said. "None of this is working."

"What do you mean, none of this is working?" She looked at a nearby ponderosa, at the wide, uneven plate of bark on its trunk. "What does that have to do with anything?"

"We can't keep these kids anymore," Roger said again, looking back down at his feet. "This warehousing. This giant hospital. This whole system is wrong."

"What do you mean?" Louise said. She stood up. "What are you talking about? About the hospital? About us?"

"We have to return them."

"Roger," she said, looking at him, aware that her arms, her legs, and her stomach were stippled with gooseflesh. "What do you mean, 'return them'?"

"I mean, they need to go back to their parents, back to society. This system is broken."

"Their families don't want them, Roger," she said, staring down at him. "We can't just give them back. That's why they are here."

"It doesn't matter," he said. "They have to take them back."

"But we took them away in the first place," she said.

"We didn't. The doctors sent them here. Warehoused 'em. It isn't good for them, Louise. Look at them. They're packed in here, surrounded by shit. Shitty laundry. Shitty food. Shitty care—and I don't mean any offense—it's just the state of things. They drug these kids to the gills and just sit 'em in an empty room and call that 'state of the art.' They'd be better off in communities or old folks' homes or with families. We're the state," he said, splashing her foot with hot water. "The family—well at least they're flesh and blood."

She wrapped her arms around her breasts. "What the hell are you talking about? For Christ sakes, they're children, Roger, not library books you check in and check out."

"I know that." Roger looked up at her, finally, from the pool of hot water. "God, you're beautiful. Right now, just like that. I love you just like this, Louise Gustafson, don't ever forget it. Naked and furious."

Of course, she realized, he was trying to tell her many things were about to change, but she wasn't listening. She didn't want to hear it. Years later, when she was in a truth-scouring rage, she could see the crumbs he left behind, beginning with that moment at the hot springs, then later on that hot summer day in August, when she was sitting on the steps of the Stone Home, sweating, watching Lizzie jump through a sprinkler as it flung water from one side to the other, like a hand waving back and forth. Mary Windy-Boy and Belle Star were nearby, shrieking as they took turns running through a fountain sprinkler. Cattle stood heavily in the distant fields. A plane droned. The sun beat down so hot and dry it seemed to vibrate the air. A car appeared, rolling up the road to the school in a cloud of dust, dream-like, and they watched it as if they were in a trance, the children still jumping through sprinklers, but more slowly as the large Plymouth Galaxy approached, its fins cutting through the heat and the stillness until it screeched to a stop in front of the school. The license plate said "Illinois."

Louise slowly rose to her feet. Lizzie stopped jumping, water running down her legs.

A tall woman with a very short skirt, large round sunglasses, and high-heeled sandals stepped out of the car. "My God, it's hot here," she said in a voice that was crisp and authoritative. "And so incredibly dry. As soon as the boy at the station washed the car windows—they were dry again!"

She looked at Louise as if she suddenly just noticed that she was standing there. "Oh, hello."

"Can I help you?" Louise said.

The woman took her sunglasses off and looked up at the building. "Italianate," she said. "Beautiful. Look at those cornices."

Louise didn't know what to say.

"Is there someone you're looking for?" Louise watched the woman step away from the car, slam the door, and look at the school: the line of white cottages, Mary and Belle and Lizzie who stood, hands dangling, staring back at her from the lawn, where the two sprinklers were running, one up and over, the other sputtering up like a fountain, with their small offerings of water.

She looked at Lizzie, who walked right up to her, and stood, staring up at the woman's short skirt and brilliant white blazer. "Were you jumping in the water?" the woman said in a voice designed to appeal to children.

Lizzie stared at her.

"You need to answer," Louise said. "Can you answer the nice lady, Lizzie?"

"Yes," Lizzie said.

The woman looked at Lizzie, then at Louise. "Have they socialized the patients at all?" she said. "I mean, they are going to have to be socialized, correct?"

"We're working on that," Louise said. "But it takes time. Can I help you?" wishing this woman would leave, with her sunglasses dangling from her hand and her cool remove, her slim hips and miniskirt. It was too hot for her, too hot for all of this. It took too much energy.

The woman, however, decided she had a mission. She leaned down to Lizzie and put her face close to hers. "When I ask you how you are, you need to say, 'fine.' Can you say that?"

Lizzie stared at the woman's red lips.

"Say 'fine,' Lizzie," the woman said and held out her hand to Lizzie's.

Again, Lizzie said nothing.

"Well," the woman said, and turned to Louise. "Can you tell me where Dr. Oetzinger can be found? Dr. Roger Oetzinger? I'm Audrey," she said, looking, really looking at Louise. "You know, Roger's—"

"Oh—Audrey," Louise said. "Of course."

Three things happened at once. Louise heard the ring of proprietorship in her voice. She saw the large diamond on Audrey's left hand. And Lizzie, dear Lizzie, picked up the woman's right hand and bit it.

Repetition and rhythm kept her moving across the chasm of that summer: walking back and forth to her cabin before and after shifts, rising and going to bed, moving to and from the fields, watching the male patients cut the hay, the haystacks growing taller as the days grew shorter, moving from patient to patient, hands forking food up and down from plate to mouth, moving across the lingering twilights where the sky turned a deep ocean blue, and then she'd think of Roger and Audrey in a sweaty twist. She imagined packing and leaving again, the caress of the road beneath her, but the thought simply hung there, with no movement behind it, as the days grew shorter and brisker, and the nights darkened from deep blue to black.

Fall, she told herself, *I'll leave in the fall*, feeling the brick walls of the Stone Home rise behind her, feeling the shift of the car into first, second, third, the roll of pavement again, and then—blank. The vision ended there. She walked back and forth to her cabin before and after her shifts until one particularly golden day, when the sun was so warm, the edges of the day so clean and crisp, the fall so beautiful that she walked more slowly across the fields, looking at the cloud-scudded sky over the Elkhorn Mountains and the valley below, and she felt as if she were cupped in the palm of a hard-hearted but benevolent god.

Later that fall, after a difficult day where a five-year-old in her care seized and suffered brain trauma, and a severely retarded twenty-year-old ate a dirt clod and had to be wheeled off to surgery, she returned home, ready to pack up.

Instead, she found Willy in his overalls and Romeos, bent over his shovel.

As she walked up, he threw down the shovel, leaned over, and stood up again, holding in each hand a long orange carrot, the tops feathering out extravagantly, each one a triumph. "Look, Miss Gustafson! Your carrots!"

She smiled. "Willard, they're beautiful."

They were beautiful. Long and straight. Orange, dirt-dusted. It was Willard in her garden, working it as he had so many seasons, keeping her in potatoes and carrots, beets and lettuces.

"You did it, Willard. You're a marvel. Once more."

His face shone. "Dang, Miss Gustafson," he said. He wiped a carrot on his overhauls, bit into it and chewed it. "And sweet? Sweet as candy."

"And look here!" He grabbed the tin bucket by his side and walked close to her, his step light, springy. He placed the pail at her feet, a pail of dirt-crusted beets, carrots, and onions that Louise would haul inside and store in a small root cellar carved out under the floorboards in her kitchen, that would sustain her through the long winter when everything, everything in the Stone Home would change, and the strike would come and the governor and the senators would investigate and find the home wanting, a place "of grey hopes and grey lives," and the ideas of "warehousing" the retarded would be debated in magazines and newspapers throughout the state and the nation. Questions would be asked and changes would be made that would forever affect all of their lives. But for now, she was here with Willard, and his triumphant handful of produce.

Louise's eyes prickled. "Willard." She paused. She felt washed clean.

Willard smiled, his gap-toothed smile breaking across his wide, fleshy face. "You got to have vegetables, Miss Gustafson."

Then he looked down, put his large foot on top of the shovel, and the metal made a slicing sound as it jammed into the dirt and stopped. Willard stood up, set it down and plunged his hands into the dirt. He smiled. "Here Miss Gustafson." He pulled out red potatoes and held them toward her. "Look at that."

"Lovely," she said. And they were. Three round red potatoes. Elkhorn rubies, as people called them. Louise took them in her hands, thinking of their weight and heft, the sum product of her summer, as good a sum as any, she thought before she set them, gently, in the pail. "Big as apples, Willard. You've got a green thumb."

He looked at his thumb and back at her.

"It's an expression that means you are good at growing things."

She went inside to make tea, listening to the steady slice and scoop of the shovel and Willard's exclamations of surprise as the kettle sang out and she filled the teapot and put in a teabag to steep. She carried the teapot and cups to the front porch and set them down.

"Tea, Willard?"

He looked at her. "I have to get back."

"Suit yourself. But thank you Willard," she said. "Growing me vegetables is the nicest thing anyone's done for me."

He bowed his head. "Bye, Miss Gustafson. I have to go now."

She watched him walk across the field. His thick legs turned slightly inward, but his body moved with surprising agility for such a large man. He turned once to wave, then turned around again, and she wondered, as she watched his broad back recede, the straps over his overalls twisted, what went through his mind as he headed back to the tall brick building that was stuck in the middle of the pasture as if it had been plucked by a cyclone out of the middle of a European city and set here in this peculiar Land of Oz.

When he reached the barbed-wire fence where he would duck between the thin strands that separated the field and the edge of the patients' exercise area, he turned back to her again, cupped his hands to his mouth, and yelled, "Happy potato!"

CHAPTER TWENTY-SIX

"Pack a bag," Bob said to Mary over lunch at home on a day in June. He had received a large settlement for the Lloyds, insurance clients who had lost an office building in a fire because of faulty wiring, and he was ready for a break. The world itself was waking up—the yard awash in crocuses and tulips, the maple trees frothing with tiny chartreuse blossoms, the deep purple and violet and white lilacs scenting the alleys. "We're going off. A little vacation, Mary."

"Bob." Mary looked up from her tomato soup. "We can't afford to go off. I don't know what you are talking about."

"Nope. You can't make that argument this time." Bob smiled across the lazy Susan. "I got that settlement on the Lloyd building, so your words fall on deaf ears. Pack a bag. Bring a swimsuit and a dress to dance in. We're going off. West this time."

Mary actually cracked a smile, something Bob felt he hadn't seen in a while. The whole venture was spur-of-the-moment—he'd seen an ad in the *Bridger Chronicle* for a spring dinner and dance at the

Davenport Hotel in Spokane and thought, why not? Of course they couldn't afford it. But the idea of sitting in that lavish lobby with its potted palms, Oriental rugs, and deep velvet chairs, drinking a cocktail, cutting into an inch-thick steak dribbling just a bit of au jus, and listening to the Ike Jones Jazz Quartet, suddenly brought forth a hunger in him for movement and color and music—and the sight of people laughing—a hunger that he hadn't known was there.

On the drive over, Mary fell asleep, her head propped against the door frame, and as Bob drove, he thought about Darius Lloyd, who had come into his office with his wife, Bette, and his son, Roger. They sat at the desk across from Bob and, as Bob and Darius talked over the particulars of the settlement, Mrs. Lloyd sat next to Roger. A plump woman with a deeply lined face, she attended to Roger, making sure he was comfortable in his chair, unsnapping her large patent leather purse, taking out a handkerchief, rising from her chair, and wiping the spittle from his face. "There, there, Roger," she said. "Don't you worry about a thing. Daddy's done in just a bit."

The boy, who Bob figured was in his late twenties by his size and the growth of his beard, looked up at her, adoring. "Mama," he said. "Can we go?"

"Roger," his father snapped. "I told you to be still."

Roger hung his head, and Bob could see a tear on his check.

"Roger, do you like trucks?" Bob said. "Do you want to look at my toy soldiers?"

Roger brightened and looked over at his dad. Darius scowled. Mrs. Lloyd smiled with relief. Bob took down his lead soldiers from the bookshelf, and Roger plopped down on the floor and began to line them up, one right after the other.

"I made those Roger," Bob told him.

"Really?" Roger said. "You did?"

"I did," Bob said. "Enjoy them!"

"Thank you, Mr. Carter." Roger had lined up the second flank.

"You are a godsend, Bob," Mrs. Lloyd said, tucking her handkerchief back in her purse with a snap. "You have a knack with kids, you know."

"Thank you, Bob," Mr. Lloyd said, his eyes apologetic. He leaned forward on Bob's desk and put his head in his hands and shook it. Then he looked back at Bob. "Are we ready to get back to business?"

That could be me, Bob thought as he navigated over the steep Montana-Idaho pass, where a logging truck passed him, spraying a fantail of muddy water over his windshield. That could be me and Mary and that child in twenty-some years. Wrinkled, worn-out, wiping up spittle.

As they stepped into the lobby, Mary on his arm, her overnight bag in her other hand, his bag in his other, the valet parking their car, she said, "Bob, you really shouldn't have," but when he looked at her face, it shone and he knew, for once, his instincts were right.

"What are we doing here?" Mary said. "You haven't told me a thing. Is this a convention? Are we meeting someone? What?"

He leaned over to kiss her on the cheek and this time she didn't flinch. They picked up their keys, stepped in the elevator, and as the elevator man in his double-breasted red jacket and matching pants greeted them, Bob told them about the roads from Bridger, how they were clear, just a tad of snow at the pass, fine except for the damn logging trucks at Lookout Pass.

They dropped their things in the room—simple with a carved mahogany bed and dresser, brass sconces, and an overhead light. Bob lay back on the bed, sighing.

"Join me," he said.

Mary went past him to inspect the bathroom. She looked at herself in the mirror, then pulled out the shaving mirror to look at herself from the back, running her fingers through her hair. "Look Bob! It has a claw-foot tub and white tile. The towels are monogrammed."

"I know Mary, but I'd rather have you lie down next to me," Bob said.

"You are a horn dog, Bob," Mary said. She sat on the edge of the bed, next to him, then carefully lay down next to him. She turned to him. "This is nice," she said. She turned and kissed him. "Thank you."

It wasn't quite what Bob had in mind, but he knew that he couldn't push her. He knew she was fragile. He knew he was fragile. Everything was fragile. Sometimes he wanted to just take a hammer and smash the world open, tell everyone he was tired, tired of being the one who was always there, always picking people up, paying the bills, asking how everyone was, but he wasn't going there now. He couldn't. The bed was so soft. His wife was so beautiful. It was just that he didn't know how to go forward from here. He took Mary's hand and turned to her. "Mary, quite contrary," he said. He turned to face her, her sculpted, pale face and full red lips. "How does your garden grow?"

She smiled. "What have you got us in for, Bob?"

"Dinner at 6, dancing at 7."

"I thought you hated dancing?"

"For you, I love dancing."

Her lips curved into a smile. She flicked her finger on his nose. "What a sacrifice, Mr. Carter."

For her, he also went shopping as once she saw what women were wearing in the lobby of the hotel, she told him her outfit was hopelessly shabby. They walked to the Bon Marché and took the escalator to the fine women's department up on the second floor—Bob taking the escalator down and coming back up again just for the novelty—and when he rejoined her she was already going through the sale racks of evening dresses. He found a chair near the dressing room and sat, waiting for her to appear, modeling a new outfit for his appraisal. For his wife, he would shop, an activity he ranked up there with having a tooth filled.

The pale blue sheath made her face look chalk white. The second, a wide-skirted, wide-collared affair of black-and-white check, was too loud. Then Mary came out wearing a high-waisted satin cocktail dress. It was lipstick red and sculpted at the shoulders, with a loose, whispering skirt.

What struck Bob the most was her expression. It was a glimpse of the old Mary: lit up, excited, her face flushed and beautiful, her brown eyes clear. She turned slowly. "What do you think?"

On the way back to the hotel, they walked down the sidewalks, Mary pointing out the gardens already blooming in summer flower. "Peonies, already Bob! Can you believe it? They are about two weeks ahead of us." She bent down to a small garden plot at the edge of a large brick church, touched the small, closed-up rosebud. "Amazing about flowers. You just forget that they ever exist during winter." She stood up again and thrust her arm in his, and they continued down the street toward their hotel. In her other hand, her Bon Marché sack crackled in her hand as she swung it back and forth, her heels tapping the sidewalk.

They walked into the lobby and up to the large, marble fireplace and plopped into velvet chairs and stared out at the enormous crystal chandelier in the lobby and the balcony with its arched porticos. Just as Bob was about to insist they go up to change for dinner, a man in a tux strolled up and unlocked the grand piano, took the lid off the keys, propped up the cover. He shook out a telescoping easel, where he placed his sign that said, with a flourish, *Piano Dave*. The final touch was the crystal goblet that served as a tip jar, with two dollar bills he pulled out of his wallet and stuffed in there.

And then he started in, "Summertime" from *Porgy and Bess*. Next he played "Rhapsody in Blue." Mary and Bob just sat, side by side, by the fire, Bob growing so heated he loosened his tie and took off his jacket. Mary was still, her sack at her feet. A muscle in her cheek twitched. *What is she thinking?* he wondered.

It was later, in the Peacock Room, where she sat at the mirrored back bar, her hair in a twist, her shoulders powdered, shining like a ruby amid the bouquets of peacock feathers, as she slowly sipped her Kahlua and cream, as they listened to the chatter around them, the bartender polishing the crystal wine glasses, that she told him how she didn't realize how starved for sun and color and music she had been. "I feel like I've been living in newsprint," she said. "Living in a two-dimensional world."

Later, she wore the shining dress into the formal dining room, where she turned the heads of so many diners as they walked to the table, a rhinestone-studded comb in her hair, the satin dress swishing, her black shawl draped over her white arms.

"Are you having fun, Mary?" Bob said, leaning over as she was cutting her steak into triangles.

"Mmm," she said. "I'm so happy to get away I don't want to talk about it."

"What shall we talk about?" Bob smiled.

"Let talk about dancing. Are you going to lead or am I?"

Bob laughed. Mary thought he loved to dance because he had booked her on so many dances when they were courting—when he only wanted to make sure that she wouldn't see anyone else. He laughed when she did lead on the waltz when the Ike and the Jazz Man played "Here's That Rainy Day," letting her guide him around the lavish ballroom with its gilded walls and crystal chandelier. When they moved into the quartet, the "Pennsylvania 6500" and "Take the A Train," he took over, spinning her around the floor until the two of them were breathless and sweating, laughing, Mary pleading for a drink of water. Bob went up to compliment the band. When the saxophone player leaned down to talk with him, Bob grew awkward. "I just wanted to tell you what a fan I am of your playing, of the Duke." The words sounded so impossibly small. How could he tell them about how those swooping notes opened something up inside him. "They just move me so much." He touched his heart. The man gave him a broad smile. "Thank you so much, sir. And give our thanks to your missus, the beautiful one in the red dress," the man said. Bob nodded. "Hang on to her, brother. You are a lucky man."

They ordered Highlander beers and kept dancing through all the sets, Bob leading, Mary leading, until the two of them headed upstairs, laughing, the same elevator man punching up their floor, and they stumbled out of the wood-paneled elevator, still laughing, and Bob turned the key in the door and as he shut it closed behind him, Mary was already stepping out of her shoes and Bob tore off his jacket and pants and the two of them unzipped and unbuttoned until they were naked and kissing, and they slipped onto the bed and under the covers to make sloppy, sheet-winding, delicious love.

CHAPTER TWENTY-SEVEN

There was a new restlessness about the Stone Home that Louise couldn't put her finger on. Maybe it was the size—the patient numbers had swelled to more than eight hundred—and with all these bodies were all these hungers and wants and needs and never enough staff. They had added a Junior Hall, where Margaret corralled kids ages three to six to separate them from the older population, but the five cottages, which were built to house fifty patients, each now held more than one hundred. They were trying to teach socialization classes—how to relate to an employer, how to handle money, why you should belong to a church—but the classes were so overcrowded it was hard to teach much of anything at all. No one was pretending any kind of therapeutic community existed anymore; there was a kind of recklessness among the doctors and staff—*Just do what you can*, they'd tell each other and roll their eyes, *Lord help us.*

A memo had been sent to the staff a decade ago from the state office informing them that the term "feebleminded" was officially replaced by the term "mentally retarded," and the mentally retarded were divided into twenty-six classes, which were placed in three broad categories: Moron, Imbecile, and Idiot. The Stone Home for Backward Children was renamed the Stone River School and Hospital for the Mentally Retarded. The staff was also instructed the "Principle of Normalization" to organize the patients—a system developed by Wolf Wolfensberger—which meant mixing up the higher-functioning patients among the lower-functioning patients.

Roger called it the Principle of Bullshit and went on treating his patients just the same. He was working in the lab with the thyrimeter he'd paid for himself, using it to develop a test for phenylketonuria, a genetic condition that Roger suspected caused brain damage, tremors, retardation. He tested the wet diapers of babies until the lab began to stink of urine. Louise threw all her weight against the heavy sash of the window in their basement lab until it budged open, and the two of them continued working in winter coats. They identified fifteen babies out of one hundred with phenylketonuria. He wrote the paper and Louise edited and typed it and it was published in 1971 in *The New England Journal of Medicine*, one of seven papers on genetic abnormalities published over Oetzinger's lifetime.

Although Audrey shared Roger's bed, Louise had become his lab assistant, working by his side, examining patients, depressing tongues, checking throats, tapping knees, and measuring gaits and tremors as he developed his tests, her handwriting growing determined and bold. Roger developed the genetics lab, and the two of them disappeared therein after morning rounds. They tested for epilepsy and enzyme deficiencies with the barest minimum of equipment—the electroencephalograph and his thryimeter. In the end this relationship was more satisfying, Louise thought, than any marriage would have been with its sink of sour dishes and fights over disappointing children.

Despite his comments about how the institution was doomed, Roger, she knew, had a vision of moving it forward, from a patient warehouse to a research center for genetic disorders. Together, they followed the mysterious spikes and slow waves of epilepsy patients on their EEG, tested urine and blood as they waded into the mysterious realm of chromosomes and amino acids and mutating genes.

Then, late in the day, when footsteps above them subsided, Roger would turn to her as she was bending over a microscope, looking at slide after slide of thread-like chromosomes, looking to identify the extra chromozone 21 that identified Downs syndrome children, the tiny scratching like pictographs from an ancient culture—*here is the deer, here is the story of the hunt, here is the story of the boy with the wide-open eyes and the round face who is separated from his family because he has that extra chromosome.* Roger would lift the hair from the back of her neck and kiss her, gooseflesh rising, and she turned back to him and the two of them kissed and began to shuck their off clothes—lab coat here, pants there, folding down nylons—like snakes shedding skins as they moved toward the day bed set up in back for physicians on a long shift.

As the school became more and more overcrowded, staffing became a major problem. Staff quit daily. Positions went unfilled. They had a permanent help-wanted ad running in the Helena newspaper. No one wanted to know exactly how many patients or how many staff there were—to know exact numbers would be too depressing, would put a number on the press of bodies and wants and chaos around them and they would quit too. There was talk among the staff of a strike if the state legislature didn't give raises—and who could blame them? How in the hell, staff was saying, could anyone live on $405 a month?

But no one took it seriously—everyone just thought it was the hippie staff workers trying act tough like the miners in Butte. "And look what happened to them!" Margaret had told them, looking around the table, daring anyone to answer back. "Yeah, sure, the miners won higher wages, and better benefits, and then, two years later, the friggin' mine shut down and left town and where was everyone then?"

But they had a point. Conditions were deplorable. The Helena paper announced that the Stone Home, with its eight hundred patients and only two hundred employees, was a barely controlled free-for-all.

"Principle of Normalization be damned," Roger said when they talked after love-making. "We're talking about children lying on the floors, tied in beds, lolling, wall-eyed on couches, drugged to the gills."

She knew she was part of it—the nurses, the staff, the doctors, they were all part of it. She knew some of the staff—but there was so much turnover that she barely knew many of the new aides—and many were out-of-work miners whose families were starving in Butte, hippies, or cowboys who'd been hurt on the rodeo circuit.

Louise still walked each night to her cabin, but the fields now were choked by weeds or leased out by the neighboring ranchers. She had taken to meeting Anna on Friday nights at her cabin for long-necks and chili because they didn't have time for coffee breaks any more, and they despised the watery coffee and the tasteless food that came out of large striped cans marked "Chili Con Carne" and "Beef Stew," and "Spaghetti with Meatballs." The cabin still had a fireplace, though Anna had been bothering her for months to replace it with a more efficient woodstove.

"Jeez, Louise," Anna said when she came one particularly cold November night—ten below zero. "You'd get a helluva lot more heat in this place if you'd get a woodstove, like my grandma."

"I like my fire," Louise would say. "I like splitting the larch, I like starting the fire, I like that comforting crackle of the fire in the fireplace."

"So did my grandma," she said, peering over her cup at Louise. "Till she got her woodstove and she was actually warm all winter."

"Good chili," Anna said, her spoon scraping the bowl. "Much better than the canned Chill Con Carne, or whatever they call it. I bet they make that stuff with horse meat."

"It's a mystery," Louise said. "Except for the fact that it's bad. Very bad."

Anna scooted the chair closer to the fire. "Louise, I practically have to sit in this fireplace to get warm." She stared at the fire for a minute, then turned to look at Louise, her eyes dark. "You and I have to get out of here."

Louise stood up and put on an eight-track tape: Peggy Lee, "I Go Out Walking."

Anna laughed. "You're changing the subject."

"What would I do, Anna? I'm single, thirty-five, where would I go?"

"You got in your Rambler and drove here, right?" Anna said. "So why not get in your Rambler and drive out?"

"I don't know if I'm that person anymore." A log cracked and split, a spark landing on the braided rug that her mother had hooked for her the previous Christmas, sending it by train with a note, *A little something for your new life. I pray for you daily.* She stamped it out with her foot.

"What're ya waiting for? Roger, for God's sake? Prince Charming?" Anna cocked her head and flashed a grin at Louise. She was the only one that knew about Louise's affair with Dr. O. In staff meetings and around the hospital and cottages, many women adorned themselves in their official roles as conspirators, talking about staff affairs, but the two of them enjoyed this intimacy of knowledge, this understanding of the weighted looks and lingering hands, that offset the days of getting petulant children to wash their faces, sit up, or shit.

"He'll never leave Audrey, you and I know that," Louise said. "And I wouldn't marry him anyway—God what an ego. As for Prince Charming, forget it. That ship has sailed, as they say. Who are you waiting for, Anna?"

"My pilot."

"You're still in touch with him?"

"Occasionally. He's coming back for me."

Louise knew not to press her, but she couldn't ignore the hollow feeling in the pit of her stomach when Anna said that. She loved Anna more like the sister she never had and to see her hurt would kill her. The pilot, she knew, was not coming back. How many white pilots came back to Assiniboine girls they'd met at a dance? How many guys came back, period?

They sat in comfortable silence for a minute, the popping and shifting of the fire between them.

"See that new guy in Spruce? And the other one—in Cottonwood?" Anna said. "Did you see their arms? They have pen-and-ink tattoos, Louise."

Louise shrugged.

"And that guy with a tear tattooed by his eye. You know what that means?"

Louise shook her head.

"Those're yard bird tattoos. That tear means he's killed a guy. A guy in prison. This place is so desperate for staff they are hiring ex-cons now. Those are our new colleagues, Louise. Give me a ranch wife any day with all their holier-than-thou bullshit. Even if they're racist as hell, you can trust 'em not to kill or rape you."

"And that Wilsall idiot? Stealing drugs and trying to sell 'em to staff?" Louise said. "Talk about shitting in his own backyard. After his rehab, he wrote Roger and asked him for a recommendation to work at pharmacy."

"What did Roger say?"

"Whaddya think? He told him to go to hell."

Anna smiled and stared into the fire. "I'm thinking I need to take Mary and Belle and split. They'd be better off on the rez."

"You'd have to get custody."

"Yeah." Anna looked at Louise, her eyes steady. There was a long rip as she tore the label off her beer bottle. "But I'm pretty sure their families don't want them back. And there's a lot of weird shit going on here."

"But what would you do with them on the reservation?" Louise said.

Anna cocked her head at Louise. "Well, miss know-it-all, what is there to do here? Drug them so they behave? Learn manners so if they get adopted they know how to say please and thank-you? Shit. Who in their right mind is going to adopt these kids? Except us? At least on the reservation, they'd be able to run around and ride horses, live some kind of a life. You can't call this a life."

"It's true," Louise said. "I could take Lizzie and go somewhere. I can always get nursing jobs. But she's got parents."

"Yeah?" Anna said.

"Look at me," Louise said. She swept her hand around to indicate her cabin. "I like order. I like neat things. I don't like to live with chaos, in spite of my job. When I leave, I want to come back to quiet, and there isn't a steady man in my life. I'm not the mother type."

"Well, Louise, you can always leave her here and just get in your car and head on out of here and hope like hell she'll be okay."

"Well, we both know the end of that story."

"Right. We don't have a lot of choices here, do we? I go north, you go—well whatever. But shit, Louise, these kids are part of us. You know it. They'll haunt us if we leave 'em. They'll haunt us if we take 'em." Anna nudged a log back into the fireplace, moving it around until the fire caught and sparked again.

"Is that supposed to inspire me?" Louise said.

"I'm not sure," Anna laughed.

The day Belle Star drowned, Louise was sitting in the cafeteria with Anna and Margaret. Margaret was reading the headlines from the *Butte Standard*, discussing how Kennedy had just given U.S. workers the right to collectively bargain, and the new movie *Cleopatra* that was being filmed with Richard Burton and Elizabeth Taylor. The sun slid through the window wells and spilled across the red-checked oilcloth.

Margaret set down the paper and started telling a story: something about a ranch hand she was dating who'd been roughed up in a bar fight last week with another ranch hand known as Stone Face, a Lithuanian from Butte, at the Mint in Stone City. He had two black eyes, a broken nose, and nearly broke his foot and had called Margaret on Sunday to nurse his wounds.

"The idiot," she said. "Fighting in a bar."

"Don't wanna mess with that guy, Stone Face." Anna looked over her coffee cup at Margaret. "He's known throughout Montana. He's got a piece of the devil in 'im."

"I guess they got in some fight over which team was better, the Bulldogs or the Custer County Cowboys—"

The three women started to laugh when Charlene came running in and grabbed Anna's arm. "It's Belle Star. The bath area."

The three of them ran down the hallway and up the stairs, Anna in front of them, her feet quick and light as rain on a tin roof.

There, floating in the claw-foot tub was Belle Star, her long knobby arms and slender legs floating in the water, her black braids snaking around her.

From the next room, a man was crying, explaining to someone that he'd just stepped out of the room for a minute to check on another patient, just one room over, and she must have seized, that was it, poor thing, how would he know, just a minute, just one little fucking minute, and he felt so terrible, terrible, terrible.

Anna leapt on him, clawing at his eyes, *ti okte*, scratching at his face, his ears, his eyes, as he cowered. He tried to protect his head with his arms, to shield his eyes as she swung at him. *Fool, idiot,* she growled. *You left her for a cigarette?*

"Anna," Louise grabbed her by the waist to pull her off the man. Anna swung around and nearly punched her.

"Anna, it's me."

Anna's face was wild. "He killed her, Louise, and he stands there weeping like a kicked dog."

Louise bound her in a hug, holding her as she shook, feeling the largeness of the grief and how it shook the small, wiry woman. The cowboy fell to his knees at her feet, pleading. She turned her head to Margaret, who was running into the room. "Get him out of here."

Belle Star's death was the first of 1973.

"Miss Gustafson!" The voice chilled her blood, following by a pounding on the door.

"Wait, wait." It was Willy, of course, but his voice was all wrong.

She hurried into her robe, disoriented. It was late, nearly one in the morning. Her bare feet flinched as she put them on the ice-cold floorboard.

When she opened the door, she could barely see Willy's face. He was gasping.

"What is it?" Louise said, alarmed. "Come in. Tell me." For a minute, he wouldn't come in, he just stood on the doorstep, gasping, his hands in the pockets of his overalls.

"Please Willy." Louise touched his arm. "It's very cold."

He moved just inside the door so she was able to latch it shut.

He began to cry, terrible tearing sobs as if his heart had been ripped out whole, his back shaking, his face contorted.

"Willy." She went to the bed and grabbed a blanket. She wrapped him up, and led him over to the fireplace. The fire was out, but she'd rebuild it. "Don't talk. Just calm down."

She took a hatchet and cut the larch into strips of kindling, first thin stick-like strips, then wider, ruler-sized pieces. His sobs slowed. She crumpled up paper and stacked up the kindling, tepee-like, around it, and lit a match. The two of them watched as the flame devoured the paper and leapt to the thin, dry sticks of larch.

Willy's sobs were quieter now. His eyes were dark, hollow, his large open face streaked with red. He sat back in the chair, never taking his eyes from the fire.

Louise sat down next to him. She patted his knee.

"Oh, oh, oh," Willy began to moan. "Oh Miss G., I done something awful." He moaned, a sound like an animal caught in a trap. "Oh Miss Louise."

"It's not as bad as you think," Louise said. She sat next to him and put her arm around his shoulder, as he rocked back and forth.

"Oh no, you're wrong about that, Miss Gustafson. It's real bad. Real, real bad. I'm in a mess. I shouldn'ta come to you, I waited real long, and it's real late and I woke you up and I'm in trouble for that too." He put his head down and a tear rolled down his red cheek and dangled off the end of his nose.

"Willard, it's okay. I'm not much of a sleeper anyway. I was just lying there, wishing I could fall asleep. So look—you didn't wake me up anyway."

"That new guy—the one with the eagle on his arm—that guy?" Willy looked at her to see if she recognized the man he was talking about.

"I don't know, Willy. There's so many new guys."

"Well, he's in the Spruce Cottage. And he has to feed the people by himself. Know how many that is? Hunnert and fifty, I counted. Actually, hunnert and fifty-three. So he asks me to help. So I say, sure! I'm Willy."

Louise waited.

"I like to help." Willy was crying again.

Louise folded her hands. The fire popped. She got up and took another log from her wood bin and threw it on the fire, smashing the tepee, the sparks flying out. She took the poker and moved the logs around until they settled into a steady burning.

Willy buried his head in the pillow while she waited for the rest. The fire crackled. The branches of the ponderosa pine knocked against the cabin.

"Well, dammit to hell, anyway!" Willy rose up from the pillow, his face flushed. "That stupid ass Rosa wouldn't eat, says that man with the eagle arm does it better, and she takes a bite. Then she spits it at me. Spits it at me, Miss Gustafson, bite full of spinach, all over my overalls. Then takes another bite, spits it at me, says she won't take food from a retard!"

Dread skittered down Louise's neck.

"So I took the bleepin' spoon and I shoved it down her throat!"

Willy shouted. He was standing up, staring at her. His face was drenched in sweat. "That's what I did, Miss Gustafson! I shoved the spoon down her throat! And she swallowed it and now I don't know what is going to happen." He buried his head in the pillow again, his large round shoulders heaving.

Louise rubbed his back. She grabbed hold of his feet, peeled off his Romeos, set them on the floor, and moved his feet up so that he was lying on the couch. Tears wet her cheeks as she went into her bedroom, opened a trunk and found a comforter, the one her mother had stitched for her hope chest so many years ago for that Blue Earth wedding, brought it back to the living room and covered up Willy.

"What's gonna happen to me, Miss Louise?"

"Don't think about that now, Willy," she said. "You need to rest now. You're a good man, Willy, and I know you didn't mean it. You shouldn't have been put in this situation. You just sleep, go to sleep now."

"I wish I could sleep forever," Willy said. "Like that fairytale." He pulled the comforter to his chin and closed his eyes.

Louise studied his face, red and splotchy from crying, his body a mountain under the comforter, the bright yellow and red tulips so jarring, and wondered what would become of him.

Roger stayed up all night, performing emergency surgeries to try to save Rosa, but the spoon perforated her large intestine, and she died on the operating table.

Willard was sent to isolation, a small windowless room in the basement of the school. Louise visited him when she could manage, reading *Hardy Boy* stories to him while he lay on his cot, his back to her, covered in a nubby army surplus wool blanket. Once in a while, she thought he glanced in her direction, but mostly he lay there, motionless as she read, and when she got up to leave, she could see his face was as grey as the surrounding stone walls, his cheek pressed against the stiff canvas, his eyes closed.

"Willy," she tried to say. "Willy, talk to me."

He would not open his eyes, but he turned his head toward her. "No, Miss Gustafson," he said in a whisper. "There ain't nothing to say."

CHAPTER TWENTY-EIGHT

"Oh moon, high in the deep sky, your light sees faraway places."

The song came back to him long after Mary had been wheeled into the delivery room, and this time he was the man behind the paper watching a new father pacing the room. When did he begin to like opera? Was this Pete's influence? This time he was the one to ask, "First child?" of the clean-shaven young man who couldn't have been more than twenty, who nodded, his Adam's apple bobbing as he swallowed, and Bob invited him to the cafeteria for coffee and pie. "On me," Bob said. They were sitting across from one another, forking up the sour-cherry pie, the kid telling him how he'd rebuilt a 1948 Dodge, when Bob heard his name over the loudspeakers. "Jesus," Bob said. His fork clattered from the table to the floor. "I have to go." "Can I eat your pie?" the young man said, and Bob waved at him as he followed the sound of the page, Robert Carter, Robert Carter, his legs wobbling as he strode across the sea of green linoleum, past nurses' stations, doctors with white coats and flapping stethoscopes and the swooping grey nuns, the back of his throat acid.

Cecil was there, waiting.

He crooked his finger at Bob.

Cecil had on another bolo tie, an arrowhead, perched on the braided leather by two silver prongs. Bob walked up next to him. The edges of the room fluttered, the aqua cushions on the sofa wavering like a dream, the lights dimming.

Cecil steadied him, slipping his arms under Bob's armpits. "Whoa, soldier. You're a little unsteady."

Bob shook his head. "I'm shaking it off."

"It's all good," Cecil said. "All good. Sit down a minute, put your head between your knees."

The blood pressed against his temples, dimming the sounds of the doors whooshing open and shut, till a high ringing sound started in his ears. It's all good. All good, he thought to himself. I am going to lift myself up and walk myself into the delivery room. It is all good. The doors opening and shutting. The quiet broken by that one note. A clarinet. Yes, clarinet. The slow, dreamy rhythms of Benny Goodman playing "Moonglow." Then the thrumming, the pounding, the insane pounding of the drums, the vibes, the horns, the mad incessant notes then heart-pounding pauses of "One O'Clock Jump." He snapped up his head.

He sat up, shook himself awake, the music gone now to that place where music disappears, and he was sitting in a waiting room, facing Cecil. "Okay, Doctor Babcock. Let's go now."

The two of them walked down that corridor of linoleum. Voyage of discovery, my friend, Bob remembered saying, and Cecil laughed and Bob was just trying to keep himself together as he walked that unending green linoleum mile.

At the bassinet marked Carter, Bob paused. Cecil patted him on the back. "It's okay, friend," he said. Bob peered over the edge to see her head, a round head. The skin, a delicate pink, the color of the inside of a seashell. Bow-shaped lips. Fingers so tiny and blue with their clear nails and creases. Eyes round. Clear and blue as a glacial lake. Limbs, toes. The nurse wound her in a flannel blanket, tucking the end in over her feet, then wrapping each side around her tightly. She handed her to Mary, who leaned forward from the hospital bed to receive the cocooned child. Mary with her black hair fanning out on the white pillow behind her. He scooted in the bed beside her.

"You did it," Bob whispered. "We have a beautiful new daughter."

"She's so beautiful." He stroked her downy head, her pink cheeks. "So tiny."

"She knows your voice," Mary said. "See how she looks toward you when you speak?"

"Hold her," Mary added.

"Really? She terrifies me."

Mary laughed. "Bob. She's an infant."

"I'll break her."

"No you won't."

She sat up. "Cradle your arms. Now pick her up. You'll be fine now. You have to get used to it. We're parents now." She reached over to the bassinet to pick up the baby and hand it to him. "You ready?"

Bob reached out for the bundle. Blood seemed to rush through him. As Mary transferred the baby into his arms, he felt the weight of her as solid and light at once. "'Bout the weight of a good-sized rainbow."

"The weight of a rainbow? What does a rainbow weigh?"

"The trout, silly," Bob said.

"Good God." Mary laughed and looked up at the baby, who

tipped her eyes toward Bob.

"Down in the meadow in a little bitty pond," Bob sang. "Swam two little fishies and the momma fishy too. Swim said the momma fishy, swim if you can, and they—"

Mary chimed in—"swam and they swam right over the dam!"

Bob stopped. The room blurred, the view out the window a riot of red and orange maple trees, the leaves stirring and rustling in the wind, dissolving into a galaxy of color and movement. It was as if the old world of streets and sky and trees had collapsed inside himself and, as he sat on the white cotton blanket with his wife and daughter in this large brick hospital, a new self was coming forward. When the nurse came for him to sign the birth certificate, he filled in his name, Robert Carter, and the baby's birthdate, October 4, 1956.

When the nurse handed it back to him and showed him his mistake, he laughed. She took out a new birth certificate. This time he wrote: Elizabeth Rose Carter, October 4, 1956.

Mary looked at him. "Elizabeth? Really?"

He looked dreamily over at her. "And they swam and they swam right over the dam."

"Look at me, Robert," she said. "Two Elizabeths? You want to do this?"

He looked at her. "I want to start over. This is my baby. Elizabeth Rose Carter."

"I guess you know what you are doing, Robert," Mary said. "Am I right?"

"This is our family now," he said.

His next daughter was nearly born on the hospital lawn. Mary's contractions came on hard and fast, and Bob wondered if the neighbors could hear her cry out through the windows, open for a cross breeze. After several hours, it was Mary this time who suggested they called the babysitter for Elizabeth. He called Mary's friend at two o'clock in the morning, "Mary Nell, this is Bob. And this is the time!"

"Well," the male voice said before he hung up. "This is not Mary Nell. And this is, most definitely, not the time."

Bob dialed Mary Nell's phone number, saying each number out loud as he put his finger in the telephone dial. She arrived minutes later and Bob and Mary packed off to the hospital. At the reception desk, where the nurses were asking for his name and his address and his telephone number and what his occupation was, Mary was holding her stomach.

"I hate to be a bother," she said, her face flushed. "But this baby's coming."

"And your insurance?" the nurse was asking.

"I'm sorry, but my wife is having a baby right now."

"Well, we need your insurance number. We need your place of business."

"You need to get moving and get her to a delivery room," Bob said. "Unless you want her to give birth in your waiting room."

Mary's groans were deep and frightening. The nurse scuttled off to get someone, and when Cecil came in, he took one look at Mary, at her body wracked by a new, harder contraction as she twisted in the wheelchair. "We have to get her in the delivery room right now," he said to Bob. He scowled at the receptionist. "What were you thinking?"

"The manager said I need all the information."

"Get it later, girl," Cecil said. "This woman nearly had her baby in your waiting room."

The doors to the delivery room swished shut behind them and, approximately forty-five minutes later, Karen Rose Carter was born, August 1, 1958.

"Chattanooga Choo-choo." "Take the A-Train." "Sophisticated Lady." The songs no longer ran through Bob's head, but he played them on the stereo on weekends as he played bear with his girls. It was a simple game where he lay on the floor of the living room and they ran past him and he tried to catch them, he the bear, they the young Rose Red and Snow White, and he'd growl and they'd squeal and sometimes he'd miss them and sometimes he'd catch Elizabeth with her braids and round legs or petite Karen with her red hair and brown glasses and he'd hug them tight as they giggled and cried to be let go.

And then came the long, blessed years of Normal. Nursery rhymes: "Mary, Mary, quite contrary"; "Ashes, ashes, they all fall down." The kindergarten plays. Measles, mumps, and chicken pox. The chalked hopscotches on the front sidewalk. The playhouse in the backyard. The walk to first grade. The report cards with S's for Satisfactory and S+s for Satisfactory plus. The school plays. The princesses. The witches. The endless shopping for dresses, ballet costumes, dress-up clothes; games at night after dinner, the plates cleared, Mary in the kitchen washing the dishes, and, over the clink of pottery against the metal sink, he and Karen and Elizabeth laying out the cards for Concentration or Hearts or, his least favorite, the board game Sorry! The stumbling piano recitals. The choir concerts in stifling gymnasiums. The report cards: "Your daughter Elizabeth is an outstanding..." and "I have been delighted to have your daughter Karen..." The church potlucks in the dim basement, Homebuilders their group was called, with the endless scalloped potatoes and beans and weenies, the kids running wild in the church, racing through classrooms and tiled hallways and shooting across the aisle of the church like comets. The camping trips to Avalanche Campground in Glacier National Park, where Karen stood over the campfire, in red braids, banging a skillet, because that's what they told her to do if she saw a bear, and Bob said, "Karen, knock it off," and she said, "Dad, bear!" and he turned and saw that she was right, it was a bear, a black bear, lumbering right toward their campsite, held off by a six-year-old redhead in pigtails banging a cast-iron skillet. The Christmas tree expeditions, all of them grumbling and whining in the car until they reached the forest west of town and hiked among the snow-hushed trees, Karen and Elizabeth, flushed and red-cheeked, saying, "This one, Dad? No! This one!" until he finally said, "Okay, this will be our tree," and they all hushed and accepted his judgment. And bridge parties, Karen and Elizabeth perched on the stairs, peeking out at the guests at their card tables with the seasonal bridge tallies—autumn leaves, Easter eggs—Mary turning the card shuffler, the cards shooting out willy-nilly, and their guests seated and sipping Sanka as he set a record on the spinning turntable and pushed a button and the arms came down and there was the scratchy pause as the needle fit into the grooved plastic and then the horns started up and the war was won and the world was right and it was Glen Miller playing "Tuxedo Junction," the slow, swinging rhythms, the bright horns, as he, Bob, stood by the maple record cabinet, his pointer finger in the air, saying, "Just listen to those horns, will you?" He added, his voice thick. "Hear that rhythm? Hear that?" And his guests never seemed to hear or feel it deeply enough.

In the middle of all that was his mother's death, Bob visiting her in a nursing home at Christmas. She had never seen Lizzie again. She was nearly unconscious, her speech slurred from the Lithium, as he held her hand, the lights from the tiny plug-in tree blinking red, green, and yellow on the white sheets. "Take care of your girls. All of your girls" as she stared at him, making a point, before she closed her eyes to sleep and that night she'd died. Even at the last, he thought, she had the ability to stick the knife in. Ah mother.

And Louise Gustafson, the nurse, kept up her correspondence, telling him how old Elizabeth was, what she weighed, and how she was slowly learning her ABC's, wasn't that great, and could he send more clothes, they were always so short—dresses and underpants and socks—and for extras like shampoo and soap, always so welcome, Mr. Carter. He always hid the letters on his desk until another one came, Mr. Robert Carter, in that slanted, precise handwriting that seemed to pierce his heart with dread, Mr. Robert Carter, can you please? And he would finally get out the Sears catalog and order underwear, socks, and a few dresses, hoping that this would make Louise Gustafson go away for a while.

The 1960s rolled in with a New Year's party at Dick Anderson's. Cecil and Arnie and their wives were there, but there were a lot of men and their wives that Bob and Mary didn't recognize, drinking martinis and laughing at Dick's new wet bar in the basement, and when Bob met up with Arnie in the narrow hallway in the basement, Bob said, "I think we're in with the jet set, Arnie, I don't know any of these people."

"High rollers," Arnie Brechbill said. "I may bankroll their houses, but man, they're out of our league, my friend. But fun, don't you think?" he nodded at the woman leaning over the punchbowl in a tightly fitting red silk dress with a plunging neckline, while Mary, next to her, looked a bit schoolmarmish in her wide-skirted dress with the Peter Pan collar.

"Too rich for my blood," Bob said, as several couples began to dance, two by two, on the floor, Cecil and his wife among them, to

Glen Miller's "In the Mood," the trombones so mellow, so sassy, Bob thought.

"C'mon," Mary came up and tugged his sleeve. "It's Glen Miller, Bob. Your favorite. This is your chance, Bob."

"Dancing," he said. His heart sank. As much as he loved the music, he was a terrible dancer, but this was their joke: he attended so many dances to keep Mary to himself in college, that she had made the mistake of thinking that he liked to dance. He loathed it: awkward, clumsy, all left feet. Nevertheless, he set down his drink and took Mary over to the floor and held her in his arms and they began to waltz in time to the music, Bob holding her hand, stopping every once in a while to conduct, until Dick came over and said, "Bob, you are wasting this beautiful woman," and he grabbed Mary and spun her away from him, and danced her around the room, his movements graceful and athletic, Mary fitting in his arms as they spun about the other couples, and Bob had the sinking knowledge that there would always be men like this—more dashing, more dramatic—as he stood patiently off to the side, waiting for the music to end.

Two days later, Dick's wife came to him at his office at noon, when the secretary was out for lunch. Her face was red, wrenched in misery, unrecognizable, her hands shaking. "It's his drinking," she said, when Bob had settled her in the chair across from his desk with a cup of coffee. Tears streamed down her face. "He's out all hours. When he gets back, he's—well—he's not very nice, I'll put it like that. Good God, Bob. We have four kids, now. He's good at making them, hell he's good at supporting them."

"What can I do? Do you want me to talk with him?" Bob said. "I'm happy to, Marilyn. He loves his family. He loves you, I know."

"It's too late." She looked him in the eye. "I'm leaving. I'm taking my kids and I'm going back to Wisconsin and getting a divorce. I can't live like this, Bob. I don't know how I'm going to support myself, but between alimony and prayers and maybe some teaching, I hope I can keep our family together. I wanted to tell you because I think you're a good man and Dick looks up to you, but he's a drunk and he's not very good to me, and I just want you—someone here in this town—to know why I left."

"Can't you give him another chance?" Bob said. "Try AA? Dick's a good man."

She set her cup on the desk. "I don't mean to be rude. But honestly, Bob. What universe do you live in?"

CHAPTER TWENTY-NINE

She found his name in the newspaper articles about the strike at the Stone Home in 1974. He was the outspoken doctor and a former head of the Stone Home for the Mentally Retarded, who took the governor of Montana to task for his shameful treatment of the patients, staff, and doctors at the woefully underfunded institution. Finding his number was a breeze: she simply called information and there he was. Calling him was something else entirely. For a week, she stared at the number, but when she tried to pick up the phone and dial it, she simply froze. She called once and an elderly man said hello and she hung up.

She steeled herself by pretending it was just any old interview. She would just write out the questions and he would just give her the answers. Easy as pie, she told herself, you've done this time and time again. She called, scheduled an interview, and put down the phone, marveling at the man's gravelly voice. Roger Oetzinger. Dr. Roger Oetzinger.

She decided she would show up as Elizabeth Blake.

She followed the Clark Fork River through the Sapphire Mountains up over the Divide, and then headed north and over MacDonald Pass, where she'd read that the pilot Cromwell Dixon had been the first to fly a plane over the Continental Divide to a bonfire at the pass and back again to cheering crowds at the Helena Fairgrounds. She descended to the gully town of Helena and continued south, to Stone City. The Stone River was rising, the water dark and turbulent with snowmelt, the cottonwoods greening out in new leaves, the hills dotted with yellow balsamroot and purple lupine. This was the time of the quickening. This was the time, after the soul-baring winter, when the world was stripped into simplicity, everything seemed to burst forth again: color, scent, movement. The time of year when she felt as if she'd come out of a long slumber, and she wanted to go beyond the smallness of winter. Was that faith? Not exactly. It was survival, but something that could be substituted for faith. One foot in front of the other, until one day you looked up and you had moved beyond the sadness of that lost child, that empty place in the womb that had each day swallowed you anew, until like Jonah you lived in it, constructed a whole life inside its whale-like sadness.

As she drove she could still feel the sorrow stitching the edges of her heart. She could feel it, but she could also feel its boundaries. That was different.

She wanted to *move*.

She wanted to unearth this story about her sister, to tease apart the strands that bound her to her sister's story. She also wanted to tease apart the strands of that other story, that story her mother and father had locked away with this child and chosen not to tell, as if they could calve off this part of their lives like ice shearing off a glacier.

Dr. Roger Oetzinger, eighty-nine years old, lived in a Quonset hut overlooking the Stone Home, the hospital where he had worked for forty years before being fired by one of the most liberal governors in the state of Montana.

She was going to introduce herself by her pseudonym—Elizabeth Blake—but after she'd knocked on the door and his son answered, and she ducked in the low-beamed entrance, and the doctor rolled his wheelchair up to her, his shock of white hair, his eyes bright behind his black glasses, her mind went blank. She held out her hand and said, "Elizabeth Carter."

His eyes flashed with recognition, but he said nothing. He held out his hand and she shook it.

He knew who she was—she was sure of it—the sister of the Elizabeth Carter who had been a patient there. But she didn't want to acknowledge this or she would fall into a pit she might never come out of. She wanted to focus, instead, on what had happened.

Dr. Oetzinger's son shook her hand and offered her a cup of coffee.

She took it, but her hand trembled so much, she had to set it down to keep the coffee from spilling.

In the kitchen, long windows overlooked raised garden beds of shriveled tomato and cucumber vines. The son was frying something at the stove, the room fragrant with the smell of oil and meat. The two of them sat at a long, wooden table, made, Dr. Oetzinger told her, by one of his sons. She looked around the room, decorated by several elk trophies, their glass eyes shining.

"Are you warm enough, Dad?" the son asked.

"Fine," Dr. Oetzinger said. His son brought him a plate of venison sausage. He offered a plate to her, the oily sausage rolling a bit on the turquoise-blue pottery.

She thanked him and took the plate he offered, and started to eat.

The meat was so rich and salty and gamey it turned her stomach. She forced herself to eat a few bites. "Delicious," she said.

"My boys make it every year," the doctor said. "Every year they get their deer and elk and they make their own sausage and jerky."

She took out her pen and paper and began asking him questions about his history at the Stone Home.

Dr. Oetzinger told her about coming to the Stone Home for the Feeble-Minded in the early 1940s, directly from his medical residency at UCLA. When he first arrived, he told her, the head nurse conducted "Sick Time" each Sunday night. The patients lined up in the parlor of the old brick building in front of a long mahogany dinner table where the head nurse stood at the ready, and she would ask them, "Where does it hurt?" The patients would point to whatever hurt—stomach, head, elbow—and the head nurse pulled out a bottle of mercurochrome—did she know what mercurochrome was?—and with a plastic wand she painted the spot red.

"Sick Time," he laughed, "as you might imagine, ended soon after I arrived. As did her career. These people had cancer. Bad teeth. Broken bones, and she was healing them with *mercurochrome*? She never forgave me."

He told her about the increase in the patient population at the Stone Home, from 30 in 1892 to 990 in 1974. He told her about the staff strike of 1974, how they deliberated, how they had tried to live off the measly $405 a month the legislature appropriated, and when they couldn't and they wanted to come to Helena to testify about needing better salaries and the terrible conditions in the homes, the legislature prohibited them time off to come to Helena to testify about what was happening at the home until children started dying, and then—fucking idiots, he said—they woke up and started blaming *them*, the staff and doctors, the very people who had been there all along, for the filth and the degradation and overcrowding when they had denied them funding all those years!

"To us, all of us who'd devoted our lives to these kids, it was worse than a slap in the face," he said. "It was sheer cruelty."

He took a drink of coffee and set the cup down on the table. He was warming to his story, describing how the staff struck and how, in his words, that asshole governor, Roy Brown, sent in the National Guard after he'd promised he wouldn't, and the guardsmen were so sweet, so caring, telling a newspaper reporter that this was harder than any combat duty they'd seen.

"What about the farm, where they worked and grew all their food?" Elizabeth asked him. "I heard they were completely self-sufficient."

"Slave labor!" Oetzinger said, his face reddening. "They worked 'em to death. Seven days a week. And this place—no basic cleanliness… it was, excuse me miss, a shit factory." He described how the feces-covered laundry was collected and piled up in a laundry truck, then clean laundry was reloaded back into the same truck. "Massive dysentery, and they wondered where it came from. Jesus."

"What about the families?" she said.

"What about the families?" he said. He looked at her, his eyes dark. He stared at her, waiting. Again, she knew he recognized her. This was the moment. She could say, *My sister was here. My father and mother brought her here. Tell me about her.*

She couldn't do it. What was wrong with her? The room wobbled. She couldn't break some invisible wall that was freezing her mind, body, mouth, making the room expand far away from her, making this man and this room filled with the heads of dead animals seem as if she were seeing it through the wrong end of a telescope. She was flushed and sweaty. Singed with shame.

Shit, what was she going to do now, cry?

"Did families visit the kids?" she finally choked.

"Some came to see kids. Some visited on a regular basis. Some picked up their kids every summer and brought them back in the fall, though honestly I think that was worse. Some never came at all. Many of the patients became very attached to staff." His face grew distant. "There were all kinds of kids from all kinds of families. A senator's kid. Indian kids. Shit, kids from some of the wealthiest families in Montana. Several staff even adopted them. Wonderful people, the staff. Wonderful."

He sighed. The light dimmed.

"You know, if you really want to pursue this, you ought to find one of my old nurses. Shit. What's her name?" He closed his eyes and held still, waiting as if for a word to flash on the dark screen of his memory. "Louise," he said. "Louise Gustafson. Came in the 50s. Great person. Don't even know if she's alive. But she really looked after 'em. She really did."

A heater came on somewhere and fans started blowing. He reached beside him and pulled out a sheaf of papers stapled together, page after page meticulously typed with dates, times, names and places, along with photographs of doctors, occasional patients, his children, fossils he'd collected. She wondered when—with his work and children—he had time to do this. "I saved this for you," he said. "It's my journal. I wrote everything. I want you to have it."

She looked at him.

"Tell the truth about all this," he said. "You're a writer."

"I'm a journalist."

"Well then," he looked at her, his eyes glittering. "Even better."

She headed north from Stone City to Great Falls, winding through the spectacular narrow canyons carved by the Missouri River and threaded by eagles. The highway rose up and up until it opened onto the plains, and the openness was startling, revelatory. She was on her way to meet Karen, her sister. She had to tell her about Stone City, Dr. Oetzinger, the newspaper pieces, the strikes. The drive was a tonic, the smooth buff-colored plains whipping by, the steady flow of semis loaded with round bales of hay, the stock trucks and pickups.

They met for drinks at the Sip 'N Dip in the Bel-Air Motel in Great Falls, a 1960s motel built like a bunker with underground parking, a glassed-in restaurant, and a turquoise-colored Tiki bar. There were no windows. They didn't build bars with windows in this part of the world because, in winter, Elizabeth mused, you didn't want to look out. You wanted to get away from the prairie blizzards and cold and, in this town, the endless wind that scattered leaves and branches and people without mercy, you wanted to gather to forget what you could as you listened to Piano Pat, the amazing septuagenarian pianist, play "Stormy Weather" and as hefty mermaids dipped and dove through the chlorinated motel swimming pool visible through a window in the bar, beating the water into a froth, blowing kisses at their equally hefty bar patrons.

Karen was at a high-top table. She'd been in town doing the monthly grocery shopping that she'd take back to Choteau the next day.

"Are you mad at me?" She looked at Karen, her back straight as she sat at the high-top table with her straight red hair pulled back into a smooth ponytail, so petite and slender in her boot-cut jeans, a down vest, and a baseball cap, the gold cross at her neck. Elizabeth could see several men at the bar studying her. Next to her, Elizabeth, in leggings and a long pumpkin-colored shirt, felt large and lumpish.

"Of course not!" Karen said. "I could never be mad at you. I'm sorry I sounded mad on the phone. The kids were driving me wild and I guess I was snapping."

Karen read the Xeroxed copies of the articles that Elizabeth had handed her. "Oh my stars," she kept whispering. "Unbelievable."

The mermaids were doing the sidestroke, light glancing off their water goggles. Elizabeth lifted her beer to them. They lifted their hands, in unison, in a mock toast.

"God, I wonder if any of these are pictures of her," Karen said, looking at the black-and-white photos of children lying on sofas, on the floor.

"Want another beer?"

"Absolutely," Karen said.

One of the mermaids looked over, smiling, and somersaulted in the water. Then she pressed her palms together and floated upward, smiling.

Karen scowled. "Those mermaids are beginning to really annoy me right now. I want them to just go away."

"They're like very large tropical fish," Elizabeth said.

"Great Falls sea life, I guess." Karen scowled and looked down at the newspaper pictures of children lying on the floor, tied up in chairs. "God." Her eyes filled with tears. "To do this to children." She was silent for a minute, turning her wedding ring around and around.

The larger mermaid sidestroked by again.

"It's horrible."

Karen folded up the paper and set her beer on top of it. She turned in the bar stool, her red hair brushing her collarbone, her dark eyes frank. "Listen, Elizabeth. I'm glad we know about her. And you're an amazing reporter. I think you should do what you want and all—and you've done an amazing job of finding all this—but don't get stuck here, stirring all this up. You have your own life. You're going to have another child, you wait and see—I've been praying about it. Mom and Dad—they were so good to us. Maybe this was a trial they had to endure so that we could have the wonderful childhood we had. They gave us everything."

"I know," Elizabeth toyed with her beer, watching the gold liquid slosh from side to side. "I feel like a shit going into this. But I'm a reporter, Karen. This is what I do. I need to find out about this. She was one of us. She's our sister. And she had this horrible life. Doesn't that bother you?"

"I think Dad did what he thought was best," Karen said as she tore neat strips up the edge of a cocktail napkin that stated, *Our local brands and we're proud of 'em!* The napkin showed the mixture of letters and symbols that comprised Montana cattle brands: *the Quarter Circle U, the Lazy J, the Pitch Fork, the Circle C.*

Karen was such a lovely woman, Elizabeth thought, so secure in her world, her children, her husband, and she deeply envied her sister's calm knowledge of herself and her easy comfort within the bounds of her world.

"I'm not saying he didn't," Elizabeth said. "But what he always thought best was to keep everything a secret. Which meant that it belonged to him. To him and to Mom. Well, guess fucking what? It isn't just theirs, Karen. She's our family too. They never thought about that."

"Well, maybe you should leave this alone," Karen was on the second side of the napkin. "I mean, I've got my girls to think about, you are going to have another baby, and you've got your job. This is just going to drag us all down. I mean really?"

"Really what?" Elizabeth was annoyed again. Karen was sometimes so smug, so unwilling to be rocked by anything outside herself.

"Well, this isn't just you it's affecting, now, is it?" Karen said.

"What about me? What about my family? Did you ever wonder if we want to be part of this? Have you thought about Tom?"

"Tom knows all about this," Elizabeth said. "He's the first person I told. At least he's behind me."

Karen's eyes teared. "It's not that I'm not behind you." She crumpled the napkin. "I'm sorry. I just feel I have to be honest."

"Karen." Elizabeth put her hand on her sister's to stop her from tearing more paper. "She's our family. And what's more, she has my name. Mom and Dad gave her my name. How weird is that?"

Karen zipped up her vest.

"Don't go," Elizabeth said. "Please don't go. You're gonna go mad and that'll break my heart. Look, I don't know what I'm doing here, I just feel like this is something I have to do and it's upended my life, and who I thought we were as a family, and I can't let it alone. You're my only family now, Karen," she said. "Please don't go."

Karen sat down, cradling her head in her hands. Elizabeth wondered if she were praying. Piano Pat was beginning to launch into a medley of songs: "Sophisticated Lady," "It Don't Mean a Thing," and "In the Mood." She lifted her head to look at Elizabeth. "Duke Ellington. Dad would have loved this," she sighed. "I miss him," she said. She touched Elizabeth's hand. "Sometimes I just wish I could hear his voice again."

"I do too," Elizabeth said. "There's so much I want to ask him."

CHAPTER THIRTY

January 25, 1974, a young girl was locked out of her cottage and froze to death outside, her fingers leaving claw marks on the door frame.

February 1, a paraplegic patient wound up pregnant, father unknown, though, Louise noted, a young intern was quickly transferred to a hospital in New Mexico.

It was as if they were under a curse and the bad news just kept spilling forth, each day darkening into the next. Every major newspaper in the state descended on the Stone Home, reporters arriving daily with their notebooks, pens, and questions, and leaving with headlines: "Grey Lives, Abandoned Hopes at the Stone Home" (*Butte Standard*) and "Who Is Minding Our Children?" (*Helena Independent*). Legislative committees from Helena conducted investigations and issued reports about the abhorrent care of the mentally retarded and the miserable or nonexistent training of the staff. Legislators, doctors, and investigators drove from Helena in their shiny cars and suits, whisking in with their notebooks and recorders and their air of breezy importance. They tried not to retch at the urine-soaked hallways and feces-ridden laundry room and Cottage Two with its torn insulation, splintered furniture, half-naked men. They clicked on their pens, wrote notes, and then clicked them off again, the women put their gloved hands on Louise's or Anna's arm, looking at them with long, sad eyes and whispering, "You are doing such important work," which really meant, "How in the world can you stand it?"

It was if the world had just discovered them.

How do you think eight hundred children arrived here in the first place? Louise wanted to spit back at them. *Who thought this was a great place to raise kids?*

She wanted to stop the reporters with their glasses and earnest scribblings, the women with their coiffed hair, the men with their smooth-shaved faces who took their tours and shook their heads then headed down the road to the nearest supper club for a steak and a martini to literally shake the stink off. *Jesus Christ, know what I did today? Do you know how those poor people live?*

The staff didn't know what to think. Their lives, which had been ignored and abandoned, were suddenly exposed and pitied. All of them, patient and staff alike, portrayed in black-and-white Helvetica with merciless, relentless, shaming pity or, worse, blamed.

"Can you describe the life here?" a young reporter asked her, his notebook poised between them, as he looked around Spruce Cottage, scribbling notes. She could only imagine what he scribbled: the first thing that strikes you is the smell: a heady pastiche of urine and disinfectant. The second, the noise: children laughing, screaming, crying, the nurses trying to play a clapping game in the back, another asking if anyone has seen Michael?

How to tell him how hard they worked—when this was all he could see. Louise looked out at the sixty children ranging in age from ten to fourteen: kids tied to chairs, kids strapped in beds. How to describe a life here? "Many of us have cared for these children for much of our lives. We have had long relationships with many of these children, with some of them since birth. It is more complicated than it appears."

The young man thanked her and moved on to interview Dr. O.

She pulled a reporter from the *Great Falls Tribune* aside. "You need to spend more time here; you need to experience these kids," she said. To another, she said, "You are targeting us—the caregivers—as if we are responsible for the bad conditions and the smell and the lousy food. You know who you need to blame? The legislature. Ask them why don't they fund this place? Why have they allowed this to happen? These kids are all of our responsibility."

"You have a good point," the reporter said, looking her earnestly in the face. He wrote a few things down and moved on.

The story about who was responsible for these children wasn't the story of the hour. The story of the hour was about forgotten children, sent down here, mistreated, locked up, put out of sight, their feces covered up in their beds each night because the staff had no time to change them, dirty and clean linens trucked back and forth to the laundry in Butte in the same trucks week after week until pretty much everyone—staff and patients all—had dysentery. Patients drugged to the gills because there wasn't enough staff to watch after them. Those were the stories on the front pages of the state newspapers and on the TV news journals. Not stories about nurses in white shoes with flat rubber soles, working their brains out.

By February, the staff was ready to strike. Matt Steele, an organizer from the Local 500 in Butte, stood on a table in the cafeteria underneath a long line of new fluorescent lights that lent an unreal, watery glow to the room. Yes, he told the assembled staff members, it was true President Kennedy had given federal workers the right of collective bargaining. Yes, it was true that as members of the union of state workers they had a right to voice their demands at the current legislative session in Helena. But this was the latest: in the wake of staff unrest, Roy Brown, the recently elected democratic governor, had issued a "stay away" order stating that any staff that missed work to testify before the legislature would be fired.

The room grew silent.

Louise felt her heart clench.

"You need this raise," he told them, looking over this crowd of people, their hands weather beaten, rough, capable. Louise looked at Anna, Margaret, and Charlene: she'd known them since she'd arrived nearly ten years ago. The large number of ranch women and daughters dressed in slacks and housedresses, the men who'd just been doing farm work, the few miners who came down from Butte, leaning against the walls in the back: there were faces she didn't recognize, but many she had known for years. They could barely afford to pay their rent and buy groceries each month.

"Did you know," the union organizer said, "you are among the most poorly paid state workers in the nation? How does that make you feel?"

There was shuffling, a few shouts.

Finally, a man in the back shouted, "Like cow dung. That's what."

"Yeah," the crowd shouted.

"You said it, Mike," a man next to Louise hollered, his voice thick, his face red.

"Did you know that the cost of living in the state is $25 a month higher than what you make? How does that make you feel?"

"Hungry!" someone else answered.

Everyone laughed.

One of the large hands from Cottage Two said, "You tell those fat asses, Matt," then he looked to Louise, Anna, and some of the other female staffers and bowed slightly. "Excuse my French, ladies!"

"Bet those fat cats don't live on $400 a month!" shouted Margaret, her face red, her grey braids swinging like bell pulls.

The organizer rolled up his sleeves. "You watch, people. This is our time." He leaned into the crowd, the light flicking gold from the hairs of his forearms. "Stone City, Hot Springs, we're joining together, and there's power there, people! We'll get our raise."

At the second organizational meeting, Matt stood on the table, hands on his hips, as the men in the room studied his boots. Workman's boots. He was an organizer, but by trade, a pipefitter.

He held up his hand. The room was silent.

"Yes, we have a pay raise. We have a pay raise, retroactive to January 1, signed into law by our governor and our fine state legislators."

Someone began to hoot, but he held up his hand again.

Margaret stood next to him on the table, her arms crossed, looking at him.

Something was up, Louise thought.

"State workers at the institutions were given a monthly pay raise of… $30."

"Huh!" someone said.

One of the ranch hands said, "Well of all the goddamn lousy things I ever heard of—"

Then everyone started to talk at once as if an electrical current had just zapped the room, the voices rising and falling, in short charged sentences.

Matt held up his hand again. "That's what I thought you'd think. Shall we tell the Montana Legislature and their governor they can take this raise and shove it?"

Louise watched the men from Cottage Two, the nurses who worked in the day nursery, the Junior Hall, the five different cottages so packed with kids they could barely control them, the kitchen staff, the office staff, the grounds men. It was the men from Cottage Two who began stomping their feet and shouting, "Strike! Strike!"

"Shall we tell this governor, and this legislature, that the work we do is some of the hardest in Montana? That the conditions are sub-human? Unsafe? Unsanitary! And that we want change now?"

The room exploded with cheers. Louise watched a large ranch woman grab one of the Cottage Two men and twirl him around. Several of the cowboys who helped Margaret in Junior Hall started yodeling. A large burly man jumped on another table and held his hands out to get others to clap. "Yes, yes, yes!" the crowd chanted, and he crossed his legs and squatted, thrusting one leg, then the other out in front of him doing his best imitation of a Russian Cossack dance until the table leg cracked and Margaret came over and told him, for God's sake, she'd institutionalize him if he didn't come to his senses and get off the goddamn table.

Louise stamped her feet along with everyone, even though she knew that she and her other nurse friends and doctors would be filling in for the staff during the strike, even though she knew that it meant the beginning of even more chaos. How in the world would their tiny group of sixty-five nurses and one doctor possibly keep everyone under control? But things were moving so fast right now that what else could she do?

Across the hall, she could see Audrey, Roger's wife, standing in the doorway, pregnant again, her fourth, her arms resting against her white wool maternity dress, her face lit with a peculiar light that Louise would remember as a mixture of curiosity and dread.

She made a fire that night in her fireplace, watching the tepee of kindling crash down into the flaming paper, holding her hands out to the heat, letting the sound of the crackling fill her. Where was all of this going to take her? she wondered. Back to Blue Earth? She shuddered. Not a chance. She looked over at the grim-faced picture of her mother and felt a door in her heart slam shut again. *Seize the day.* Where had she heard that? Her mother had died a year ago, and she'd taken the train, arriving in time for the funeral at the windblown church, where the pastor's words reminded her of those long, bleak summers in Blue Earth—how could words from worlds away be as bleak as the Minnesota prairie?—and as soon as she was able, she settled her mother's affairs and headed back to Montana. She looked at the flame licking the paper, the clean split larch, the way the flame flickered yellow with a heart of blue and green.

What would happen to Lizzie?

That day Roger and the nurses met to split up the patient files. "This is the time," Roger said, "when we've got to return these children. They've got to go back to their families, however temporarily. This system is failing. This is it. This is the apocalypse." They'd split up the files among them. A letter went out from Dr. Oetzinger and the hospital director to all the parents, including Lizzie's.

> *January 15, 1974*
> *Dear Mr. Carter,*
>
> *I am writing concerning your daughter, Elizabeth Carter. She has been a patient of mine since 1954. She is a very*

sweet girl, likes to sing, enjoys swinging. She experiences seizures frequently, sometimes once a week, and is a level II Down syndrome child, which means that she has been able to learn her letters and some basic words. We had put her on Luminal, but changed her medications to the more currently used Dilantin, and her affect is greatly improved.

But I am writing to you about events currently facing the Stone Home for the Mentally Retarded. We will shortly be facing a strike and we cannot guarantee the safety of your daughter now or in the future. It would be best if you could come and pick her up at your earliest convenience.

Sincerely, Dr. O

CHAPTER THIRTY-ONE

From the front room, Bob could see the tall alpine fir Mary had set up in the living room. It was a beautiful room, he thought, with its lush green velvet sofa and Oriental rug, and the Christmas tree, its branches drooping with tear-shaped bulbs and ornaments. Mary had done the work, stringing the branches with colored lights and shiny red and green bulbs, miniature knit stockings, and crocheted stars from the Methodist ladies' craft fair, a few antique angels and a hand-painted glass Santa Claus that had somehow survived being handed down through his family. He walked into the dining room where the long oak table that had belonged to his grandmother Carter, that had been sent all the way from St. Louis, Missouri, to Fort Benton on a paddleboat and then carried by mule to Bridger, was laden with ham, scalloped potatoes, carrot Jell-O salads, and Spritz cookies that Karen and Elizabeth had made, swearing and laughing at the cookie press each time they turned the crank at the top and the lid popped off and small white dough wreaths and Christmas trees emerged on the cookie sheet below.

All he had to do was play his part, when the guests arrived, greeting them at the door, and dropping the needle on the record in the walnut cabinet: "Sing Along with Mitch 1973." He stood in the living room, waiting. This was his favorite part of parties: the moment before, when the house was quiet, the table set, and there was this calm before the guests came tumbling in and everything was set into motion again.

They were having their annual open house for Bob's insurance clients as well as their neighbors and friends. The house was clean and decorated, waiting and ready, Elizabeth upstairs singing as she primped in the upstairs bathroom, Karen, her younger sister, pacing the living room, rehearsing her part for the high school Christmas play: "Behold Shepherds! Upon your watch! Behold that star in the distant sky!" Mary was in the bathroom, sliding the mirror on the metal vanity back and forth, spraying herself with his favorite perfume, "Charlie," as it mingled with scents of ham, pine needles, and wood burning in the fireplace. He had invited all of his friends and their wives: Cecil, Arnie, even Dick, though in truth he was a little nervous that he would actually show up.

It was the time of year Bob loved best, his girls lovely in their finery, the smells of ham and cookies in the oven, the richness, all of them cozy in this house and distracted from sadness by the bright season.

As he wandered through the living room again, he looked at the fireplace mantel, at his armies of lead soldiers that he had made from old toothpaste containers, pouring the lead into molds, then painting each soldier, and lining them up, one battalion after the next, the lieutenants and captains and colonels, forever in lockstep, forever facing west. He wandered to the piano, looking at the stacked music books, the bright red leaves of the poinsettia, and then peered out the front window to the grey streets, looking for cars.

As he waited, he glanced up at the black-and-white photograph of his mother, her broad, lined, kindly face looking out over the room in the house she had loved so well, looking out at the porch where she had rocked each evening with his father in that brief time after he was back from the war and his father was still alive and his mother was well, looking at the street where once Studebakers, and now Volkswagen bugs and Chevy trucks, ran in a steady stream. He missed her, missed her sharp observances of the things in his life. He wished the girls would have known her when she wasn't so sick—when she was livelier and funnier, back in the days when she would do things like take him for an unexpected train ride. They knew her as a large, sad woman, thick-tongued with Lithium. She would have approved of this scene, right now, the house waiting, waiting for the girls to come down the stairs, for the guests to fill up the foyer with their hats and coats and their bright holiday conversation.

The letter had come today, December 21, 1973, from the nurse at the Stone Home, Louise Gustafson, asking for money.

> *The ten dollars you sent to buy Elizabeth something for Christmas was received, and Elizabeth will be enjoying Canteen visits...not to mention a visit to Santa Claus when he comes to visit all of the patients at the Stone River School and Hospital, something that our patients look forward to very much. Santa delights them with treats and toys which they then enjoy for weeks on end.*
>
> *Elizabeth, I thought you might want to know, is a good natured happy child who attends school Monday through Friday, from 9:35 A.M. to 4:10 P.M. She goes to shows and*

church weekly and takes part in the Recreation program. We are building a new carousel, which we expect to be open this summer and we think the children will really enjoy that. If you would send this Canteen money regularly that would be ideal, as Elizabeth does not have any money in her account.

Jesus. His heart darkened. Just when you think you're opening up, enjoying things, allowing a little happiness and ease back in your life, another letter arrives from the nurse, reminding you, you're not quite done, buddy. You still have obligations. Okay, you say, I'll read a little report and then I'm done with it, and instead they say, no. Not enough. You give them $10, they want $20. You give them a dress, they want coats, hats, boots. You agree to the Canteen, they want you to take the kid home for Christmas.

There was the letter before that, December 15, where she pushed him even harder.

It would be much better for Elizabeth to go home for the Christmas holiday, with her own family, which we strongly encourage.

—Miss Louise Gustafson

Home for the Christmas holiday? To the family that didn't know about her? To his girls, Elizabeth with her long brown hair, wide green eyes, and avid, intense face; Karen with her red hair and her doll-like figure. Both of them so fresh and beautiful in their Christmas dresses, with their plays and rehearsals and Christmas concerts. How could it be fair for this child, this stranger, this ghost sister to appear from nowhere? How could she possibly fit in to all this? Where did she fit in—and he was being kind to her here—as all of them gathered around this dining room table, serving ham and potatoes, this daughter, this sister, who had only known an institution? How would that ever work? *A child was born*, he thought to himself and felt a darkening sink through him. A child to unravel everything, everything he'd worked for, the sorrow he'd worked to press back, the ravening, the ravening.

Bob wrote Louise Gustafson on December 22, 1973.

> *Here is the $20 for the special shoes. I have, once again, ordered what I hope to be suitable dresses, panties, and a coat from Sears to be sent to this address. Christmas at our house, however, is not possible. I am trying to provide for my children, including my Elizabeth Carter, her older sister. These children are unaware of her and I wish this to remain that way—a decision I have thought long and hard about. But I do not want to neglect my responsibilities. I am enclosing a check for $10 and would appreciate it if you could buy Elizabeth some suitable Christmas presents. It will not be possible, however, to bring Elizabeth to our house.*

The shadows in the room lengthened. The Christmas tree, which moments ago looked lovely, suddenly seemed scrawny and bare on one side—goddamn Mary and her love of alpine firs. Couldn't we once have a big, full Scotch pine with big, full branches that didn't bend with the lightest of ornaments?

He turned the tree slightly toward the wall to hide the bare side.

A blue bulb with a silver stripe fell and shattered.

"Jesus Christ!" he murmured.

"What is it, Bob?" Mary said from the bathroom, her voice distracted and vaguely annoyed. "Stop fussing with things. Everyone's going to be here in just a minute."

"The tree is too scrawny," he said.

"Just get the broom and clean up your mess," she said, coming into the living room and giving him the look he knew too well, the look that said, you are behaving like a child and so I will treat you like one. "C'mon, everyone is going to be here."

Bob got the broom and the dustpan. He wasn't going to give her that one. And just as he was emptying the glass shards into the garbage can, the doorbell rang.

It was, of course, the Brechbills.

He put on the Christmas record on his way to the door, and the Mitch Family Singers burst into "Deck the Halls."

He didn't know when he started dreading Arnie and his wife. When had Arnie grown so officious? When he was promoted at the bank? When he took over as president of Kiwanis? He always enjoyed Arnie in the past—he was quick and funny—but it seemed every time Bob ran into him now he was going on about his latest win on the stock market or his recent foray into real estate, Arnie growing balder and shorter as his wife grew wider, her sausage-like body encased in tight-fitting suits with loud chunky jewelry and her endless, tasteless remodeling of their split-style ranch and their large, talentless children who somehow pushed their way into the finest schools. But there they were, brightly clad in the colors of the season, their large, potato-like faces peering up at him through the peephole in the door, fishbowled, imperious, and at the same time as certain as cattle that the door will open because they expected it to.

Bob opened the door, stepped back, and swept his hand into the house in a welcoming gesture. "Well," he said, "if it isn't the Brechbills! Who'd a guessed? Come in! Merry Christmas! Let me take your coats!"

The Brechbills scooted into the hallway, where a candelabra snaked shadows up the walls, and heaped their coats on his waiting arms.

"Mary—the Brechbills are here," he called, hoping this message conveyed both his urgency for her company and his desperation not to be left alone with them. "Mary!" he added, thinking, *Mary! Help! Get down here fast!*

As he hung up their coats, the four Brechbills moved into the living room, Mrs. Brechbill clasping her hands together. "I love these old houses," she breathed, the buttons on her tight red suit jacket rising. "With the fireplace and the wood-framed windows and the high ceilings. Oh my goodness. It's just so darn charming, isn't it, Arnie?"

"Yes," said Arnie, and Bob imagined him sizing up the square footage, the squareness of the room, the potential for remodeling. "So much you can work with, old man." Arnie nudged him in the side. "Rates are low if you want to remodel."

He, of course, was referring to the vast improvements he'd made to the 5,000-square-foot house they had built on the hill with a triple garage, the daylight basement with the pool table and a wet bar, the four bathrooms, and a mother-in-law unit for when, as Mrs. Brechbill was heard to say, in a deep, dramatic whisper, "the time comes."

Bob thought if he were Mrs. Brechbill's mother, he'd rather be dead than have to live with Mrs. Brechbill when the time came.

"Well," Bob said and resisted the urge to nudge Arnie back. "I'll take that into consideration." Remodel over my dead body, he thought, so I can have wall-to-wall cheap-ass carpeting and popcorn ceilings and an aquarium of ugly-ass fish in my living room? Jesus.

He followed the Brechbills into the dining room, wondering if he dared call Mary again and wondering where the girls were and why everyone had chosen to abandon him at this particular moment, and poured Arnie and his wife and himself large cups of brandy-spiked eggnog. The Brechbill kids, who were standing at the table sipping the punch of cranberry juice and 7-Up, were already looking down their noses at the spread—which he could see was a bit thin, damn it, why did Mary have to economize at the worst moments—the teenage boy putting his thick fingers around a piece of ham and lifting it to his face when Elizabeth walked in the room.

"Hey Sam," she said. "How's the ham?"

The boy stopped to look at her, dressed as she was in a long denim dress with a low-cut lace collar, her hair swept back from her face and shining, her eyes bright and amused.

The mother and father Brechbill looked at her as well. Their daughter, Emily, was bound for some eastern college, Bob couldn't remember which, where the girls wore kilts to play lacrosse and learned skills and attitudes they could come back to lord over the rest of their small-town friends when they returned.

"You must be a fan," Elizabeth said to Sam and then smiled, a sunbeam of a smile, to show him she was just kidding.

Sam looked at the ham in his hand as if he couldn't decide whether to put it down or go ahead and eat it. He ate it, then reached over and delicately picked up another and ate that too.

Bob enjoyed the awkward pause as Sam struggled to come up with a rejoinder, his parents pretending not to notice that their son had the manners of a warthog, while Emily, on the other side of the table, didn't miss a beat, but instead reached over and grabbed a piece of ham and plopped it into her mouth and ate it. "I'm a fan, too!" she said.

Everyone laughed. Tension dispelled. Poor Sam was now free to eat all the ham he wanted, though Bob knew when he got home, his mother would scold him.

Bravo, Elizabeth, Bob wanted to say, just as the doorbell rang and several groups of people swirled into the front hall: Cecil and his wife, Dick with a young redheaded woman on his arm. Elizabeth swept her friends into the dining room and handed them plates. There were boys in ragged jeans and army jackets and several girls, one in a miniskirt with a peasant top embroidered with flowers, another who seemed to be bursting out of overalls, a third in a sweeping velvet gown and long, black hair who looked as if she should be holding a candelabra in a haunted house.

"Kids," Mrs. Brechbill said to Bob, as she looked over at the crew, as the boys clustered in one part of the room, the girls in the other, like charged particles that immediately moved apart, then gradually collided and bumped into one another amid the lumbering adults. "You'd think they might dress for a Christmas party, but then, Robert, perhaps we should be happy they are dressed at all." She tittered at her joke.

Bob looked at her. "Are you trying to scare me to death?"

Mary joined them as Mrs. Brechbill gushed about the tree, the decorations in the house, the lovely spread, then asked Mary, pointedly, about how the family was doing.

Mary stiffened and held out her hand to indicate Elizabeth and Karen. "They are just fine. Busy. Lots of activities."

Mrs. Brechbill put her hand on Mary's arm. "You know what I mean, dear."

Mary looked at her. Her eyes glittered. "I do, but I'm telling you my girls are just fine."

Mrs. Brechbill threw back her head and laughed. "Oh Mary, you are such a delight."

Mary patted her arm. "May the peace of the season be with you. A cookie?" she said, grasping a plate of the red-sprinkled Christmas wreaths that Karen and Elizabeth had made.

"Oh, I shouldn't," Mrs. Brechbill said, her fingers arching over the plate. "But I just can't resist."

Mary, Bob thought, took some kind of comfort from watching the crumbs of cookie gather in the corners of Mrs. Brechbill's bright red lips.

One of Elizabeth's friends, the tall gawky one with the bright eyes who, Elizabeth had told him, was rumored to have the highest scores in town on all the college tests, a perfect grade point, as well as a swimming scholarship from Brown, bounced up to Bob. "Hello, Mr. Carter," she said. "Don't you think we should sing? Doesn't every party need singing? A Christmas party particularly, to bring us all together?"

It seemed to Bob that she was turning into a matron at the age of seventeen. She rifled through the stacks of music on the piano and pulled out a book of Christmas carols. She set it on the piano and opened it to "Jingle Bells," and, after rolling an arpeggio and playing a scale, began to play.

"Oh, oh, oh." Mrs. Brechbill hurried over to the piano and clasped her hands to her heart. "I just love singing carols." She launched into "dashing o'er the snow" in her wobbly soprano. Then stopped. The pianist kept on. "Hello dears," she said to the crowd. "Aren't you going to sing with me? It is Christmas and this dear girl is playing for us."

From his spot in the dining room, next to the table, where he and Karen were filling a plate with Ritz crackers and cream cheese, Bob watched the party-goers move into the room. Elizabeth, his daughter, who could sing the moon down out of the sky, if you asked him, was first, followed by the Brechbill kids and some others, and even the ragged-looking young men, though one was muttering that it was hard to be filled with joy and peace with a crook like Nixon as president.

"You're Karen?" said Cecil, who had slipped in and draped his coat on the couch before he came to stand by them.

"I'm Karen," she smiled at him, and Bob's heart swelled at her. "One and the same."

"That's Karen? My God," Cecil was saying about his lovely curly-headed daughter. "My God, she's beautiful. Last time I saw you—" Cecil touched her on the arm and turned to Bob. "Last time I saw her, she was in pigtails. Now she's all grown." With a start, Bob could see that she was attractive, sexy, and he wasn't prepared for that thought.

Karen bowed out and went to join the party at the piano, which was now onto "We Three Kings of Orient Are," the old singing with great earnestness, the young tilting their heads, singing with as much irony as they could muster.

In all of this, Mary sashayed back and forth to the kitchen, ferrying in new plates of celery with cream cheese, banana bread sandwiches stuffed with cream cheese, more cookies, and more chocolate torte, and when she thought no one was looking, a pale exhaustion washed over her face.

When he saw that, Bob went to her and said, "Forget about the food. Everyone's fine. Go sing. I know you want to."

"No, no," she said. "We're out of punch."

"Hell with the punch. I'll make the punch," Bob said. "Have fun. It's your party too."

Mary scowled at him as if he'd said something incredibly stupid.

"Mary, come here." He grasped her by the elbow and steered her toward the crowd of people at the piano who were singing his favorite carol, "O Little Town of Bethlehem." He wanted Mary to sing, her voice pure and high, her face lit up as she sang, transformed by the music, and he nudged her toward the piano even though he could feel her resist.

"You're singing," he said. "You can't get out of this one."

He positioned her in the center of the singers, and put his hands around her waist, still slender under her red wool dress that flared out at the knees, and he felt her turn her head to the music, draw a breath, relax, and begin to sing: "Above thy deep and dreamless sleep, the silent years go by." This beautiful old hymn, he thought, about this quiet and peaceful town, the way any good town should be. A hymn that, when he heard it with its slow, minor chords, was probably the closest he ever got to believing in God. Outside of jazz.

As the group sang around him, he glanced at all of the people in his living room, his daughter Elizabeth, whose face was shining as she sang and turned pages for her friend singing beside her, with a deep bass voice, wild curly hair and silver tooth, and an electricity between them that he was trying not to see, and Karen, gliding through the visitors clumped on the edges of the room, sylph-like with her red hair and silver tray of Ritz crackers with pimiento cheese, the sound of the singing so lovely, in this deep, dark living room.

I thought you would want to know, the nurse said, *Elizabeth does like toys of almost any kind—anything you could send would be fine. Toys that are durable are the best here.*

CHAPTER THIRTY-TWO

It was summer, and Elizabeth and Tom were in their Dodge Dakota driving I-15 north from Butte over the Continental Divide. The windows were rolled down, the wind fluttering Elizabeth's hair and fanning her bare feet that rested on the glove box as they wound through the narrow canyons along the Stone River. They were driving, listening to Les McCann's "Compared to What?" She was going to research the files at the Stone Home, then they were continuing on to a hot springs resort, Potosi, where they would celebrate the summer solstice and their wedding anniversary.

They were driving to the Stone Home for the Mentally Retarded, renamed the Montana Development Center, which was located outside the small, windswept town of Stone City, between Helena and Butte. Dr. Babcock, the retired family doctor, had told her when she interviewed him that children listed as "withdrawn" in the hospital records in the 1950s were institutionalized here. "It was a different time then," he told her as she sat in his starched blue living room, his wife serving them coffee. "Don't be hard on your parents, Elizabeth.

You've got to understand what they were facing. Those children were not accepted into normal society. There was nothing for them like there is now—no programs, no special services, nothing. If you kept those children, you were social outcasts."

"Those children?" she asked. "Who are 'those children'?"

"Down syndrome children, severely epileptic, paraplegic children, you name it," he said. "Pretty much anyone who wasn't what our society would call 'normal.'"

Dr. Babcock went on to talk about her parents, what fine people they were, telling her about a snowshoeing trip he'd gone on with her father, long ago, when her father had saved a mutual friend from drowning. But what she really wanted to ask him was this: How could anyone in the 1950s define "normal" after going to war against a man who had killed six million people he didn't think were "normal"? It was as if an entire society had adopted the rigid definitions of normality they had gone to Europe to fight against. When she thought about it now, she realized how deeply ingrained and fragile and neurotic and pervasive this idea of "normal" was in her childhood of the 1950s. It was as if the definition of a human psyche was a light switch that could easily be turned from one side to the next: happy/sad, normal/abnormal, good/evil.

Tom steered the truck down the off-ramp and they rolled onto the main street of Stone City. It was a pretty western town. Lined with ash trees, the four-block main street had a hardware store, café, grocery, several bars, and a tire shop and was inhabited by dogs, kids on bikes, and a few adults who dashed out from pickups angle-parked at the curb. They drove by one-story brick homes with hollyhocks as backdoor sentries and large vegetable gardens in the backyards. The road headed out of town past the fairgrounds. Then they were there: the Montana Development Center, as it was called.

The sign for the center was next to a large gate made of tamarack poles painted white that framed the entrance to the campus. Her stomach knotted as Tom turned down the dirt drive, lined on either side with neat one-story brick administrative buildings with gardens of nodding petunias. White clapboard cottages with jaunty names—Spruce Cottage, Cottonwood Cottage—lined a grid of short streets of the Montana Development Center. Elizabeth wondered which one her sister lived in. In the back, towering over all, was the historic Italianate building. It was like something out of Dickens, Elizabeth thought, a hulking, three-story brick building that looked as if contained a hundred years' worth of screams.

"I think I might throw up," she said.

"You're doing a really brave thing," Tom reached over and squeezed her hand.

He parked their truck in the gravel lot at a brick building. Elizabeth stepped out of the cab and shut the door, the metal on metal resounding. The two of them walked across the gravel to the back door of the large brick building. The lawns were bright green and freshly mown. The windows shone. A few orderlies hurried from building to building, but other than that, there weren't many people around. As she and Tom approached the door marked "Records," there was a group of what looked like staff members gathered outside, smoking. They grew quiet as Elizabeth and Tom passed by, only the smoke from their cigarettes rising.

Elizabeth smiled. "Howdy."

A few nodded and looked away.

The sun was very bright. Her heart pounded. Tom grew silent beside her, his hand on the door.

The door opened with a sigh. She walked in and immediately couldn't see. The smell of disinfectant washed over her. When her eyes adjusted to the dimness, she saw a chalkboard in the hallway where someone who signed his name "Dr. Know" had written: "Thought for the Day: 'A person who wakes up in the morning is a new creation.'"

"Good luck in there." Tom tapped Elizabeth's arm. He looked as if he were drowning. "I have to get out of here," he said. "I'm sorry. This place gives me the creeps."

"You're leaving me?" she said. "You're not going to stay?"

"Take all the time you need, Elizabeth. I'll be in the car," he said, then he turned and his broad back receded down the hall. The doorway opened, the bright day flashed before her, and he disappeared into it. She knew he would be there, asleep in the cab of the truck when she emerged, blinking, several hours later. They would drive to the hot springs, where they would drink wine by the river, and that night, she and Tom would undress and slip into a hot pool in a small cedar cabin with a window onto a nearby creek where a pine siskin would hop from ponderosa to ponderosa and a squirrel would scurry through the kinnikinnick burying nuts for the impending winter. The hot water, Elizabeth would notice, made their skin appear rippled, greenish white, ghost-like. The water would slide through her body like a drug, weighting her limbs until they were heavy and slow.

"It's hard to believe," Elizabeth said.

Tom put his fingers to her lips. "Shhh," he said. "This is *our* time."

"But—" Elizabeth didn't have the starch to finish her sentence. The water was too warm. She felt as if her bones had dissolved into rubber.

Tom kissed her, his body weightless but large. She heard the *tat-tat-tattting* of a woodpecker from far away, and a chickadee calling *pho-ebe, phoeee-beee.* The scratch of his beard. The loud whoosh of the water as she and Tom climbed out of the pool onto the bench, the water slopping over the edge of the tub, the two of them trying to find purchase on the rough wood planks of the bench, the image of the other Elizabeth hovering over her like a moon that stays out during the day as they made love for the first time in months.

But that would come later. She still had to walk in the door, wondering: *Will I come face to face with her*? Her shoes tapped on the shiny linoleum. It was so eerily quiet. At the sound of footsteps behind her, she jumped.

A tall, white-haired man with a hooked nose peered down into her face. "Who are you?" he said in a slow, deliberate voice.

Elizabeth Carter, she was going to say, then thought better of it. She told him she was looking for the records room, and he walked her there, making sure she didn't stray. When they entered the room, he presented her to the several tired-looking women who sat at desks before flanks of filing cabinets. The cabinets were piled with manila files, stacks of green hanging files. Sun filtered into the room through tall, streaked windows on the side and pooled on the linoleum. On the wall was a cartoon of a man holding his sides, laughing, with the caption, "You want it *when*?"

Elizabeth looked up at the woman, her blood thumping against her temples, and asked her for the files of Elizabeth Carter. There was a woman in the back, typing, wearing a Sturgis T-shirt. The receptionist, who wore a T-shirt that read, "Nice Days are for Wimps," asked her if the patient was still at the Stone Home.

The woman with the Sturgis T-shirt flipped through some papers with a practiced hand. She had straw-like hair, a weatherbeaten face, but her voice was kind. "Discharged '91, looks like. That's the last I have of her. Meadowlark Group Home."

"Meadowlark Group Home," Elizabeth repeated. "Do you know where that is?"

"Choteau," the woman in the Sturgis T-shirt said.

"Where?" Elizabeth said. She shook her head, trying to clear it.

"Choteau," the woman said. "A ways from here."

"You said that, didn't you?" Elizabeth said. "I'm sorry."

"I did." The woman's voice was soft.

"Do you have a phone number?" Elizabeth asked.

"You'll have to look it up, hon," the woman said. "We don't keep track of 'em from here."

"Does she have files?"

"I'll see. Are you family?"

"Her sister."

"Driver's license?"

Elizabeth showed her driver's license. The woman looked at her name and shook her head. She disappeared into an inner room. She was gone for a long time. While she was gone, Elizabeth watched the receptionist cut plastic strips in small lengths for the tops of hanging files. Then she labeled them, inserted a paper strip, and affixed them to the top of the green files. Patient files. Each one a rough story of a life.

"Here you go, hon," the woman said, when she finally emerged. She set two enormous battered files on the counter with a thunk. On the outside of one, a card was stapled with all of the patient's essential information: Elizabeth Finch Carter, a/k/a "Lizzie." Birthdate: February 4, 1953. D/o/d: ??

"A bit of reading, eh?" the woman said.

Elizabeth nodded.

The woman came to the edge of the counter, opened a small gate, and let her in. She pulled out a molded plastic chair from a counter.

"Here ya go, hon." Her voice softened. "You want a cup of coffee?"

"Please," Elizabeth said. The woman was right, she thought, nice days were for wimps.

Elizabeth drew a breath and opened the first file. The first thing she saw was two black-and-white Polaroids. Her sister. In the top photo, a large girl in her late teens with short dark hair stared up at her. Her face was round, her eyes turned up at the corners, and she had a short, uneven haircut as if she'd tried to cut it herself. She was a presence, solid, blunt as her hair.

The other photo was dated September 26, 1981, the day Elizabeth had started her job at the *Chicago Tribune*, after graduating from Northwestern. On the back, an inscription: "Lizzy Carter, from Louise Gustafson." Her sister was wearing a sweatshirt featuring a silhouette of a black-and-white cow. Her mouth was pulled down in a frown. Her eyes were narrowed, her faced clouded, angry.

Deal with me, the picture seemed to say.

As Elizabeth stared at this image of her sister, she felt the world drop away from her. It was as if she were looking down a great long tunnel running the length of her life, and at the end was this sister.

Elizabeth felt she had fallen to the bottom of a well. Here was the other Elizabeth, the one who was always lurking around corners, around the edge of sleep, of consciousness, full-on, in her cow-sweatshirt picture, in a dusty archive in a backwater town. *Deal with me.*

Elizabeth wanted to reach through the great tunnel of time and space to her, to touch her, to feel her skin, warm the cold distance between them—this sister who was not at all the benevolent, smart, pretty older sister Elizabeth had always dreamed of as a child, who would travel and talk into the night with her, giving her advice on everything from shoes to literature, but a furious, flesh-and-blood sister who stared up at her from a Polaroid taped to the back of an institutional hanging file.

What childish notion could have possessed her parents that, somehow, if they disappeared this child and gave her, the next child, the same name—the world would be right again? Is that what "withdrawn" meant?

Elizabeth turned to the sheaves of papers, nearly three inches thick in each file. She read years of doctors' notes, daily nursing logs, medication listings, seizure reports, and the saddest thing of all: a greying copy of something called a "Gift Report," with a grid and a space for checkmarks for each holiday—Christmas, Easter, Thanksgiving. Each Easter, there was a checkmark for one Easter basket. Each Christmas, one Christmas stocking.

In the next file, the correspondence: the letters between the doctor and her father, between the neurologists, nurses, and social workers, but more haunting than anything, an exchange of letters between her father and a particular nurse that kept resurfacing, letters between Robert Carter and a Louise Gustafson, RN. As Elizabeth read, the ringing of phones, the slamming of file drawers, the clacking of computer keys receded to a sound like blood rushing down tunnels of veins and arteries, the mad swim of sperm and eggs, the swing and dash of chromosomes, the eerie squeaking and bubbling of DNA forming and reforming like tiny planets swimming in a dark beating universe, the wet bubbling of the zygote just before it split into two.

CHAPTER THIRTY-THREE

In Helena, the legislature was rushing to get through the bills on the floor. They were not going to revisit the pay raise for workers at Stone Home for the Mentally Retarded or Hot Springs, and on March 15, 1962, they adjourned with an amendment promising the staff at the two state institutions better benefits and pay raises retroactive to January. That was all they had: a promise.

On March 16, Matt Steele stood on the cafeteria table at Stone City and held a strike vote.

156 to 42.

The strike began on March 17, 1974, when 350 members of the Stone City staff joined the walkout of another 750 state hospital workers, defying a state court order not to strike. As Louise trudged to the hospital from her cabin that cold spring day, the grounds looked almost festive. Overnight, pickets had blossomed like night-blooming flowers outside the hospital fence, held by staffers bundled in winter coats, army surplus wool pants, and hunters' hats with ear flaps.

Parents and relatives of patients from the nearby towns of Basin and Wilsall, Jefferson City and Clancy joined the strike with homemade signs, exchanging stories as they warmed their hands over the fires that leapt up from dented oil barrels. A Butte diner, Tony's, sent sheets of homemade beef pasties. The Stone City Ladies Aid brought vats of coffee and shoeboxes of homemade cookies. When it came to strikes, miners' families and friends knew full bellies equaled support.

Louise cheered them on as she crossed the picket line and headed up the stone steps into the hospital—the picketers politely stepping aside and cheering as she followed Dr. O and the other nurses. They were not as friendly to the group of Helena government types who stepped through the lines just after them, hoping to slipstream in their wake. They were booed by the strikers, the men turning up their collars as they hurried toward the protection of the thick oak doors at the front of the building. Inside, Louise leaned back against the oak sash of Dr. O's doorway, watching the herd of men in dark coats as they piled inside, and stood for a moment, blinking, as their eyes adjusted to the dimness of the wide hallway.

For the next few weeks, the days rolled in and out on waves of exhaustion, bathing, feeding, diapering. Anna, Margaret, and Louise crossed the picket line in the mornings, lunch pails in hand. "Hey Louise," she heard someone call out as she passed through the strikers, the forest of pickets. "Tell 'Lizabeth I'm thinking about her." It was Nora, the woman who staffed Lizzie's cottage at night. Louise nodded and moved on, slowly up the walkway, knowing a sixteen-hour day lay ahead of her, research, nursing, everything abandoned. It was merely survival here, feeding, cooking, diapering, trying to keep patients clean and fed and alive, she and the other nurses flying by each other in the halls at a near-run, rolling their eyes, their faces grey, moving to the steady chant of the strikers outside, as they held their signs and moved around and around the front gate.

At night, Louise went to Lizzie's cottage to check on her. Once she had a new bruise from a seizure and fall and when she questioned the nurse in charge, she apologized, her brown eyes filled with tears. "I'm so sorry, Miss Gustafson, she started having her fit when I was helping someone with their bath. I couldn't get there fast enough."

Louise patted her shoulders.

She went to Lizzie's bed in the crowded room, took her hand, and led her over to the rocking chair. Lizzie was exhausted from her seizure and didn't want to talk. Louise lifted her onto her lap and rocked her, one of the runners squeaking, Lizzie filling up her entire lap, and the two of them rocked.

"Weezie," Lizzie sighed. "I hurt, Weeze."

"Baby," Louise said, rocking her. She smelled the top of her hair. It smelled like antiseptic. She stroked Lizzie's hair back from her face. "You're tired, sweetie."

She had Lizzie lie down in her bed, and as she smoothed Lizzie's hair back from her face, she told her, "'Night, Lizzie. Go to sleep now."

Lizzie shut her eyes, the thin, delicate skin laced with purple veins.

When Louise stood, the others cried out, "Rock me! Me! Me! Me!"

She tried to pat heads, squeeze hands, as she walked by the beds of the children on the way out of the cottage. She had to physically restrain herself from running from the sound of their voices as they trailed her out into the starry night, her heart still beating as she walked across the field to the transcendent quiet of her cabin. When she got there, she sat on a chair on the porch, just sat there, until the sounds of the voices receded, until she could no longer feel their hands tugging hers and her heart beat slowed and she could breathe normally again, filled with nighttime quiet.

CHAPTER THIRTY-FOUR

There were always bills.

Stacks of bills. Leaning towers of bills.

And Bob was the pillar among them, the one who had looked back and turned to salt, except that he had to somehow lift his weighted hand and open a checkbook and write—bills for his daughters' endless dance and music lessons, clothes and shoes, coats and dresses. There was the roof over their heads and the car they drove, the groceries and heat, the water and gas, bills to the tax man and garbage man, bills from the hairdressers and the symphony tickets, bills from the veterinarian for the damned flea-bitten dog. Bills from doctors for sore throats and coughs, and the female ailments he didn't know the names of. Then bills from the state: past due bills from the state hospital for the insane for his mother, from the state hospital for the mentally retarded for his other daughter. What kind of normal family paid bills like these? Then the letters, which he kept pushing down to the bottom of the stack.

Dear Mr. Carter, we have conducted a test on your daughter, Lizzie; we have measured her intelligence. IQ: 80. Retardation: profound.

Dear Mr. Carter, we have trained your daughter to feed herself.

Dear Mr. Carter, your daughter can identify the colors of green and blue, and can dress and toilet herself at the age of 16, but can only utter a few words.

Dear Mr. Carter, your daughter has exhibited aggressive behavior.

Dear Mr. Carter, we have need of dresses, size 12.

Dear Mr. Carter, your daughter has fallen again and we have taken the precaution of fitting her with a helmet.

Dear Mr. Carter, we have not heard from you in some time and we are in urgent need…

He put the letters back near the bottom of his inbox, where through some miracle of science they rose again to the top, rising above the bills and the insurance claims, rising to prick him again and again. But today he turned away from them and walked the three blocks home through the crepuscular light—it was winter and dark at five—where the cars hissed through the streets, turning into the gloom to hibernate at home, to wait it out—they were all waiting it out, he thought—until spring was here again.

He opened the front door of his home, a solid oak door, and was blasted with a high C.

High, strong, and clear, her voice demanded everything.

It was Elizabeth. His Elizabeth. She was standing by the piano, this young woman in her ragged jeans and long brown hair, her round clear face and bright green eyes. She was wearing his grandfather's WWI army jacket, ragged at the sleeves and hanging off her, which she wore to protest the Vietnam War. She looked, he thought, like a street waif in a Dickens novel, except that she was singing a high C, all of her poured into that single note that filled this old house with its lovely sound, chasing away the ghosts of disappointment and loss. She was practicing "Come, Dawn," for her solo at the high school's spring concert.

Bob waited by the front door until she was done.

Then she stopped, gasped for breath.

"Wow." Bob walked toward her.

"Dad," she said, her eyes suddenly focusing on him. "You scared me."

Where did she go? He wondered. Where did she go when she was singing like that?

"That was exquisite," he said. "I can't believe I have a daughter that can do that."

"That was shit," she said. "I blew it on the C. *Je suis gai quand je te vois*. I am gay when I see you." She flipped her long hair over her shoulder, owning the world at eighteen. "The concert's in two days and my teacher thinks I'm ready and I'm bustin' my butt, but I'm not. I sound like a goddamn mule braying."

"Don't swear," he said as he tucked a stray hair behind her ear. "But I don't think you sound like an ass."

"Ha. Ha."

In the hall he peeled off his coat, glanced at his haggard face in the hall mirror—his eyes puffy, his chin jowly, his cheeks grey and stubbled—a horror really—then turned back to the more cheerful sight: his daughter's face. "And remember, you're always more ready than you think you are. You especially."

She looked back at him. "Is that supposed to help me?" She cocked her head, her hair falling sideways across her delicate features, her eyes focusing on his and then darkening.

"Where's Karen?" he asked.

"Dance team."

"When's she getting back?"

"Seven."

"Where's Mom?"

"Don't know. Don't care." She cocked her hand on her hip.

Bob put his hand on the door to the kitchen and sighed. "What'd you fight about?"

"You don't want to know."

You're right about that, he thought. Over and over again, he watched Mary and Elizabeth burst into passionate, inexplicable fights about hair and hem length, curfews and music practice, their words hot and fast, the passion between them singular and ferocious, but if he tried to burst in, if he tried to say, "Is this really worth it?" they turned their fury on him as if he had started the fight in the first place, as if he had interrupted them at the climax of a movie written for only the two of them.

"She's made me stay here and practice," Elizabeth said. "She won't let me go out with my friends or shop or get out of the goddamn house. She enjoys imprisoning me. She wants me to be her little trained monkey."

"Calm down. Your mother only wants what is best for you. Finish up, then go take a walk. Jesus, Elizabeth. You can do better than this."

"Go to upstairs to your office and calm down yourself!" With that she spun on her heel and headed toward the front door.

"Elizabeth—" he called out, but he could already hear the door slamming as she stomped out into the cold. He could picture her heading down the alley, punching her arms in the pockets of her jacket and pulling a watch cap over her head. *Walk it off*, as she liked to say. *Walk it off.*

In the kitchen, the counters gleamed. The oven was cold. His heart sank. Where was Mary? Out again for bridge? Running a bake sale? Raising money for the symphony? Now that Elizabeth and Karen were in high school the causes proliferated—which meant cold rushed dinners, an empty house, lots of poster board and cash boxes, and an endless stream of well-meaning women in and out of the house with their pots of tea and tinned cookies and sly jokes that were meant to tease, and then dismiss him.

As he predicted, the note was there: "Meatloaf and potatoes in the fridge. Put in a 350 oven at 5:00 for one hour. See you at 6:00. —M."

Recipe for a marriage, he thought.

He took his work upstairs and sat at his desk, opening the folder on a complicated case, the insurance claim for a construction job where a worker was killed when he stepped backward and fell from an unfinished second floor to the concrete slab below. The construction worker's family sued for a quarter million dollars and the insurance company didn't want to pay—though Bob thought they might consider a settlement. Mel Rains, in the Idaho office, sent it over to him, saying, "Hey Bob, you're the expert—this one's for you."

Bob stared at the words. Claimant: Tom Baumeister.

Life insurance policy: $20,000 upon death.

Cause of death: Construction accident.

Doctor's statement: Broken spinal column due to fall at construction site. Death, instantaneous.

Poor bastard, he thought. So his wife and kids get $20,000. Tom gets life hereafter. A cold spot in the dirt, formaldehyde in the veins.

He began filling out forms: address, date of birth, cause of death, amount of claim, reason for claim.

Here he was in the middle of winter, in the middle of Montana, filling in a form for a dead man. He stared at the empty blanks under employment, income, family—and stopped. He looked out the window at the grey skies, the grey buildings that rose on the other side of the grey river. There was something about winter, he thought, that reduced a man to the size of a pebble.

On the radio, more news about the break-ins at the Watergate headquarters of the Democratic Party. More news about workers threatening a strike at the state mental hospital and the home for the retarded. Some asshole giving an editorial about how even the retarded had civil rights. Mentally ill? Civil rights? Jesus, they could hardly talk. With all the problems in the world, why did people have to go stir things up there, of all places? Pretty soon, they'd be voting, getting married, running for office. It all exhausted him. Maybe this Mr. Baumeister had the right idea—step backwards, break your neck, and you're off duty. No more bills. No more people yelling. No more people saying, this is your job, you have to do this, it's all your responsibility. It's all up to you, Bob. Step up and take one for the home team.

He stood and looked out at the alley, the garbage spilling out of one can, sniffed by a spotted dog with a ribcage harp-like with hunger. Next door, another neighbor's Ford pickup and Chevy Cavalier were up on blocks next to their snowed-in garden with ghostly stalks of hollyhocks and frosted tomato vines.

He was looking for his daughter, who liked to wander, when he spotted her green army coat. She was leaning against a telephone pole in the middle of the alley. Next to her was a man in a black pea coat.

They were leaning into one another, their heads wreathed by clouds of breath.

He leaned in closer for a look.

Or was it smoke?

He scraped frost from the window and squinted.

It was smoke.

Or were they kissing?

His first instinct was to run outside and punch the guy out.

She would never forgive him. He dug his fingernails into the windowsill, making half-moons in the soft wood.

Now he could see they were passing something back and forth, a cigarette? Smoke rose up between them, curling grey into the sky.

His lips. Her lips. The hands in between, the fingers pinching, faces together, laughing, the way the young man's face bent down to hers, and the look he gave her, soft, predatory, hungry as they passed the cigarette back and forth.

Bob stood there, frozen, feeling everything crumble around him.

Elizabeth, Karen, they were everything to him, and here she was, in the alley, with a strange boy, kissing, smoking. He wanted to thrust open the window and yell at her to stop, to come home, to come to her senses, but at the same time, he could see, even from here, the softness on her face when she looked up at the man, the yearning that pierced his father's heart with the knowledge that she was moving away from him, toward a world where she was no longer a girl, no longer his and Mary's, and the knowledge made him sink into a nearby chair, as if the wind had been knocked out of him.

Outside, Elizabeth and this man were bending close together, laughing. Elizabeth's face was shaded, conspiratorial—not at all the open, sweet face that, minutes ago, was singing "The shepherdess who I find dear has vermillion cheeks like you."

Bob turned away from the window and walked into her room and sat on the rocker, the same rocker where he used to rock Elizabeth to sleep each night, singing the Lord's Prayer. He rocked for a long time as the room grew dark, the runners squeaking, until he finally heard a door open and slam shut downstairs, and Elizabeth called, "I'm home Dad!" and he heard the banging of kitchen cupboards and the ring of a pot on the stove.

"Okay," he yelled back, but he wasn't okay. He was back in that hospital room where it seemed as if he and Mary had been given a second chance, this time a baby arriving, good news, the nurses patting him on the back, no silent hurried walks down the hallways, Mary exhausted, but smiling, as he sat next to her holding the brand-new Elizabeth Carter, holding the tiny child with her perfect fingers, toes, belly, arms, eyes, and round, dimpled face. *You are a miracle*, he told her. *Right, Mary?* he said to his wife, and she looked up and gave him a weak smile.

CHAPTER THIRTY-FIVE

The Meadowlark Home. That name has possessed her over the past few months. The Meadowlark Home. As she slogged through a series Ruth had assigned her on the increasing particulate count in the air over the past ten years—the owner of the local paper mill of course denying this—she kept thinking about it. Could it be that her sister had been there all along, right over the Continental Divide? Would her parents have known this? Were there other little secrets tucked away that she'd discover—an angry client? A lover? Tom was busy, starting up the year at the Hastings School, meeting with the new faculty and kids at the beginning-of-the-year retreat at Seeley Lake, where they gathered to kayak and write poetry and do art projects, and, at night, sit around the campfire.

It was a lingering fall day, the cottonwoods and aspen a bright yellow against the upended stone backbone known as the Rocky Mountain

Front. Elizabeth sat on the porch of her sister's bungalow in Choteau, watching the leaves scatter across the sidewalk, remembering the creations she and Karen used to make each fall, ironing colored oak leaves between sheets of waxed paper and hanging them in the kitchen windows so the sun would shine through them, illuminating their delicate spines, creations they treasured until the leaves dried and turned brown and the waxed paper separated and, one day, they disappeared, their mother having thrown them in the trash while they were in school.

From the porch, she could hear the comforting sounds of football on the television inside Karen's house. Her house was lovely, brightly painted tangerine and mint, decorated with Mexican tiles and pottery. Tom, Karen, Karen's husband, Bill, and her two children, Jessie, three, and the baby, Emily, who had just turned one, were gathered in the family room around the television watching the annual cross-state rivalry between the Bridger Bruins and the Meriwether Cougars. She could hear Tom's voice, then Bill's, in a counterpoint of cheers, Jessie shouting after them, "Yeah, Daddy, yeah?"

Elizabeth excused herself, saying she had to run to the store for groceries. She did not want to involve Karen in this now. She had clearly washed her hands of Elizabeth's explorations—and although she was hurt, Elizabeth knew that Karen had plenty to cope with, a new baby, a three-year-old, a husband who worked full-time, and all of the cooking and cleaning and parenting and managing that took. And she did it well—her house was bright, her kids content, she seemed happy in her marriage. Elizabeth wished she could do the same, that she wasn't such a malcontent. It would make her life so much easier. She sat on the porch for a minute, letting the fall sun wash over her, warming her, watching a neighborhood kid pedaling down the sidewalk.

The screen door squeaked and Jessie peered out, hanging on the door for safety, her hair plaited into two crooked braids, and dressed in overalls and a plaid shirt.

"What are you doing, Aunt Lisbeth?" she said.

"Sittin' here," Elizabeth said. "What are you doing? Want to join me?" Elizabeth patted the bench beside her.

"I'm watching the football," she said, swinging on the open door and staring at her. "I'm yelling for Bruins."

"Are they winning, Jessie?" Elizabeth asked.

"Don't think so," Jessie said, swinging on the door, pushing it forward with her round tummy. "Are you my mom's sister?"

"I am. I used to braid your mother's hair."

Jessie looked down at her braids and back at Elizabeth. "Were they as pretty as mine?"

Elizabeth laughed. "Well, almost."

Jessie looked at her oddly. Then, someone inside the house told her to shut the door, she flashed Elizabeth a heartbreaking smile, and with a flourish disappeared inside, the door banging shut behind her.

Elizabeth walked down the sidewalk through the crackling leaves, got into the car, and drove down the ambling streets of Choteau with the 1890s brick storefronts and comfortably worn houses flanked by rattling hollyhocks and wire and post fences and hardscrabble yards and bright pots of flowers, with the ragged spine of the Rocky Mountain Front as a backdrop.

She glanced at the address scribbled on the scrap of paper, and as she got closer, her stomach knotted. The Meadowlark Home.

She turned in to a gas station to buy a pack of cigarettes, despite the fact she hadn't smoked for years. She knew she would hate herself for smoking again. But she had to. She was a wreck. At this moment, her body was aching for nicotine, aching for that slow, smooth, calm inhale, the rush of the exhale.

She opened the car door and a man in a cowboy hat sidled up next to her just as she was about to stand up. She thought he was about to say something friendly, something about her car or her river sandals, so she smiled up at him. He scowled. "Just because you're from Bridger—you think you don't have to park your car like the rest of us?"

She looked back. She had parked the car across the painted yellow stripes in the lot. She nearly burst into tears. "Sorry," she said. "I didn't see the lines—" the last part said to the greasy ponytail that swung back and forth as he walked into the store. And then she wanted to add, "Asshole!"

She waited in the car until he walked out, shoving a Skoal can in the back pocket of his jeans, then went in for her Marlboro Lights and matches and lit up in front of the gas station in a patch of sun, taking that first deep, hot draw, feeling the guilty swirl of nicotine run down her throat, the heady, almost sexual pleasure of succumbing. Here I am again, old friend, she thought. And then that almost immediate sorrow, all the while contemplating what waited for her across the street in the green house with the red door and the ramp that said Meadowlark Group Home.

Was Elizabeth Finch Carter, a/k/a Lizzie, sitting there, watching TV? Would Elizabeth and Lizzie look at one another and recognize they were sisters and discover that after years of separation they used the same toothpaste? Was this too cruel, Elizabeth wondered. Maybe her sister was right. Sleeping dogs and all that. Was it wrong to open the door to these lost years, to satisfy her curiosity, her need for atonement?

If she opened this door, Elizabeth knew, she couldn't shut it.

Why not, instead, just leave this poor woman alone, in her group home, with the friends who have cared for her, who have taken her in?

Elizabeth was already dizzy, but she lit another cigarette, watched a pickup rev its engine and run down the street. How strange this all was, her sister and husband on one end of town, watching football, eating pizza—and Elizabeth on the other end, preparing to meet this lost sister, unraveling this hidden past, all of this going on not ten blocks apart, all of this going on in the same sun-stippled fall day.

She knew how uncomfortable Karen was with all of this. With this idea of undoing the image of their past, their parents as two loving people bringing them up just so—Karen was a very orderly person—and Elizabeth suspected that she just didn't want to open this door. Earlier, as they stood side by side, smashing avocados and squeezing lemons for guacamole, blending together black beans, hot sauce, and salsa, there was still a quiver of tension between them that wasn't quite overshadowed by the shouts of the husbands and kids watching the game.

Elizabeth listened to the heavy, clacking sound of geese passing overhead. It seemed to her that she could almost feel the way their wings beat the air to keep their dark bodies flying. They honked as they flew, moving quickly over this strip of pavement called a street, above the building that housed her sister.

Instinct, she thought. That's why I can't leave this alone. She watched the geese heading south to the Missouri River, a flyway where they would join the other flocks heading south, this great journey initiated by a genetic compass located in their brains just behind the eyes of each goose. *Flugwahren* it was called, the neurological itch that lifted each and every one of these geese up and out of the great waters of the Northwest and returned them each year to the Gulf of Mexico.

Like those birds, she thought, we share a common mother, father, DNA, and this name that lifts me out of ordinary life and onto this journey: Elizabeth Carter, six syllables of history, six beats of blood.

She stubbed out her cigarette, put her hands in her pockets. She looked both ways across the street, though in Choteau on a Saturday, she knew, that was not always necessary. A border collie, two blocks down, sauntered across the street and then, in the middle, plopped down and rolled over on its back and began slowly wriggling in the dust.

She walked up the ramp to the green house and knocked on the door. She had not called ahead, afraid that if she had, if she had made an appointment, she would lose her nerve.

The woman who opened the door was short, her tightly curled hair had roller marks in it. She wore a form-fitting aqua-blue polyester top and pants that made her vaguely resemble a detergent bottle. She looked at Elizabeth, top to toe, cocked her head, and said, "You the new housekeeper?"

"No," Elizabeth said. Her stomach, roiling already from cigarettes and nerves, churned at the smell of old cooking and disinfectant and old clothes. The Bruin-Cougar game was on television here too, the same burble of cheering fans and announcers and whistles, but this time the Cougars were ahead. "I'm here to look up a family member."

"Have to do that Tuesday," the woman said, as several people wandered past and Elizabeth eyed each one, looking for a familiar face. "Have to go through proper channels." She closed the door until the space was only five inches wide.

"Please ma'am," Elizabeth said. "I'm up here from Bridger, and I won't be here Tuesday. Could you just answer a question?"

"I don't know. It ain't policy." The woman cracked the door wider but stood in it to block Elizabeth's entrance. She called to someone in the kitchen. "Hey, Marie, are you going to get lunch anytime soon?"

Someone yelled back, and Elizabeth saw residents circling around the kitchen in the back, two large men with pants belted high on their waists who inched around in walkers, a woman with a palsy who looked Elizabeth directly in the face. An older man sat on a chair, softly hitting himself in the chest.

Another women came out of the kitchen. She wore a large faded sweatshirt that said, "Californians: Gut Shoot 'Em at the Border." "Lunch in five minutes," she said. She looked at Elizabeth, then at the woman in blue who'd answered the door. "She stayin'?"

The woman looked at Elizabeth. Something wordless had been decided between them. "Would you like to eat with us?"

The thought turned her stomach another notch.

"No thank you," Elizabeth said. "I have to meet my family," a statement that already felt loaded.

The woman in the sweatshirt gave a curt nod and disappeared back into the kitchen.

"I'm looking for Elizabeth Finch Carter," Elizabeth said to the woman in the doorway. She's called Lizzie. Is she here?"

"No," the woman cut her eyes at Elizabeth, suspicious again. "Not now."

"Oh." Elizabeth's stomach seemed to drop. "Do you know where she is? Please?" she said.

"Hey," the woman called back into the house. "Do you know where Lizzie went? Remember her? Big gal."

Elizabeth heard a gravelly man's voice in the back yell something.

"Wait here." The woman opened the door just wide enough to let her into a foyer with light blue shag carpeting. Elizabeth felt she had to stand exactly on this spot. She heard a scrape of chairs, a clatter of dishes, murmuring voices. As Elizabeth stood there, the residents circled around her on their way to the kitchen.

"Why are you here?" asked a man with large glasses.

"I'm looking for my sister."

“I have a sister,” he said. “She gives me red licorice. She comes and she takes me to the store, but she says, ‘Roger, don’t take things that don’t belong to you.’”

Another man glanced at her, then whipped his head back to the television screen in time to see the Bruins score a touchdown against the Cougars, bringing them into the lead.

“Yes! Yes!” he cried. He stood up and roared, “Bru-ins! Bru-ins!”

The curly-haired woman scurried back into the foyer, wiping her hands on a towel. “That’s enough, Ralph. Keep it down until dinner.” She turned to Elizabeth. “She got moved. Henry here thinks Libby, we don’t know. But we got lunch to get.”

Elizabeth turned to leave when the man with the glasses came right up to her and peered intently in her face. “Say hi to your sister,” he said. “When you find her, bring her licorice. She likes it.”

“I will,” Elizabeth smiled and reached out and shook his hand.

Back in the car, Elizabeth watched the play of shadows in the windows of the Meadowlark Group Home, the leaves of a large cottonwood brushing the roof. Minutes ago, she stood on the porch, her heart thundering in her chest, waiting for her life to change. Now she was back in the car, and the day had a crack in it—a rift that could have widened between her life before and her life after—had closed up, and once more it was an ordinary day in Montana with her family.

In a few minutes, she would be back in her kid sister’s living room, and the football game would be in the fourth quarter, and everyone would look up as she came in the room and say hi, how are things in town, and Elizabeth would say something pleasant, then their eyes would move slowly to the screen, trying not to be too impolite, and things would roll on until dinner, and the moment the cavity of the family could have been cracked open would have passed.

But before she could face the chaos of the house, Elizabeth lit up her fifth cigarette, felt the bittersweet rush of smoke.

What if the other Elizabeth had been there? What if the door had opened and there she was—her sister, three years older, round-faced, round-bodied, but with the same arched eyebrows and bow-shaped mouth and white skin and brown hair.

"Elizabeth?" she'd say.

"Who are you?" the other Elizabeth would answer, her blunt eyes staring, asking, "Why should I care about you?" And she'd be right, Elizabeth thought. Why should she?

Because I'm blood? Family? Your sister?

Whatever that meant.

And then what? What would she say to that frowning face that she knew only from a Polaroid picture at the back of a file?

There wasn't anything to say, she knew that now. But what would she have done in that moment? Elizabeth liked to think she would have overcome her fear enough to take in her sister's face: the stout, angry face that took in the world just as she saw it, just at that moment. She liked to think she would hold her sister's hand and she wouldn't say anything, just offer the comfort of a hand, of skin on skin, warmth.

But she would be a stranger.

The other Elizabeth might be afraid.

"I'm your sister," she would say.

Go home, have a baby, Elizabeth thought. Give this up. Stop thinking about the lost sister.

Back at her sister's, the family had moved closer to the television. Tom, Bill, and Karen were in the living room, shouting at the football game on the television, and when Elizabeth walked in, no one looked up—

the score was in favor of the Cougars, but it was the fourth quarter and they were just a touchdown ahead. Karen's face was flushed pink, a pretty contrast to her auburn hair. "Arrg," she said to Elizabeth. "The Cougars are winning!"

Elizabeth joined Jessie in the kitchen, where she was seated at her drawing table making placemats for dinner, spelling out her name, a spindly J with lines after it, working hard as she bunched the crayon in her fist, her blonde braids slanting forward as she leaned over each placemat. Kate, the baby, looked down at her from the high chair, her brown eyes quick, and when she dropped her rattle, Elizabeth picked it up and then Kate, with a toothless smile, dropped it again.

Elizabeth scrunched up in a little chair and watched Jessie press her hand onto the butcher paper, outline it with a crayon, then draw a wattle off the thumb.

"See!" Jessie said. "A turkey. I'm making one for each of us."

"Sure enough," Elizabeth said, and Jessie colored each of the outlined fingers a different color, scribbling the turkey body a deep brown.

"Now you do one."

Elizabeth took a red crayon and outlined her hand on the paper. She drew a wobbly waddle down from her thumb and outlined her fingers with a purple crayon.

"Aunt Elizabeth," Jessie said primly. "That is a weird turkey."

There was a roar from the living room and Elizabeth could hear Bill shouting, "Yes! Yes!" The Bruins, she figured, must have scored a touchdown.

"Why do you think my turkey is weird, Jessie?" she said. She lifted up Jessie and placed her on her lap, smelling the top of her head.

Jessie laid her head on Elizabeth's shoulder. "I dunno. Maybe your turkey is sleepy."

"Do you want me to read to you?"

Jesse nodded.

Elizabeth picked her up and carried her to the rocking chair in the corner of the living room, but Jessie hopped off to run to her room. When she came back, she had *Frog and Toad Are Friends* in her hand. "This one," she said, crawling back in Elizabeth's lap.

Elizabeth rocked, reading about the Frog who asked Toad if he could tell him a story, Toad answering, "Yes, if you know a good one," and Jessie's lanky body fit into hers as they read about the lean sprightly frog and the long-suffering toad, as the burble of the football game continued across the room, the chair creaking as they rocked back and forth, Jessie growing groggy, Elizabeth settling back into herself as she thought, *I can do this, I can do this*, and she wasn't sure if that meant a baby or a sister, but, in this moment, with Jessie's sweet weight heavy in her lap, she wasn't sure she really cared.

CHAPTER THIRTY-SIX

She slipped into Roger's office, sitting in a chair, waiting until the thudding of their footsteps came closer.

There was a light knock.

"Dr. O, I presume," said the appointed spokesman, a round, hearty-looking man. "I'm here from Roy Brown's office. Can we step in?"

Louise stood up and held out her chair to the men.

"Come in, come in," Roger said. "It's a delight to see you. This *is* a historic day everyone—take note—March 21, 1974. I've been waiting for years to see a member of the governor's office down here."

"I'm here, as an appointee of the governor, to see what we can do to stop the strike," said the man.

"I see," said Roger. "Well." He turned his back to the men and looked out the window for a long time. Everyone waited. Louise wondered what his ploy was: Was he composing himself? Stalling for time? Finally, he swung around again, the leather chair squeaking.

"What you want to tell your governor," she heard Roger say, "is that this is basically a shit factory where the mentally retarded have been locked up forever and that none of this is working. Tell your governor that until he learns to pay his staff a decent wage, these deaths are going to continue, sad as they are, because we don't have enough people to adequately take care of the patients. Tell your governor that right now nurses and doctors are changing diapers and feeding patients because our entire staff is out on strike because they make less than a kid at a hamburger stand."

Flashbulbs popped, and a lone reporter scribbled in a notebook.

Louise sat with Roger that evening in his office, to hear the 5 P.M. local news out of Butte. The reporter announced, his face close to the script in his hand, that the governor had ordered the state workers back on the job. The strikers had refused to settle until the state had agreed to a 10 percent pay raise and to improve conditions at both the Stone Home and Hot Springs. Governor Roy Brown had talked about calling in the National Guard, but in a phone call to Roger, he assured him this would not be necessary. Roger told Louise this as she sat across the desk from him.

"He assured me," he said.

He held his hand across the desk.

Louise put her hand in his.

"Louise," he said. "My dear Louise." His eyes watered for a moment as he looked across the desk at her. "I feel like I know you better than anyone. I know this must be hard for you, with Audrey and all. Shit. It's hard for me. I'm sorry."

"It is what it is, Roger," she said, and cupped her hand around his.

He leaned over the desk toward her and she leaned toward him and there was something in the kiss—something so familiar and old and comradely—she knew that their affair, the physical part of it anyway, was over, and it dug at her. Why was she losing everything at once?

"Kiss me again, damn it," she said. "You can at least do that."

He leaned over and kissed her, the scatter of patient files, state order, pens and pill bottles beneath them, and he pulled her toward him and up on the desk and lifted her legs around him.

That night, Louise and Roger were working in Cottage Two. The cottage was a two-story building, with the harder cases upstairs, where they tied the men into their beds. Several men barely had a brain; one cried nearly the entire time they were there. Two rocked in the corner, in their blue hospital gowns. One large, hairy man in the back of the first floor had a mattress he flung at the wall, picked up, and flung again.

Roger firmly grabbed a large, black-haired man who was lying in bed and kicking his legs up and down, making the bedsprings shriek. His calves were thick—round as tamaracks and hairy. Despite her training, Louise felt repulsed by the size of them. Roger quickly grabbed a leg and tied it neatly to the iron bedpost. "You learn to be quick," he said and grabbed the other leg and did the same. The man looked at him, captured, and grunted.

Louise was helping a man who was sitting up on a reinforced bed. He was a mountain of flesh, with a neck that lapped into his body, and a body that lapped over his legs. Why was he tied to a bed? Roger, who had a hypodermic needle poised in his hand as he stood on the other side of the bed, said, "He's the shoe-eater." He punched the man's arm. The man bellowed, as Roger's thumb slowly pressed the plunger and then quickly withdrew the needle.

They were pushing a bed to cover the fire escape where one patient had escaped the night before, when, beneath the scraping of the iron on the wood floors, they heard another set of sounds.

Roger froze. "Do you hear what I hear?"

"Yes." Louise could make out the distant purr of the motors.

"Those aren't cars," Roger said. "Those are big motors."

The purr grew into a loud grinding of trucks gearing down, the crunch and pop of gravel as vehicles, lots of them, slowly made their way up the dirt road. Louise, who was attaching a restraint to an iron bed, looked at Roger across the man's shoulder.

He walked over to his black leather medical bag and shut it with a snap. "He lied to me, Louise," he said. "That fucking hypocrite Roy Brown lied to me."

The governor, of course, had called the National Guard anyway. Later Brown told Roger he did so to calm the public and to keep the union off-balance, but Roger said, "Bullshit." The governor's office wanted the advantage of surprise.

"Why wouldn't they want to move the patients?" Louise said. "If they get hurt, they'd look bad."

Roger looked at her, his eyes bright. "No, Louise. If a patient gets hurt, it makes the union look bad. That's what the bastards are thinking."

The patients quieted down, listening to the sound of the motors. Even the large, hairy man who threw mattresses against the wall lifted up the striped mattress and paused, listening, as the low buzz grew to a loud clanking rumble, accompanied by squeaking springs, men's voices, tires scraping on the dirt road—magnified it seemed in the dark night. Then, as if on cue, he threw the mattress against the wall, where it hit and slumped down to the floor again. The other men grew more agitated, moaning, crying out, rubbing their fists in their eyes and crying.

Roger stood at the head of the room. “Quiet now,” he said fiercely, as two large men who worked in Cottage Two came running up the stairs. “Frank and Earl’re here and there’s nothing to worry about.”

“Thanks guys,” Roger said. “This is between us.” Louise knew he’d had to pay them separately—working was strike-breaking but they had no one, literally not a single person—to take over Cottage Two, and it was too dangerous to leave these men alone.

Earl held out his hands to the men, palms up. “Hey! Guys!”

The men grew quieter.

“Bob, stop throwing the damn mattress and sit down.” The mattress man sat on the floor. Earl looked around and clenched his fists. The men looked back at him. “That’s more like it.”

“Go,” Roger told her. “I’m right behind you.”

The two of them walked out of Cottage Two into the dark. Roger held his bag in his left hand and with his right reached out for Louise’s. They linked hands as they walked along the dark path from the cottage until they reached the bridge, where they let go of one another, as if by agreement. Up the road stood the main Stone Home building, silhouetted by thirty pairs of headlights that snaked up the road behind that gate. Engines idled, like dogs panting.

“Want me to come?” Louise said.

“I can handle this,” he said.

Louise watched his back as he disappeared into the darkness. He walked in a straight line, no deviation, his steps even, determined, as he strode across the main campus to the gate and into the headlights, his short powerful body a dark mass, his fists clenching and unclenching. She could hear the engines chuffing, an owl calling in the distance. He unlatched the gate, walked it open, then walked to the first truck, where a door opened and a man jumped down to talk with him. Louise watched their heads as they leaned together, nodding, then moved apart. The man got back in his truck, waved to the others. Roger walked across the road, pointing to the empty baseball diamond, where the trucks filed in, one after the other, lining up in neat rows. Engines quieted and the soldiers piled out of the trucks, dozens of them, and set up tents, shook out sleeping bags. As she moved toward her cabin, the mown hayfield scratching her ankles, she could barely make out Roger's form as he walked the two-lane road to his ranch house, to his wife Audrey and his children, his body a hazy black shape, blurring into the darkness.

CHAPTER THIRTY-SEVEN

Three months later, Bob received another letter from Louise Gustafson. He read it at the end of a dreary day, March 4, 1974, in a month when the world seemed to be going mad, the Arabs threatening an oil embargo, the recession deepening, Elizabeth roaring home from school each day with some new tidbit about Watergate that just made him weary, Karen running around the house in slit Capri pants and a bikini top for her role as a harlot in *Jesus Christ Superstar*, Bob telling her for God's sake, just put on a bathrobe, will you? Workers at the state institutions were demanding the legislature sign the bill increasing their pay before they broke for Easter—and who could blame them—for God's sake, some of them made a paltry four hundred dollars a month. The reporters started crawling around the Stone Home with their notebooks and cameras, writing stories about how understaffed and overcrowded the place was, about the strung-out patients, the rooms with no furniture where patients slept on cushions on the floor, and he lived in dread that one morning he would open the paper and stare at the face of the daughter he had left behind. A young woman choked to death on a spoon. A convicted rapist was hired as an aide and impregnated a patient before they caught up with him. It was like terrible music coming up the street toward him, and hard as he tried to concentrate on the good things in his life—his beautiful family, his business expanding so that he had to hire two other agents and move into a larger building out on the strip where there was more parking, he couldn't ignore the strident sounds approaching.

He spent the day ignoring the letter, working instead on an overdue claim, death benefits for a woman who had been widowed when a logging truck jackknifed in front of her husband's car and he couldn't brake fast enough. In the quiet office, the other agents gone, water dripping from the eaves, the secretary out early for a doctor's appointment, he picked up his letter opener, a miniature sword that had been his father's, and slit open the thick white envelope.

Dear Mr. Carter,

I am writing to ask that you fill out this form so that, in the event that the staff goes on strike at the Stone Home, your daughter Elizabeth can be placed in a foster care situation. She is 4' 10", approximately 108 pounds. She displays the typical facial features of Down syndrome. She is a trainable adult, she has been in an institution for 20 years, and she desperately needs to be in a home—your home if possible—but if that is not possible, another home. We need you to fill out this form in order for her to be placed, perhaps in foster care, but again, it would be best for you to have her to your home. She is a lovely girl.

Sincerely,
Louise Gustafson

Bob glanced at the form, the blank space for patient name, address, parents, medical condition, and felt a weariness steal over him. Four foot ten, 108 pounds. A trainable adult. What did that mean? Why was this woman, this Louise Gustafson, always at him, always telling him to send money, toys, clothes, nothing ever enough, and now this: bring her home? He had seen a picture of her once, sent by this Louise. The girl stared straight at the camera, her hair chopped off, her eyes angry, her mouth pulled down in a deep frown. Have her at the dinner table with Karen and Elizabeth and Mary?

Never.

He would do what he was required to do, he would pay her keep. When she was born, Cecil had instructed him to take her to the Stone Home and start over. And he did. And now this Louise Gustafson was going to change all that? Because they decided that now it didn't all work? Just when he felt like he was getting ahead, his kids were doing well, Mary beyond her sadness, and he actually had some money in the bank, why did everyone suddenly decide to change the rules on him?

One day, he and Mary were at a stoplight in downtown Bridger, on their way to dinner with Cecil and his wife, when an older woman, hand-in-hand with a young girl, crossed the street in front of them. The young girl looked at the woman as they crossed, her eyes clear and trusting in her round, flat face, as they slowly walked in front of the cars, rumbling with exhaust.

"Do you have regrets, Mary?" he said. He turned to her, his hands gripping the steering wheel.

She was silent. A muscle in her cheek twitched.

Bob knew he shouldn't have asked. When this topic came up, Mary just disappeared somewhere. Her eyes followed the woman and the child as they reached the sidewalk and the girl skipped up on the curb.

"Do you think I'm doing a bad job as a mother?" she said. Her voice was icy. "Do you find me lacking?"

"Mary!" Bob said. "That's not at all what I'm asking."

Mary watched the girl and the woman move down the sidewalk until they disappeared inside the Penney's building.

She snapped her head around. "I can't answer that question."

They drove on to the restaurant, where Bob welcomed the clatter of plates and glasses to drown out the static between them. They put their menus up like shields, waiting for Cecil and his wife to arrive.

He set the letter in his inbox. Bring her home. This was the latest thing. This new director said all these patients needed to be home. With their families. They shouldn't be here. Jesus. First they tell you, by law, this is the best thing to do with your child—and you do that—and then, twenty years later, they try to turn around and tell you, guess not, time to bring these kids home, folks.

Under the letter were claims from the past winter. The season had been particularly damaging: heavy wet snows in February caused a lot of roof cave-ins on barns among farmers and ranchers in the Bitterroot and the Flathead. An early spring hailstorm ruined fields of winter wheat just as they were ready for harvest.

Bob picked up the form from Louise Gustafson, studied it, and set it down again. Name, address, parents, condition. He wondered what the child looked like now. He wondered if he would ever tell the other girls, but the idea made his blood run cold. His family was his family: Mary, Elizabeth, and Karen. This child was a bad dream, a false start. He got up, pacing the office, overtaken by restlessness. Who was this Louise Gustafson who was always writing him? Didn't she get his checks? Didn't she know how hard he worked to keep up with all this?

He walked to a filing cabinet and pulled out a claim report. He slammed it shut. Damn self-righteous busybody. He was going to make it right for this farmer, for the wheat he'd lost—poor guy, a whole year's work down the drain. He copied out the man's name, address, filling in all the details of the storm and the acres of damage the farmer had sustained, and as he worked out each line, his anger subsided.

He, Mary, and the girls visited the farmer in Arlee that weekend. His farm was at the end of a long, curving road to the base of the Mission Mountains, and as Bob sat at his kitchen table drinking coffee and visiting about the storm damage, Mary and the girls walked along the road, laughing and pointing at his small herd of cream-colored Charolais cows. The farmer showed him pictures of the fields, first waving green sprouts of grain, next a field of mush, flattened by hailstones. The farmer told him he'd replanted soon after, "on a wing and prayer," and was hoping for a beautiful crop. He shrugged. "But that could change in a minute." Bob stood and shook his hand. After his meeting, the family drove on to spend the night at a nearby hot springs, soaking in the oily-feeling mineral water, Elizabeth and Karen the stars of the pool in their skimpy bikinis, as he and Mary grew red and limp in water that smelled of sulfur, and later, as Karen and Elizabeth laughed over Monopoly in their room, he and Mary quietly made love deep under the covers, their skin smooth and shiny and smelling of rotten eggs.

Of course, when he returned to the office on Monday, there was another letter waiting for him, dated March 10, 1974.

> *We desperately need to get your permission to move Elizabeth in the event of a strike. The staff at Stone Home regret such a move, but we have to do it. The legislature that is currently in session has not approved additional funding*

for the state institutions at Stone City, or Hot Springs. The staff feels they may be forced to take such measures as a strike as $125 a week is not enough to live on for such difficult jobs. Please help us, Mr. Carter. Please help your daughter.

Can't you just take five minutes of your time, Mr. Carter? How long do you expect an institution to wait for you to fill out a simple form?

Regards,
Louise Gustafson

He set the letter on the stack of papers in his inbox. He must answer her, he knew. He would do it at 3 P.M. He heard the irritation in the woman's voice. She was right, after all; it would take five minutes. Her irritation stung and cornered and infuriated him. Why did he have to keep answering this question about the other Elizabeth? When he and Mary had taken her to the Stone Home and signed the papers, he had thought that was all behind him. He had his Elizabeth, his lovely talented Elizabeth, and he had Karen, a curly-headed sprite, but somehow this was never enough.

He was all for the staff getting better salaries. Of course they should. The salaries were pittances—beginning at $425 a month. He'd write the governor, his legislator. But bring the child home? The letter seemed so pointed, annoying, mingling the way it did with the insurance claims and the newsletters from the Rotary and the chamber of commerce and the zoning committee that he'd recently taken up with, the inbox always churning over and over, like waves spewing up dirt and old seaweed and ship's garbage and tossing it on the beach for all to see, the letter getting buried and then, just a few hours later, resurfacing, glittering and nasty, and containing new meanings each time he read it. Louise Gustafson and her huffy name, her self-righteous, annoying tone: "How long do you expect me to wait?"

Jesus, didn't he help out?—working for the city on the litter drive, volunteering for the pancake sale at Kiwanis, selling tickets door to door in his neighborhood, raising money for the disadvantaged youth basketball tournament where the boys were so poor they wore cut-off socks around their wrists instead of sweatbands. He helped the neighbor woman—whose husband was a drunk and who worked as a waitress—take her kids to school each morning, packing them in the car with his girls, the young boys stroking the leather seats of his Thunderbird and one of them whispering, when they thought he couldn't hear, "Your dad is rich."

"My dad isn't rich," Elizabeth said to the thin, yellow-faced boy who clutched a black metal lunchbox to his chest. "He just saves his money."

"No," the kid said bluntly, looking from their spotless wool coats to the leather seats and back to their clean shiny hair. "Your dad is rich."

Elizabeth comprehended what he meant, and said quickly, "Your dad has that cool red pickup."

"And it makes that great sound," Karen leaned over the seat to add. "*Grrrrr.* Like a bear."

The boy beamed. Bob felt his heart swell with pride.

Bob shoveled the walks. He made fried eggs and toast for breakfast in the morning as Mary tunneled further into the bed for an extra fifteen minutes of sleep and he bundled the girls up and took them to school. He worked late at night winding up insurance claims. Because Mary was busy with her bridge club and her symphony committees, he drove up to Seeley to see Pete at the sawmill, where he kept on his metal desk a picture of his son dressed in his captain's uniform, saluting. "Kid's in 'Nam, just made captain," Pete said. "Damn kid. Didn't think he amount to anything for a while there, Bob."

But when he returned to his office, several days later, the form was still there in the inbox, staring at him. He looked at it. This is ridiculous, he told himself. Fill out that damn thing. What are you afraid of? Some damn officious bitch of a nurse with her stupid lines like, "How long do you expect an institution to wait?"

He walked to the bay window of his office, the office he made in an old building, its shelves filled with legal codes and torts and models ships he had built and an old fan given to him by a Japanese woman several lifetimes ago after his Liberty ship had landed in Okinawa Harbor. The other two agents were firmly ensconced in offices upstairs. This was his business. Over the years, he had tripled his accounts. So why was he undermined by this question: "Can't you just take five minutes of your time?"

How could he say to Louise Gustafson that every time he picked up this form his mind went black and his hands and legs turned to cement?

Four days later, another letter from Louise Gustafson. His heart pounded as he looked at it, the mail-o-gram, the address peeking through the window in her curt, angry writing. He looked at the form. Patient's name. Age. Father. Mother. He ripped the letter open, hands trembling. He pictured her, as he read it, her lips pursed over the typewriter as she pounded the keys. He was ready to write her supervisor. The tone she took.

March 20, 1974
Dear Mr. Carter:
I strongly advise you to take Elizabeth for the duration of the strike—that would be infinitely better than a hospital

or foster situation. I would also appreciate any additional information you may provide me about Elizabeth.

This time, no salutation at the end. Just: *Louise Gustafson.*

He cringed, imagining her, her face red, signing the letter with her slashing signature, furious, and she was right, of course, but he buried this letter too. Instead, he headed to a nearby drive-in, where a large-breasted teenaged girl, with eyes outlined in black eyeliner and long, droopy brown hair served him two cheeseburgers and a chocolate milkshake and a large order of fries. When she handed him the crackling paper packages, dotted with grease, he told her, "My wife is going to kill me. I'm not supposed to be eating this between meals—not good for the waistline, but you know, some days—you just need a little pick-me-up," as he looked at her face, her chest, her grease-slicked fingers, then down at the hamburgers.

The girl looked at him, her eyes flat, as she said, "Well, if I were you mister—I wouldn't tell your wife. Not that it's any of my beeswax."

On March 23, 1974, he picked up a pen and legal pad and in the deep gloom of his office, he began to write, looking across his desk at the scattered claims for damages—hail damage, snow damage, damage from fallen trees and lightning and storms— writing as fast as he could before he lost his nerve, crossing things out, writing until his hand cramped, stopping every once in a while to listen to his heart thump. He got up, peed, poured himself more coffee in the delicate eggshell porcelain teacup that was all that was left of his great-grandmother's Dresden china, and looked out the dirty window of the coffee room to stare at the brick wall of the building next door, then he walked back to his office, shut the door, and wrote again.

The next day, he paid his secretary extra to skip her lunch hour and type the letter. He felt badly that she had to read his messy handwriting, but he paid her well to translate a three-page draft—with additions and corrections, arrows going all over the page like some kind of hieroglyphics—into a neatly typed collection of thoughts. The type was all caps, the font on one of the first correcting typewriters made in 1972, which rendered the chaos of his thoughts into an orderly and rather oddly decree-like-looking document on the stationary that featured the Robert Carter Insurance logo.

"Please," Bob said to her as he handed her the letter at her typewriter, the woman looking up at him, her hands in her lap. "Please keep this to yourself."

"Yes, Mr. Carter." She looked at the letter, instead of at his face, as if avoiding eye contact somehow made this more private.

She began to type, the loud hum of the motor and the tapping of her red fingernails against the keys steadying him, each sentence punctuated by a clean *ding*. He told her he was going out to lunch as she completed the letter.

He walked to his Tuesday Kiwanis meeting, past the ice cream shop where the old man was known to have a meeting of leftists in the back, past the furniture shop with its white- and gold-trimmed bedroom sets, and the electrical store where grim-faced men in coveralls came in and out. He went across the bridge over the river, where a small island of ice dotted the dark water, past the theater where he was planning to take Mary to see *Murder on the Orient Express*, though in truth the movie he really wanted to see was *Death Wish,* with what looked like its satisfying take on revenge, but Mary told him no, it was too violent. At the meeting, he put on his badge, Bob Carter, stood for the Pledge of Allegiance, bowed his head for the prayer, and put in a dollar for the Happy Bucks so that he could brag about Elizabeth's upcoming recital, another dollar to brag about Karen's play; these were his daughters, he thought to himself, looking out across the room of men who, in turn, paid Happy Bucks to brag about their own children—before sitting down to eat his gummy Swedish meatballs, listening to the biology professor's program on the health effects of smoke from the local paper mill.

When he returned, coming in the office, up the peeling steps that led up the back way, hanging up his jacket on the hook, bringing in a cup of coffee that had soured on the burner, he settled himself back at the desk. She brought the letter to him, neatly typed on his letterhead, tucked in the fold of a Carter Insurance envelope, smiling as she handed it to him, patting him on the hand, then softly closing the door as she went out, her heels dully scritching across the carpet.

He read the first paragraph.

> *March 23, 1974*
>
> *Dear Miss Louise Gustafson:*
>
> *Your letter regarding Elizabeth has been received. In regard to a visit to our home, I am afraid we cannot agree to this. When Elizabeth was born, we discussed this with our doctor and many others who had similar problems, and our decision was not to keep Elizabeth in the home. Our doctor advised against it. Our doctor said that the best thing for the mongoloid baby and for us was for us to send her to the Stone Home for the Mentally Retarded because they would now care for her.*

He brought up the issue with Mary the night after the dinner with Cecil and his wife. They had just settled themselves into bed, snapped on the bedside lamps, and Mary had opened *Dr. Zhivago*, when Bob broached the subject. Bring her home? Mary sat up abruptly and pulled the chenille bedspread over her as if she'd just taken a chill. "She's seventeen now, Bob. She's been in an institution her whole life," Mary said. Her face softened. "Though if you want it,

I guess we could put her in the back bedroom. I do wonder about her. But how do we break this to the girls? Our lives will totally change. How do I care for her? Do I stay home with her all the time? What if she has a seizure?" She looked at Bob, her face white, her eyes panicked. "No," he held out his arms and held her to him, her body still slender after three births, her soft breasts pressing against his chest through the thin cotton of her pajamas. "This isn't wise. We made our decision, Mary." "I know," she said, her voice muffled in the covers. "We made our decision."

He looked down at the rest of the letter.

We further decided that, despite the risk of having another retarded child, we would have more children. We have two lovely daughters who are superior students, one who sings like a meadowlark, the other dances on the drill team: she can kick her leg over her head and do the splits all the way to the floor. They do not know about their retarded sister. I do not think, at this late date, it is wise to discuss this sister with them. We named our oldest Elizabeth because we loved the name. It is a family name and while we thought of naming her something else--we did not want to. You can see how awkward it would be if they would meet. Two Elizabeth Carters.

I have supported my family the best I know how and they have had a wonderful childhood. I have supported my mother, who was manic-depressive and suffered from stomach cancer, a long sad death, supporting her in the end at an expensive rest home. It was something I wanted to do, of course, but I was trying to do my best.

I have seen many families where they keep the retarded child, and the results are unfortunate. My wife is an excellent mother, but she could not take the added burden of another child. I am trying to be a good man and make a better world by raising my children the best I can. I am trying to instill in them the idea of love and of being a good, conscientious member of our society. I hope you will try to understand this.

I am trying to be a good citizen.

We feel, rightly or wrong, that I am making my contribution toward society by raising my beautiful daughters, in whom I am trying to instill ideas of good and evil, and right and wrong, and those values that are important to maintaining a good society. I hope you will understand my feelings and we can cooperate with each other on this basis.

Sincerely,
Robert Carter

Bob looked at the letter, typed in all caps, and next to it, the yellow legal paper of his draft, curling from the weight of his handwriting that marched across it in orderly rows, the scribbles, the cross-outs, the circled insertions crawling across the page. This, as much as anything, he thought, was a declaration of his life.

He sat in his office, knowing that he needed to go home to the dinner that Mary would have prepared for exactly six o'clock, when all of them—he, Mary, Elizabeth, and Karen—would wearily gather around the table for meat, vegetables, salad, and baked potatoes, the precise balanced meal Mary prepared each night. They would converse about the day, and how would he put this one into words?

After he signed the letter, he folded it in thirds and sealed it, along with the form, inside the Carter Insurance envelope. He then sat, watching the room darken as the sun reddened the horizon through the word "Insurance" on the glass. On the street outside, the traffic lights shone red, yellow, green in the plate-glass windows of the lighting store, and the hiss of traffic picked up in the slushy streets outside. The traffic was thinning, which meant that he really needed to go. He shoved himself out of his chair and shut off the lights and shut down the coffeemaker, and walked out the front door and down the street to the mailbox, where he opened the metal door and watched the letter slip down into the darkness.

It was a day he thought about years later, when his Elizabeth asked him, "Do you think life is generally sad or happy?" He paused a long time before he answered. "Generally sad," he said. She kissed his cheek. "But you're such a happy daddy, Daddy," she said. "That doesn't make sense."

"You're young," he said and kissed her head.

"While I accept your statement about your contribution to society," Louise Gustafson wrote back on March 25, 1974,

> *I cannot accept the position that you so quickly deny your responsibility to Elizabeth. I'm sure if your other Elizabeth, whom you have discussed in previous letters, needed these things—you would not deny her.*
>
> *P.S. Elizabeth is also in need of all type of clothing such as: dresses, slips, panties, half socks, tights, slacks, blouses, sweaters, and a jacket. Perma-press or wash and wear clothing would be appreciated. She has grown and takes a size-12 chubby.*

That night, he told Mary he had a meeting and snuck out to the Fox Theater. He hoped that no one saw him—it wasn't like he was going to see porn—it was just that someone was likely to ask him where Mary was, and he'd have to lie, and he'd already told Mary a lie, but he just wanted to see this movie, *Death Wish*, so here he was, and he bought a giant buttered popcorn and sat in the front, righteous and guilty, as Charles Bronson cocked his pistol and began to look for the criminal who had murdered his family. A warm, delicious feeling of revenge stole over him.

When he got home, Mary was up. "Where have you been?" she said. "I've been waiting for you."

"A meeting," he said, and turned to the sink so she couldn't see the flicker across his face.

"Dick's been frantically trying to reach you."

"Dick?"

"He called from home. From the Frontier Lounge. And this time from Eddy's Club. Here's the number." She thrust a scrap of paper into Bob's hand. "I cannot talk with him again. He is very drunk and isn't making a lot of sense and seems to want to talk to me about a philosophy of life or some such nonsense, and I'm going to bed." She kissed him on the nose, turned, and proceeded up the stairs.

He called the number. Dark images of wet New York streets, Bronson's narrowed eyes, still crowded his brain as a voice answered, "Yup. Eddy's" and Bob asked for his friend. "Oh that guy," the bartender said. "He's right here."

"Bob, my friend, my port in a storm, my knight in shining armor," Dick said when he got on the phone. His voice was slurred. Clearly, Bob thought, he'd been there for a while.

Bob laughed. "What is it, Dick? How can I help you this evening?"

Dick whispered something indistinguishable from the background noises of glass clanking and voices shouting.

"I can't hear you," Bob said.

"I need you to get me, Bob."

"Don't you have a car? Can't you drive?"

"I need you to get me, Bob," Dick said again. "I can't explain."

Bob was at Eddy's in ten minutes, annoyed by having to come back out so late, but determined to help his friend. Dick was in the back at a table, his long legs sticking out, his work boots pointing to the ceiling, his arms dangling. He looked up as Bob approached and tried to stand up, but he knocked the table over, his beer bottle clanking on the floor. He pulled the table to rights and sat down and, when the barmaid came to wipe up the foaming beer, held up his finger and said, "One more and one for my friend here, miss."

Bob sat down. It had been nearly a year and a half since he'd seen Dick and he was shocked by how he'd aged, his nose purpled, his eyes bloodshot. Dick waited until the beers were in front of them. He smacked the table. He leaned over to Bob. "I want you to know, formally, or formerly," he said and smiled. "I've made a fucking mess of everything, Bob." Bob started to shake his head. "Don't even start," Dick said. "I'm a mess. I messed up my marriage to a beautiful woman—you know that—she came to see you." Bob startled. "Yes, I know about that, how can you keep a secret like that in this town? But I appreciate it, my friend, she trusted you and so do I. That's why I'm telling you this. That girl you saw me with at your party? Dumped me. 'You're a drunk, she said. So did the other dame I tried to see. I'm a fucking mess, Bob. A failure."

Dick looked at him. He placed his hand on the table. "And now I go calling you late at night, keeping you from your beautiful wife and girls. You did everything right, Bob. Shit, look at Arnie, chairman of the bank and all, little Arnie from the Northside. Why is that?"

"Jesus, Dick," Bob said. "Don't be so hard on yourself."

"No, I'm serious. I'm washed up. Over. Over and out. *Sayonara*, isn't that what the cartoon guy says."

Bob tried to tell him things he had to live for: his kids, his business, heck, women he hadn't even met yet, but Dick would have none of it. They were sipping their beers when a small man in a ragged green leprechaun's hat came up to them. Dick motioned him away, but the man wanted money. Bob reached in his wallet to give him a dollar and the man snatched it out his hand and laughed. "You," the man's eyes bulged as he looked close into Dick's face, "are a muddle. And you," he swung his head to Bob, "are a puddin' head."

"And you," Dick said, with perfect timing, "can go fuck yourself."

Bob and Dick laughed, and Bob told him he'd give him a ride to his house.

The next day, at noon, he got a call from the Bridger Police that Dick was dead. He'd been found by a neighbor who'd heard a shot the night before. Gunshot wound to the head.

Four days after that, Louise Gustafson wrote to say that she felt, since he had neglected his parental responsibilities, that she had no other options. She would like to take custody of the child. On March 29, 1974, he signed an order granting this woman, Louise Gustafson—this irritating, nagging woman with her needling, impatient questions, whom he had never met—custody of his first daughter, Elizabeth Finch Carter.

CHAPTER THIRTY-EIGHT

Ruth put her on the "Special Lives" beat, which was depressing because Clayton was researching grizzly bears on the Rocky Mountain Front, another assignment she had wanted, but they were down another reporter and, Ruth said, she simply didn't have anyone else to do it. She was writing about the citizens of Bridger who had passed away, leaving in their wake stories of military service, business careers, hobbies. The World War II vet who built model train sets from London, Paris, even Edinburgh in his basement. The nineteen-year-old mother who died in a motorcycle crash, leaving behind a nine-month-old baby and her epitaph: "Holy Crap, What a Ride!"

In November, Ruth, at last, assigned her to cover an unusual weather event that had impacted a forest outside Seeley Lake. Elizabeth met a forest service ranger at the roadside turnoff to Inez Lake. She locked up her car and hopped into the cab of the ranger's four-wheel-drive pickup to head down the snow-covered road, wheels spinning in a couple of deep spots. After driving for a while, they arrived at a thickly timbered curve near Inez Lake. The ranger stopped the truck. The two of them sat in the cab and looked out at the forest, dead still in the grey afternoon.

"Amazing, these microbursts," the ranger said. "They're like a little tornado that just sets down in one place. Then it picks up and goes away. My pal tells me there's another place it set down, further up in the mountains. Strange, ain't it?"

"When did it happen?"

"Last night. We had a big rainstorm over Seeley so thick, man, if you walked outside, you'd be soaked in a minute, and gusts of wind up to—I dunno—hundred miles an hour. Shit—excuse my language ma'am—there were branches flying around everywhere. I never seen anything like it." He looked out the window and shook his head. "Probably never will again." He laughed. "I hope. It's like some whirling dervish just set down in the forest with a buzz saw and started cuttin'."

That was exactly what it looked like to Elizabeth. In a thick stand of tamaracks that extended from the road down to the lake, a swath of trees were broken off in the middle, as if a giant hand had come by and snapped them in half like toothpicks. She grabbed her notebook, stepped out of the cab, and walked a few feet until the crosshatch of fallen timbers prevented her from walking farther, writing notes about the fallen trunks, broken limbs draped with the pale green lichen they used to call "witch's hair." The piles of tree limbs were ten feet high in places.

She returned to Bridger on the heels of another storm, the snow pelting down so hard it was hypnotizing as she inched along the chain of lakes—Summit, Alva, Inez—to Seeley, then past a car that had slipped off the road and an overturned semi. When it was a near-whiteout at Ovando, she pulled over, looking out at the jackleg fences and wide-open pastures where the snow was rapidly piling up. In the distance she could see the huddled cattle. When the snow lightened, she continued south along the Blackfoot River. By the time she reached the river's confluence with the Clark Fork, she was exhausted and running late. She quickly made it to the office, put together her story, and filed it.

She knew Tom and Nonny and Lucinda were waiting for her at the annual Day of the Dead potluck, where kids and adults alike ate tofu casserole and chocolate and read poems about departed grandmas and grandfathers, ghosts and goblins.

When she showed up, the party in the gymnasium was under way. The Day of the Dead ceremony was over—the kids having read their poems—and people were lining up at a table laden with bean and pasta dishes and thick hunks of homemade bread. Parents were dressed in their best Guatemalan fare with a few vintage velvet dresses thrown in. Many of the children had faces painted white with blacked-in eyes—their ghostly cheeks smeared with chocolate.

Elizabeth paused before diving into the cacophony of shouting children, banging silverware, and thunking guitar music. She watched two girls with wild, curly hair holding hands and dancing by the boom box. Mothers were dishing up tin plates of food for young children.

"Pasta, Seth?" one mother said, holding a plate for her distracted son, who bounced up and down next to her in his top hat and skeleton T-shirt. "Yummy pasta? Or yogurt and banana?"

Seth looked at her as if she had two heads and shouted, "Cake!"

At one of the long Formica tables where families and children sat elbow-to-elbow, Elizabeth squeezed in next to Tom.

"You made it." Tom glanced at her and squeezed her hand.

"How're the roads?" He lifted her hat from her head and smoothed her hair. "Did you get caught in the snowstorm?"

"Knuckle-whitening," she said. "But I made it."

Nonny was across the table. She leaned over, her grey-streaked blonde hair brushing her shoulders. "Lord, girl, I can't believe you drove in this. But look—what lies before you! Student singing!"

Next to her, Lucinda smiled sweetly. "That's code for drinks at our house afterwards."

"But I love the singing," Elizabeth said. "It makes me cry." It brought up her sense of those lost days when she was on the stage, singing about the faraway moon, her father sitting in the back of the audience clapping, always clapping for her.

"That makes one of you," Lucinda said.

"Two of us," Tom added.

"Tom's such a softy," Nonny said and rolled her eyes. "He's almost too much for us."

Tom shrugged and smiled at his friend and colleague, Nonny—the long warm friendship between them encapsulated in their easy smiles. "I suppose."

They moved through the potluck line to eat their fill of green salads, rice salads, pasta salads, and baked ziti, and then they moved on to the meat of the dinner—dessert: rich chocolate cakes decorated with skulls, beautiful hand-painted cookies with black frosting and bones, white-and-black kisses—before they settled in for the last item on the program, the singing of "Bones, Bones, 'Dem Bones."

Elizabeth held herself close. She watched mothers spoon-feeding their babies, the mouths closing around the silver, the food dribbling this way and that, and felt a sadness welling up in her. *Stop*, she told herself. She hadn't been like this for so long, what was wrong with her? Was it the relief of getting home after driving those hideous roads? This was a show, she told herself; children are children. She listened to a little girl who started the group off singing, "The ankle bone's connected to the—thigh bone." The girl's tights had smudges of black at the knees. Then the other kids stood up, one by one, until they were all singing the song.

She watched their wriggling bodies, the pigtails, the soft faces, and she thought of her story on wind: how, when the temperature changes and a front is coming in, it is often borne on a stiff wind, an Arctic front from the north, or the warm, dry Chinook wind blowing down the east side of the Rockies, the breath of the world, each one bringing its own set of temperature changes, the air unsettled and churning.

Everyone stood at the end of "'Dem Bones," clapping, the parents wiping their eyes, Tom's students yelling for him, the little ones jumping up and down as they had the year before. Maybe, she thought, this is what traditions are all about. Rituals to prop you up, year after year. Actions and reactions to keep you hurtling through time and space, to keep you moving until the blood comes back into your fingers, until your heart begins to thaw.

It came on suddenly. Her face grew damp and she hurried through the crowd, heading for the bathroom, past the mothers washing their children's hands at the sink or changing diapers at a table, diving into a stall. She locked the door, sat on the toilet, her head on her legs, her back shaking as she tried to bury her sobs in her Levis, the image of that face swimming before her, the ragged hair, the frown, the eyes point-blank. Angry.

Later that night, she and Tom went to Nonny and Lucinda's house, a sweet red craftsman bungalow tucked at the end of Lilac Street against Mount Jumbo, where they hiked each day with their dog, Butternut. Nonny brought them glasses of cabernet. Lucinda curled up on the blue couch, Tom across from her on a tattered leather chair that had belonged to Nonny's father, the judge. Elizabeth was next to Lucinda. Nonny hovered, serving cheese and crackers, adjusting the music. It was a chilly evening, so Nonny got up and made a fire in the fireplace.

Elizabeth knew that everyone could see she had been crying—her eyes and nose were red. They were all careful with her, even Tom asking her nothing in the car, as if he somehow sensed she needed quiet.

"Sit down, Nonny," Lucinda kept saying as Nonny jumped up to fiddle with the pillows or to get more cheese. "Everything is fine."

But Nonny kept on, asking everyone if they wanted to hear jazz or classical guitar, bluegrass or fusion. "And we need more wood," she said. "We need more wood."

"What we want," Tom said, "is for you to sit."

"Second that," Elizabeth chimed in.

Butternut, a pound dog from the Blackfeet Reservation that was the color, it was true, of squash, paddled her feet in her sleep.

"Okay, I'm sitting," Nonny said and sat, though they could tell by the way she perched at the edge of the chair, it was temporary. "Look at Butternut. She's running in her sleep. Chasing squirrels, probably."

"What I wonder," said Tom, "is if they ever catch them. Dogs are always chasing things in their sleep, it seems, but if they catch them, do they wake up?"

Lucinda laughed. "Like when we fall off a cliff in our dreams?"

"Precisely," Tom said. "Like when we fall off a cliff in our dreams."

When he turned to her in bed that night, Elizabeth held him for the first time in months, feeling the warmth of his flesh, the nob of his backbone, the thin mantle of hairs covering his stomach.

The language of bodies, she thought.

"You okay?" he said. "I was worried about you."

"Everything just caught up with me," she said. She still felt raw, though the wine had taken the edge off. "The baby, this other Elizabeth, and then hearing those sweet children singing—something just snapped."

"I'm glad you're okay," he murmured, arching his back against her. "This is lovely."

"Mmm," she said. Between them, the touch of fingers, brush of hair, skin. He turned to face her and began to massage her breasts, the nipples growing erect, all of her warming. Then she recoiled slightly, the frozen place there again.

He stopped.

A quiver of sorrow between them.

"It's okay," he said. He stroked Elizabeth's back, though she could tell he was hurt.

"I'm sorry," she whispered.

"This doesn't have to happen right away," Tom said. "Go easy, Elizabeth."

And then it did happen, the coming together, the deep-at-night, under-covers love, the tangle of limbs and sweat and breath and the sweet sink into sleep.

The next morning, Tom came upstairs to bed, bearing coffee and the newspaper. "You're on the front page. But check out this story—I'm so glad you are home—two teenagers walked into a bar in Stone City—The Lounge—looking for cash, and, when they didn't produce any, they murdered the owner and his wife, Terrance and Marie Duffy, with a shotgun. Their son is Patrick Duffy of *Dallas,* the TV show."

CHAPTER THIRTY-NINE

There was no answer to the letter that she'd sent two months ago, or to any of Louise's follow-up notes, even the one where she lost her temper and wrote, *For God's sake, Mr. Carter, how long does it take to pick up a pen and tell us yes or no?*

Finally, Robert Carter's letter about citizenship. About his fine family, introducing her to each child and the wonderful things they were doing in school. And this other Elizabeth. Really? She wanted to scream. You have another child and give her the same name, as if to wipe your past clean? What were you thinking? Of course she sings soprano, gets good grades, takes the lead in the school plays. And her sister, Kim, Kelsey, Karen? Her hair the color of fire, whose math scores were top of the class. And how he tried to raise a good family, be a good citizen, a good man. Please try to understand, he'd implored.

Citizenship? She wanted to scream back at him. What in the hell are you talking about, *citizenship*?

She wrote back a quick note. *I bet if your other Elizabeth needed you, you'd help her.*

No reply.

She put another log on the fire, watched as it sent a shower of sparks up the chimney. She looked around the cabin, at the quilt, the pictures, her rocking chair. She had come all this way, created a life for herself that had enfolded her, embraced her, supported her—Roger, Lizzie, her friend Anna—but suddenly she could feel it all cracking around her. And this guy whose child she had basically reared wanted to talk with her about citizenship?

A week into the strike, the National Guard was called in to serve as staff. At first, the picketers at the gates booed the guardsmen from their tents at the Stone Home's gates or went silent and stone-faced. But as word got around about how the men worked in the main home and the cottages, changing beds, diapering children, overseeing nurseries, feeding patients, wiping up spit-up and puke and shit, they earned the respect of the nurses and later the staff who were picketing outside the gates of the Stone Home. Many of the guardsmen wore clothespins on their noses as they worked. One whole unit was organized just to mop—cottage floors, the brick administration building—another unit organized just to do laundry. One crew was assembled to cook, and they bought groceries from the local farms so that on top of the canned dinners, at least the crew had fresh eggs and bacon for breakfast. The young children loved the soldiers in their uniforms who taught them to salute and to drill. They followed the guardsmen like flocks of starlings as the young men cooked up impromptu games of hopscotch and flag football for some of the more ambulatory patients or carried babies around on their shoulders like sacks of potatoes.

The strikers continued, writing letters to the *Helena Independent*, the *Butte Standard*, tirelessly driving up to Helena where they'd carry pickets in front of the statehouse.

When his office announced that Governor Roy Brown would visit, Roger was incredulous.

"Roy Brown's coming here?" he said to Louise as she and Anna stood in his office at 10 P.M. one night, sipping from a bottle of whisky Roger produced from his desk. "This ought to be entertaining."

Louise waited with Roger in his office until the governor's entourage arrived with several newspaper reporters, a photographer, and his press secretary, a statuesque blonde in a lime green minidress and a look of barely disguised horror. The governor's long lanky form filled Roger's office door. He was dressed in a dark blue, double-breasted suit, his jacket slung over his shoulders, his bell-bottom pants fitted around the hips, his sideburns trimmed.

"Well, if it isn't Governor Roy Brown," Roger said. "Welcome to Stone City, governor. What a pleasure."

"Doctor Oetzinger," the governor said breezily. "This is a grave situation here. I admire your commitment."

"Nice to see you at my door. Seems like when I'm in Helena, I can't get past your door."

Governor Brown cleared his throat. "I want you to know," he said, looking at Roger straight in the eye, the air thickening between them, "I'm more aware than ever of this situation—the patients, the laundry, the staff shortages. I want to help."

"Are you going to settle this strike by increasing the pay for these workers?"

"We're considering our options, doctor," the governor said. He stood straight, a concerned look on his face, as a flashbulb popped.

"In that case," Roger said, "I invite you to my gallery."

The governor looked puzzled. He took a quick look at his thick gold watch. "I was hoping to tour the facilities—I don't have a lot of time."

"It's okay—" Roger said, his voice so light, so breezy, Louise felt a numb dread crawl down her spine. "I know you are a busy man, sir. It just takes a minute." He pushed himself up from his chair, stood and held out his arm, sweeping it around the large oak-paneled office. "Welcome."

The governor bowed his head.

"Now I'll direct your attention to my exhibit," Roger said simply, holding his arm out to a series of black-and-white Xerox copies taped on his wall.

As the governor walked past the chair where Louise was sitting, she could smell his spicy aftershave. He walked close to the Xeroxes, his face frozen into what she would describe as an "art appreciation" smile, which slowly disappeared as his face flushed a deep red as he studied the black-and-white photographs that seemed so abstract at the onset, and gradually recognized the photographs for what they were: butts—old butts, young butts, wrinkled butts, hairy butts—lacerated with burns, scabs, and welts.

"This is my butt gallery, Governor Brown," Roger said. "Do you remember those radiator covers that I requested? The ones that cost only $10 a piece? The ones that you never supplied? Well, this is what happens without them. This is what happens when patients accidentally sit on radiators. Their butts get burned. I know it seems odd to take a photograph of them—but it was the only way to get your attention."

Roger and Louise, even the photographers and journalists, paused.

Louise sensed they were all waiting to see how the governor would handle this—the bluntness of these angry welts, these burns, this distasteful human flesh. The governor straightened up, brushed his trousers. "That is appalling, Dr. Oetzinger." Then he told his press secretary in the lime green to make a note to call the Office of Institutions and the Department of Health.

He turned to Roger, stiffly holding out his hand. "You care deeply for your patients, Dr. Oetzinger," he said, the smile gradually returning to his face, just as frost returns each year.

Roger shook it, looking up at him quizzically.

"You've made me think," the governor said. "We'll put the whole force of the governor's office behind you."

As he turned to walk out the room, he caught Louise's gaze and she could feel the shock of his blue eyes going through her, the power of them, as he touched the earring in her left ear and said, "Yogo sapphires, aren't they? I know them when I see them."

"Yes sir," Louise said and was immediately ashamed.

Then he pivoted on his Italian leather shoes, a full 180 degrees, and walked crisply out the door.

That night, the evening news showed footage of the governor coming out of the building as well as images of him shaking hands with striking staff members and National Guardsmen. A veteran reporter asked Captain Bill Yaeger of the National Guard what his men thought of these jobs at the Stone Home, where the patients were helpless and soldiers were called upon to change diapers of young and old alike.

"Most of these soldiers wouldn't have one of these jobs if you gave it to them," said Captain Yaeger. "This is the hardest work we've ever done."

The union official called a general meeting in the cafeteria. Roger and Louise walked to the cafeteria that day with the therapists and nurses and technicians and the wind-chafed strikers, all of them clattering down the hallways of the Stone Home, where she'd come so long ago. Patients, too, were streaming toward the cafeteria, where the National Guardsmen were cooking spaghetti, the air rich with smells of hamburger, fried onions, tomato sauce, and the pungent smell of garlic. They were celebrating their last night: the next day they would pull out and, ostensibly, life at the Stone Home would go on again without them.

Over the clatter of the trays and silverware and heavy plastic dishes, Matt Steele stood on a table and announced the news: On March 30, the governor and the union had settled the strike with an across-the-board monthly pay raise to $650, with housing provided. The room exploded, people tapping forks on trays, till the patients got so excited one of the epileptic girls began to seize and Margaret stood and scolded them.

"You are our hero," she said to Matt, looking up at him. "But you should know better than to stand on a table in front of the patients." Matt smiled at her, got down, and tweaked one of her braids.

The room exploded into a circus-like atmosphere. At the kitchen window, the guards dished out trays of spaghetti noodles and sauce to patients, staff, doctors, and nurses. Someone found a radio and turned it on just as Little Eva's "Loco-motion" came on and some of the staff started to dance.

Louise helped Lizzie through the line, helped her sit down with the tray of spaghetti. She sat next to her and tried to show her how to twirl the spaghetti with a fork, but Lizzie was intent on sucking up each noodle, laughing as the noodles grew shorter and shorter, until, then, magic! were gone.

Then one of the nurses gasped, "Oh my God."

Everyone seemed to turn at the same time.

At the doorway of the cafeteria was Ida, a non-amb. She was naked. She had scooted herself from her room, just down the hall, along the floor on her butt, her small breasts jiggling as she moved toward the cafeteria, this room of music and food and laughing, her eyes fixed ahead of her.

The voices quieted. Someone snapped off the radio.

"I'm hungry," she said.

A guardsman got up from the line, took his jacket off, and wrapped it around her. He picked her up and set her down at a cafeteria table. "Turn the radio back on," he said, and waved to the room at large.

Got to do the loco-motion, Little Eva crooned.

"Go back to what you're doing, damn it," the guardsman shouted. "It's fuckin' rude to stare." After he settled her at the table, he proceeded to feed her, twirling his fork in the spaghetti Italian-style, he said, the same way his grandma from Black Eagle had taught him, telling the girl that she could just eat as much as her heart desired, and the girl looked at him, between bites, her face shiny with red sauce.

CHAPTER FORTY

The story of the strikers at the state mental hospital and the home for the retarded had been in the news all winter, along with calls for Nixon's resignation, reports about student riots in India, and, one Sunday, a picture of a completely see-through Volkswagen bug built of white wrought iron. The opinion page was filled with letters from nurses and aides telling stories about patients who were drugged and tied in beds, dressed in filthy clothes, day after day. There were articles about the Stone Home featuring the pictures of slack-faced children tied in chairs in empty rooms, and interviews with doctors who talked about the *broken system*.

It was as if Bob's past crept closer with each newspaper, each needling article about the doctors crying foul about the abuses at the Stone Home, the reports of the legislators shocked at the filth and neglect as if they had only just discovered that children and the mentally ill were held in institutions. Journalists, emboldened by the success of the strikers as well the brand-new state constitutional convention that upheld civil rights for blacks, women, Indians, even the mentally challenged, were writing investigative pieces, interviewing nurses, doctors, even patients. One morning, he went to get the paper from the front porch, settled into his chair, unfolded it, and there was the other Elizabeth, her body slumped in a chair, asleep. "The Lost Children," the article was headlined. The superintendent from the Stone Home noted this warehousing of patients no longer was effective, because, he said, "retarded citizens had the same rights as others." Jesus. When he heard the door to the bedroom open and Mary's footsteps in the hallway, he crumpled the paper and stuffed it in the garbage can.

When she asked, he told her he found the paper under a juniper bush, waterlogged—he said he'd call circulation and complain—then he slipped out the door, hoping like hell she didn't pursue it, see this article with their child's body slumped in a chair. "The Lost Children." What nonsense.

"They should let them die at birth," Bob lectured his girls that night at the dinner table, when Elizabeth brought up the subject of the strike at the Stone Home. "I know it sounds cold, but it would be a blessing. It's what the Greeks used to do."

Mary looked across the table at him when he said that, her eyes glittering.

"I know it's cruel." Bob looked back at her. "But what good to society are they? Really? Think of the heartbreak it would ease."

"Think of it," Mary said drily.

"Dad, you are so heartless." Elizabeth piped up. She set down her knife and fork. "And who makes that call? Who defines what's good for society? Really? Hey, you're retarded. You die. Hey you, you have cancer, we can't keep you—out!" She jerked her thumb over her shoulder. "Pretty soon, it's hard to decide who stays and who goes, who's normal and who's not. You know who wrote the book on that, Dad. Right? Hitler. Right? Didn't you go to war to fight that guy?"

"Yeah," Karen piped in. "Your mother had manic-depression. Would they chuck her out for that?"

"I went to war to save our democracy," Bob said. "You don't know what you are talking about." He carefully drew the carving knife down the roast, enjoying the curl of flesh against the knife—his grandfather had taught him how to carve at this very table using this very bone-handled knife and it pleased him to be here, passing on this tradition—and he pressed the thin slice between the point of the knife and his fork and set it on Karen's plate. Then he placed a slice on Elizabeth's plate. Then Mary's. This is what he did: he provided.

"What's important," he said, as he set down the carving tools and everyone paused, "is that you are both so intelligent. Intelligence is everything."

Elizabeth looked up at him, her face framed by hair, parted in the middle, her eyes level. "You are so elitist, Dad. Just because you got all the breaks in the world, what about people who didn't? What about compassion? What about caring about your fellow man? Or woman?"

"Elizabeth," Mary's voice was sharp. "Be respectful."

Elizabeth shook her head as if she were about to retort, but Mary's glance stopped her.

"Eat your meat," Mary said.

They concluded the meal, the silverware conversing in chinks and scrapes with the plates.

Bob hardly recognized Pete's voice. The gruff baritone was so strangled Bob thought at first it was a crank caller. *What is it?* Bob asked Pete several times. Then Pete told him. It was Danny. He'd been missing in action for several months, and then a reconnaissance team discovered his bones in a prison camp near Binh Dinh province in a cell the size of an outhouse. Along with Danny's remains, they sent Pete and Cora Danny's journal from the base, where he had made pencil sketches of Pete's cabin, the woodstove, the woods outside, marking off the days in drawings of loons, bears, deer, chipmunks, even voles.

Bob and Mary drove north in the Volkswagen bus he'd bought in exchange for his Thunderbird to attend the service several days later in Seeley Lake. It was held in the rough-hewn Baptist Church, surrounded by tamaracks, overlooking the lake that, in spring, was chopped by wind into a white-flecked green. The church was full when they entered, but Pete had saved them a seat in the front. Bob saw immediately the way Cora leaned into Pete, her body weighted by sadness. She dipped her head to Bob and she and Pete scooted over to make room for Bob and Mary. When Bob sat on Mary's left, she squeezed his hand. "It's good you're here," she whispered. Pete nodded. He looked terrible. He seemed to have shrunk into himself, his chest caved in, his face hollowed by grief. Bob patted his back and the two of them sat, side by side, through several hymns and the sermon, Pete breaking down as the minister talked about his Danny playing as a forward for the Seeley Lake Blackhawks, and his service as a Ranger, graduating from special forces at Recondo School at Nha Trang, then patrolling along the Ho Chi Minh trail until he was captured. An old World War II vet played taps on a trumpet and handed Pete the three-cornered flag, thanking him for his son's service. One of Pete's lieutenants played an imitation of Jimmy Hendrix's "Star Spangled Banner" on an electric guitar.

Cora rose to go out in the courtyard. She rested her hand on Bob's shoulder. He warmed to the weight of it. "You stay here with him, hon," she said. "I'll go out with the rest."

Mary stood by Bob, her hand resting lightly on the pew, her head bowed. When Bob went to sit by Pete, she nodded at him and motioned her head toward the door to indicate that she'd be outside.

A thin spring sun slanted along the wooden aisle between the pews. Bob looked out at the lake as he sat next to Pete. Dressed up in his bolo tie and his wool suit, Pete hunkered down in the pews next to him. "I ain't a Baptist," Pete said finally, his hands propped on his legs, his eyes scanning the choppy surface of the lake through the window. "I only come in this church when Cora insists—Christmas, Easter. I don't understand it here, Bob. I'm raised Catholic. You are what you are. There's no saving, just confessing."

"How can I help you, Pete?" Bob said softly. "What can I do?" He turned his head to his friend, this man he had known and loved for nearly twenty years.

"I lost my boy." Pete looked down at his hands. His face collapsed. "I lost my boy in that war, Bob. That god-damn, ginned-up, stupid war."

Bob folded his hands between his legs. "You can be so proud of him, Pete. He died serving his country."

Pete peered closely at Bob, his eyes two stones. "I used to think I understood things. Now I know it wasn't worth it."

CHAPTER FORTY-ONE

She followed Tom through the woods, her feet in snow up to the sides of her boots as she walked through the narrow canyon bordered by tamaracks. They'd driven up a small dirt road, just off Highway 12, the route of the explorers Lewis and Clark. She had the forest service tag for the tree and they were walking among the seedlings, looking for something suitable. Tom would have grabbed the first decent-looking Doug fir that was full on all sides. Elizabeth was more particular.

Ahead of them were hundred-foot-high granite boulders that looked as if they'd been dropped here and there in some giant's game of marbles, overshadowed by ponderosa pine trees, needles dark against the bright sky. Elizabeth was starting to heat up, which wasn't saying much, she was running warm already, but as she walked she began shedding things: hat, scarf, mittens.

"See anything?" Tom shouted back to her.

"Those are too small," she said, pointing to the waist-high Douglas fir.

"Of course they are," he said. He smiled. "They always are."

This was an argument they had every year: he wanted a small tree, something not too hard to carry or strap on the car, she wanted a large Doug fir, larger and fuller than the ones she remembered from her childhood, one that dwarfed the living room with long graceful branches, the pine scent wafting through the house. This year, Karen and her family were coming. She'd invited them and was so surprised when Karen accepted, saying that Bill needed a change of pace and the girls wanted to come and see the new carousel in town. Elizabeth wanted to do it all right: the dinner, the presents, the decorations. And especially the tree. She'd found a box of old ornaments in the attic: a tin soldier, some needlepointed crosses that must have been stitched by Methodist church ladies, and a strange hand-painted ceramic angel. She intended to surprise Karen with all of it, even the old felt tree skirt with a pattern of miniature toy trains stitched into the fabric.

But at this moment, her resolve was waning. They'd been hiking for half an hour, and in the snow, it was more work than she'd expected, and she was tired.

"Wait here," Tom said. "I'm going to scout up higher and I promise I will find one." He stopped, unbuttoned his flannel shirt to wrap around his waist.

"I want to see it!" she said, but she was too tired to follow.

"I'll be right back," he said, "with the most wonderful tree." With that, he disappeared around the high boulder and was gone. She walked further into the middle of the woods to a rock shadowed by a group of ponderosa trees. She peeled a small piece of bark off a tree to smell it. It was supposed to smell like vanilla, but the only scent she could detect was that of toast. Buttered toast. She picked up some needles, three to a bundle. Three sisters, she thought as she settled herself on the rock.

She remembered the years she and Karen had traveled in the VW bus up the narrow road with her father and mother to get a tree, near this very spot, her mother filling thermoses with hot chocolate and coffee, her father hurrying everyone into the bus so they could get in and out of the woods before dark, her mother picking out an alpine fir, she loved alpine firs, and her father grumbling at the tall, sparsely needled tree, but he chopped it down anyway. Maybe they had been in these very woods, walked up this very trail. On one trip, she and Karen had brought their sleds, and they coaxed their mother into sledding with them down this narrow road, first Karen, then Elizabeth. Her mother had sat on the Flexible Flyer behind her, Elizabeth in front, steering with her feet. The sled sank into the snow and they went nowhere. We have to push, she told her mother, and her mother jumped up and pushed from the back of the sled and, as it started to pick up speed, she jumped on. Elizabeth could feel her arms around her stomach, yelling, "Oh, oh, Elizabeth, we're going too fast, we're going to crash," and Elizabeth yelling back, "It's fine, mom, just hang tight," as they moved down the bumpy, snow-covered road, taking one curve, then another. They passed her father, who stopped to watch them, his axe dangling from his hand, laughing. They zipped past Karen pulling her sled back up to the road. Her mother was laughing in a loose, zany way Elizabeth had never heard before, and Elizabeth remembered wishing it would go on forever and wishing, too, it would stop, when the runners hit a rut and they were upended, dumping both of them on the road. Elizabeth sat up on her elbow to look behind her, at her mother. "You okay, Mom?" Her mother was laughing, but tears sparkled across her cheeks. She quickly put her hands up and wiped them away. "Terrifying," her mother said. "I almost want to do it again."

Elizabeth picked up the rope handle of the sled and began to walk up the hill, her mother beside her. "Let's go."

"I don't know," Mary said. "I think we'd better think about heading home."

"C'mon Mom," Elizabeth said, and plucked her mother's sleeve. She studied her face. It was as if a mask had descended over her openness, her laughter. Where did that other mother go? Did her mother retreat back to that moment when she was told she had to give up her baby?

Her parents worked so hard to create this lingering, carefree childhood for Karen and Elizabeth with the music lessons and dresses and trips. But, in so doing, the four of them were bound in a tight circle, as if they were gathered around a campfire in a dark forest, warming their hands over the fire, but deadly afraid of what lay in the woods beyond the light of that campfire.

She thought she could hear Tom's footsteps, crunching through the snow in the distance. Was that an axe ringing? Maybe he'd found a tree.

For now, she was just content to sit. She hadn't told him her news. She knew right away that she was pregnant this time, feeling the blood rush through her and the tweak of nausea each morning, but she wanted to keep it to herself just a little bit longer. She loved walking to work, turning on her computer, following leads, wrapping up stories, and sending them up the pneumatic tubes—*phhhfftt!*—to typesetting, the whole time knowing that there was this child growing inside her, and, for now, it was just the two of them, and she was vaguely superstitious that she'd risk losing it again if she broke the news, though she knew that was ridiculous. It was intoxicating knowing that at any moment she could break forth with news that would change things, her life, Tom's, but she chose not to. Was this a shadow of how her father felt? She knew he had kept his secrets out of fear, but still they were powerful secrets.

In the last few weeks, she had been hibernating at home, drinking tea, not going out, crawling into bed first thing at night, telling Tom she was sure she was getting a cold. She felt herself preparing for a long journey ahead, while questions dogged her: Would she be able to nurse? What about her work? What if she found her sister? Would she bring the other Elizabeth to live with them?

In these woods, the questions seemed very far away.

As she sat, a light snow began to fall. The woods were so quiet, she could hear the sound of the flakes arriving on the ground, like many small breaths. The branches of a ponderosa swayed as if a presence had passed this way. Something fluttered. A pine siskin, a small grey-streaked bird with yellow-tipped feathers, hopping along the branches, feeding, its eyes bright, twittering to others on the branches above.

She wanted to sit with that now, in this silence, on this rock, just her and her baby, snug inside her.

She heard a shushing sound. It had to be Tom. She stood up, then saw him round a bend far up the hill. He was dragging a large Douglas fir by the trunk, the wide green branches splayed out on the hillside behind him, his face triumphant, the axe swung over his shoulder as he moved down the hill toward her.

"There!" he said when he walked up beside her. He stood the tree up, holding it by its trunk and shook out the branches. "Whaddya think?"

It was enormous, full and fragrant. Elizabeth said, "It is perfect."

He smiled at her.

She smiled back. "Guess what?" She told him her news.

"Really," he said. "Really?"

"You have to promise not to tell now," she said.

At the holiday party at the gymnasium at Hastings, the students dressed in their finest and the parents brought casseroles of their famous soybean turkey roast with cranberry sauce and stuffed tofu peppers and squash soup, and the same hapless parent brought a bucket of chicken legs, which Elizabeth eyed first thing as she headed down the aisle. The little kids were leaping and hopping about, the girls in their velvet dresses and candy cane tights and the boys in elf hats and red vests, several of them with felt reindeer antlers on their heads. The men had exchanged their Guatemalan vests for crazy light-up ties and the women had on Honduran sweaters and velvet skirts. Someone was playing the guitar in the corner, which was barely audible over the noise of the crowd.

Elizabeth followed Tom through the line and over to the table next to Nonny and Lucinda. She sat next to Lucinda, across the table from Nonny. Nonny was elbowing Tom and giving him a hard time about skiing this year, claiming that he wouldn't go with her this year because she beat him down the hill every time.

"You won't wait for me, Nonny," he said. "You just take off. How fun is that?"

"I pay you back in beer, Tommy," she said.

He nodded. "You do, that's true."

She lay her head on his shoulder, and he patted it. "You can't help it if you're a speed demon, Nonny."

Elizabeth was quietly eating the fried chicken, thinking she would like to write a thank you to the parent who had the foresight to bring this crunchy, fat-laden, delicious bowl of meat to this all-vegetarian meal, when she was startled to hear Tom say, "Hey, we have news."

She tried to catch Tom's eye. She took her chicken bone and pantomimed drawing it across her neck like a knife. "No," she whispered.

"No?" he said. "Okay, I'm not supposed to say."

"What? What?" Nonny hopped up and grabbed Tom by the elbow. She leaned across the table to Elizabeth. "What is it? No. You didn't take another job." She stared at Tom in horror.

He shook his head.

Lucinda leaned to Elizabeth. "C'mon, we're your best friends. You can tell us. Please."

"Not here," Elizabeth said, scowling at Tom, but she couldn't help smiling too. That night in front of the fire at Nonny and Lucinda's, they told their friends, who swore themselves to secrecy, and they opened a bottle of champagne and toasted. "I swore I wouldn't tell," Tom said. "But I couldn't help it. I'm so excited. But that's it, Elizabeth. My lips are sealed." Oh dear God, Elizabeth thought. Help us all. But she drank her ginger ale and toasted them all.

All four of them worked on the Christmas dinner, while the girls played with their new toys: Jessie was dressing and undressing her new Polly Pocket doll in her soft plastic jackets and pants, and giving her rides around the Christmas tree in her pink VW bug that stretched out into a limousine with a swimming pool inside of it. The baby was content in her bouncy chair, moving up and down to Nat King Cole singing "Deck the Halls" as she stared at the tree lights. Tom was braising the turkey, Elizabeth was putting the finishing touches on the sweet potato casserole, and Karen was making her famous mashed potatoes. Bill was making Manhattans for everyone except Elizabeth, because, he said, Christmas came just once a year.

Joy, pure joy, Elizabeth thought, as they moved through the kitchen, bumping into one another, bantering. Karen had clasped her hands to her heart when Elizabeth told her the news, tears in her eyes.

"I knew it, I knew it." And Bill patted Tom on the back and told him they were in this parenthood thing together and they high-fived each other and Bill made Tom another Manhattan.

As she moved through the kitchen and into the dining room, carrying the Spode that her father was so proud of, she thought of all of her family who had eaten in this room, holiday after holiday, Sunday dinner after Sunday dinner, this long oak table with the carved claw legs that had been the center of so many conversations and silences.

When they were all seated around the table, Tom and Elizabeth on opposite ends, Karen and the girls and Bill on the sides, the crystal shining in the candlelight, each china plate with the prairie rose in the center just waiting to receive food, Jessie's eyes bright, Tom said he would say the blessing, asking God or the Great Spirit to bless this gathering in this house where so many had gathered before, generations and more generations to come. This was what it was about, bringing everyone to the table, Elizabeth thought, mothers, fathers, sisters, brothers, aunts, uncles, in-laws and out-laws—and certainly lost sisters. Elizabeth added, "I want to say a grace for our other sister, the other Elizabeth, wherever she is." Karen looked over at her, startled, then turned her face back to her folded hands, just in time to say, "Amen." Jessie looked up at her mother's face, then over to Elizabeth's, then down at her folded hands. "More sisters is good," she said, and everyone laughed.

CHAPTER FORTY-TWO

She was dreaming about a horse galloping, its hooves clattering across the rocks, its mane fluttering in the wind. Then she woke up and realized the clattering was someone knocking.

Louise sat up.

The knocking was light, but urgent.

"Who is it?" she called out. She stepped out of bed and dashed for her robe on the hook behind the door. Then she looked for her slippers, by the bed, under the bed, by the stove. Where were her slippers? "Who is it?" she called as she scurried around the cabin, half asleep.

"It's Anna." The voice was so quiet Louise almost didn't hear her.

The sound of Anna's voice panicked her more. To hell with her robe. She headed straight for the door, heart beating.

"Anna?" she said, as she pulled back the heavy wooden door, feeling the cold air on her face. "What the hell—"

"I came—" Anna said, as she stood there, a small bag in her hands, "to say good-bye."

"Why? They settled, didn't you hear?"

"It's not over," Anna said. "You haven't heard the latest."

"What's that? What happened? Why are you here in the middle of the night?" Louise stepped back into the room so Anna would follow her.

Anna walked into the room, stopping to secure the door behind her. Louise followed her back to the bed, and as she sat with her back against the log headboard, the covers still warmed by her body, heat rising up to her like the edges of a dream. Anna sat across from her on the bed, stretching her boots out across the quilt.

"What?" Louise said. "What is it?"

"It's Roger," she whispered. "He quit."

"Quit?" Louise felt a dropping sensation in her stomach. "Roger? Why? What happened?"

Anna wound her braid around her neck and started rubbing the bristly tip of it against her cheek as she talked.

"It was tonight, after you left—he was calling in a prescription to Whitehall after the meeting, and when he picked up the phone, the governor was on the party line."

"The governor?"

"He was talking to the director, Roberts."

"And?" Louise said.

"He was telling Roberts to get rid of Roger. He said he didn't think he had the "right attitude" or was appropriate in his dealings with the state and he wanted him out of there, post-haste."

"And Roberts? What did Roberts do?"

"He said, 'Yes, Governor.'"

Louise's heart stood still. Their research was finished. They were finished. "What is going to happen to him? To us? Shit." She felt dizzy suddenly.

Anna put her hand on Louise's leg. "Things are changing fast here, Louise."

"So what did Roger do?"

"He quit." Anna shook her head. "I saw him in the hall, afterwards, and he asked me to come into his office as a witness. Right there and then. He told me to stand there as he wrote his resignation letter, totaled up all of his vacation time, and then—he quit."

"What's he going to do?"

"I don't know, Louise." Anna shook her head. "I didn't ask him."

"What are we going to do, Anna?"

"I'm leaving. I'm taking custody of some Indian girls and I'm leaving."

"Everyone's leaving. What about me? About Lizzie?"

"You have to figure that out, Louise. You're smart. You'll come up with something."

Anna stood up and walked over to Louise and embraced her in her flannel nightgown, her braid sliding down to thunk Louise on the back as they hugged.

Shortly after that, they all split apart and entered different lives, different worlds, as if they had been water skippers, skating on top of a lake, suspended above another world until the surface tension broke and they finally tumbled down into another, watery world just beneath them.

Roger's resignation made all the state papers—he'd essentially run the Stone Home for twenty-seven years—and the public outcry forced the governor's office to improve the governor's measly strike offer, but it was the nail in the coffin for the Stone Home. Roger left the Stone Home for the Mentally Retarded on April 10, 1974. He left for a genetics conference in Iceland, with a suitcase of thirty brains of Down syndrome patients that he'd used in his trials. On April 15, he was hired to start the state's first genetics lab in Bozeman, Montana, to further the genetics research he had pioneered at the Stone Home, then moved on to found Shodair Hospital in Helena. In the following twenty years, he identified seven different chromosomal abnormalities, several of which were named after him. He had eight children. He remained married to Audrey, until she died in 1986 of a pulmonary edema.

Louise saw him once, briefly, at a medical conference in Billings, where they met at a cocktail table, Roger handing her a full glass of red wine, his hair gone white and stiff, but still that intense gaze as he held out the wine and asked how she was holding up, telling her that she, at sixty, was still an eyeful, and in that moment, before she took that glass and his wife, Audrey, joined them, all of the past trembled between them, then she took the rounded glass to her lips and drank.

The Stone Home limped along for a while, staffed with workers that were bused in from Butte and Helena and Townsend, but it was hopeless. The age of institutionalizing the developmentally disabled, as this population was now known, was over. Patients were gradually moved into group homes, scattered throughout small towns in Montana, where they lived with perhaps ten patients and a few nurses.

The summer after Anna left, Louise was out with Lizzie's group, watching the adults wade in the Stone River. She was sitting on a blanket, feeling the sun warm her white legs, watching Lizzie splash in the river with one of her friends, when she heard a plane overhead. She didn't pay it much mind as she sipped her cola and watched an ant pick up an enormous bread crumb and carry it across the bumpy sand. But the buzzing grew closer. She looked up again. It was a red-and-white biplane, tiny against the blue canvas of sky, moth-like, and it looked as if it were headed right for them. Then, as she stared, the wing of the plane dipped. The plane circled back, and then came at her again.

Louise stood up, shielding her eyes. "Oh my God! Lizzie!"

Lizzie stood in the middle of the stream, her hands dangling, as Louise pointed up at the plane.

The plane buzzed down closer. She could the outline of two people in the cockpit. She didn't know who was in the co-pilot's seat, but she was almost sure it was Anna in the cockpit, waving. But how could she be sure?

"Wave," Louise said, not bothering to explain why. "Wave as hard as you can, Lizzie."

And so they stood, Lizzie in the rippling river water, Louise on the green wool army blanket in her red bathing suit with the white sash, and they waved, flinging their arms from side to side, Louise even doing a few jumping jacks while the patients laughed at her, covering their mouths, and whispering to one another, "Look at Miss Gustafson!"

She could only imagine how they must all look, specks against the river and the rocky bank, as the plane dipped a wing one more time, then, with a buzz, flew up and over the rounded back of the Elkhorns.

Of Margaret and Charlene and the other nurses, Louise was the last to leave that spring. She adopted Lizzie, writing Mr. Carter one last letter.

> *I would like to serve as a foster parent to your daughter, Mr. Carter. I think you should know she is a lovely girl.*

She loves picnics by the river. She loves music, especially country western, and she likes to sing with the radio when we drive together in the car. No, I am not the perfect foster parent. She is very retarded and very frustrating, getting mad when she doesn't get her way, throwing food sometimes, and pushing other patients. But then, guess what? She's still a good girl, Mr. Carter.

And so, later in May, when he signed the release, she packed the car with all of her belongings and this foster child, and, twenty years after she had driven in, Louise drove out the entrance of the Stone Home, Lizzie at her side. Lizzie with her small round body and fierce, flat face. As she headed west, with Lizzie at her side, she said, "This is the world, Lizzie."

Lizzie gazed out the window, saying "Cow," "Barn," "Horse"—everything she had seen only in picture books. It was exhilarating. In the course of a year, Louise would meet a man and marry him and would be surprised, at thirty-nine, to become pregnant with her own her own child, a son. Lizzie began having daily seizures, then tantrums, and when she tried to throw the baby out the second-story window, Louise had to put her in a group home, first in Great Falls, then Libby, where she visited her as often as she could—but that was all ahead of her. For now, she was leaving the Elkhorn Mountains, heading west over the Continental Divide to the other side, where the rivers grew wide and fat and the sun burned red across the horizon.

CHAPTER FORTY-THREE

Three days later Bob was driving with Elizabeth from Butte, where he had met with a client, to her state music festival in Helena. He and Elizabeth had had fun. He drove them up to the hill above the town, where they stopped and climbed up a hiking trail to see a panorama of the mile-high city scraped out of a mountain and dotted with headframes of old copper mines, where they could look down and see the narrow roads lining the Berkeley Pit, where trucks crawled further and further into the bowels of the earth. They'd lunched in Anaconda, at the Parker Hotel restaurant, a narrow restaurant with a wall-sized photograph of the Pintlers and the most ancient waitress the two of them had ever seen, Elizabeth joking that she must have to go back to her coffin in the back room and have transfusions in between serving them, her heavy, deliberate movements so slow as she hovered over them in her pink waitress uniform asking them was it chicken or egg salad and was it coffee or tea, and each time getting it wrong. They had dinner that night at Lydia's, an old Butte supper club, with its leather banquettes and stained-glass windows and sunken dining room, the waitresses swinging in and out of the kitchen with enormous platters of spaghetti and glistening steaks and chicken Marbella. Across the table Bob watched his daughter diving into the relish plate—exactly four carrots, four pieces of celery, four slices of salami, and four radishes—before they ordered New York steaks. His Elizabeth, whom he loved to spoil, his lovely, spirited, vibrant Elizabeth. After dinner, back at the hotel, she would practice from her book of Schubert arias back at the hotel, preparing for the competition in Helena at the Civic Center.

The next morning, washed and dressed, filled with bacon and eggs, he and Elizabeth climbed back into the Volkswagen bus to head to Helena. It was snowing lightly as they left town, but as they started to climb up the Continental Divide, the snow grew thicker and they could feel the drop in temperature through the sides of the bus as the road narrowed and they pushed on between the thickly forested hills. The bus slowed to a crawl, Bob gearing down from fourth, to third, as they passed the old silver mining town of Basin, which seemed to be gripping the side of the hill, and on up Boulder Pass. The snow pelted down, the wipers were going fast, but seemed useless against the onslaught. In the dim light, he could see Elizabeth's profile, her turned-up nose, her clear skin, her body tilting forward, her face so alive as they drove past the thick stands of ponderosa and rocky canyons of the Boulder Batholith, where magma poured out so many years ago and slipped between the tectonic plates and solidified.

"We're leaning forward," Elizabeth said in the darkened car. "Did you notice that?"

Bob looked over at her. He sat back against the seat, his arms stretched out on the wide steering wheel in front of him. "We are.

I guess we're trying to keep up the momentum. These VW's aren't made for speed."

"That's for sure." Elizabeth looked out at a Lincoln town car that seemed to effortlessly sail up the hill past them. "Sometimes I want to put out a tow rope and see if they'll help us up."

"True," Bob laughed. "But they'll be the sorry ones at the gas pump."

Elizabeth shook her head. "It's always about money with you, Dad."

As they climbed, the snow let up, and their visibility cleared so they could see out over the hills. As they approached Stone City, they started to see signs of the strike: a hand-painted banner fastened to the guardrail: "Honk for Stone Home Pay Hike." Several miles on, another that said, "Justice for State Workers." As they slowly chugged up over the hill, the VW crawling, Elizabeth saying, "Dad, I think I could get out and run faster than this," the wind sighing around them as if it, too, were impatient with the speed of their travel. At the top, when the bus began to pick up speed, Bob pointed ahead to the long, wide valley, threaded by a river, the cluster of hospital buildings close to them and, further away, the orderly streets stretching out from the road that cut through town.

"You can see the strikers from here," Elizabeth pointed to people holding pickets who were grouped around barrels topped with flames and a plywood shelter. In the nearby hospital yard were clumps of National Guardsmen, the dull green of their uniforms standing out against the white snow as they moved from building to building. "Let's go see them, Dad. I want to see them. I've never seen a strike. Please."

"No," he said. "We don't have time." He flushed.

"Dad, why not?" Elizabeth looked over at him, surprised at the tone of his voice. "We're not hurting anything? Why not? C'mon."

"Oh God, Elizabeth." He felt himself sweating. His heart hammered. Jesus. "I just know we're running out of time. We need to get you to your competition."

"Oh, Dad." She waved the air as if she could push his worries back into a bottle somewhere and stopper them up. "We've got plenty of time. We have all the time in the world. Relax. I practiced. I could sing this song standing on my head. C'mon, let's go down there. It looks exciting."

"We're not getting out. I'm driving by and then we are driving right out of this town." He took the exit off the highway and wound down the hill and through the town, remembering the trip long ago with Mary, holding the child between them, looking out at the hardware store, the café, the ice cream store where—in the middle of winter—a young girl stood, licking an ice cream cone.

Beside him, Elizabeth was glued to the window, commenting on how small the town seemed, and pointing out the antiques store where an old woman was just setting out a rocker on the porch among silver milk cans, despite the snow.

As they wound their way out of town, they crossed a small bridge. A sign said, "Stone Home, 300 feet." The drive seemed surreal to him, the way the snow filtered down past the old man stumbling out of the Union Bar, past the old post office with its wind-whipped flag, past the cottonwoods along the river, their branches grey against a white sky, the way the snow and the grey and the dark seemed to erase time and he was here with a child and his young wife in the seat beside him, trying to hush her, this child that he was going to drop off at this place, this child who had been born with eyes too wide and ears too rounded, and he felt her presence curl in his stomach like a cancer until he shook his head. "We'll go for just a moment. I don't want to stay, Elizabeth. I know you are curious, but things happen at strikes. It may be dangerous."

He drove down the dirt road to the gate of the hospital, where the crowd was gathered, Elizabeth chattering away beside him, her eyes glued to the strikers dressed in overcoats, hats, and gloves against the bitter wind as they carried signs or fed logs to the fire in the oil barrel or handed out pasties from the trunk of a car. On the road ahead of them, several television trucks were parked, with cameramen on the back, filming the strikers, and reporters mingled in the crowd, holding microphones and asking questions. In the distance, guardsmen moved from the main hospital to the cottages, carrying diapers or dishes, patients or medicines. He looked out at the nurses and aides, tall and short, women with tight permanents, men in long ponytails, some Indians, a young man in a Local 352 hat and a bullhorn shouting something and he felt he had to tell Elizabeth something about them. How they filled him with disgust and sadness because they were scroungy and protesting, because they thought they were better than he was, and because they were right and, in his heart of hearts, he knew it, and he hated them for it.

They had lingered, he felt long enough, though they had probably been there maybe all of fifteen minutes.

"We have to go now," he said. "Right now."

Elizabeth heard the strain in his voice, and rebuckled her seatbelt.

He and Elizabeth stopped at the service station on their way out of Stone City to fill up. He could see the fire-filled barrel of the protesters from the station. "Hear there's been trouble," he told the gas station attendant.

"Can't say I blame the folks," the man said. "They've been workin' for nothin' and the state ain't ready to give 'em a break, them fat cats in Helena."

"Well," Bob shrugged. "I guess you have your opinion."

Elizabeth followed him into the lobby of the small station, where he was getting out his credit card to pay for the gas, when the service bell rang again. The attendant hurried out to help a woman in a Rambler fill her car with gas, and soon she too crowded into the small, brightly lit station, waiting to pay.

"Ladies first," Bob said, stepping aside.

"Thank you." She took a sharp look at Bob. She was a handsome, older woman with thick red hair and smooth pink skin and a piercing way of looking right at him. "I'm filling up, just in case I need to clear this crazy place," she said. She nodded her head and stepped up to the counter, holding out a coin purse and looking directly at the attendant. "Did you check the oil? I've got to get somewhere, Ed, and I got to make sure the engine's in shape."

"Did that, Louise," the man said as she paid up and left, the glass door banging shut behind her, the attendant saying, "It's $12.50, sir. Sir? Is there something wrong, sir?" as Bob followed the swing of the woman's brown coat as she walked across the snow-dusted asphalt, opened the door, and got in, turning the headlights on despite the daylight. He continued to watch the car as it turned out of the station, and, just as the right taillight blinked red, signaling a turn, before the car slowly headed out on the highway, picking up speed as it made its way up the divide to the pass, Bob saw, just above the bench seat, the rounded bump of a passenger's head.

At the end of the day, Bob would sit in a scratchy velour seat in the Helena Civic Center, the odd Moorish building with its one minaret, where his daughter was competing in the vocal category for the state music competition. He would sit in the dark, where no one could see him weep as his daughter walked across the stage to stand in front of a microphone. In her ankle-length black velvet dress, her hair tied back from her face, she would stand, breathe deeply, and bow to her audience, three stern-looking judges, music professors from various Montana universities. She would fold her hands together, nod to the pianist. When the pianist hit a chord to begin, she would take a deep breath, press her shaking knees together, and sing Franz Schubert's "Liebe Schwärmt Auf Allen Wegen."

His face would grow wet as her voice faltered at the start, this creature, this child of his. Even from the back of the theater, he would see her steady herself as she sang, gripping her hands tighter, reaching farther inside herself for breath as she sang.

Love wanders on every road
Fidelity lives by herself alone;
Love advances swiftly to meet you,
Fidelity must be sought.

But that hadn't happened yet. Robert was still back, climbing Boulder Hill, shifting the Volkswagen into third, then fourth gear, as Elizabeth was asking him about the past, how he and Mary had met, how they courted, what Mary had looked like, and Bob was trying to describe how achingly beautiful she was: black hair, the red lips.

Elizabeth asked him if he and Mary ever slept together before they were married.

She asked Bob about where they were married.

He gripped the wheel as he answered the questions slowly, cloaked in the privacy of the late afternoon dusk, driving the car, the engine whining to keep up with the drive, but steady, he had to give it to the old VW.

He told her about the wedding, how the photographer put the film in the camera upside down and no pictures survived, and about the basement bedroom in his parent's house where, yes, he and Mary made love before they were married.

And then she asked him about when he knew Mary was pregnant.

And there it was, the moment.

Something trembled between them, something round and wet and lovely, a child with webbed fingers and toes, turning over and over, the see-through umbilical cord twisting, this lovely small astronaut in its salty universe, sleeping, waking, turning, moving, developing as they started around the bend past Stone City, past the pool of lights, freeway exit, and gas station, past the long main street with brick buildings, past the home of that other Elizabeth, who, Louise said, she was taking to her house, somewhere, where they were forming a group home, where she'd learn to use utensils and to write, maybe read, and he could feel that bubble press against him, waiting to be born.

"So tell me, Dad," this Elizabeth said and looked out the window at the lights. "What was it like?"

As they drove past Stone City, he told her about Mary's pregnancy and the trip to California and the campground and Mary telling the rowdies her husband had a gun and he'd use it and her terrible, terrible sickness.

"So who was she pregnant with?" Elizabeth said.

The invisible child trembled and glistened in the space between them.

"You have a sister," he says.

Elizabeth paused. And then she swatted his arm and said, "Well, of course I do, silly. I know that."

And with that, the moment passed. He drove on, tires slicking the pavement, seeing only the road in the headlights in front of him.

CHAPTER FORTY-FOUR

When the roads cleared enough, she traveled north along the Clark Fork River. The river was fat with snowmelt, the lawns in each town brightening from brown to green, the calves sturdy and ready for market, the cows slow-eyed with nursing. The sun warmed Elizabeth's face as she drove past the signs for write-in sheriff candidates, past homes hidden in the timber, past bighorn sheep clambering down from the rocky cliffs with their lambs to drink snowmelt from the Bull River. This country was wild and barren. People survived by cutting out parts of the country each year—timber, rocks, minerals from deep in the earth, exporting generosity as well—and yet, there was gentleness where the sun lingered, in this place so removed from the rest of the state with its slow-moving rivers and high rock walls and grassy hillsides. This was a place people came to with a purpose—logging, mining, ranching, hiding.

She was nervous as she felt the baby turn in her belly, felt the pressure of having to pee again, despite having stopped at a gas station just ten minutes ago. She was nervous, but driving steadied her. A song entered her head, the Schubert lieder she used to perform—"Liebe Schwärmt Auf Allen Wegen"—and her heart swelled at the memory of standing on the stage in the Helena Civic Center Auditorium, knowing her father was there, sitting on a chair in the auditorium, sitting in the dark, sitting there for her, and her alone—*love wanders on every road, love advances swiftly to meet you*—her father who had been dead for so long now.

What if the people who knew Lizzie didn't want to see her? What if they hated her? *You are from the family that abandoned her?* She wanted to explain everything to them: her parents, the antiquated rules, the terrible absence, the guilt, the silences at the dinner table inhabited by the absent sister, but in the end they were just words. These people raised her sister. There were no words to substitute for that. All she could offer was the knowledge that she had a family. She had family who wanted to see her. A sister, in fact, who shared her name: Elizabeth Carter.

Plains, Paradise, then Thompson Falls, where a spring sun lit the streets, and part of her just wanted to check into the Rimrock Hotel perched on a bluff over the Clark Fork River, which ran green and fast beneath the bank of motel rooms. She wanted to stay there forever, spreading out on the bed or soaking in the tub, watching her toes wrinkle.

But she drove on, following the road inland, through the thick forests interspersed with the occasional small farm or boarded-up gas station that paralleled the Bull River, then Bull Lake. It was a world of deep green, shadowed by the Cabinet Mountains. It was mid-afternoon when she passed the billboard at the edge of town that proclaimed the area home of the Libby Loggers, and she headed for the main street downtown, presided over by an iron eagle.

She was looking for the Evergreen Home, which the receptionist had told her was just off the downtown. She slowly drove down the main street, with its hardware stores, grocery store, sporting goods store turned high-end women's boutique, interspersed with antiques shops and secondhand clothing stores. The senior center was housed in what looked like an old grocery store, done up with leftover cutouts of Easter baskets. At the end of the block was a flower shop, Bette's Bouquets—which had a huge display of silk sunflowers, carnations, roses—that endured on in the graveyard across the street.

The Evergreen Home was on a side street, overlooking a large ravine above the Kootenai River. She pulled up the car. Elizabeth looked in the mirror. She took out a brush and brushed her hair. Was her sister inside? Her hands were unsteady, and when she put on her lipstick, she smeared some above her lip and she had to wipe it off and start again. She didn't know how much more of this she could do. Maybe Karen was right, she should just settle down, accept things as they are, and focus on the baby turning and growing inside her.

The Evergreen Home was housed in what looked like an old supermarket, with large plate-glass windows, now festooned with taped-on notes: Mondays, dollar days. Tuesday, all pink tags half off; family session, Thursday, 6:30. The front was a brightly lit used clothing store, filled with racks of sweaters, baby clothes, women's shirts and dresses, men's shirts and coats. The decaying smell of old clothes was so overpowering Elizabeth walked back outside to clear her head. She gulped fresh air. She stood on the street, looked at the river below and the small storefronts that lined Main Street—an electrical shop, the *Libby Eagle* newspaper office, a Home Treasures shop. Then she opened the door and walked back in.

She sauntered through the racks, pulling out a dress here, a shirt there, trying to gather her courage.

She sat on a duct-taped chair in the lobby.

Her stomach twisted.

Her hands shook.

Finally, she stood up, walked to the counter, and asked for the woman she had talked to on the phone, a woman named Nancy. The man, dressed in a ski sweater, looked her up and down.

"I had a sister here," Elizabeth said.

He must have seen something in her face, the way she kept her voice low so it wouldn't wobble.

"I'm not sure she's here, but I'll check," he said. Then he stopped and turned around. "Why don't you just follow me?"

She followed him through the hive of offices, portioned off with particleboard and decorated with posters that said things like "Helping Hands Are Helping Others!" and "Kind Hands, Kind Hearts!" In a small ramshackle office in the back, he stood by a doorway and held his hand out.

"Nancy—?" the man said. "Meet—excuse me," he said. "I didn't get your name."

Elizabeth paused. From a distant room, she could hear television music start up and an announcer's voice cried, "Iiiiit's time for Let's Make a Deal!" and Monty Hall's lively, "Thank you, thank you, thank you..."

In a small, windowless office, a slender woman with a narrow, sculpted face and dark eyes looked up from her desk at her.

"I'm Elizabeth."

"Nancy." She jumped up and shook Elizabeth's hand, smiling warmly. She had strawberry blonde hair in a short cut and wore dangly earrings. She had a quick smile. "How can I help?"

"I'm Elizabeth Carter," Elizabeth repeated. "I'm here to find out about my sister. My sister, the other Elizabeth Carter."

The woman's eyes grew larger. She stared up at Elizabeth, studying her. She put her hands on each side of her face as if she needed to cradle it. "Amazing," she said. "I really see it."

"See what?" Elizabeth said.

"The resemblance."

"How?"

"The brown hair, the freckles, your build. I guess I shouldn't be saying all that."

"Hey, it's okay. I want to know about her."

"I'll leave you two," the man said and disappeared down the hallway. The two women didn't turn their heads.

"I've been looking for her for a while," Elizabeth said. "Stone City. Choteau."

Nancy jumped up, scattering papers to the floor like confetti. "Oh, my God. Oh, I'm so rude. I'm sorry. I'm kind of in shock. Listen, sit down. I have some things to show you. Do you want tea? Water? Make yourself comfortable. I have a few things to do and I'll be right back. This is just amazing."

Elizabeth could hear her feet tapping down the hallway. A file drawer opened, then shut with a wheeze. There were murmured voices. Another door shut. She sat still in this room, wondering if her sister had sat here. This place, these photographs, even this woman Nancy, her warm, brown eyes, weren't at all what Elizabeth had expected. What had she expected? A hospital-like atmosphere, something antiseptic, cold. She gazed at the poster on the wall—"Hope is not optional, it is a necessity"— and the silk roses stuck in a ceramic cowboy boot.

She looked around the desk, crowded with papers, pictures of residents, calendars, party hats, even a baseball cap crocheted out of strips of cut-up Budweiser beer cans, crayon drawings of rainbows and Christmas trees and a poem scrawled in stilted, childlike letters:

To Nancy, Who Flies
like a bird
from me to the sun,
brings me happiness
Jacob

When she swung back into the room, Nancy plopped down in her chair and swiveled so that she and Elizabeth were face to face, without a desk between them. "I'm still digesting this," she said, her eyes bright. "But I think you are so brave."

"I'm not feeling very brave at this moment," Elizabeth said. "I'm frankly so terrified it's all I can do not to get up and run out of here. So thank you for saying that." She gave her a weak smile. She had to hold herself still so she wouldn't fall apart—she couldn't fall apart now, she only had a few minutes, arriving like she did in the middle of this woman's afternoon, and she couldn't skew it all by crying—this woman was being kind enough after all, putting her work aside to talk with her, so she swallowed. "I know I am infringing on your time, but I'd like to know more about her."

The woman touched her leg. "You know she died in March. It's just seeing you here, it's like a ghost appearing."

Elizabeth nodded. "She died?"

"I'm so sorry." Nancy's eyes filled with tears. "But she was so loved here."

"I thought I would walk in and see her."

"I'm so sorry." Nancy paused and looked down at her hands. She looked back at Elizabeth, brightening. "But I knew Elizabeth very well and I'd love to tell you about her. She was full of piss and vinegar, you know. She was very, very funny. And so sweet. She loved to hug you. She'd hug you in the morning. She loved to cuddle up on the couch when we watched movies or read together. I have to find this picture for you."

Elizabeth nodded. "It took me a while to find her," she repeated. She explained that she hadn't known about her, that the family had kept her existence secret. As Elizabeth talked, her face grew stiffer, stone-like, and the room seemed to swim away from her. "I can't believe they'd just abandon her like that," she said. "They were good people, good parents. But to pretend to start all over like that—"

Elizabeth thought she was going to faint.

"It happened a lot then," Nancy said. "These people were doing what their doctors told them to do."

"Nancy!" a man shouted from the other room, his voice slow and childlike. "Na-ancy!"

The woman put her hand on Elizabeth's knee. "I have to get him a hot dog—it's his lunch time—but I'll be right back. Don't go. I have so much to talk with you about. But know this—your sister was so loved here. Can you wait?"

"Of course," Elizabeth said, resting a hand on her stomach.

She saw the hand.

"You're—?" She looked at Elizabeth's rounded stomach.

"Yes." Elizabeth smiled, feeling the pleasure of her pregnancy flush her heart all over again. "I'm pregnant."

"Oh honey," she said. "That's so great. How far along?"

"Four months."

She smiled again. "There's nothing better than a new baby," she said. "Oh, that's simply marvelous for you. The best thing that could ever happen."

Elizabeth wanted to tell her everything—about the years of waiting and how this was such a surprise, but she just said, "I wasn't sure it was going to happen, and then it did. I'm thrilled."

When Nancy returned, she sat down, clasped her hands together, and looked intently at Elizabeth's face. "She was pretty messed up when she came here. Couldn't talk much. Had to be strapped in a bed because she seized so much. Very angry," Nancy said. "But she came around. She settled down, grew a lot calmer. We loved her here. She got stabilized and then she could move around more freely. She loved music—her favorite song was 'My Home's in Montana,' which frankly we all grew to loathe. She loved the hokey pokey and the cowboy two-step. She lived here fourteen years."

Nancy paused. She knit her fingers together, pressed her two pointer fingers together and looked at them, then back at Elizabeth. "It's hard to sum up a person's life, isn't it?"

Elizabeth nodded.

Nancy spoke softly but firmly, her eyes growing watery. "She loved Halloween, and every year tried to wear something different—she was a witch, a dog, and her favorite—a ghost. She loved to surprise people—jumping out from behind filing cabinets, furniture, and beds. She worked putting clothes in the store. She loved meatloaf, mashed potatoes. She had seizures. She liked to watch the goldfish in the day room."

Elizabeth pictured her, the goldfish sailing around the bowl, the long fins fluttering, her finger on the glass.

"She used to tease one of the other patients by hiding his stuffed animals, setting them around here—we'd never know where." Nancy said. "She liked pranks. She liked birthday parties. She had a lot of friends among the other residents. She helped bake cakes for the other residents' birthdays—sprinkle cakes, chocolate cakes, crazy cakes."

They talked for what seemed like hours, though in actuality it was forty-five minutes, Elizabeth conscious that she'd walked in on this woman's workday and apologizing, Nancy watching the time and finally settling Elizabeth in with some photo albums while she finished her work. As Elizabeth studied the photographs of residents at birthday parties or dressed in fuzzy red-and-white Santa hats at Christmas dinner, or sitting in the grandstand at a local rodeo, what drew her eye in every photograph was her sister, her sister's face round as her own, with the same dark slash of eyebrows, same pursed lips, same oval-shaped eyes, her wide red lips turned down as she stared at the photographers as if to say, "Here I am."

Elizabeth realized that, coming here, she was expecting the worst, another nightmarish encounter with her past. But her sister looked happy here, and for that she was immensely grateful.

"She died last spring at St. Luke's." Nancy put her hand in Elizabeth's. "Is it okay if I hold your hand? Forty-three. Pneumonia. That's a long life for someone with Down syndrome. We were all there," she said, her eyes tearing. "Her mother, Louise Gustafson—you know that your father signed over custody, right? She was here. She was very good to her, you know. Sad, she had to institutionalize her again after her son was born—Lizzie tried to attack him as an infant. I'm probably not supposed to be telling you all this, but you came here, you're the sister, you have her name."

"Louise is here?"

"She'd like to see you. She's just twenty minutes away."

The house was a simple, clapboard one-story with a string of Christmas lights outlining the eaves of the porch and turned on, despite the fact it was spring and early afternoon, and as she lifted the latch on the chain-link fence, Elizabeth could hear barking from inside the house. The river behind the parking lot, the Kootenai, which poured down out of the mountains glacier-green and slippery, burbled steadily in her ears. She thought she felt her child flip in her stomach, but it might have been sheer nerves.

The knock on the steel door. The waiting.

The woman who opened it was old, her face lined, her hair a pouf of white held back in a pink clip that matched the thick terry slippers on her feet, her eyes a dark, intense brown. She had a cocktail glass in her hand, ice cubes rattling. "It's okay, Wade," she called back to someone in the house. "I got it."

"I just had to say something to get him back out into his workshop," she said in a conspiratorial whisper of white wine and perfume. Then she raised her voice again. "If you're here about the boat, I'm so sorry but it's sold."

Elizabeth opened her mouth but no sound came out.

The woman looked at her and shifted her glass from one hand to another. "Well. We finally meet."

"Miss Gustafson—"

"I only know you as Elizabeth Carter." The woman looked at her sharply. "There is a shocking resemblance, you know. Same eyes. Same nose. You're thinner of course, much better skin, but then I can imagine things might have been easier for you."

Elizabeth's stomach went cold. "I did try to find you—I saw your name on the letters between you and my father. I had no idea that you had adopted my sister." *Yes I am the other one*, she wanted to say. *The one you mentioned in the letter to my father: I bet if your other Elizabeth needed clothes, you'd get them*. "I've just found out about you. I wanted to meet you."

"For example, when you needed clothes or medical care, I bet you got it," Louise said.

Elizabeth stood on the porch, feeling the coldness of the cement rising through the soles of her shoes.

"And I know you were so talented, so accomplished. A singer, right? Your father was very proud of you."

Elizabeth gripped the wrought-iron railing. "I am not my father."

Louise straightened up, set her glass down on the carved oak piano that stood by the door. "Wait," she said. "This is going badly. Why don't you shut the door, take a breath, and knock again."

Elizabeth said, "What?"

"Just do what I say."

Louise carefully shut the door. She stood there, swallowed by the darkness of the winter afternoon. She considered just getting back in her car, driving down that highway along the river, and heading home, but she wanted to complete this odd journey. She faced the white metal door again and knocked.

Louise opened it. "Welcome! I've been expecting you. Let me take your coat." She held her hand out for Elizabeth's windbreaker. "Thanks for indulging me. I'm an old woman, hardened in my ways."

"Thank you for having me in," Elizabeth said. She looked around. She noticed the pictures on the piano, studio photographs of a young man in a blazer and suit and tie, smiling—he had Louise's dark eyebrows and dark eyes, even as a teenager; and then Lizzie dressed up, sitting on a chair as a young woman, her head tilted, roller marks in her straight hair, a wide grin on her face, her patent leather shoes shining. There was a large Shaker clock on the wall and a print of Degas's *Woman Ironing*, and hand-crocheted afghans in the most hideous color combinations (maroon and yellow, green and purple, red and pink) covered every couch, chair, and ledge in the room.

Louise moved aside and gestured toward a comfortable-looking couch decorated with yellow sunflowers. "Come in."

She sat down on a wing chair across from Elizabeth and stared at her. "I'm sorry. "I'm Louise. I'm sorry I was a bitch," she said. She leaned forward and touched Elizabeth's knee. "I guess I'm like an aunt to you. I raised your sister."

"It's okay." Elizabeth felt like she was going to explode. Can a human explode in a living room with shag carpet, with a maple dining room set, and a husband busying himself in the garage?

"I just didn't know how to explain all this over the phone," Louise said. "It's complicated."

"I don't know what to say either," Elizabeth said. "I've done so much research; I've tried to find my sister, I've seen her pictures, I'm going to her grave tonight, and all I have is this—" She held up the copy of the obituary that Nancy had given her.

"Your family didn't want any part of her," Louise said.

"I know."

"And you have the same name," Louise said. "Why in Christ would your parents do that? I kept trying to get your father to take responsibility for his kid, Elizabeth. We had a strike; he wouldn't take her. Then the whole institution fell apart and he wouldn't take her. Finally, I realized that when the state said it was responsible for her—back at her birth—that was it for him. He was done. He wanted to erase everything and start over again and she was a burr in his side and so—goddamn it—was I. It was like all or nothing for him."

"This is so shocking for me," Elizabeth said. "I think he thought that was right. I think he thought that was right for the rest of us. But here I am."

"He may have been a great father to you—but he was a shit to this child. I'm sorry, but it's true. Both things can be true," Louise said. "Excuse me for my language, Elizabeth. I'm sure you're a lady and all."

"Not really," Elizabeth said and smiled. "My mother used to tell me I swore like a sailor." She wanted to embrace this woman in her purple jumpsuit with her long red fingernails and her deep voice. "He was a great dad. Then there is this."

"To be fair to him—which frankly I'm not very inclined to be—the state told him from her birth that he didn't have to be a father to this girl. That's what they told all of the parents of these Down syndrome children. Leave them, send them off, the state will take care of them. Well, my friend, I was the state. And I'll tell you what: the state did not take care of them. They dumped them in rooms, fed them shit, doped 'em to within an inch of their lives, and many of them died young. So I took her on."

"I know that," Elizabeth said. "I found the letters."

"So you need to know what happened. I became her guardian after the strike, because the whole place fell apart, Elizabeth." Louise went on to explain that Dr. Oetzinger, who held the place together, resigned and left for a genetics conference in Iceland with a suitcase of thirty brains of Down syndrome patients that he'd used in his trials.

"You did a great thing taking my sister," Elizabeth said. "I can't even begin to thank you."

"Well, we all failed Lizzie one way or another," Louise said. "In the end I had to give her up too. She tried to hurt my kid. So I guess that makes your dad and me not that different. But I tried. And I never stopped seeing her." She looked at Elizabeth, reached over and patted her rounded stomach. "I'm sorry to touch you, but I can't resist."

She got Elizabeth a 7-Up, then plopped down on the couch and patted the cushion next to her. "C'mon, I'll show you some pictures."

In the late afternoon, with the sun slanting through the plastic blinds at the window, Louise showed Elizabeth pictures of her sister, Lizzie. Lizzie holding her new baby brother at the hospital with his red, squinched-up face. "That's about the time we had to put her in the group home," Louise said. She cleared her throat and looked at Elizabeth. "When I had Riley—after Wade and I got married, she tried to throw Riley out the window when he wouldn't stop crying."

Lizzie standing next to the Rambler as the two of them were leaving the Stone Home, her hair in pigtails, wearing a blue princess-style coat Elizabeth recognized, with a shock, as one of her castoffs. Lizzie and Louise's son, Riley, at three years old, at Christmas, nestled under an alpine fir, his arms around a large toy fire truck, Lizzie at sixteen holding up a Monkees album and a record player. Lizzie in the hospital, threaded with tubes, an IV drip, surrounded by an adult Riley, Louise, and Nancy, embracing her, Lizzie in bed, one hand in Louise's, one hand in Nancy's.

Then Louise looked at Elizabeth and snapped the book shut. "That's it. The rest are mine," she said.

Elizabeth's head jerked back, stung.

"You people," Louise said. "You people think you can come in here and scoop up her life after all that?"

The lump was rising in her throat faster than she could help it.

"It's okay," Louise said. "I know it wasn't you. But I've got to get on now. Wade needs his dinner. And if I keep looking at these, the two of us will stay on this couch forever, bawling."

As Elizabeth got up to leave, Louise plucked two snapshots from the album and handed them to Elizabeth, placed them in her hand and pressed her other hand on top, lightly. "These are my favorites. They're better with you than in some dusty photo album."

The first was a black-and-white portrait—Lizzie in her early twenties, staring at the camera, her round face fringed by black hair. Her expression was serious, poised, her face soft. The look of blunt misery from the photograph stapled at the back of the patient file from the Stone Home was gone.

"This is my favorite." Louise pointed to the second picture that, she told Elizabeth, was taken during a party for Lizzie, judging from the "Happy Birthday" banner. She was wearing a shiny blue bike helmet adorned with sparkly red pipe cleaners twisted into coils and was sitting at a table in front of a large cake with her name, *Lizzie!* scrawled in pink icing. She had tilted her head to the camera, pressed her hands to her chest, smiling.

"It's hard to believe she's gone," Louise said. "Spirit like that."

Elizabeth started to cry.

"For God's sake." Louise looked at her, her eyes kind. "Don't. It's too late for all that."

She found Libby Community Cemetery, tucked behind the Wilkommen Motel, and drove through the cast-iron gates to try to find her sister. She wandered through the rows of tombstones—tall obelisks, short lichen-covered markers, one new granite piece carved with a mountain and elk for a recently departed hunter—until she found the flat gravestone on the northwest corner. She bent over the granite marker, Elizabeth Finch Carter, and placed a coffee can of bright silk sunflowers near a bitterroot etched in the stone. Elizabeth Finch Carter.

It was quiet. She could only hear the sounds of the passing cars on the main street of Libby just blocks away, the wind shushing the pine trees next to the field of graves decorated with hanging baskets of silk geraniums and sunflowers and daisies, some in the shape of hearts, others spelling out "Mom" or "Dad." Clouds turned from deep red to pink to purple to black. It was strange to think that this was where the journey ended, her feet on the grass above her sister's bones.

She knelt to touch her sister's tombstone, plot number 10, squeezed between the graves of a certain Eleanor Biggerstaff and a Thomas McCutcheon, a new child fluttering inside her. She touched the black-flecked granite carved with a single bitterroot, the small pink flower with long roots, *rediviva* or resurrection flower, which was known to be able to regenerate from dry, almost dead roots into a lush, wide-open pink flower that grew almost flat to the ground.

She hoped she was touching the spirit of her sister. She wondered if her father helped pay for the grave marker. She wondered at a world where a girl who survived such hardship could smile, crookedly, at the camera.

Her knees were growing wet. She lay down on the grass, on top of where she thought her sister would be, imagining her small frame deep in the ground beneath her. Her body over her sister's. Her child, herself, her sister, one on top of the other, like a set of wooden dolls, one fitted on top of the other, like some ancient riddle.

Elizabeth looked up at the sky, where she could see a new moon appearing. She wanted to tell her sister she had a niece on the way and that she'd be an aunt and that she could come visit whenever, and that she hoped her child had the courage that she, Lizzie, did. Hell, she hoped *she* had the courage that her sister did. But she was tired of words. That would come later, when her child was older, when she felt she would have to learn a whole new language, a new alphabet of genes, to understand this mystery, to capture this story—as ephemeral as the mist now settling over the grass—in black-and-white marks on the paper.

Leaves were falling from a few maple trees at the edge of the graveyard, a slow whisper. As she lay there, in the dim graveyard, with the deep stillness of the mountains and valleys of this place entering her, she saw the deer at the edges of the forest, saw the way they floated in silently from the trees toward the cast-iron fence and then jumped over, like a breath, as if there were no boundary there at all.

Here I am, Sister, was all she wanted to say. *I found you. We found you.*

Before she left Libby, before the long drive back to Bridger, she hiked down to the Kootenai River and stood there on the long, rickety swinging bridge that spanned the rushing water. It was reckless, standing there, pregnant, suspended over this wild river, studying the cliffs of red, amber, and green rock where the aspen had turned shockingly yellow, looking to the north to see the huge boulder that hugged the shore, and then to the south to see the way the river took a horseshoe turn and swung out of sight.

She stepped onto the middle of the bridge, holding the wire cables, and bounced, feeling the child in her sway with the bounce of the bridge, listening to the river's roar, looking into the jade-colored water—glacial melt—washing over huge boulders far below the water's surface. There was something so alluring about those boulders under the water—so deep and smooth and eternal.

She checked the guy wires at the side of the bridge. Through the slats of the bridge, she watched the white rapids below her. This was wild, she knew, but knowing her sister had been happy here, had had people who loved her and took her on trips and made her birthday cakes made her giddy. Her sister's happiness, just a portion of it, was like those tiny microscopic beings that crawled between the layers of dirt from the aquifer to the stream beds to the lakes and streams to purify water. Here they all were, little creatures, her mother, father, sister, all of them, each trying their best, and if someone dumped something like chlorine in there trying to sterilize things—it killed all the microorganisms that made their water the source of all life, for trees, humans, and animals.

How like family, she thought. Here she was, suspended over the roiling, heart-stoppingly cold water on a swinging bridge. With one snap, the guy wires could break and she'd fall headfirst and be crushed. Or she could fall, then float, broken, but alive, on currents that would bear her downstream. Or, just as easily, she could jump on the bridge, and the guy wires would hold and her child's heart would beat inside her like bird wings, as light played off rock and water, a map of the world beneath her feet, and as the river rushed on and wrapped around the bend and out of sight, she would jump again. She would jump again because she wanted to. Because she liked knowing that above the turmoil of the green water and its promise of a sudden, swift death—she could jump and the bridge would bounce and sway and hold her.

AUTHOR'S NOTE

This book began with car trip across the Continental Divide in a Volkswagen van with my father. I was sixteen; my father was forty-seven. We were headed to Great Falls, Montana, where he had some legal business to attend to and I was participating in a high school drama meet. As our headlights tunneled through the darkness, I peppered him with questions about his early days with my mother: their romance at the University of Montana, their wedding photographer who put the film in upside down. He told me about their first car trip to San Francisco, and my mother's terrible morning sickness. "She must have been pregnant with me!" I said.

My father cleared his throat. "No," he said. "You have a sister."

"Cathleen?" I said, referring to my younger sister, already knowing the math didn't work out.

"No," he said."You have another sister."

Her name was same as mine: Caroline Patterson.

Upset and confused, I flooded him with questions. Where was she? Had he seen her? Could we go see her? He told me she had been institutionalized from birth. That it wasn't a good idea to see her because it would open up an old wound. This would be too difficult for all of them. The doctors told my parents that the best thing for this child and for them was to take her to the Boulder School for the Mentally Retarded (as it was known then) where they could take care of her. This was what families were told by their doctors in middle of the twentieth century. Institutionalize the child; wipe the slate clean, and move on.

I was overwhelmed by this revelation. I had a missing sister. An older sister. Not only an older sister, but an older sister who had my *name.* My father had asked me not to tell my siblings or friends. I immediately told them. I simply had to begin to try to understand this news by talking it over with my brother John and my younger sister Cathleen and with my close friends. John, Cathleen, and I had a few awkward conversations with my parents about this "hidden" sister, about why the doctor had told them to institutionalize her. My brother, on a field trip during a high school psychology class, met her at the Boulder School for the Developmentally Disabled, as it was renamed. After this, the silence about her seemed to close in again. She remained a mystery at the very core of our family, which, on the surface, was filled with graduations, marriages, and grandchildren, but was also beset by depression and dysfunction. After all, as Linda Wood noted in her excellent article about Doctor Philip Pallister and the institution at Boulder, "Given the pervasiveness of imagined associations between feeblemindedness and degeneracy, shame was a natural response."

When I began suffering from panic attacks of my own—while I was a Stegner Fellow at Stanford University— an astute psychotherapist asked me about the relevance of this missing sister with whom I shared a name. I was struck dumb. That night, I went home and had a dream where I was being chased by someone I could not see. At the end of the dream, when I turned around, I knew it was my sister. When I looked closer, I saw that it was me, with my skin turned inside out. That was the beginning of my search.

Every person in this story is part of a larger narrative about the terrible, dehumanizing treatment of individuals who had any kind of condition that was not understood by medicine in the twentieth century. We were cogs in a wheel of fear: me, my sister, my parents, the doctors, and the nurses who were trying to do the best that they could at the time. There were bad decisions, horrible decisions, and inhumane decisions about these children who were institutionalized. But there were many doctors, nurses, assistants, and social workers who did their best to provide their patients with comfort and dignity. I hope that I honor both the institutionalized children and their caregivers with this book.

Silence was the way my family coped with the story of my institutionalized sister. In 2002, my father surprised me by giving me access to her files in the Boulder School and Hospital archives. I sat in that office for hours, surrounded by banks of filing cabinets and ringing phones as I was "introduced" to my sister for the first time. I read her medical files, I read of the Luminal she was given, her membership in classes for etiquette and music, her seizures, her adoption by a foster parent, a possible ectopic pregnancy that was discussed then dropped, her return by the same foster parent, then the move to a group home in Great Falls, where the file ended. When I emerged in the hot August light, I felt stripped of my own identity. The wonderful women working in the archives copied hundreds of pages of my sister's files: medical records, letters, and the heartbreaking chart of gifts received: Easter basket, check; Christmas stocking, check. I attempted to find her in the Great Falls group home, arriving without an appointment, where they graciously told me what they knew about her. It wasn't until I located her at the last group home in Libby, Montana, that I was able to catch up with news about her. A lovely women there, whose name I sadly did not write down, filled in her backstory. She told me how funny my older sister was. How much she loved music. How she liked to play practical jokes. The woman even gave me a picture of her on her birthday, wearing a helmet that was decorated with red hearts and sparklers. Then she handed me her obituary. She told me she had died of pneumonia. She told me where her grave was and I was able to visit it that day. I now visit it once a year.

This story incorporated events from my family's past, as well as events from Montana's past, but these were fictional springboards. I exercised my license to invent as needed as a way of moving this story forward. I love library archives, and I spent a good deal of time in them researching this book. Archivists are a writer's best friend: the way they engage in your search in a professional and dispassionate way; the way they find things that you couldn't and pile files on your desk. And here is the hard thing about a fiction writer's research: you unearth all of this material and then, you have to leave it behind as you forge ahead, hoping only that all you've learned has somehow seeped into your narrative. I visited the archives at St. Patrick's Hospital (now Providence) and the Missoula Public Library to compare the notices of my sister's birth and my own birth. This was where I began to see how systematically she was "disappeared." In the mid-1950s, there was a newspaper column "In the Hospitals" about people going into the hospitals (particularly for births). Then a second note about the births or hospital discharges. My mother's entrance into the hospital was noted; but the birth of my sister was not.

From the Montana Historical Society Archives, I ordered oral histories of nurses who had worked at Boulder Hospital. One of the best papers I unearthed and used was Larry Burton's "A Historical Brief of Montana's Services for the Mentally Retarded" written in 1976, which provided a comprehensive history of Montana's institutional treatment of the developmentally disabled from 1889 to 1976—a hair-raising account of the warehousing of such individuals. From the Mansfield Collection at the University of Montana Library Archives, I found hundreds of letters of constituents writing Senator Mike Mansfield about the terrible conditions at Boulder. "Dear Mike," so many of these letters started, "This is one of our most digrashful [sic] programs in the state...we don't take care of our kids." This particular man was writing to protest the firing of his friend, who refused to work when he was asked to take care of 176 patients one night. By contrast, I was also able to get a copy of the "Boulder Star," a cheerful mimeographed newsletter from 1966 about from Superintendent Al Price and staff about the state of education for the "mentally retarded." The ever-changing name of the Boulder School is, in itself, a lesson in how attitudes toward people with special needs patients have changed: from its beginnings in 1889, it was known as the Montana Deaf and Dumb Asylum, the School for the Feebleminded (which graded children in this fashion: idiots/low-grade imbeciles, middle-grade imbeciles, high grade imbeciles, and backward children); The School for Backward Children; the Montana Training School for Feebleminded Persons; the Boulder School for the Mentally Retarded; and the Montana Training School and Hospital. In 1974, eight patients died and a nineteen-year-old patient gave birth after being raped by a staff member. Hundreds of staff initiated a strike which brought the institution to a standstill, at which point the governor called in the National Guard. The complaints about overcrowding, patient abuse, and neglect initiated a Department of Justice lawsuit. Overcrowding, bad press, staff strikes, and changing attitudes toward the developmentally disabled resulted in a long period of downsizing at the institution. Finally, on November 1, 2018, the Montana Developmental Center closed. A government report that year concluded that "an institution can never be a substitute for parental love."

The eugenics movement, so prominent in the early twentieth century, informed so much of the thinking about the care for special needs children. The excellent documentary, "The Eugenics Crusade," by Michelle Ferrari details this dark chapter of American life. We all know how devastating this mistaken idea of a pure gene pool can be, but it pervaded American thinking long before World War II. Witness this quote from Montana governor Joseph Dixon, who in his 1923 message to the eighteenth Montana legislature defended the construction of buildings at Boulder because "society must, in self defence [sic], if from no higher motive, protect itself against this on coming [sic] crop of morons and feebleminded, else we contaminate the whole and the race itself will ultimately degenerate and perish."

I took road trips to interview people who could help me understand more about this story. The first was just across town to interview Mary Cross, the wife of my veterinarian. Not only did she open her home to me, a stranger, but she was open-hearted, kind, and willing to educate me about raising her daughter, who has Down syndrome. It was so revealing and healing to see what could have happened in a different time with my sister: in this bright kitchen, Mary and I talked at the table as she fed her daughter who was smiling and clapping in her high chair. She was very understanding about the choices my parents faced in the 1950s and she helped me to understand them as well. She also connected me with a local group, The Down Syndrome Connection, of which she was president at the time. She was the one who met up with parents of infants who had been diagnosed with Down syndrome soon after their child's delivery. Andrew Solomon's *Far From the Trees: Parents, Children, and the Search for Identity* was an excellent resource on contemporary thinking about raising children with Down syndrome. Also the website for the National Association of Down Syndrome (nads.org) has a thorough history of the treatment of children with Down syndrome.

I drove to Boulder, Montana to interview Doctor Philip Pallister, who had been the lead doctor at Boulder Hospital for many years. Known as the father of Montana medical genetics, he had identified seven previously unknown genetic disorders and went on to found Shodair Children's Hospital in Helena. At 94, he was sharp and deeply passionate about his patients. I at first thought I'd interview him under my married name, Caroline Haefele, to keep from getting too emotional at the interview, but abandoned that at the door. He knew who I was and I knew that he knew—but the conversation was all about his time at Boulder, starting in the 1940s through the strike in 1974, until the time he left in 1976 and went on to found Shodair to continue the genetic research he had started at Boulder. His perspective on the care of patients, the institution, and the strike were essential to this book and I am so grateful to him for his honesty and generosity. For an incisive, thorough, and beautifully written account of this remarkable doctor, look no further than Linda Sargent Wood's article, "We Had to Start Treating Them as Human Beings," published in the Spring 2017 issue of *Montana: The Magazine of Western History.*

This story itself has been a journey of almost fifteen years. Through that time, I have had some very astute readers who helped shape this narrative. Fred Haefele, my husband, has lived this with me, on the page and on the road and has given me excellent feedback. William Kittredge, my wonderful writing professor, gave me dead-on advice over drinks at the Depot. To live in Missoula, with such smart readers (and writers) at hand is a gift: thank you Beth Judy, Jenny Montgomery, Amy Ragsdale, and Janet Zupan.

Julie Stevenson, my agent, as well as Diane Goettel, my editor, rescued me from despair about publishing this book. With Julie's excellent editorial suggestions I was able to complete a solid final rewrite at the VCCA in winter 2019, after a previous rewrite there in 2016. I was on the road from Polebridge in June 2020 when I heard I'd won the Big Moose Prize, and I feel so grateful to have been in the capable hands of Diane Goettel. I thank the Montana Arts Council, Ucross Writing Residency, and the Missoula Writing Collaborative for their support. Many thanks to Ann Seifert and Angela Leroux-Lindsey and Diane Goettel, for their sharp-eyed edits.

Finally, I want to thank my wonderful kids—Phoebe and Tobin—for their patience with this long process. They are the joy of my heart. The companionship and conversation of my younger sister, Cathleen, sustained me as we talked through family history. Jack and Laura were wonderful, complicated parents and this is my attempt to understand them. My brother has shared my interest in getting to know the story of this hidden sister. Finally, words are not enough to embrace my older sister, that other Caroline, who is still a mystery and sadness at the core of my being.

I plan to donate a portion of the proceeds of this book to help families through the Montana Down Syndrome Association, *mtdsa.org*.

AUTHOR INTERVIEW

1. You have written in your author's note that this story was inspired by the discovery, when you were 16 (year 1972), that you had an older sister, Caroline, who was institutionalized. What was the discovery like?

When my father told me this, as we were driving together to Great Falls—I was on my way to participate in a drama tournament, in our Volkswagen van, my father on the way to a deposition in Great Falls—I was dumbstruck. Especially when he told me that the two of us shared a name. As I mentioned, he told me not to tell anyone. But I immediately told my brother and sister, and my friends. It was the only way I could begin to even process it. I also realized I had had sensed her presence—when I pretended to have an older sister as a child and my mother reacted strangely, when I noticed in my father's ledger book my name written twice with two different social security numbers. But I think that fact of this secret was very damaging to my sense of trust, confidence, and self-efficacy. My quest to find her in my early thirties became a passion, although it was utterly terrifying. And it shook to my foundation my understanding of my family.

My parents worked very hard to provide me, my brother, and my sister good childhoods. They provided us good educations, college, musical training, sports opportunities, and a wonderful home. We skied, sledded, visited a family cabin, and took trips around our state and to Europe. Yet there was always a strain of sadness around our family that I felt but did not understand as a child. When I learned about this other sister, much of this unspoken sadness became clear.

2. Why did you decide to write this story as a novel instead of as a memoir?

I thought about writing this as a memoir, but I didn't want to tell the story that way. I simply couldn't convey enough of the story in memoir. From the start, I felt this story needed to be told from multiple points of view to embrace the complexity of the characters and to portray the treatment of the developmentally disabled at the time. Fiction gave me a larger canvas. I could explore through fictional characters, such as Louise Gustafson, and how she became attached to this abandoned child; I could explore the child's father, Robert Carter and why he was led to make the decision to institutionalize his firstborn; I could explore the compulsion of Elizabeth Carter, the journalist, who, after losing a child, becomes obsessed with finding this missing sister.

3. Montana in the 1950s seems to operate almost as a character itself in this novel. Can you comment on that?

Characters are molded by time and place. Montana in the 1950s was isolated, largely agricultural, but moving toward more centralization in its towns. Characters like Robert and Mary were college-educated, upwardly mobile parts of society, but very bound by convention. Louise Gustafson, who leaves Minnesota to travel to Montana to start a new life of her own, discovers this isolated, beautiful, completely involving environment of The Stone Home. I think my sense of this time is of characters who were still dwarfed by the immensity and intensity of the place. It created a kind of fatalism I often observed in my own parents. Also, I felt that in this rough place of extractive industries—mining and logging—that humans too were treated as raw materials.

4. The Carters in this novel were advised when their first daughter Elizabeth was born to institutionalize her because she was a child with Down syndrome. Was this common?

Doctors across the country told their patients with Down syndrome (originally referred to as mongoloidism) that their children should be institutionalized. It would be better for the parents, the medical establishment advised, and better for the families. And, it must be remembered, there were very few if any social services to help parents or children at that time. Families were completely on their own. My parents, like so many others, were doing what they thought was the very best thing based on the medical advice they were given. At the same time, these institutions were a horror, particularly as patients were increasingly warehoused.

Parents did defy the medical establishment, but it was rare. The National Association of Down Syndrome was founded by Kay McGee, in 1960, when she gave birth to Trish McGee, and her doctor told her to institutionalize her child. Instead, she and her husband, Marty, formed a wonderful national organization that provides information, education, and support for families with Down syndrome children.

5. According to your author's note, you did quite a bit of research about the history of treatment of special needs children in Montana. How did this influence the writing of your novel?

I love research. I love archives. I love archivists, because they get excited about the things that you are researching, and then they help you find more material. I have files full of research, quotes, letters, etc. The most difficult thing, however, as a fiction writer is that you do all of this research, then you have to put it behind you and hope that it seeps up and infuses writing. Certainly, there were things I got from research—information about the staff strike at the hospital, many details about the treatment of the patients—but I had to let the material float up so that it was serving my narrative, and not the other way around. Also, I found there were such horrifying details particularly toward the end of the warehousing movement at Boulder, I had to leave them out or the manuscript would be unreadable.

6. There is a lot of discussion in this book about what constitutes a mother. Can you comment on that?

Society expects so much of mothers. Mothers expect so much of themselves and we all feel as if we are failing at some time or another. Motherhood is so complicated, all-encompassing, and so fraught with peril. Mary does what society tells her is the best thing for her child—giving her up to an institution—and pays for it psychologically. Louise falls in love with a child that is not her own and ends up adopting that child. Elizabeth Carter, vulnerable after having a miscarriage, is pregnant as she tried to find her lost sister. As she is starting her own family, she wonders how this family tragedy marks her.

7. Do you think Robert Carter's experiences in the war affect his decision to institutionalize his daughter?

I do think that Robert, like so many men of the Greatest Generation, returned from war anxious to put everything behind them and start new lives. The vigor with which so many of these men dove into their education, business lives, marriages, and families was amazing. At the same time, the 1950s was such a period of homogenization in America. I was intrigued by the fact that, after a veteran like Robert went to war to defend America against Hitler—this man who tried "cleansing" a society by first murdering the mentally ill, epileptics, developmentally disabled, then 6 million Jews— would then return to America and subscribe to this idea of what a "normal" family would look like. At the same time, that need to have a "perfect family" creates a great deal of anxiety within Robert; he is haunted by his decision to give away his child and becomes more adamant about it only because is he has to continually reassure himself that it was the right choice.

9. How is Louise Gustafson's choice to leave her home in Blue Earth, Minnesota connected with her decision to allow Lizzie into her heart?

Louise Gustafson is someone who takes her life into her own hands. She hated what life held for her in Blue Earth, Minnesota—with her religious mother, her bleak marriage prospects, and boring job—so she got in her Rambler and left. She works, she is unmarried, and she is strong-minded. She lives outside of the 1950s conventions of womanhood. She knows her own strength. When she sees this lovely child who has been abandoned, she nurses the child back to life. And in that essential moment: the woman nursing the child to life, an unshakable bond is formed.

10. There is a lot of underlying tension about what constitutes "normal" within this book, whether it refers to behavior or medical conditions. Can you speak to that?

In the 1950s and 1960s, there were so many pressures to conform to a larger society that was booming economically, with its sunny portraits of families and new cars and pastel-colored houses in suburbia. On a local level, there were so many pressures in small town life to belong the right club, church, or clique. And there were so many ways to fail. As a society, we weren't having open discussions about gender roles, marriage, sexuality, mental health, medical conditions, so anything that touched on these subjects was often whitewashed. Why did we have that pressure to conform? What is normal? I couldn't describe it in high school, but I was sick inside because of the pressure I felt to conform. I told a therapist once my upbringing was "normal." What I think I meant was that I came from a white, upper-middle class family. Then I began to tell her about that "normal" history in my family: mental illness, suicide, an institutionalized child, abandonment. In short, my family was anything but normal. But then, what family is normal? What does that even mean?

In those times, we vanished the people we considered abnormal. As Wood notes in her *Montana Magazine of Western History* article, "We Had To Start Treating Them Like Human Beings," those with intellectual disabilities were locked away. She writes, "In the mid-twentieth century in Montana, as elsewhere, the diagnosis of disability was fluid, determined by social values and perceptions. The definition proved so elastic that it could be and was used, especially by eugenicists, to include those deemed 'socially deficient,' 'delinquent,' and 'depraved,' individuals judged so intellectually and morally bankrupt that they must be incarcerated to protect society."

11. Family secrets and how they are held and perpetuated are central to this story. Was it difficult to wrestle with this in this novel?

On one hand, because it was a novel, I felt I had more ability to make up characters and stories that freed me from the original narrative and the original story, as it were. On the other hand, it is amazing how deeply ingrained the family "silencer" is. I can't tell you how many times I have lost files, misplaced manuscripts, had profound feelings of acute disorientation in the telling of this story. The family code of silence is a profound one, even if you don't think you abide by it. I had to plunge through these blocked moments. I still do. But I now feel that this fear is important, like a light guiding me to material that needs attention. So I try to plunge on.

12. If you could see your sister, what would you do?

It would be impossible to atone for everything she had to endure. I wish I could envelop her with love. Hug her. Apologize. Hold her hand.

Caroline Patterson is the author of Ballet at the Moose Lodge and two children's books on the natural world. She edited the literary anthology *Montana Women Writers: A Geography of the Heart*. Her short fiction and essays have been published in journals including *Epoch*, *Outside*, *Southwest Review*, and *Seventeen*, and have been included in anthologies including *A Million Acres*, *Montana Noir*, *Bright Bones*, and *The New Montana* Story. A graduate of the University of Montana creative writing program in fiction, she was awarded the Wallace Stegner Fellowship in Fiction at Stanford University, the Joseph Henry Jackson Prize from the San Francisco Foundation, a Vogelstein Foundation Award, and the Montana Arts Council Fellowship. She's received residencies at Ucross, the Virginia Center for the Creative Arts and Ragdale. She is currently the executive director of the Missoula Writing Collaborative, which places writers to teach creative writing in more than 34 elementary schools in rural, urban, and reservation schools across western Montana.

She lives with her husband, writer Fred Haefele, in the Missoula home her great-grandfather built in 1906, which he built on the banks of the Clark Fork River where, he told his five-year-old son back in Chicago, they could throw stones in the water and the family could come and "cut out all worrying." Her two grown children visit on Sundays for dinner and laundry.

www.ingramcontent.com/pod-product-compliance
Lightning Source LLC
Chambersburg PA
CBHW030603310726
48979CB00003B/550

9781625571465